SUNSPHERE

Nicholas Mark Harding

London

First published in 2011 by Mutus Liber

BM Mutus Liber
London WC1N 3XX

ISBN-13: 978-0-9555230-5-2

www.mutusliber.com

For AB
The true Grail

Umberto Eco – who was closer to the truth with that list of his

Family and friends – supportive throughout the lean years of which, and on reflection, there were too many

Numerous thanks to Sean Martin whose research into the Botticelli Operation proved invaluable.

Dedicated to the memory of Larry Hooper.

"The Christian religion and Masonry have one and the same common origin: Both are derived from the worship of the Sun. The difference between their origins is that the Christian religion is a parody on the worship of the Sun, in which they put a man whom they call Christ, in the place of the Sun, and pay him the same adoration which was originally paid to the Sun."

Thomas Paine, *The Age of Reason*

O what a tangled web we weave
When first we practise to deceive…

Sir Walter Scott, *Marmion*

The World is still deceived with ornament.

The Merchant of Venice

But now I have come to believe that the
whole world is an enigma, a harmless
enigma that is made terrible by our own
mad attempt to interpret it as though it
had an underlying meaning.

Umberto Eco

If they can get you asking the wrong
questions, they don't have to worry
about answers.

Thomas Pynchon,
Gravity's Rainbow

Key: This symbol may be improved to impress upon the mind of every brother the importance of those secrets, which have been transmitted through thirty centuries, amidst bitter persecutions, for the benefit of the sons of light. As we have thus received them, untarnished by the touch of profane curiosity, and unimpaired by the revolution of time and empires, let us deliver them, in all their purity and perfection, to succeeding brethren, confident that they will never be divulged to such as unworthy.

A Dictionary of Freemasonry, Robert McCoy, 33rd Degree (1815-1895), New York: Bell, 1989

"The very word "secrecy" is repugnant in a free and open society; and we are as a people inherently and historically opposed to secret societies, to secret oaths and to secret proceedings. We decided long ago that the dangers of excessive and unwarranted concealment of pertinent facts far outweighed the dangers, which are cited to justify it."

President John F. Kennedy

Address before the American Newspaper Publishers Association,
Waldorf-Astoria Hotel,
New York City, April 27, 1961

Prologue

The phone rang. I didn't answer it, fearing an irate client. It was Gus.

'Hey, it's me. Just found something you might be interested in. Need it valued and dated and verified properly or whatever you call it. Bloody interesting. Reminds me of a book I read last year - a novel called *Sun*–something or other. I'll be in touch. Just down in the West Country. Back tomorrow.'

Secretum Secretorum
Venice, 1587

Some distance below, he could hear the sounds of idle chatter fluid in its Italian cadence, describing the humdrum, the ordinary, the familiar. Businessmen negotiating last minute deals with merchants, the shouts of oarsmen, bosuns, or itinerant sailors looking to be hired for a ship's crew. Crass insults and friendly banter echoed along the ancient city walls against which the lapping of the water created an undulating hypnotic rhythm, with the creaking of rigging and the crack and flap of sail tugged by a night breeze rich in aromas of exotic spices from distant lands.

It was an obvious place to hide deep secrets, but with an element of arrogance to it. A golden sphere supported on two carved figures for all to see; perched high above and in plain view on the roof of the Venice Customs House with its statue of Fortune casting her mute blessings down upon the city. She reminded him of Lady Alchymia, the mythical figure who presided over his own path – that of alchemy. The two women held secrets that he was determined to discover. But for now, his mind was not on his alchemical operations.

He reached into a pocket and pulled out a key no longer than his small finger. At its head was an ornate sun

11

symbol that had fine radiating lines spreading from its circumference. It was gold in colour but was obviously not forged in that element. It was certainly heavy for its size but he had seen and coveted enough of the precious substance in his time to realise that the key was fashioned in another metal. Not that it mattered. All he wanted was to find the lock built somewhere into the sphere.

Pulling himself up, he positioned his wiry frame beneath the ornamental sun and began running his hands around its surface hunting some obvious seam or opening in which to insert the key. Finding nothing obvious, he paused to think. His thoughts flashed briefly to the tattered manuscript replete with clues, half-truths and hidden meanings, many of which he had failed to decipher. One page flashed into his mind's eye, a fine ink representation of the Sunsphere. He remembered that there was a small triangular mark above the equator and in the western half of the bronze globe. He shifted his attention to that part of the sphere and after a few moments found what he was looking for.

He ran a fingertip along the gentle triangular depression in the surface. It was probably an inch and a half along each side and felt as if it might give beneath firm enough pressure. His hand balled into a fist for a moment with the tension. He closed his eyes and pressed with his left thumb.

There was soft click then something sprung up and pierced the skin. He recoiled but he knew he was too late. The poison was fast acting. He took a step back, his mind already in a fog. He felt his throat close and his muscles begin to tighten.

His eyes rolled up and the light of a thousand distant suns, the high heavens above him, span as he slipped from the roof. For a brief second before the light of life was extinguished, he stared wide-eyed into the infinite and saw a flash of lightning.

The key slipped from his hand and tumbled; lamplight spilling and sparking across its surface as it spun in freefall. It bounced once on the street below before dropping unseen into the dark waters of the Grand Canal.

Uniform Behaviour
Dallas, 22 November 1963

The Chevrolet four-door Impala sped down the Interstate, out of Dallas. The passenger, wearing a cop's uniform, felt uneasy. There was something about the driver he didn't like. Suspicion ran high in his line of work and he'd learnt to listen to his intuition, which was now warning him in no uncertain terms that the driver was trouble. Despite being clean-shaven and wearing a smart tailor-made sports coat, the man had dirty fingernails as if he were nothing more than a downtown backstreet car mechanic posing as someone of a higher social standing.

"I'm taking you to a place where you can get rid of that uniform," Sports Coat said.

"You got the rifle away?" The Cop asked, his attention on the road ahead. He was thinking his way through all the permutations that the situation could play out into.

"Yeah. You won't see that again. That uniform suits yah." Sports coat smirked.

"No, it don't. I'm usually runnin' from them." The Cop said.

"Well it don't matter anyhow now. You're a free man. Ain't nobody gonna be chasin' you now."

The man's accent was not hard to place. Deep South, but where exactly the Cop could not quite fathom. "You from New Orleans way?" he asked, trying to sound as casual as possible.

"Hey, you know the way these things are supposed to go. No questions. You don't know me and I sure as hell don't know you. That's the way they want it. You know that." The last three words were tinged with threat.

"Just makin' light."

"After today, man, I don't blame yah. Everythin's just apple pie from now on. See, I told them I didn't think you had the balls big enough to do what you just did. But now I know you were just one gutsy character."

"I get paid to do a job, that's all," the Cop said.

"But what a job! What a job. I mean for one split second there you were the most powerful man in the world."

He was not sure what Sports Coat meant, but then replaying the events of the last hour in his mind, it dawned on him that the statement was indeed correct.

"The man who takes out the most powerful man in the world is the most powerful man in the world." Sports Coat grinned. "For a second. Then it's done and he's back to being a John Doe."

"A John Doe?"

Before the Cop knew it the snub end of a revolver was up against his brow.

The Impala came to a stop on the edge of the construction site. Sports Coat jumped out and made his way swiftly over to a man in a dark blue suit drawing heavily on a cigarette.

"How'd it go?" the Suit asked.

"You ain't been listenin' to the news?" Sports Coat looked at the man incredulously.

"I make it my policy never to listen to anybody or anything." The Suit threw his cigarette into wet concrete.

"Whatever. The cargo's in the trunk. But burn this separately." He handed over a dark police uniform. For a second the November sun flashed across a badge, the badge of the Dallas police.

Arrival

A series of staccato stings cracked against the fuselage and the Blackhawk bucked as the pilot, alerted by a proximity siren, steered his craft out of the line of fire. Hannah Franklin, eager to see the source, shifted her body and looked out of the cabin windows just as a low calibre SAM rocketed past, rising on a loose-spiraled plume of white smoke. A Hughes 500, one of their escort helicopters, was already in the process of peeling away in an attack manoeuvre. Streaks of exhaust blasted rearwards as it fired several of its TOW missiles at some hidden target beyond her line of sight.

"Insurgents?" Hannah asked.

"Yes Mam. They're always trying to bring one of our birds down." A well-built, taut-muscled man dressed in desert camouflage sat opposite her and chewed gum lethargically. He opened his eyes. His name strip bore the name *Forster*. "We should flatten this city. End the problem." More bullets stung the side of the Blackhawk. "If it was up me I'd nuke the place and then leave it to rot." The soldier grinned.

Hannah wasn't sure if he was joking or not. She took one last look out of the window at the fractured buildings of Baghdad then sat back in her seat and rolled up a sleeve. Her watch, given to her by her father, was a family heirloom. She had expected to come into its possession only after her father's death but he had insisted on her having it for her twenty-first birthday. He had also told her, somewhat cryptically, that there might come a time when it would save her life, if a special set of circumstances occurred. She had no idea what he had meant but it was comforting to have something of his so far from home.

Not that she was sentimental. Far from it. Her tough ambitious drive had won her few friends and much of her time was spent preoccupied with her own activities, isolated from others because that was how she wanted it. Yet neither was this a mask for some inner sensitivity. She was, as her mother had described her, a bitch to the core.

Hannah looked up and caught Forster examining her. He wore a tight lustful smile; one she had seen a thousand times. She knew she had the power to attract men but it was never a conscious thing, unless of course necessity required it.

"Like what you see?"

The soldier ignored her question for a second or two.

"You'll do."

Hannah raised an eyebrow.

"I don't believe someone like you has the ability to discern good taste." She could see his mind working, trying to fathom out a sharp reply, but he chose not to respond. She decided to change the subject. "How much longer?"

Forster sat upright and looked out of the cabin window.

"Two minutes max," he replied.

The high concrete barricades of the Green Zone reached up beneath them as the Blackhawk lurched into a descent pattern that would bring them, in a low sweeping flight path, to the landing site.

Forster leant over and heaved open the door. A blast of warm dry air beaten by the blades of the Blackhawk burst into the cabin. As the helicopter neared the ground boiling plumes of dust kicked up in sweeping arcs that curled away and dissipated in the hot Iraqi afternoon.

Forster stood up, one hand on a support handle watching the ground. The helicopter touched down.

"Mam." Forster turned to his charge.

Hannah unclipped the seat belt, reached for her backpack and without missing a beat stepped down into the scorching heat.

Pausing briefly, she cast her eyes around the buildings and watched as a distant sand coloured Humvee drove towards her through the shimmering heat haze.

She turned slightly and looked back at Forster, who grinned, spat his gum out into the whirling vortices beneath the helicopter then spoke into his headset. A second later the machine rose into the air.

By the time the Humvee drew up, Hannah was alone in relative silence. Sweat was beading across her forehead and, despite a long shower and fresh clothes not an hour before, all she could think about was repeating the process. The passenger door was opening even before the vehicle stopped.

A tall man, dressed in desert camouflage with colonel's rank insignia leant out. His silver hair was tightly cropped, but was obviously younger than his appearance suggested.

"Miss Franklin?"

Hannah looked around, her body portraying something of the sarcasm that was about to be aimed in the Colonel's direction.

"You were expecting more than one female visitor today Colonel -"

"Rushent."

"Colonel Rushent." Hannah stared at him.

"No Mam. Apologies. Will you come with me? It's not wise to stay in the open."

"I thought this area was secure." She looked around; her body language once more revealing her barely contained impatience.

"Nothing is ever secure." Rushent stepped to the back of the Humvee and opened the rear passenger door. "Mam."

Hannah made her way to the back seat. Rushent attempted to take her bag but she quickly snapped it out of his grip.

She shook her head.

Rushent exhaled noisily as he shut the door behind her. Clambering into the front passenger seat, he glanced quickly at the driver who gave him a knowing look. The man's eyebrows snapped up briefly.

As the Humvee headed back towards a series of battle scarred buildings, Rushent reached for a bottle of water from a cardboard tray covered in plastic. He cracked the lid and offered it to his passenger.

"A peace offering." Rushent smiled.

"Are we at war, Colonel? Personally, I mean."

"Mam, I've been asked to make you as comfortable as possible. I have also been given strict orders to assist you." He held out the bottle a little further towards her. "You have to keep your fluid intake high out here."

After a moment's pause, Hannah reached forward and took the water. She examined the label.

"Malvern spring water? Where's that?"

"The UK I think. I won it in a poker game with some Brits."

Hannah nodded appreciatively and took a long drink. She poured some onto a hand then ran her palm across her face.

"You have time to play poker?" she asked.

"Sometimes."

"For water?"

It was a low building that had bullet marks peppering all of its walls. At the base of one was a medium sized crater with a corona of black scorch marks. It was an obvious and open reminder to everyone that, despite being in the Green Zone, the threats were real, immediate, and more importantly, within range. And despite the optimistic notion that the official war was over, the hostilities were definitely not.

The driver brought the Humvee as close to the entrance of the building as possible. Rushent jumped out and whipped open the passenger door.

"Mam. Quickly." Rushent's eyes darted around as if he expected something to happen.

Grabbing her backpack, Hannah slipped out of her seat and in one swift movement was stepping over the threshold into the comparative safety of the building. Rushent slammed the door then banged on it. The Humvee sped away.

Rushent stepped after Hannah, moving quickly to keep up.

"We've assigned you quarters in here." He overtook the young woman and pointed towards a shattered safety-glass windowed door.

"Salubrious," she sniffed.

"The best we can do, I'm afraid. If we come under attack stay in there until someone comes to get you."

"Do I hide under the bed?" Hannah cast her eyes around her small makeshift quarters. Her tone kept its edge of sarcasm.

Rushent ignored her. It was easier not to engage this woman in verbal jousting. He guessed, rightly, that he would always be on the losing side.

"Can I get you anything, Mam?"

Dropping her backpack on the regulation forces bunk Hannah turned to look at the Colonel.

"You're very conciliatory for a high ranking officer."

Rushent tipped his head.

"Like I said, Mam. I'm here to make your stay as comfortable as possible."

"If you say so."

"Is there anything you need?"

"I'm sure I'll think of something."

Rushent looked at his watch.

"We'd better get going." Rushent's voice trailed away. His eyes rolled heavenward and he turned his head to listen.

Hannah was, for a moment, mystified, then an odd sound caught her senses.

"GET DOWN!" In one swift movement Rushent grabbed Hannah and dropped her to the floor just as the first explosion crashed through the building. What remained of the safety glass in the door erupted and blasted in a shower of bright lethal shards across the room. Smoke, dust and debris boiled through the fresh opening, causing both to cough violently. Hannah panicked. The dust was cloying in her throat, threatening to close the airways to her lungs. The weight of Rushent on top of her added to the sense of claustrophobia. Her hands reached up to push him off but he would not move.

There was a second explosion, more distant this time followed by a third and a fourth. Rapid gunfire burst into life, a rattling sporadic response to the unseen enemy. Oddly enough, there was no shouting, just well-rehearsed responses to something that was familiar and everyday.

Realising that the attack was short and sharp, Rushent quickly stood up. Hannah, still on the floor, was having difficulty breathing. Her hands were clutching at her throat. Rushent helped her to her feet but she pushed him away and ran for the door gasping for breath.

She staggered down the hallway and, slamming the door open, stepped into the sweltering heat. She breathed in sharp lungfuls of air, her throat tight and unwilling. As Rushent caught up with her, he saw her reach into a pocket and fumble for an inhaler. The woman had a weakness after all. The small cylinder in its dark blue plastic sleeve clattered onto the ground. Rushent stepped up and reached for the medication. Hannah grabbed it from his hand, swung away and administered herself three rapid shots. With hands on knees, bent over, she tried desperately to breathe, her body heaving with the effort.

Knowing that all he should do was allow her the space, Rushent cast his eyes around at the aftermath of the attack. A group of soldiers were pointing in a westward direction. One or two of them, with weapons raised, were studying the distant defensive wall through barrel-mounted sights. Military vehicles were driving rapidly in the direction of the attack, roof-mounted heavy machine guns at the ready.

Behind him, the building was now missing half its roof. The frame was blackened, twisted and bent. In some places flames had caught roof beams. A thick industrial smoke was climbing into the perfect blue of the sky.

Rushent switched his attention back. Hannah was still coughing violently, her body turned away from him wracking with each convulsive hack. Her defences were down. He knew she was suffering in more ways than one. She was obviously used to being seen and respected as a tough woman. But, as Rushent knew, even the hardest of personalities had an Achilles heel, to be sought out and exploited. He knew this because it was part of the art of war and therefore part of his training.

But this was a secondary issue. The main thing he could not fathom, even with all his military Intel training, was the reason for her being here. What on earth was someone like her, afforded the very highest security level, doing in a hellhole like Iraq? He knew she was coming. He had taken the call, his superior briefing him over the phone. Asking questions went against established protocol. But why her, why here and why now?

A Mystery Thickens

It was the fifth prepuce I'd seen that year. Okay, so what? You'd be right to ask that. It was yet another wrinkly bit of dried skin, sheep gut most likely, that was supposedly snipped from the infant JC. I'd seen quite a few before in jars or crispy darkened lumps like decaying pork scratchings tucked away in small half-rotted wooden boxes on the shelves of convents and churches around Europe.

I'd even seen one at a car boot sale just outside Swindon. It couldn't have been real as the fat, balding moron, dressed in a Brighton and Hove Albion football shirt, who

21

was trying to sell it, had it tagged for £4.50. I made the mistake of enquiring about its provenance. This sent him to a flurry of apoplectic tizziness, partly, I sussed, from his complete failure to understand what I meant. He then regaled me in front of his equally obtuse family as to the slim and highly dubious facts relating to its supposed discovery in a small village near Carcasonne.

'Provenance mate? That's a sauce ain't it?' the Rude Mechanical asked.

'Yes, indeed,' I said.

Hearing the sarcasm in my voice, he lifted the matchbox off its display stand and hid it in the back of his faded red Renault hatchback.

I moved on. Swindon was not (and probably still isn't) a holy relic hotspot, as far as I know, and, besides, there had been second-hand Pink Fairies albums to be sought out elsewhere at the car boot. I'm wary when confronted with artefacts of that ilk.

But I digress.

I put down the hinged box containing a piece of sheep-gut, akin to the one I'd seen in Swindon, and was handed a small glass phial by a desperately nervous priest, his forehead and neck speckled with sweat. The glass had clouded with the centuries and was positioned within a small cage of silver, encrusted with a few jewels of the orient. Well, I say jewels. They were probably made of cheap glass from a Venetian window, like those on the reliquary that housed the finger of St Dubious of the Holy Stick, which I'd once seen displayed high above the altar in a recess in a church wall in a small Polish town, the name of which always escaped me. I'd seen a good number like this and my expression revealed to the tentative priest my complete and utter detachment.

'15th Century. Forgery, most like.'

'Really?' The faltering question stammered out of his mouth. He reached for a hip flask and took a swig.

'It looks like the work of the master forger Duprés of Arromanches. Tricky bastard.' Which was of course true.

Duprés possessed the great skill of making even his genuine articles look fake and, of course, vice versa. I think in reality he spent most of his time in his cups, and therefore his relic creation was something of a random hit and miss affair. The old soak was eventually to meet his comeuppance after being caught red-handed doing a touch of the Burke and Hares during their leaping-out-on-living-individuals phase. Duprés was drowned in a privy near Tours, as his biography was at pains to mention.

'So I spent a lot of my money on a fake?' The priest fingered his collar. The poor man was sweating.

'Actually you spent of lot of the Church's money on a fake. Looks like you're off to some dusty parish in the heart of Afrique old chap.' I couldn't sweeten it up for him. That's not my way. If you've been in this game long enough you begin to remove all the soap and honey when dealing with Mister Charlatan and his chums. This had a habit of spilling over into dealings with those caught up at the manky end of the deal.

I can't blame him though really. His parish here was dying on its arse. He needed something to bring the congregation back. Some focus point of adoration. Bits of the true cross wouldn't swing it. Not these days. That cross on Golgotha must've been 800 feet high with a span of at least 400, to judge from the amount of wood kicking about the Kirks of Europe claiming to be such. One even turned up in the States last year. Then someone found out it was a chunk of giant redwood. Imagine that on the hill of skulls... *Hey Pontius, I can see your house in Rome from here...*

'What is it?' the priest asked.

'You paid two hundred thousand Euros for fake blood. Well not actually fake blood. It probably belonged to a long-dead feline that was caught half-inching the fish from an Abbey pond.' It was like disappointing a child.

I had a vague idea where the sucker had bagged this nonsense. Or rather from whom. Tarquin Hale. Ex-Harrovian, all-time rogue, and one-time acquaintance. Tried his hand in the mercenary business for a while, until a bullet nearly did for his inheritance. He plied his trade in all kinds of places, mostly the Middle East, and it was here that he had picked up his lust for pumping money out of the gullible after he was stitched royally with a collection of duff old scrolls. Seeing how easy it was, he'd started in the rarefied air of the arts. After he'd weed liberally and metaphorically in the bathwater there, he moved swiftly on to antiques. Then for a short while he ran a boudoir in the Smoke, until the police turned up and seized most of his stock. Bankrupted, he went into the black economy. Or rather, further into it…

'Are you sure? I mean how can you tell?' The priest put both hands up to his mouth.

Poor bastard. There was panic written all over him. The same thing had happened only a few weeks before, when I'd been asked to authenticate what turned out to be a turd. It didn't belong to Timothy of the Utterances but to a dog, probably an Alsatian, an assumption based on a few canine hairs attached to it. The poor nun was heartbroken. If you'll pardon the expression, it had Tarquin's grubby hands all over it. If I'd looked harder, I might have seen the bastard's finger prints.

'Experience. They churn these out in villages in China, at least the silver bits. I say silver, it's mostly lead.' I had to be honest.

'It looked genuine.'

Well of course it did, mate. That's why you bought it. That's what it is supposed to do. Make you think it's an original.

'They always do,' I said, feigning sympathy.

'The glass. It looks old.'

'The have techniques to age it. Acid, for instance.'

'Christ.' He turned away, arms over his head, hands knotted in angst. 'I'm screwed.'

And he had been. Big time. If I'd offered him a revolver and a bottle of brandy now he would have willingly accepted both.

You wouldn't have thought it in this day and age. Or am I being horribly naïve? Probably. I'm sorry, there's no other way to put this, but weak minds attract this kind of deception. I have no idea why he and his kind need all this iconic clutter. Fingers of saints and rings of famous Bishops always turn out to be monkey digits and sow's bums. All those people prostrating themselves in front of stained bedsheets or handkerchiefs or snotty Veronicas shouting hallelujah!

Big time daft.

I can't complain though. It keeps me in consultation fees.

'Do you think I could sell it?' The priest turned and looked back at me with pleading eyes, like those of a puppy.

A desperate man going against his own teachings. No surprise there.

'No one's in the market for blood at the moment. Especially holy blood. All that *Sang Réal* crapola.'

'You sure?' He asked. 'I thought it was you know... I mean my superiors have spent millions trying to repress that novel...'

'You're always playing catch-up in this market.'

He offered me a slug from his hip flask so I duly accepted, took a swig then stepped away from the cabinet, a ghastly affair – as they often are – full of little figurines of teary-eyed women on their knees, hands slapped together in prayer. There was even a little diorama of JC's tomb depicting the man in question with his hand raised to a doe-eyed bint. *Noli me tangere* and all that. I even saw once saw, in a shop in Thailand, I kid thee not, a model of Jesus riding a bicycle.

I was being dismissive for a reason. It's part of the buying-selling toe to toe. You have to do it. The perverse psychology of selling.

For dramatic purposes I ran my hand around my chin and pretended to think. The cunning and, to me at least, very obvious bluffing of the salesman, was underway. I played for time. The panicked mind clutches at straws. Which of course is why religion is so popular.

' Could you...?' he asked somewhat over-eagerly.

'It won't be easy and you won't get all your money back, but I'll have a go.'

'How much?

'Three grand.'

The colour drained from his already blanched face. Sounds impossible, but I watched it happen. A miracle no less... if that's how you want to see it.

'Three gr-!' He couldn't complete the sentence.

'The holy blood market's drifted a bit. Two years ago or more, bang on. But now... Interest, like it is wont to do, has drifted on to the next shiny bauble.'

'Surely not? I mean I get papers through the door every week from higher up demanding I tell my congregation that this holy blood line thing is utter nonsense.'

It was a bit odd, all this piss and wind about a novel. I couldn't give two hoots, mind. I'd read it and ended up thinking, why not. Just as likely. But there you go.

'Best I can do is try. How's that?' It was sort of a compromise.

'Do it.' His reply nearly snapped his neck in two, such was its force. 'Get as much as you can.'

'How long are you giving me?'

'Bloody ASAP!'

That long eh? I needed at least two months. But I couldn't tell him that.

When I got home a few days later, horror of wretched bloody horrors, there was an answerphone message. Nobody calls me to be nice, so I was reluctant to press the button. There was also some post, including a jiffy bag plastered in thickly-written orders, to be careful with the contents. What was it? Semtex? I'm sure this type of thing is a red rag to old postie. I heave-ho'd paperwork off the desk and slumped into my chair. It ejected a little puff of dust by way of a threadbare welcome.

I took out the phial of crappy blood from my jacket pocket, knowing full well that I wouldn't get fifty for it, even in Swindon, and tossed it in the bin.

Pressing the answerphone's button engaged the clonky mechanism. Off it span.

'Hey man. It's me.' It was Gus. 'I've sent you a package. Read it. Interesting, I'd say. It's from a novel I found in a chest of drawers. Must be two hundred years old. The chest, I mean. Rich bitch chucking out heirlooms to pay off her dead husband's debts. Rumours on the old grape he was murdered. Found his car in a field, crashed through a wall. Anyway picked it up for a whistle. The chest, I mean. See what you think. Then I'll come round and we'll crack a bottle or two. Discuss partnership. Ttfn!'

I tore open the jiffy bag, pulling out 20 or so pages of photocopied A4. There was a note with the MS:

I think this is bloody amazing. Clues to a secret I reckon. You know, some lost treasure. Give it a once over and see what you think... Gus.

And there it was. A section of some wretched novel that Gus was convinced contained clues to a genuine secret. Frankly I was sick of the whole nonsense. Secrets and conspiracies. All a pile of over-worked guff if you ask me. *The Garden of Earthly Delights*. Oh well. I had nothing else to do that evening.

The pistol nestling in the fold of his breeches was a masterwork of precision, made all the more desirable on account of its exquisite beauty and silver inlay. A more-than-casual observer would see etched with great care and labour the name Thomas Hiddon across a finely-decorated escutcheon. The firearm itself was manufactured – a harsh word for something so exquisite –

by Gabriel Szhell, the famous Vienna gunsmith, who worked only on private commissions for gentlemen of means.

I paused to unplug a bottle of Italian Red, drained a glass, then continued:

Despite its, some would say, delicate appearance the pistol was a firebrand, a kindler of strife for those upon whom it was turned. It took the form of double barrels, with firm and optimum rifling, mounted on an oak stock inlaid with certain exotic woods of the colonies of Great Britain. The marquetry, like the stock itself, was the work of Isaiah Hamilton of London, he who had once recreated some of the great paintings of the Masters using only wood inlays, so that, at a certain distance, his works were indistinguishable from the originals. His most famous renditions were Hans Holbein's *The Ambassadors* and Mabuse's (Jan Gossaert) *Adoration of the Magi*. All met with high acclaim until their destruction in a conflagration. The fire had started in the tavern below the lodgings in which Hamilton had sought refuge after a run in with a bellicose Catholic secret society, The Order of St Patrick of the Revolution. It was rumoured that one piece had survived, a copy of the *Adoration*, in which Hamilton had made subtle changes to enshrine certain secrets of a heretical kind, possibly alchemical.

In certain popular and well-frequented coffee houses, word spread that the fire was the work of Catholic conspirators and had been started with deliberation, to rid the world of such devilish works. But the true cause of the inferno never became known; it only could be surmised from deeply dubious and circumstantial evidence.

The dispiriting loss of Hamilton's masterworks had, with certain alacrity, added to the value of Thomas Hiddon's firearm, to the point where the weapon itself had been sought by at least one Protestant group for its supposed talismanic properties. Hiddon himself had been set upon near the Inns of Court in London by certain individuals keen to acquire the pistol. In the foray, the weapon had spoken and two of their number fell dead.

To avoid legal difficulties, Hiddon fled to the estate of a previous employer, one Bartolomeo Xavier Marillo, an émigré Spaniard raised in St Petersburg, who had made his fortune in rare minerals. Marillo was married to the widowed Lady Esme Buonarroti, whose Italian husband had died at the skilled hands of André Laplace, a Frenchman well versed and practiced in the arts of duelling. (The reason why the two men engaged in a duel is lost to history, but there were rumours of sacrilegious practices.)

Desperate for financial succour, Hiddon took on the task of surveying the grounds of Marillo's estate. Marillo had grand, and for the most part, unworkable designs for improvements: ornamental fountains, an artificial lake and several grottoes, as was the fashion, as a way of expressing his love for Lady Esme.

But, with his finances collapsing, the Spaniard failed to execute these plans. He rewarded Hiddon anyway with a handsome purse of diamonds and other fine gems, and the two continued in friendship and mutual respect.

One of those diamonds was eventually set into the base of the stock of Hiddon's pistol now pointing directly at the stomach of the man across the table. The weapon was out of view beneath the card table, a baroque affair that shocked the senses with its ornate garishness.

This particular gambling table's genesis had taken place in a small border town in the Tyrol. It was created by one Antoine Dax, an eccentric Belgian carpenter with sympathies for certain outré modes of thought. It was rumoured that he had created a number of disparate items of furniture, which, if brought together, formed a great tableau illustrating some startling heresy concerning the Lord of Hosts.

There was no proof of this, as only three chairs have ever been in the same room at any one time. Dax was condemned as a lunatic, and he took up that mantle with a bitter and eager vehemence. In later life, his skill began to fail. His furniture took on an unbalanced appearance due to failing eyesight, poor judgement and an illness of the mind, liable to erratic outbursts not too dissimilar from Tourette's. He earned the epithet *The Lord of Misrule* for his efforts.

His card tables were indeed second to none, hence their popularity with certain miscreant aristocratic individuals throughout the upper echelons of Europe. This was due in part to the fine slots carefully hidden within the carved female figures, rich in embonpoint, at the capitals of the legs, into which certain favoured cards could be slid during sessions of gambling. Only in direct sunlight were the openings to these caches visible; by candle and tallow they were lost to the naked eye. A certain sprung mechanism, released by pressing a switch, each one unique to the table and concealed within the anatomies of the plump naiads, brought the hidden card back to the game.

Hiddon had observed this on more than one occasion but it was not his principal concern, not today at least when the stakes were higher, in a manner of speaking, off the table than the fall of cards upon it.

The gentleman opposite him, Frederick Ketzer of Westphalia, a tall man with broad shoulders, an engaging smile and curt eyes, wore an air of drunken contentedness edged with a steely undercurrent as if, at any moment, he might be spurred into violence by the simplest disturbance. At his left was a cream skinned, raven-haired beauty who leant and whispered into the man's ear, uttering words that had about them the nature of advice and strategies. Through her hair were ribands on which small devices had been exquisitely embroidered, finely stitched suns with radiant beams, as if she wore the figurative impressions of the enlightenment.

To Hiddon's left was Count Memlinc, a robust man with a face weathered by a thousand storms and ten thousand decanters of port. He was staring blankly at his hand; the perplexed look of someone who, with continual shuffling of their cards, hoped that on each pass, new ones might somehow magically appear. His wig, a scudding cloud, had dislodged somewhat and was drooping across his furrowed and sweating brow.

On Hiddon's right was Wilhelm Wespe, Bishop of Leipzig, a man of bitter countenance. The winnings on the table before him were as large as those of Frederick. He gazed impatiently up at the ceiling, as if in private conversation with his god, picking at his teeth with a thumbnail grown too long for common decency. At one point, without lowering his head, he cast sour eyes in the direction of Memlinc. He exhaled noisily and spoke firmly in the direction of the count.

"Would you prefer to engage in a fierce round of Troll-madam, Memlinc? A game more suited perhaps to your fevered incompetence."

"And dash to your impertinence Wilhelm," Memlinc spat, his face deepening to an apoplectic purple. "Were that your sportsmanship was to the fore!"

Frederick snapped his fingers at the nervous quartet of musicians huddled near the south wall, beneath a trompe l'oeil of Arcadia in which cavorting satyrs advanced on unsuspecting women, in the style of the Sabines, washing at a river's edge. This work had been painted not two years past by the peripatetic artist Ferronneau, famous for his raging libido and his restoration of the ceilings of Chateau Charles near Amiens. His insidious activities were immortalised in the bawdy and ribald English satirical comedy, *The Painted*

Brush of White, a troublesome play, not least for its dubious title and replete with double-entendre.

To a man, the musicians coughed, nodded at each other, shifted sheet music and commenced a Rigaudon (*presto*) in the manner and style of Handel.

"Tell me Sir, you are a skilled cardsman yet you hide your gambling prowess as if it were a bright light beneath a bush," Frederick announced to no one in particular, and waved an attendant over. The young man nodded and approached the table. Twenty at most, he bore a salver on which was perched a large and singularly impressive bottle of brandy, the label of which was adorned with the image of Louis IX of France. "You have played safe, yet cunningly."

Hiddon looked up from his cards.

"Yes, you sir," Frederick continued. "There is about you a self satisfied demeanour as if a well practiced skill and guile were your constant companions."

"I play, sir, with some efficiency, but I am not as blessed with guile as you so deem," Hiddon answered.

"Yet there is something about you that I might conclude to be nothing less than furtive. If you will forgive the word-play, you keep your cards close to your chest." Frederick, with mock suspicion, tipped his head to one side but kept his attention firmly on the man opposite.

"I am but an amateur and seek nothing but a modest win, that I may hold my head a little higher in the presence of such accomplished players as yourselves."

"False modesty sir, befitting of a charlatan such as yourself."

Memlinc and the Bishop were surprised.

"Frederick! The man has done you no disservice." Memlinc shifted his scurrilous wig back up onto his head. "You accuse him of fakery."

"I do sir and with good reason. I would have the man examined for concealments." An ebullient Frederick, puffing his chest out, shifted his hands so that they rested on his thighs.

Unbeknownst to Hiddon, two uniformed men of Frederick's own militia had positioned themselves furtively beyond the double doors of the parlour. Hearing Frederick's accusation, the pre-approved verbal signal, they entered with muskets aimed.

At this key juncture, I toddled off to the bog to aim mine. Five minutes later I got stuck in again. It was all very *Barry Lyndon*:

Hiddon, somewhat perturbed, remained passive in his chair.

"You accuse me, sir, of wrong doing?" Hiddon said. He knew that, if he were to lay his cards upon the table, he risked a pronounced acceleration in the precipitousness of the situation, and so remained the picture of stoicism.

"I do, sir, and I ask that you surrender yourself willingly to examination," Frederick continued. "For I am in possession of knowledge as to your true purpose."

"Are you sir? And pray tell me what is my true purpose?" Still Hiddon remained as unmoved as a millpond on a quiet autumn morning.

A wide expansive grin fell upon Frederick's face. His yellowing teeth were like serried ranks of standing stones upon the plains of Western Europe.

Hiddon noticed the raven-haired beauty bore a look of satisfaction. In her he sought evidence for the possibility of betrayal. Yet he did not know her, nor could he recall having seen her before.

"Sir, would you kindly remain where you are while my men subject you to a rigorous and thorough search for any paraphernalia unwarranted at a game such as this."

On a sign from Frederick, the men of his militia advanced upon Hiddon whose hand now, in a manner of speaking, had been forced. Dropping the cards, he stood up. Expertly, he raised his pistol firmly in his right hand.

Without pause he fired twice in quick succession hitting the trigger hands of the militiamen. Both fell away in agony, dropping their muskets, one of which hit the floor with a loud report. The ball was loosed and struck a servant in the shoulder, whereupon the man fell back against the mural of Aphrodite's temple, the painted steps of which were struck with sunlight, dappling the flows of fabric about the ladies at their bath. Sliding slowly to the floor, the man left an arc of red to mark his passing through the dress of a virgin.

Memlinc disappeared beneath the table, where he found, with great relish and at odds with the situation, an ace that had slipped from his grasp half an hour before.

Wespe, on the other hand, revealed his familiarity with such scenes by remaining unmoved upon his seat.

The musicians stumbled to a stop but Frederick turned to glare in their direction, enough indeed to stimulate them into renewed vigour. This time they made haste about a menuet in G major.

Turning back, Frederick looked indignantly at Hiddon. Both barrels of his ornate pistol were still smoking.

"Now we both possess no advantage, please sit and let us discuss terms."

Hiddon reached into a pocket while simultaneously snapping the breech of the weapon to reload. This had a marked affect upon those in the room still standing. Further was the puzzlement still as Hiddon removed two lead shot mounted in small brass casings and inserted them into the pistol.

"Alas, I feel the advantage remains with me." With a subtly wrought smile, Hiddon snapped the breech shut and pointed both barrels in the direction of the incensed Frederick.

"This is a vulgar display not befitting of men of our learned disposition and may I say, status." Frederick thus attempted to woo Hiddon with sweet words of favour but they fell short of their mark.

"I would have the debt you owe honoured sir. That is my task in hand. Although I fancy you already knew this, or at least had fair warning." Hiddon turned his attention to the raven-haired beauty. "'Tis an onerous one on many levels yet I am oft richly rewarded for my endeavours."

"Who sent you?" Frederick's dander was up.

"Do you mean, sir, that you have more than one creditor?"

"I have none, you serpent of the garden!" Frederick spluttered. "You spread lies and inconsistencies about your betters like rain from a cloud. I took you for a gentleman but you are nothing more than a hired hand, a mountebank and a blackmailer of the worst kind. You sir, are an accursed nobody."

"Cursed maybe, and there are many who would agree with that, myself included, but I am here for one reason and that is to secure recompense for my employer."

"Damn you! Reveal his name!" Frederick leapt from his chair, spilling it backwards. A servant stepped forward to catch the wayward stool. "Reveal his name so that I might seek redress for this outrage."

"I maintain my silence about his name to spare you further embarrassment, your name and indeed reputation, if there is one to be saved within your favoured social circles. Monies are owed. They must be paid."

"There is not one gentleman in this land who does not owe in one monetary form or another. My name is safe."

"Debt or death, that is the contract," Hiddon said. He cocked the weapon and aimed the precision piece at Frederick. "To your heart, should you have one, I will loose a shot." Placing two fingers of his left hand, palm reversed, behind his back, he found his secret cache of reload in a fold of his dark blue jacket (a tailoring masterpiece from the skilled hand of Dachstein's in London) and readied himself should the necessity arise.

"You would deliver death so swiftly on one who is deemed innocent by all his colleagues? That, sir, is an act of malicious failure in moral rectitude. You, sir, are a tawdry ne'r do well. I am called to remember the Brothers Kandinsky, who were sent on a similarly reckless exploit on behalf of the Duke of Lombardy."

"Then you admit previous wrongdoing?" Hiddon ventured. A verbal ruse to bait the hook.

"No sir, I do not. And they too, like you, will fail." Frederick raised himself from his seat and held out his left hand. A servant, somewhat ashen in demeanour, stepped forward. In his hands a silver box reminiscent of those used to contain the surgical tools of Dr Jose De Jaime, notorious practitioner in the arts of auto-de-fe. Its minute and exquisite filigree work called to mind the engravings of Jeremiah Hansard, whose skills were sought for the manufacture of coffers, chests and other storage items, all sprung with cunning protective devices.

Hansard designed the basement cache for storing the treasured possessions of one Heinrich of Danzig. He then went into hiding for five years to avoid the fevered machinations of his client, trying to rid the world of the only other man who had the skill to bypass the locks. Hansard was eagerly sought by all manner of cutpurses, jealous rivals and certain members of the clergy, all well aware of Heinrich's vast wealth and keen to relieve the man of a large proportion, if not all, of his monies. This meant Hansard could retire a wealthy man if he chose to comply with certain nefarious invitations. Hansard fled, but it was rumoured he paid an assassin to off Heinrich, later found dead on a gold chaise longue, his engorged mouth stuffed with grapes, his chin a staid torrent of purple, poisoned by certain venoms from the East and by gluttony.

"Now sir. Which is it to be? Will thou reach deep into your pocket or hurry on towards your maker?" Hiddon's hand was steady, the weapon still. To show the slightest tremble would allow a casual observer to infer that all was not well in hand and thus mind. Hiddon himself practiced late hour exercises in which he would stand still amid his chambers, pistol in hand, unmoving against all disturbance and interruptions. Guests who called during these interludes were left none the wiser as to why their potential host remained tacit and unfamiliar behind the door.

Frederick, labouring under a forced and indeed strict reserve while his mind sought a strategy, reached for the box the ashen servant now placed upon the card table. Memlinc, smiling upon his treasure, stayed on his knees, eyes wide and fearful, unwilling to draw himself up further into the line of fire. Wespe, somewhat displeased, clasped his hands across his ample lap and with a look of seasoned disdain watched, as if he were the sole observer at a private showing of a *Revenger's Tragedy*, the unfolding of the drama.

"Do you owe, sir?" Wespe asked of Frederick.

"No sir, I do not. Tis a ragged slurry of half truths and bedevilled lies." Frederick remained calm, giving Hiddon no advantage.

In an ornate sequence of manipulative and dexterous finger positions, Frederick released the box's locking mechanism under the concealments of the lid. Hiddon, tense as a fox in the field hearing the hunter's horn, steadied his position.

"The box, sir. Thus payment can be found within?" asked Memlinc. "If so then hurry and be done with such matters so that we may return to the game."

Frederick paused, barely able to contain his anger, and edged his mouth into the briefest of smiles.

"In a manner of speaking. But we shall not return to the game today. The reasons are several. Not least for your rediscovery of that wayward card."

Memlinc looked surprised. Lacking the skills with which to bluff efficiently, he sheepishly returned the card to the table, sliding it across the surface as tentatively as a nervous child eager to avoid punishment.

Hiddon, eyes sharp as a hawk, his manner taut as the strings of a viola, watched as Frederick lifted from the box a gold key no longer than the smallest of his fingers. Upon one end was a likeness of the sun, crafted with great precision. Like that of certain sharks of the Oriental Oceans, Frederick's smile became such a grin as would reek of menace to all who knew him.

"A key be damned. What debt might exist that a payment of a key would suffice?" Memlinc reached for his brandy and swiftly drained the glass.

Wespe impatiently exhaled.

"You state sir that you owe not, yet you produce such trinkets as if to admit guilt in this matter."

"Not trinkets." Frederick held his hand forward towards his accuser, the gold clef across his palm.

Hiddon knew the device. Such a thing was mentioned in certain hidden documents he had been party to at the Worshipful Company of Goldsmiths in England's capital. The Warning Carriers brought news of the theft of numerous gold items from the coffers of Lord Isaiah Penbury, a high ranking Freemason – that secret society new in the country, which claimed the heritage of the Cathedral builders.

"This item is known to you, is it not sir?" Frederick kept his hand out towards Hiddon as if to tempt him further.

"In name only. I have never set my eyes upon it, but yes sir, I do possess knowledge of such an item."

Memlinc, mopping his brow with a delicate lace handkerchief scented with oils of lavender and rose, looked from one man to the next.

"Do you not see this for what it is?" Memlinc asked Hiddon. "Take the key and be done sir."

"You will not regret such an action." Frederick maintained his eyes upon his opposite.

"Sir, your bravado knows no bounds. I am charged to recover a debt, not fall prey to a bribe."

"Yet you yourself owe a princely sum to others." Frederick played his first ace upon the table of circumstance. "So much that they hound you across Europe?"

"I cannot deny the accusation. But I, sir, am attempting to repay that which I owe, not offer others temptations and petty baubles."

Frederick nodded and gave Hiddon a smile to acknowledge the score he had made.

"Limited by time no doubt. A month, two? A year?" Frederick raised the ante. "With this you will know wealth beyond earthly avarice."

"'Tis not the key to the vaults of Heinrich. For that is lost at sea." Hiddon had studied the histories of all the vaults of Europe and knew their cunning portals. He knew the fates of those involved and the whereabouts of all the keys connected to them. Long nights of study under taper had led him thus far. Yet not for gain had he sought this knowledge, but to assist those who might yet one day suffer such from brigands and mountebanks.

"Your vigilance does you justice. You are indeed correct. Yet I wager that this key is unknown to you. If you can deduce its history I will summon my accounts and return that which is owed without question, and with gratuities and interest upon said amount."

Hiddon remained tacit; his honour set upon a blade.

Frederick opened up his hand to reveal all his cards, aware that none could trump the decorous arrangement he had proposed.

"Sir. I know your history. Accepting this will free you from those who have ensnared you. By claiming this, you may release the bonds and chains that are about you. You may live your life as a gentleman, no longer caught between your debtors and those who desire to exploit your knowledge of fiscal matters among the great."

"Answer the man and we can return to the game." Wespe reached for the Brandy bottle. "I do not wish to hear further from the whining Memlinc with this continuous jeremiad."

"You pompous, effluvial jetsam, sir. I take deep umbrage at your accusations." Memlinc banged his fist on the table with a loud report that had the fallen musket bearers flinching in response.

Ignoring the ignoble outburst, Frederick continued, "Do you accept the key? A seemingly trivial device to reveal a great secret...'

Right. So Gus was in a flap about an old novel in which a debt collector, himself up to his oxsters in fiscal calumny (I know that one), is offered a key to a great secret. Spiffing. I had a mind to phone the bastard up and tell him what I thought, but resisted. I was after all trying to cut my use of Alexander Graham Bell's plastic virus to avoid clocking up a fat bill next quarter. I didn't want broadband. That would inevitably lead to a wasted life online. The domain of paranoiacs and middle aged men who won't grow up, insisting they really must virtually blast mouthy little twelve years olds from Iowa on right wing anti-pacifist shoot 'em ups. Conspiracy theories, penis spam and viruses, much like marriage, was all the web was good for these days.

Sod it.

I drained my glass, refilled it, drained that, then slipped off to the Queens Arms up the road for last orders.

But not before rescuing the fake relic from the bin. Maybe I could sell it at the pub.

Discovery

Josh Madsen revelled in the grey skies of a wet early morning; the walk along the beach had been perfect. He was not a melancholic person although in recent years he had begun to wonder if age was starting to make him so. There was something about this landscape that worked better in the rain. He told himself that it was his Scandinavian, northern melancholic genes kicking in and coming back to haunt him.

He had bought the house on the wooded north side of the hill so that he could look across the bay to the headland beyond. A location away from the crowds, somewhere to walk when he was tired of people. Very few came to this shoreline. Access was difficult at the best of times. It made him harder to reach. This he found ideal.

But now, in the middle of the beach, his cellphone chimed. The modern world had a way of finding him.

"Josh melancholic Madsen."

A familiar voice greeted him. "What?"

"Never mind."

"Listen, we need you back as soon as possible."

"Chris, I'm not coming back to Boston for another week." He felt his heart sink.

"We've got structural problems. The pilings aren't deep enough."

"That's nonsense and you know it. Besides, you don't need me for that. You made the drawings and I know they're right. If the pilings are too shallow then someone's not followed the plans."

"That's just it. That person was me. I followed my own plans."

"Chris, I'm not coming all the way down to Boston just to get you out of the crap. Again."

"For your old friend?" Chris adopted a voice like a whining five year old.

"No. For once sort it out yourself." Madsen snapped the cellphone shut. He walked on, but the mood was ruined.

Up ahead he could see a shape on the sand. As he approached, it resolved into something dark and long, nestling in a small depression. A large dog paced around the form, sniffing and growling. It looked up, dropped to an aggressive posture and bared its teeth. The thing was a body. There was a pool of water around it as if it had been there some time, the surface of which rippled in the gentle onshore breeze.

Madsen slowed his pace, held out a hand. He scanned the beach for any driftwood that he could use as a weapon, but there were only pebbles. He lowered himself and began selecting a few of the more sizeable ones. The dog shifted its position, snapping a warning.

He was not convinced launching a salvo of stones at the beast would do either of them any favours in the long run. And if he managed to reach the body, he was not sure how much help he could be, assuming the person was unconscious rather than dead. He already felt, though, that the figure was dead.

He threw the largest of the pebbles at the dog, which backed off, barking. But its courage returned and it lunged at Madsen, forcing him to retreat.

"I'm only trying to help!" The words sounded ridiculous spoken out loud.

Raising himself to his full height, Madsen shouted as loudly as he could at the animal, while simultaneously throwing a handful of pebbles. The dog recoiled. Madsen's stomach turned at the hollow sound of the pebbles hitting the dog. The salvo did the trick. The dog turned and fled off down the sands.

Madsen approached the body. He could see now that the skin was bleached and bloated. Whoever it was had been in the water for some time. He had only seen a dead body once, lying in a street in Boston, a fresh gunshot wound to the head, the skull cracked open. It was one of the reasons why he had left the city, exhausted by the activities of his fellow men. He was angry at their cruelty, arrogance and stupidity. More evidence of which probably lay before him.

He reached for his cellphone.

In his study that night he mentally replayed images of the head wound victim in Boston and the body on the beach. Looking out of the window, he felt a sense of subtle violation. He would never look out on that view again without being reminded of that afternoon's discovery. He chastised himself for feeling that way when somebody's loved one was now lying on a mortuary slab. He stood up, angry at himself, his mind an angular dance of contradictions. A knock on the front door echoed up the stairs and along the upper hallway. There would be no solace here this evening.

The Sheriff looked up as Madsen opened the door.

"Evenin', Josh."

Madsen's heart sank a few degrees. He had told the Sherriff's department everything earlier. "I don't know anything else, Lee."

"You mind if I come in?"

"Sure."

He led the Sheriff through into the living room, where a floor to ceiling window overlooked the bay. The room's mute dark tones gave it a sombre, serious atmosphere. The plain furniture had a simplicity that added to the effect. Architectural prints on the walls had been chosen to match the mood.

"Would you like a drink? Soda? Tea?"

"I'm fine Josh."

The Sheriff sat down, dropping his hat on a low dark wood table. Madsen positioned himself near the window and looked out. Thick grey clouds were coming in off the ocean, an approaching storm.

"It's not the body Josh. It's what we found on it."

Madsen's eyes remained on the sky. He had the sense that he was being slowly enveloped in something beyond his control.

"What did you find?"

"This." The Sheriff reached into his coat pocket and pulled out a sealed evidence bag. "I need you to take a look."

Madsen turned.

"You were the only person I could think of who might have any idea about what it is – or where it is."

The Sheriff placed the transparent pouch on the table and slid it around one-eighty degrees.

Madsen made his way over and looked down at the evidence bag. What he saw surprised him. Half-prepared for something gruesome, what he did see still provoked a strong reaction.

"It was in an inside pocket," the Sheriff added.

Madsen slowly sat down. He picked up the bag and stared at the contents.

"Do you know what it is?"

It was a vellum parchment roughly the size of an A4 sheet of paper. On it was an exquisite sepia coloured drawing of a sphere with ornate decorative work, including two supporting statues and a larger one above. It had been drawn by someone with great artistic knowledge and architectural precision.

"Yes I do. It's the gold sphere on top of the Customs House in Venice. The Dogana del Mare. These are two bronze representations of Atlas and this is a statue of Fortune, there, I guess, as a blessing on all who trade in and around the city. There's some writing which I can't translate. Italian, I think... This was in the pocket of the dead man?"

44

"Yeah. But why is the next question."

"What do you mean?"

"It's – he's a John Doe. Caucasian, aged somewhere between forty and fifty and that's about it. No ID, nothing. He ends up on a New England beach with that in his pocket and only that."

Madsen's attention returned to the drawing.

"Any idea if anything like this has been stolen?" the Sheriff asked.

"Art theft is out of my range, even art connected to architecture. It's a sheet of vellum. Without analysis there's no way to tell just how old it is."

"Does that make a difference?"

"To collectors. Provenance. Like paintings."

"If you say so. Could it be a motive, if it was stolen?"

"It may simply be his and that's the end of it."

"Yeah of course. Can't rule that out. But..."

Madsen deliberated. He knew he was about to cross a threshold. If he became involved then he would have to stick with it to a conclusion. Or he could say nothing and return to his own private world. But would that be it?

"Alright, Lee. Let me do some calling around, see if anyone knows what this is."

Madsen paused.

"It might add up to nothing more than a simple burglary," the Sherriff said, but his tone of voice suggested he was less than convinced. "Followed by some misadventure on behalf of the John Doe now in the morgue."

"Or it's his. But you doubt that."

"Of course I do."

"And you have to follow every lead."

The Sheriff nodded.

Madsen handed back the evidence bag.

"I don't know how long this might take."

The Sheriff grabbed his hat and stood up. "It don't matter. Nobody coming looking for this guy, Josh. Missing

Persons has drawn a blank so far. If you get anything, you let me know."

"As soon as. Can you get me a copy of that drawing? Scan it and email it? I'd like to study the picture some more."

For the next few hours he sat in silence, a pile of books at his side. Their predominant theme was architecture, varied in approach from historic to aesthetic perspectives. Three were already opened on Venice, as Madsen searched through every book he had in an effort to learn all he could. On the whole it seemed the Customs House in Venice warranted little attention. It was not as instantly recognisable as the Doge's Palace, the Ca'd'Oro or the Rialto Bridge. In every book it seemed to have been ignored or, at best, only merited a passing mention. Drawing a blank, he eventually picked up the phone and dialed a Boston number.

After some delay a sleepy voice answered.

"Chris Gregory."

"It's Josh. Did I catch you asleep?"

"No, not really. Well okay, yes but hey that's the perils of the job. You calling to bitch at me?"

"No."

"That's a change."

"I need your help"

"What? Now *he* needs *my* help. Go on."

"Do you know much about Venice?"

"You taking the staff there on vacation?"

"I'm serious."

"So am I. Which bit of Venice?"

"The Customs House."

There was silence at the other end.

"Dona-danago – something."

"The Dogana del Mare. What do you know about that building?"

"Not much, but I know someone who might. That postgrad doing some in-house experience? She's wrapped up in the Renaissance. About the only passion she has, mind..."

"What postgrad?"

"Josh man, this is why you should spend more time up here. You're losing touch with your own business."

"Can you call her?"

"Now? It's past midnight. Leave it till the morning. Come to Boston. We'll talk about the Whalen contract, meet this intern and then go to lunch. You're buying."

"Do I get a choice?"

"Not really."

"Yeah, right, OK, Chris. See you tomorrow. At the office."

✠

She could hear the soldiers making lewd comments about her presence. Her bunk at the end of a barrack block was functional and not very private, cordoned off only by a thick military issue blanket. Not that she cared much. She was used to solitude and was used to being the brunt of small mindedness. It was rare that any sharp word pierced her armour.

She was thinking instead about her Achilles heel, her asthma. Whether its roots were genetic or repressed emotion, it was a flaw that she despised in herself. She envied people who could run great distances, who could travel without having to carry medication. Her inhaler was a burden. Of late, it was beginning to feel more like an emotional crutch; a shorthand for her weakness.

She sat up and felt her throat starting to close up. She fingered her pocket for the shape of the inhaler, but refused to succumb to the urge to use it. She could beat it. Suppress it even. It would not control her.

She heard the footfalls of an approaching soldier.

"Excuse me Mam."

Hannah quickly stood up and pulled the blanket curtain back.

"Yes?" Her face was stern again.

"We're ready to go."

Hannah considered the soldier. He looked nervous for someone with combat experience.

"Will you follow me please?"

She gestured to suggest he lead the way.

Hannah climbed into the back of the Humvee. Idling some distance away was a Blackhawk. Its airframe had a menacing quality; not so much a helicopter as a brutish machine engineered to terrify from above as it attacked below. Hannah knew this was a deliberate effect. She had read an internal document some years before about the CIA's psych-war unit. New military vehicles had to instill in the enemy fear of a power greater than themselves, beyond that conveyed by sheer weight of numbers or technical superiority. The design concepts, colours and notions of stealth were there as a pre-strike ideological weapon, playing on deep seated fears.

She knew that the technology of stealth was, on the whole, useless. The Brits had proved that shortly after the Stealth Bomber was made public. A missile battery had tracked the aircraft, supposedly radar invisible, for hours as it approached the British mainland. When the United States Air Force were handed videotape of the radar track, incredulous officers were dumbstruck. But the powers-that-be knew that this was not the issue. To an enemy, the idea that their defense systems might be useless against supposed American technological superiority was enough. The Stealth Bomber, like the Blackhawk, was also a weapon of the mind.

Hannah, backpack over one shoulder, took a step up into the cabin of the transport helicopter and saw two men, both wearing regulation sunglasses, camo-jerkins and Heckler and Koch machine guns. They were watching her intently. Hannah inwardly smiled. CIA. But were they there as a protective measure or to watch her?

She did not engage with them at first, but sat down and buckled herself in. Only when the helicopter took off did she turn and introduce herself.

‡

Madsen sat in the boardroom. Its one large window looked out over early morning Boston. The polished dark wood table was circular, born of the policy that all the partners were on equal footing. Although Madsen was the boss – it was, after all, his company – he knew that, without his colleagues, it would not be the success it was. Ten years after its founding, it was still the top architectural partnership on the East Coast.

He preferred to stay out of the limelight, though. He found it was safer mentally. Although he was no Howard Hughes, he enjoyed his anonymity, shunning all kinds and all levels of social gathering. All he wanted was the respect of his staff and the ability to hide away when he so desired.

The round table had inspired one newspaper to call the business an 'Architectural Camelot', which provoked a stream of good-natured banter throughout the company. But King Arthur he was not nor wished to be.

Chris Gregory burst through the door in that boisterous but breezy way of his. He reminded Madsen of confident boys at school, who seemed so sure of themselves and their abilities. There never appeared to be any doubt in Gregory's mind about himself or what he was doing. He was already talking, as usual, in that easy fluid way of his. He never seemed short of words about anything.

Madsen saw he was leading in a young Asiatic woman in her mid-twenties. She seemed a little irritated, perhaps due to Gregory's exuberance, enough to exhaust even the most enduring of souls. She wore grey trousers, a white shirt and a dark blue cardigan, giving her a quiet, studious look. The thin wire frames of her glasses added an academic quality, but she was graceful nonetheless and not at all awkward.

"Hiroko, this is the main man. Josh Madsen. He really is an all round sound dude despite his tendency to hide away. Josh, Hiroko Nezu."

Madsen stood up. This young woman captured his attention. He had experienced that jump in the heart a few times before, and it worried him.

"Hello." Madsen held out his hand. She took it.

"Hiroko is the intern I was telling you about. She's an expert in Renaissance Italian Architecture." Gregory moved to the coffee machine and began filling three cups.

"I don't know much about Italian architecture from that period, which I'm rapidly regretting," Madsen smiled; to disarm and put at ease. He pulled out a chair and offered it to Hiroko.

"Mister Gregory said –" she began.

"Call me Chris." Gregory waved a cup in the air.

"We don't stand on ceremony here," Madsen added, sitting back down in his chair.

"Okay," Hiroko smiled. "Chris said you wanted to talk to me."

Madsen looked across at Gregory's back and guessed that he was smiling.

"I did. I like to get to know everyone who's working here."

Hiroko nodded and gave half a smile.

Madsen reached over for a folder and slid it towards Hiroko. "Do you know what this is?"

Hiroko picked up the folder, opened it and studied the contents. There was a photocopy of the vellum parchment.

"The Customs House in Venice. Or rather the ornamentation on its roof. The Dogana del Mare is on the confluence of Giudecca Canal and the Grand Canal. The building underwent various renovations, then in 1677, a design by Giuseppe Benoni was used to build a square tower of Istrian stone. On top of its roof was placed a bronze group composed of two atlantes, who support a gilded sphere. On top of this balances the figure of Fortune, created by the sculptor Falconi, who was living in Padua."

Gregory, setting down the coffee cups, sported a Cheshire cat grin.

"We know that already. I'm sorry, my apologies," Madsen tried to smile.

"So how can I help?" Hiroko was totally nonplussed by Madsen's attitude.

"You know, I'm not actually sure. I'm sorry." Madsen pushed his chair back and stood up.

Hiroko reached for a cup of coffee. She remained doggedly unphased.

"Come on, Josh. What was that late night phone call all about then? You seemed all into it then." Gregory sat down a few seats away from Hiroko.

Madsen ran a fingertip across his brow and sat down again.

"A body was washed up on a beach not far from where I live. The original was found in his coat pocket. The man had no ID, nothing. Just that."

Hiroko studied the image again. "How old is the original?" she asked.

"Without forensic testing, I don't know. It's being held as evidence. The only fingerprints they found belonged to the dead man. And that's about it."

"This drawing is certainly post Renaissance. I'd say eighteenth century." Her voice was confident.

"Any idea what the Italian says?" Madsen leant back in his chair. He still felt a deep reluctance to get involved. It would be simpler just to return home and tell the sheriff that he had no idea what the drawing meant and dismiss the event from his life.

Hiroko rotated the image in her hands.

"The calligraphy says what I expected it to say. This is an image of the Golden Orb or sphere on the Customs House in Venice – or thereabouts. It's the handwriting that interests me."

"Handwriting?" Gregory leant in.

"Faint, but definitely handwriting. Any idea what the word 'Ordines' means?" Hiroko looked at Madsen, who shook his head.

"Ordines? Latin for 'Order', isn't it? Something like that. What does the rest of it say?"

"You know Latin?" Madsen looked at Gregory skeptically.

"The only way I can get you to smirk is by attacking my education," Gregory retorted in mock defiance.

"Well, it's understandable. You have more bushels to hide lights under than anyone I know."

"I have that ability." Gregory drained his coffee and stood up. He made his way over to the machine for a refill. "Trouble with you, Josh, you don't get to know people."

"Shall I go on?" Hiroko looked up over her glasses.

"Sorry, yeah," Madsen said.

"This drawing had been commissioned by someone called Dashwood," Hiroko pointed. "This writing here, though, is modern. It seems to give a brief history of the document." Hiroko tapped the base of the image.

"Seek and ye shall find," Gregory said. He returned to the table and sat down.

"I'm sure this is later than the drawing." Hiroko placed the sheet on the table and ran a finger along the text. "This translates roughly as 'the original drawing employed by the men who built the Customs House'. Someone called Dashwood used it during his restoration of the church."

"Who's Dashwood?" Gregory asked.

There was a long silence.

"Anything else?" Madsen toyed with his coffee cup.

Hiroko gave the image one last examination.

"That's it for the writing. But the original itself might be a palimpsest." She looked up at Madsen to see if she would have to explain the word.

52

"Could be, I suppose."

"A what?"

Hiroko half turned towards Gregory. "A parchment that's been used for a second time after the original text has been rubbed out."

"Hidden meanings?" Gregory's eyes widened.

"Let's stick to what we know. I don't want to get too fanciful here." Madsen tapped the table with a forefinger.

"Shame," Gregory grinned.

"It's a shame we can't look at the original," Hiroko said, picking up the drawing again. "I might be able to deduce a bit more if I could see that."

Madsen thought for a moment. "Maybe I could arrange that."

"There may be more to discover. For example, this edge here may have been torn."

"From a book?" Madsen asked, meeting her eyes and quickly looking down again. She was an attractive woman. Her eyes were hypnotic. Intense, and warm at the same time. He felt that he was approaching some kind of turning point.

Hiroko nodded.

The Key To It All

'What did you think?' Gus was whittling up, in a flurry of elbows, one of his eight-egg omelettes with peppers, cheese and chilli. Fine if you like that sort of thing. I did as it happened.

'What am I supposed to think? It's an extract from a two-hundred year old novel.'

'The key, man. What about the key?'

'A writer's device. A plot point. The *whateveritscalled* that hooks the reader. The hook that keeps the reader hanging on until the next writing course paragraph cliff hanger drug rush. I think Hitchcock called it a maguffin.' I reached for the half empty wine bottle, white this time, not my fave, and refilled my glass. It's a shame there's no breakfast wine. The Danes, ever a civilised country, have breakfast beer, so why can't the French do vin au matin?

'But?'

'But what? It's a bad novel. Reads like a pastiche.'

'Finish up the vino, I've got another one chilling.' Gus shuffled the mound of egg around the pan then hoicked it out onto two plates with a deft use of an encrusted spatula.

'If you had the whole manuscript maybe you could entice some publisher to give you a monumental advance. Then you split it with me and we'll sod off abroad before my ex hears about the windfall. Cayman Islands might be an idea. Do they have an extradition treaty with Blighty?'

'How much of an advance could I get?' Gus dropped a plate onto one of the Victorian pornographic place mats in front of me. 'Get stuck in.'

'I have no idea. Do you have the whole book?'

'Erm, no.'

'Know where it is?'

'I had a bloody good rummage through the rest of the heirlooms, but zilch.' Gus sat down opposite. Wielding his cutlery like a ninja in a badly dubbed film, he set about his brekkie. He had about him that barely contained excitement of someone about to blab about a secret. He would look up at me between mouthfuls, smiling.

'All right. What is it?'

'The novel's not all.'

'It's not a novel. Just an extract.'

'The key.'

'Eh?'

'The key. I've got the key.'

'Key? What key?'

'The one in the book. In the extract, I mean. The key Frederick offers to Hiddon.'

'How do you know it's the same one?' I chipped at my food with a fork. I wasn't all that hungry as it turned out.

'The image of the sun.'

'Come on mate. That's stretching it a bit.' I stood up and made my way to the fridge. I returned with a cool bottle of off-licence-on-the-corner white. 'Where's your bottle opener?'

'It's a screwtop. It's definitely the same key.'

'A story. It's pushing the bounds of probability to suggest it's the same key.' The white wine stung its icy way down my oesophagus.

Gus twitched his head as if to say that's your opinion. It was. I attempted a few mouthfuls of omelette then decided the wine would set me up better for the day.

After a few quiet moments punctuated by the clack of fork on plate I asked:

'Where did you find it? This key?'

Gus was instantly animated again. Even if I was feigning interest, at least it gave him the opportunity to hold forth, which he always loved to do. Sometimes verbose was his default setting. Other times he was as morose as a dictator with no one to suppress.

'In a small box in the same secret compartment in the chest of drawers. That rich girl didn't even know it was there.'

'Or maybe you're a thief.'

'Pots and kettles.'

Touché!

'Okay. So we – you – have an extract from a supposedly two hundred year old novel and a key. How's that going to help the world and his wife?'

'I'm going to start digging around and see what comes up. And – '

'This'll be another of one your dead loss pursuits. Running around for three years chasing your tail... again.' I paused. 'And what?'

'Thomas Hiddon was a real bloke.'

55

It was going to be one of Gus's mad whims. I couldn't afford to get involved this time. Gus was a touch more affluent than yours truly, inheritance don't yah know. But me? Organ donation was on the cards.

'Were did you find that out?'

'Linda.'

'Linda?' Another mutual friend. Despite her supposed academic credentials, Linda's attitude to history was, shall we say, a touch hysterical. No seriously, it was. She was a bit over zealous in her interpretations and famed for her rejection of the orthodox. Academic historians, to her, were all patriarchal, bumptious and wrong. She started her career writing articles for an alternative history magazine – you know, Knights Templar introduced chips to Christendom, or Atlantis was a real place, kind of guff. Now she spent much of her time wallowing around in precarious waters – the fringe of the fringe of the fringe.

'Turns out Hiddon was a Freemason.'

Here we go.

'Not your normal Freemason but something pretty high up. Grand Elected Knight of the Kadosh or something.'

'The what?'

'Something like that. I dunno. But to get there he must have been raised through a host of degrees. One of which was Knight of the Sun.'

'Knight of the Sun... The sun on the key.'

'Symbols within symbols.'

Or total horsecock. 'The plot thickens.' My tone was deliberately dismissive.

'Do I detect a hint of cynicism?' Gus reached for a gummed-up bottle of tomato sauce.

'Really? I thought I'd done ever so well to conceal my disdain.'

'As we age, our skills diminish.' He squeezed out a great eructation of red sauce.

'Where's this all going?' A bloody good question.

'I'm meeting Linda this afternoon. She's been digging around some old contacts. You can come along if you like.'

The agony of choice. 'If I hear the name Leonardo Da Vinci just once mind, I'm off.'

'Can't promise that.'

Ye gods!

We ran into Linda in the high street on our way to the café-cum-bookstore. She was making her way out of a newsagent.

'You all right Lin?' Gus touched her shoulder. She hadn't seen us at first and was in a right old two and eight. She jumped.

'Oh! I'm trying to find a copy of *Codex*.' It turned out this less than plausible mag of little merit had just published her latest screed and she was after bagging a copy. Sadly this particular rag merchant didn't stock the journal in question, leaving Linda somewhat agitated.

We the spent the next hour trundling around Sittingbourne, my hunger growing ever more acidic, on the quest for a monthly periodical that frankly I wouldn't hesitate to hang in the bog as emergency wipe. As it happens I hadn't actually bought toilet paper for years. An old chum had hurled a great collection of naff paperback books in my direction and for as long as could remember they had sufficed. That ever-growing perverse side of my nature thought about writing to the respective authors telling them how absorbing their work had been. My propensity for using printed matter had started when as a youth I had sat on the throne to read about the Earl of Clancarty and his UFO obsession. My naked knee was perilously close to an exposed wire that had yet to have a light fitting attached. Yep, zap! There's obviously something Freudian about it all... I digress...

'Buy it off Amazon or something.' I was starting to sound not that dissimilar to a whining 6 year old. I know; I should have downed my omelette brekkie. The smell of coffee and bacon was cajoling my senses as we hovered within a few feet of a bijou food emporium. 'I'm feeling a touch peckish. I'm in here for a butty.'

Setting the pace, I crossed the threshold and made for the menu, a blackboard edged in yellow emulsion pretending to be flowers. Some of the chalky enticements had been rubbed out. Off the menu, I assumed. I hovered inexpertly to make a choice.

Linda drifted in behind me stepping almost backwards into the café as she spoke to Gus. 'Could we go down to Faversham or Rochester later?' Out of Linda's view, Gus rolled his eyes heavenward but replied in the jolly old affirmative.

I, of course, was going nowhere out of my comfort zone today. I rummaged in my pocket for a few coins of the realm, meandered purposefully to the counter and ordered a plate of lasagne. Not very adventurous. As is often the way, I just plumped for something I knew. I can't stand that hoohah in an eatery where you fark about with the menu unable to make a choice, oddly jealous of the chums you're with who have made up their mind within fifteen seconds. Then you feel pressured into jumping to a choice. And then spend the rest of the evening wondering whether you should have had the steak.

I sat down.

'Are we staying then?' Linda seemed a little surprised that I had made myself comfortable in the window. Always my choice, in case any conversation goes belly up. You can then entertain yourself counting the bricks of the building opposite.

Linda sighed.

'Can you get me a coffee Gus?' She moved to sit opposite me. Seeming not to have heard, Gus nonetheless ferreted through his pockets in search of funds.

'What's the article about?' I didn't really give a toss but I felt politeness was the order of the day.

'The Knights Templar,' Linda said.

'Again? I mean, really?' Linda had a thing for Templar Knights. If she could find a real one she'd drop her knicks for him on the spot. Her last article about them related to their involvement with the psychological destruction of the NHS. Through the media, they were instilling the idea that it was falling to pieces in an effort to get us all to go private, thereby playing into the hands of the Blue Meanies.

'Via the Freemasons and that novel that Gus found.'

'You know about that?'

'Shouldn't I?'

There wasn't really any reason why not, but for some weird perverse moment I thought it was just special knowledge between Gus and myself. Freelancing was a ghastly whore of a mistress and you had to do whatever it took. So I can't blame her for cracking on with getting some mileage out of the *Garden of Earthly Delights* extract. It was a bit of a sod, though. I'd thought about doing the same myself.

'What's the main thrust of your argument this time?' I sounded all cod serious.

'The character Thomas Hiddon and his involvement with the Freemasons. I've done some research but I can't find any reference to him.' Linda adopted that pinched face she developed when musing over an unexpected hurdle to another one of her grand plots. 'It's like he never existed.'

'Maybe he didn't.'

'So who wrote the book?'

'Maybe someone just used the name.'

'Ooo, there's an idea. Maybe they stole it.'

'Or just made it up. Maybe Thomas Hiddon was writing a book about a character called Thomas Hiddon. But then, why didn't he write it in the first person, like a diary?'

Gus placed a cup of coffee on the table then moved back to the counter.

'Maybe it was his son.' Linda picked up the spoon and stirred her brew, her eyes lost in the swirling pale brown fluid. She was circulating the event horizon of the

59

conspiratorial maelstrom. When she was like this it was hard not to tell her just to snap out of it. But I'd learnt just to let her get on with her musings.

Just for the hell of it I tossed out an idea. Coffee shop conspiracy. 'What if it was a disgruntled Freemason, or Templar Knight, revealing secrets, but in a roundabout sort of way?'

Her face lit up. 'Hey that's a thought. That would make more sense. Confuse the eye and confound the teller.'

Gus sat down next to Linda and opposite me.

'Come up with anything?' His question was aimed at the air.

'Possibly.' I could hear the cogs in Linda's head cranking round. 'The novel extract may itself be nothing more than a piece of fiction.'

'That's what you're suggesting?' Gus wasn't too pleased about that idea. 'I dunno. I was hoping there would be more.'

Taking out a notebook with a rather incongruous magnetic latch, Linda began to make notes. It was already bulging to capacity with ideas, many of them linked with arrows to suggest a connection or two between one set of possibilities and an equal confusion of implausible notions. Tatty Post-it notes protruded from nearly every page. New World Orders rubbed shoulders with MMR jabs, alien abduction scenarios with toothpaste, and twelve-foot lizards with the head of the UN. To her, and in many respects Gus too, the whole of the modern world was one monstrous über-reality in the grubby and manipulative hands of *Them*.

Gus was especially hung up with the ever-popular one-size fits all *Illuminati*. I had regaled him on at least seven occasions, the pair of us under the influence of cheap plonk, that yes, there used to be a group of lads who called themselves the Illuminati, but over two hundred years ago. They were nothing more than a group of swots who got together, in the age of Enlightenment, to broaden their minds and subvert the narrow minded bigotry of the Church.

But he wasn't having any of it. No sir.

I also made it clear that most, if not all the rantings about so called secret societies, were nothing more than thinly disguised theistic right wing anti-Semitism. It was always Jewish Freemasons, sometimes even Jewish atheistic Freemasons, who were behind every bloody dopey presumed revolutionary plot to take over the world. Take the American Revolution for instance. There were Freemasons on both sides, many of whom wanted to keep the ties to the Mother country, which kind of negates the twaddle the conspiracy loons propagate. One berk even drummed up a pyramid of power in which Templars controlled Freemasons and Bilderbergers controlled the European Union. Right at the top was a big fat question mark to represent the real controllers of the world... the dudes who ran everything. The masters. Ladies and bigots, I give you the Jews.

Having a mother who was from a long line of Ashkenazis and with, if I might say so, *moi* being something of a non-believer, I found it equally troubling and a right royal pain in the cheeks. Did Linda and Gus suspect me of being involved with the Man? Were they even now tying me into some grievous duplicity without my knowledge? Maybe they thought my cynicism was just a diversionary tactic. I wondered if there was a Post-It note with my name on. Perhaps I was just being unnecessarily paranoid – like a great many of my fellow Brits these days.

Shrine

Hannah watched the shadow of the Blackhawk undulate over the irregular surface of the desert. She ignored the tacit CIA operatives alongside her. They had been flying now for fifty minutes or so in a roughly northeasterly direction. They had passed over Ba'qubah some time ago. From her mental map, she worked out that there was still about an hour's travel ahead of them before they touched down outside Kifri, their destination.

It was hard to imagine that below her was Mesopotamia, birthplace of Western civilization, now, thousands of years on, busily being torn to pieces by rival ideologies.

She reached for her backpack and unzipped a side pocket. Tucked neatly inside were several folded printed sheets, which she laid out flat on her thigh. She read enough Arabic to know that these documents were part of an archive from the city museum in Baghdad. They came from a haul of so-called confiscated materials lifted from the vaults of the building a decade and a half ago. Tons of paperwork had been plundered; a cultural heritage torn to pieces. *Dust lust*, as a leading newspaper had branded the relentless thieving of ancient artifacts. A museum was no guarantee of safety and no defence against the dollar. Many treasures were lost to private collectors who had agents working for them on the ground. Shadowy figures, at the pinnacle of the financial elite, did not frequent the halls of auction houses like Sotheby's or Christie's. They were powerful enough to influence the architects of foreign policy. They were rich enough to pay whatever was required, to secure investment trophies for their crass home museums.

She knew her father, for instance, had acquired a number of such pieces, but at least he was wise enough to know their importance to the history of humanity. They were locked away in a bank vault out of the way of prying eyes and the public gaze.

Some of the pieces lost to the world were magnificent in appearance, masterworks of art. Hannah was lucky to have seen many of them. The CIA was in some respects quite accommodating to archaeologists, albeit ones with powerful fathers.

The top page of her packet listed a long melancholy role call of missing artifacts. At its foot several lines of names had been blacked out to protect certain sources. Archaeology was a modern science in a modern world and had been corrupted accordingly. Money, not history, investment, not science, was the way things worked. Hannah briefly wondered how many lives this list had cost. The number was, in the cold light of day, irrelevant. The ends justified the means.

The second page consisted of a crude hand drawn map. There was no sense of scale. Baghdad occupied one corner and Kifri the other, the Diyala River almost connecting the two places. Next to a small cross marking Kifri was a rough rectangular shape, a building of some sort. As to what that building was, there was no clear indication. Underneath, written in a precise hand, were the alternatives: *Church? Monastery? Shrine?*

On the third sheet was an expertly executed drawing of a stone artifact labelled in the same handwriting, *'4th Century AD shrine or altarpiece. Cut from imported marble. Purpose and deity represented unknown. Believed to be Roman with local cultural influence. Information indicates object found in shrine, Kifri, NE Iraq. Cult symbol? Possible marker? Likely GPS Co-ords below.'* Hannah knew that the experts were at a loss as to what the object was. It was undoubtedly late Roman, due to the motif of the golden sphere supported by two figures. But her father obviously knew otherwise. To him it was obvious.

She ran a finger down the left-hand side of the paper. A ragged line gave the impression that the illustration had been torn from a book. Could an anonymous office clerk, who had made the copy, have done that or had the drawing been found that way? It didn't matter. Her sole purpose was to locate the place where the object, it was claimed, had been found. If, as her father insisted, it was a marker for a more important artifact, then she must find it. The course of history depended on it.

‡

"What do you think?" Gregory was crouched beside a large model of a series of angular buildings created from modeller's card and clear plastic.

"Too much like Frank Lloyd Wright?" Madsen offered.

"Not the model." Gregory shifted his position to give himself a top floor view looking down a tree-lined avenue. "Hiroko, you loner." He closed one eye. "I think that plaza should be more to the left. The symmetry's better."

"No it isn't."

"Don't avoid the question."

Madsen folded his arms.

"She's fine, I guess."

"Come on man. She's right up your street. You always liked the quiet strong intellectual type." Gregory stood up and walked around the model. "For those dull conversational evenings."

"I'm not interested."

"You really are a dim bulb sometimes. I'd jump at something like that. Besides, she's hot for you." Gregory waved a finger in the air. "Boy, is she hot for you."

"That's just your fevered imagination. When are they due for presentation?"

"I told you to stop avoiding the subject. You know damn well when the clients are due. In fact I think I detected a little thaw in you. You didn't look at her too often."

"Meaning what?"

"Meaning? Meaning, you've got to come down from that ivory tower of yours and rejoin the human race. Stop being such a damn isolationist." Gregory dropped down to street level again and closed one eye to look along the avenue from the other side. "I think we should do something really subversive, something sexy."

"She wasn't into me." Madsen moved to the other side of the model.

"You're hooked already. It's easy. Boy climbs out of his own ass, boy meets girl, boy gets girl, happy ever after. I've given her your number."

"Drop it, Chris."

"Josh, no. You *are* ready. Leave what's in the past in the past. Move on. Life's too short."

"You're like spouting clichés."

"Saves you the trouble. I also told her that you're expecting her for dinner tomorrow evening. And before you say anything, she's coming up to your place. You can mope about in the dark – together if you want to."

"Call her and cancel it."

"If I were a teenager I would say, 'way!' Just get used to the idea that it's happening. Maybe we could tell the client that this building embodies the essence of Marilyn Monroe. These two buildings represent her titties."

"Chris, you can be a prize ass at times."

"And this triangular park here represents –"

"Enough!" Madsen put his hands up.

"Hey, when L'Enfant designed Washington, he's supposed to have drawn in all this occult symbolism."

"That's crap."

"I thought I could pay homage to the old Frenchie with the female form. And look at the street plans of Sandusky in Ohio or Bath in England."

Madsen turned and moved towards the double doors of smoked glass.

"You my friend, must cut down on your sugar intake."

Gregory looked up.

"It's the only thing keeping me going. I told her eight o'clock and to bring her own red wine because you were so cheap."

Madsen found himself smiling reluctantly, and quickly directed his smile at the smoked glass doors, where a group of expensively dressed men and women were being ushered in by a secretary. He'd get back at Gregory later.

‡

A gruelling hour or so later, he made his way back to his office to check his emails and phone messages. There were enough of each to keep him busy for the rest of the day. Suddenly all he could think of was Hiroko. As he forced himself to concentrate on business, the more her face haunted his thoughts. Perhaps Chris Gregory was right. It was time to jump back in. But he had been on his own for so long. He wondered if he had become too stuck in his ways to accommodate anyone else in his life again. His current life was on an even keel. A woman would only upset that balance. Then maybe that was exactly what was missing. Some randomness, some imbalance. Some life.

He checked his watch. Unable to settle he stood up, grabbed his coat and made his way out into the design pool. He missed being out here in front of a drawing board. Running the partnership isolated him from the creative side, now in the hands of a superbly talented team. All he did these days was act as middleman between client and senior staff. Maybe he did need fresh stimulation.

Turning left into the elevator bay he saw Hiroko, her back to the glass partition of an office. She was attending a design meeting for a residential block on the edge of Boston. He slowed, then cursed himself for doing so.

He walked quickly across the plaza in front of the building, crossed the road and entered a small coffee house. It had that feel of old Colonial Boston, somehow surviving the in modern world. It was another sanctuary for him. A place with a sense of permanence suited his outlook. Odd, he often thought, for someone who designed modern buildings. There were two sides to his character; one hanging onto the past, the other tearing it down to put up the future.

Taking out his phone to check for messages, he dropped into a chair at his favourite table and nodded at

Boris, a big Russian bear of a man behind the counter. He gave Madsen the subtlest of nods by way of a reply.

The first message was from Hiroko, thanking him for the dinner invitation and accepting. Her voice was sensual but not overtly sexual. He knew it was starting to resonate with him. He recognised familiar but long lost feelings sweeping through him. So it began.

As he looked up, playing the message for the second time, his eyes caught those of a well-dressed dark-haired man sitting several tables down towards the front of the coffee shop. This individual was studying Madsen closely. Irritated, Madsen lowered his phone and stared back, Hiroko's voice formed a soft distant accompaniment to the exchange. The well-dressed man stood up, adjusted his long dark coat and made for the door.

Underlying his anger, Madsen felt a sense of unease. Gregory would put it down his loner's existence. But there was more to the encounter. The man's demeanor held an underlying threat.

Boris came over and placed a mat, then a cup of coffee, down on the table. "Hey, chief."

Madsen did not look up at first.

"Boris, that man sitting over there. Did you know him?"

Boris turned his head to look back down the bar towards the front door and the busy street beyond.

"Nah. He bought a tea, drank it, that's it. Never seen him in here before. Why d'yah ask?"

"I thought I knew him. Maybe an old client." Madsen pulled the coffee close.

"You look a bit spooked chief," Boris said, headed back behind the counter, reached down and pulled up a bottle of brandy. He returned to Madsen's table and dropped a shot into the coffee. "I'll leave it there. You help yourself." He headed off to clear a few tables.

Madsen closed his eyes and ran a hand over his mouth and down his chin. He was opening up to emotion, and it was making him paranoid, fearful of the world around him. It was no good; he would have to go home. He drained the brandy-laced coffee, left a few bucks and made his way to the front. At the stranger's table, he saw a black case. He turned to the bar.

"Boris, that guy left his brief case on a chair."

"He'll be back for it."

Madsen nodded. He stepped out into the street. A light drizzle began to fall. He walked maybe ten yards when he was blown off his feet by an enormous explosion that ripped out the heart of the coffee bar. A rain of glass fell from every window within a block.

Picking himself up, Madsen, concussed, was aware of a parked car moving away from the chaos. The man in the back was the stranger from the coffee bar. He was smiling.

‡

The Blackhawk slowed and slipped into hover mode. About a hundred feet below a large building stood on the rocky landscape against a low cliff peppered with large calibre gunshot craters. There was a ragged hole in the roof and black blast marks scorching two of its walls.

"Insurgents holed up here," one of the CIA men shouted. He leant out as the helicopter descended. His eyes scanned the ground. Suddenly he yelled into his headset, "Move forward! Move forward!" The Blackhawk lurched, its nose dipping for a second as the pilot edged back up. The CIA agent pointed to the ground for his colleague to see. Hannah guessed there might be some ordnance or a booby trap lying down there.

Moments later they touched down further away, both CIA agents training their weapons in tight staccato arcs. Happy it was safe, they signalled to Hannah to follow. She dropped to the ground, looking around for whatever it was that had alarmed the agents. To her left a dozen yards away a fuel can lay propped up against a small cairn of rocks.

68

"Mam, I can allow you only thirty minutes max before we have to leave," the first agent said, keeping his gaze firmly on the landscape. The second agent was already out walking towards the ruined building and checking the door.

Hannah made her way swiftly to the building. The second agent held up a hand for her to wait then slipped inside. A moment or so later he came out and waved her inside. He would stay at the door. That was the deal.

She stepped over the threshold, pleased to feel the cool of the shadows. The interior was damaged. Quite what it had been used for was not clear. It looked like a school, yet there were alcoves full of religious relics none, at first glance, familiar to her. On the wall opposite was a low heavily bolted wooden door. The timber was aged by centuries to a deep rich ebony and on its surface a circle was carved deeply into the wood. The hinges were thick iron yet despite this, the door looked as if it would give way without any great effort.

Hannah studied the door briefly then kicked out sharply. It cracked and folded in on itself, revealing a long passage cut into the rock of the cliff beyond. She pulled out her flashlight and switched it on.

The torchlight picked out small alcoves for lamps cut into the sidewalls of the passage. The rock was cool and dry. A draught blew gently along the tunnel into her face, suggesting a large space somewhere up ahead. Hannah walked along until she came to another door set as awkwardly in its frame as the one she had just destroyed. Once more a circle was cut into its surface, this one inlaid with gold. She traced its shape with a finger, feeling the cool of the metal. Why was it still there? Perhaps the reverence for this place was greater than she had imagined, or were the inhabitants of Kifri, a few miles away, not aware the place existed? It seemed unlikely. There were the obvious signs of conflict. After the invasion, many resistance fighters had fled into these mountains. The Blackhawk pilot had known exactly where to go. It seemed, at least, that the military knew the place existed. It was pointless to speculate.

She pushed her weight up against the door and felt it give a little. Taking a few steps back, she kicked heavily into the wood. A crack opened up across the gold circle. With a second blow the door collapsed.

Stepping over the threshold, she swung the torch around. The room was larger than she had expected, probably thirty feet along each side. Three steps led down into a small arena. Against a far wall was a statue of a young man wearing a Phrygian cap, a tunic and a mantle over his left shoulder. The figure was in the throes of plunging a sword into the neck of a large bull. Before them was an altar – worn, but plainly in use relatively recently. Dried blood had puddled in its basin and in the sand.

The symbols in the other room suddenly made sense.

"Mithra," Hannah muttered, shaking her head slowly. The religion died out a thousand years ago, but here it was, at least until recently, apparently alive and well in modern Iraq. This was, after all, the birthplace of the cult, ancient Persia. From here, Mithraism had spread to Babylon, then to ancient Greece and on into the Roman Empire. There it eventually confronted Christianity and became subjugated by that cult-turned-religion. But until the 5th century, it was almost as powerful as the faith of Christ. The Church stamped out the cult of Mithra: Hannah remembered that the Vatican itself was built on the site of a Mithraic temple.

She stepped down into the small arena and cast her torch beam around the floor. Footprints in a thin layer of sand looked recent. For a split second she panicked, fearing she might not be alone. But there was no way out of this cave other than entrance passageway. No hidden doors or secret tunnels, as far as she could tell. She deliberately slowed her breathing and chastised herself for being jumpy. She shone the torch around again. Set into the right-hand wall were a series of alcoves of the kind which might once have contained scrolls. She ignored them. She had her priorities.

Mithraism had three sacred symbols, the bull standing for virility, the hammer representing man's creativity and the crown, an image of the sun. Before he hanged himself, the man in the cell had told his CIA captors that they would never find "the crown" because the old gods were keeping it safe from the corrupt hands of the profane in a distant and secret stronghold. Hannah, present throughout the interrogation, took that as a challenge. That challenge had led her here.

Against the back wall, behind the statue of Mithra, the rock face was decorated with more arcane symbols above a long low bench. Built into this were three small doors, each bearing a skilful representation inlaid with gold. One showed a bull, head down in a charge. The next was a hammer. The third was a crown, depicted as if it were the corona around the sun.

Hannah paused. She thought she heard a short sharp crack echoing down the passage behind her. She moved towards the bench then stopped again. There was a second sound, a distant dull thud. Then an erratic burst of machine-gun fire. Thirty minutes had become five. She moved swiftly to the door that had the crown sigil on it. Crouching, she tried to open the door but it wouldn't give; there were no obvious locks.

She heard the CIA agent call out for her to hurry. But Hannah had not come this far just to watch the prize slip from her fingers. She stood up and kicked hard. Third time lucky, she hoped, but the door held fast.

There was an explosion. The shock wave blasted down the passage nearly knocking Hannah down. The statue of Mithra toppled from its plinth then tumbled to the floor breaking into numerous pieces. Frustrated, Hannah delivered a succession of kicks to the small door but it resolutely refused to open.

There was another blast of machine-gun fire, then a few moments later the CIA Agent appeared.

"Mam, we have to go, now!"

"No!" Hannah snapped back.

"Mam. We have to!"

"I'm not leaving."

The Agent grabbed Hannah's arm and pulled her up. Angered, Hannah turned and punched out at the man. The blows connected but he seemed impervious. In the struggle she dropped the torch and it smashed against the ground.

"Sorry, I have my orders."

He pulled her back along the passageway. Hannah resisted as best she could but the man was immune to her efforts.

"Orders from who?" Hannah panted.

"Your father."

Who would be looking out for her only for his own selfish reasons, of course. She knew he was powerful, now his reach seemed practically limitless.

There was a burst of gunfire from outside, almost drowned out by the roar of the Blackhawk's rotors. Thick blasts of dust were boiling through the ruined windows into the derelict building as Hannah and the Agent reached the main door.

"Stay down!" he barked.

Pushing her against a wall the man crept to a window and looked out. Two mortar rounds detonated a few yards from the helicopter; the black acrid smoke kicked away in the wash of the rotors. He saw his colleague firing short sharp bursts in a number of directions.

"Mam, we're going to have to make a run for the bird. I'll go first, then stop to protect your back." The Agent went to the doorway. Nodding at Hannah, he started to count down from three to one. He was suddenly cut short when the main door exploded in an onslaught of gunfire. Bullets and fragments of timber stung the air and punctured the man's body. He was dead before he hit the floor.

Blood began to pool in the dust. Hannah closed her eyes for a second then reached for the fallen agent's weapon. She made up her mind. She was not going to leave.

Ducking, she moved to the window and looked out. The first Agent was limping towards the Blackhawk, firing as he went. He clambered into the rear cabin just as a round smacked him hard in the back. He rolled over jerking in agony and lay still.

Hannah was willing the helicopter to take off, to abandon her, but it resolutely refused to leave. The pilot glanced over in the direction of the building. She could see him wracked over the decision. Their eyes met although she doubted he could see her. Then his body was instantly wrapped in flame. She watched his eyes widen with abject fear just before the helicopter exploded, showering the area with angry chunks of hot metal. Something large and heavy smashed into the front wall of the building. Hannah scrambled away and made it back into the passageway before the wall behind her collapsed.

Coughing in thick dust, she staggered down the tunnel and fell into the inner sanctum. She lay at the bottom of the three steps fighting for breath, one hand scrambling to find her inhaler. Her fingers wrapped around the instrument. She closed her eyes and brought it to her lips.

Madsen sat on the edge of the plaza with a foil blanket around him. A medic attended to a cut on his forehead. All around the plaza, people were being treated for cuts and burns. Stretchers were being loaded into ambulances. Across the street was a gaping ragged hole, its edges blackened and burnt. Where once there had been a place to hide in the city. Madsen felt guilty. People died here and he was concerned about was his own minor loss. It was pathetic.

Madsen pushed the medic away.

"Aren't there people worse off than me?" he snapped.

The medic shook his head a little.

"It's a normal reaction," he said. "Just sit tight."

Madsen relaxed a little, enough to allow the medic to continue. There was so much going on in the street, so much fevered activity, that he could not really take it all in. Fire fighters hosed down the blasted ruins and rivers of black ash and soot flowed across the sidewalk and into the road. There was a constant chatter of radio communication, chirps and whoops of sirens and the shouts of policemen as they tried to bring order to the chaos. There were so many emergency vehicles that the walls of the buildings in the plaza and the street beyond were lit with an erratic and hypnotic dance of blue and red.

A figure picked its way through the crowd and resolved into Gregory.

"Are you OK? Jeez, what a mess. Chance for some redevelopment. Maybe we could pitch for the job."

"Chris."

"I know, I know. A quip too far." Gregory sat down.

"Nobody's talking."

"The cops?"

"No, I mean everyone else. No one's saying anything."

Gregory listened. He studied the faces of the people around him. Apart from a few sobbing individuals everyone was relatively quiet.

"You're right. Strange. Are we getting used to this kind of thing?"

"I hope we never get used to it." Madsen lowered his eyes. "I saw the man who did it."

"What?" Gregory asked, his voice quiet, reserved.

Even the medic stopped.

"I saw the man who did this. I saw him sitting a few tables away."

"You'd better tell the cops. You sure?"

"I'm sure. When he drove away he was smiling." Madsen paused. "I think that bomb was meant for me."

Hannah sat up. She was not aware of having lost consciousness, but she felt disorientated, as if stirred too soon from sleep. The dust had settled. A fog of motes hung in the air picked out by the paltry light from the passage. Her throat felt tight. She reached for her inhaler and administered successive blasts of vapour.

She breathed a little easier. Standing up, she hesitated. Then she went back down the passage to the outside world. Carefully she looked out beyond the first door. Most of the right hand side of the building was nothing more than rubble, completely hiding the Agent's mangled body. Keeping to the shadows, she stared out. She had no idea how much time had elapsed, but all seemed quiet. She was puzzled that no one had clambered into the ruins. Maybe they were just opportunist insurgents who had stumbled upon the helicopter. Perhaps they were protecting the sacred site from the profane. If that were the case, where were they? Either way she would have to work fast. Her mind fixed once more on the task in hand, she once more returned down the passage.

How would the priests of Mithra open the doors in the bench? Holding the agent's gun, she aimed it at the small door. She hesitated. What if someone heard? She risked alerting anyone within earshot. She would have the contents in her possession, but for how long? Hannah lowered the weapon. No, there must be a safer way.

She put the weapon aside and dropped to her knees. Running her hands over the door, she searched for anything that might indicate a means of entry. Her fingertips traced over the image of the crown, and found a shallow triangular depression in the circlet.

Hannah was about to push the indentation but pulled back. She was not a believer in the sixth sense, but an inner voice warned her to be careful. She retrieved the gun.

With the muzzle, she pressed into the indentation in the crown. There was a soft click and the door opened. Pulling the gun away she could see a small metal pin jutting from the circlet. She had been right to be wary.

Enough light filtered in from the passage for her to see inside. It was empty. Hannah sat back, exhaled and swore under her breath. All this way for nothing. Was the information wrong? The altar just a decoy? Had the informant given bogus directions when he claimed it came from this shrine? More worryingly, had someone beaten her to the prize? She was not convinced.

Using the muzzle of the gun, she found a thumb-sized depression in each of the other inlays. A gold bull and a silver hammer lay behind their respective doors. Was the third box something similar to a Buddhist koan, designed to awaken the mind? If so, then maybe what she sought was still actually here, just not where she expected it to be.

The alcoves were too obvious a place for concealment if, of course, what she was looking for was a definable object. It might be an idea, something intangible, remote, like all the so-called divine knowledge of secret societies.

There was only one place left to look. The statue of Mithra, now shattered upon the stone floor of the inner sanctum. Using the butt of the gun, she turned the fragments over, but there were no hollow cavities within. Her attention turned to the head with its Phrygian cap, a symbol of liberty. She gave a brief ironic smile, and brought the gun down hard.

The head cracked open. It was hollow. Inside there was a key not much longer than her little finger. Its bow was an ornate sun symbol with fine lines radiating from its circumference.

Further Extracts

That evening, I was unwilling to cope with anything more adventurous than a sandwich, but I abandoned it half way through construction and ordered in a pizza. I lounged about in my study making phone calls to various back street antiquity dealers who might part with a few shekels for cat's blood in a fancy container.

After the fourth call – still no takers – the phone rang. Linda's voice was hushed and nervous.

'You alone?'

'Except for a soggy half-eaten pizza, yes.'

'Is it all right if I come round?'

'This time of night?' I sounded a shade dismissive. Not my intention at all. The question came out wrong.

'Is that a problem?'

'No, not really,' I said. Linda never left the house after nine o'clock. Not since that time when she thought she was being followed. She wasn't, but who am I to make light of someone's fears, particularly a woman's?

Half an hour later I opened my front door to a furtive-looking Linda. She clutched a large manila coloured envelope that had obviously been opened and closed many times before. I saw her name on it, written in a thick black felt tip marker.

She glanced over her shoulder then crossed the threshold.

'This was pushed through my door.' She sat nervously on the edge of my chaise longue (covered entirely in old copies of the Indy and the Grauniad).

I opened the envelope and slid out the contents.

Another novel extract. Or rather a photocopy.

'I don't know who it's from. It was there when I got home. Shoved through the letter box.'

THE TALES OF THOMAS HIDDON
(1749 –1790)

The following manuscript has been pieced together from several found in the library of Hiddon's biographer, my father, Wendell Partridge of Chew Magna. He sought out the various tales, collected and written down by a number of authors living in the county of Somerset, pertaining to the activities of one of the region's most famous inhabitants. This explains the variations in writing styles.

It appears that the writers were all colleagues of Hiddon's who vowed, after his passing, to gather their various recollections of his adventures into narratives of their memories and conversations with the man. Due to the vagaries of life none of his erstwhile companions were able to complete their respective tasks. The record of his activities here has been compiled from their notes.

Although not a native, Hiddon adopted the land of the summer people as his home until the end of his days. On his death his heart was taken to the Americas and laid beneath the foundations of Washington D.C. in honour of his earlier surveying work and his Masonic connections to the gentlemen of that capital including, it is rumoured, Benjamin Franklin. My father made the assumption that Hiddon was introduced to Franklin via Sir Francis Dashwood, infamous rake of Hell Fire Club fame. Although older, Dashwood, like Hiddon, had passed through the hallowed doors of Eton College. Hiddon was expelled from his *alma mater* for atheism.

Ptolemy Partridge. 1897

SUCH TASKS ARE GIVEN

From the manuscript by Tarquin Benbow

On the morning of June 28th the good barque *Andrea B* docked in the port of Bristol after a long journey from the American colonies. Having sought a last minute passage back to England from Boston, Mass., one

Thomas Hiddon alighted upon dry land. He immediately fell into the clutches of certain fellows of distinctly low moral fibre congregated near the moorings of the recently unladened *Bonhomme Charles*. Shouts of 'stowaway' had been offered by certain members of the group in an attempt to make good their arresting of Hiddon and to avoid unwarranted attention from the crowds of merchants, deck hands and others who lurked upon the waterfront seeking profit by whatever means.

Placing upon his head a thick hoodwink and a coarse ragged rope, while his hands were bound, Hiddon was swiftly inverted then bundled to a cart and thereunto thrown in a disgraceful and boorish manner. Throughout he remained stoic and indeed tacit, for he had returned to these shores full of apprehension and doubt, fearing that which had just befallen him.

Some short passage of time later he knew that his captors had brought him into Clifton as evidenced by the laboured effort of the horse, slipping as it did often upon the cobbles and the bounteous hills of foetid manure, and his sensing of the steep rise that had made up the majority of the journey.

Upon stopping, Hiddon was lifted out by two fellows whose arms were of immense strength and exceeding girth. Expecting to be dropped to the ground, he was alarmed by the fact that he was transported like a butcher's carcass over the threshold of a house where his head collided with the door jamb. For the first time he feared for his mortal existence, as now certain murderous deeds could be performed beyond the eyes of the outside world. There would be no one to witness such acts or requests for mercy.

Boldly, he had returned to the country of his birth to meet justice. He feared he would simply now be released from this mortal coil at the hands of unknown assailants without settling that which he owed, for he reasoned, and not without good cause, that he had been restrained by rude mechanicals on the orders of the man to whom he owed certain monies. He hoped it was he, for to him at least he could offer bargains and compromises. How this man knew of his return, to the hour, was beyond his comprehension. Spies must be abroad with alliances to certain wealthy gentlemen of Boston. Hiddon had made acquaintances there in his attempt to survey insect-infested swampland for development – some were considering it a site for the Colony's capital. There was the distant thunder of revolution in New England, allegiances were tested, allies made and friendships lost. Turncoats and profiteers were prolific with bigotry, propaganda and lies. Men, as they always do, turned their heads towards greed, casting aside their principles and feigned morality so that they might gain advantage from the loss of others. History paints a picture of a repressed population eager to rid themselves, in a Republican cause, of the king of their motherland. Indeed, but history is never that simple. Many sought to maintain their allegiances to the motherland but their role is now suppressed. Many would mourn, well into the future, the passing of the crown in the New World.

Still blindfolded, Hiddon heard a voice.

"See the man returns to meet his justice." The voice was effeminate, like that possessed by a fey but sordid headmaster, and drifted through the air like women's perfume, thin in nature as if cheap and short lasting, failing to mask the odours beneath.

Hiddon turned in the direction of the voice to face his unseen restrainer.

"Do I know you sir?" Knowing not his fate, the young man took a diplomat's course in an effort to weasel himself from dark confinement. For all he knew daggers were about him like a steel cage. Hiddon set his hand upon the air as if searching for a tip of steel; he found none.

"Do you know me sir? Do you know me?" The manner of utterance was like that of a peevish child. "If thou didst know me I fear your course of action would have fallen stillborn from the printing press."

Printing press.

Two simple words to reveal a great mystery.

"Ah..." Hiddon held out both hands. A gesture of placation. He resisted the temptation to fall into pleading.

"You wretched mountebank, I could have you hung for blasphemy, at the very least! For defamation of my character!"

It was the Bishop of York. Here in the city of Bristol.

Reaching up, Hiddon's fingers tugged at the rope around his neck.

"Scurrilous words demand harsh recompense," the Bishop said and crossed the room. At the table, he poured himself a victorious tot of French brandy, from the caves of D'Aurillac, whose ancestor, Pope Sylvester II, was accused of selling his soul to the devil and dabbling, for profit, in the alchemical arts. "Now I expect nothing but excuses and I will accept none. For they would be empty words, as hollow as your sacrilegious attempts to demean the words of our Lord." The Bishop sipped his brandy and stood gloating over the moment, as a man may do when securing victory over a rival.

"Many men have tried to deny the truth and have set hard upon the task of undermining the soul and morality of this country with immoral learning. You are just the latest in a list of deceivers. If your devilish non-belief sets you free, why are you now here within the confinement of these walls, before thy judge? Thy sins shall find thee out."

On many occasions Hiddon practiced mental arguments to counter any such theistic pronouncements, but now found himself tongue-tied. Weary journeys do not facilitate engaging in round housing with spiteful men of the cloth, who, as any right thinking person can attest, possess an answer for everything.

"I had taken you for a Catholic," the Bishop continued. "A revolutionary one at that, yet your words are not those of a Papist. And indeed no Catholic would denounce the teachings of our Lord." The Bishop turned and faced his quarry. "Thou art an atheist."

Beneath his hoodwink, Hiddon's expression turned defiant.

"I am a man of the Enlightenment!"

"Dangerous to admit such. I could embellish the whole affair to encompass treason and revolution as well as blasphemy. You tread on thin ice Hiddon, held up by the treacherous and betraying hands of Satan himself."

The young man was unwilling to surrender to the manipulations of this man of York.

The Bishop went on.

"You will spend eternity in the fires of hell. You are doomed. So I hold before thee an offer. A form of penance. Yes. Penance so that you may replenish your soul a miniscule iota in the eyes of the Lord. I will pray for you if thou offer up to me your sun key. And Master Hiddon, do not pretend to deny such an item for I know it exists and that before you left for the colonies you got it from that rogue Frederick. Bring it to me and I will offer not your traitorous corpse to the authorities."

It was not an elegant choice for any man. But a trapped animal may seek any exit thus given and will follow any seam of light that presents itself.

"I have it in safe keeping," Hiddon said, "and ask that I may be freed so that I may bring it hence."

Hiddon was transported with bag still about head and by the same swarthy riff-raff to a back street and deposited unceremoniously at the exterior of a costermonger's by the name of Leech. The man was much

82

puzzled to find that a young durgen had taken up residence in the reeking effluvia in front of his shop.

Assuming the coast to be clear, and having removed the bag from his head, Hiddon studied his environs carefully. Despite his position few gave him a second look. He knew he was on a road somewhere east of Park Street.

Yet, on standing up and before he could compose himself fully, he was set upon by a contingent of be-muscled hirelings who proceeded to re-hoodwink him in an equally brusque manner as that of the original riff-raff. A vulgar lobcock took a cosh to the back of his skull.

Hiddon fell back into the dark.

Hiddon woke to find himself cast down upon another floor. He heard those who had borne him over the threshold leave. Figuring himself to be alone, he made moves to upright himself and sat there upon the tiled floor wondering as to his predicament. He tugged at the rope set tight upon his wrists but it moved not.

"Mister Hiddon." The voice was rich and stentorian and was of course not unfamiliar to the bound captive. "Your efforts are in vain."

The young man froze, his senses heightened.

"My journey in darkness must have been longer than I realised."

"You are aware, no doubt of whom you are addressing."

"Indeed sir. You are a gentleman of London. Or my memory fails me."

"Levity, thy name is Thomas. Stand up."

With care, Hiddon raised himself to his feet and stood swaying a little with fatigue, like a sapling in an evening zephyr.

"You must understand that I headed to the colonies with the sole purpose of redressing certain deficits in my fiscal affairs, to whit that which I owe you sir," Hiddon said. The hoodwink still about him, he aimed his words in the direction he thought they would best be received.

"But that was three years ago. Not one correspondence did I receive expressing any strategy of repayment. Therefore I assumed you have reneged on our deal."

"'Tis true. But there were sufficient reasons that barred my efforts."

"Not even revolution could throw up redoubts high enough to stop a man from contacting his creditor."

"You know of the impending revolution?"

"Mister Hiddon, I am a man of great resourcefulness. News travels slowly but it does travel, and you are not the sole keeper of such tidings. There are men of my association in the burgeoning republic. Men who will continue to secure the bond with his majesty, who wish to maintain the status quo."

"And these men were set about me as spies?"

"Indeed, Mister Hiddon."

The bound debtor sighed and, realising that fate had positioned him on this course faced, as a gentleman should, his punishment.

"My lord Flute. It seems as though I am fated. That I could not, even if I wanted, escape destiny for she has seen to square all her duties in the course of time. Even in light of my misdeeds, I beg mercy that I may honour that which I owe."

That request met with nothing but silence for several minutes. It was then that Hiddon became aware of ephemeral mutterings; the room contained more individuals than just Lord Flute and he.

Suddenly there were hands about his neck working upon the rope. With a dexterous flourish, the hoodwink was removed.

Standing about him were nine men of noble standing and learned disposition whose tailors were of the highest class. About their waists were aprons of white calfskin adorned with gold brocade and certain sigils of symbolic meaning.

Lord Flute was sat upon a chair of such regal countenance that for a second Hiddon thought he stood before his majesty. The carving brought to mind the work of Seraph of Milan who found fame and fortune in bouts of Papal extortion, claiming, it was said, to be in possession of *manuscripts of the flesh*. The floor was a black and white checkerboard. Mysterious symbols adorned the walls. Above, the curve of a dome was bedecked with astrological symbols surrounding an embossed pyramid and cloud from which a single hand emerged, as if to bless all those beneath.

"Thomas Hiddon," Flute said. "I thought long these last three years as to suitable acts of reparation on your behalf. At one time I had bounty laid upon your head."

"I reasoned that. I was hounded by an assassin on leaving an inn on the turnpike around Marblehead."

"I recalled him after consultation with my brethren here."

Hiddon cast his eyes upon each man ranked around the throne, as if awaiting the painter's hand to move upon a canvas.

"My escape led me into the back streets of Boston. I assumed I outwitted my nemesis."

"No sir. You had not." Lord Flute adjusted his position slightly and cast a frown in Hiddon's direction. "My colleagues and I all share a most profound similarity. We are all owed certain monies, in varying amounts, but nonetheless enough to make it worth our while pursuing those debts."

"I most humbly beg…"

"Silence." Flute's upheld hand was enough to render the young man mute. "Do not render yourself as a supplicant. The damage is done. You will pay back that which you owe, in a method of our choosing."

"I am at your service. For that which I have done, and indeed failed to do, I will undertake anything." Hiddon's tone was subservient. He bowed to add emphasis.

"Young Hiddon. Your words are those of a mountebank and a pettifogger. You cast your sentences as a maid wooing a rich man of fancy. We will set you hard upon a task whether you wish it or no. You are to be dispatched to recover all the money that is owed us."

Hiddon, much taken aback, had feared retribution of a more permanent kind.

"When all the money is returned I will consider that you have paid your debt to me and will thus set you free. Cross me again and the consequences will be dire. I have set certain spies upon the road to ensure that you execute the task in hand. Six months you are given."

"All I ask is that I may be allowed to visit my home and my possessions." Something familiar, Hiddon thought, might bring respite to his heavy heart.

"My boy. You have no home and all your possessions are within these walls, not that they amount to much less than a coffer's worth of personal fripperies. I would have sold them if they were of any value. I offer you one item and one item only. You may earn back what you have left."

"I lack one item only to assist me in my endeavours."

"Name it. It shall be yours."

Nursing two regal swollen bruisings upon his head, souvenirs of one tumultuous day, Hiddon was escorted off the premises – a fine house of good standing upon the hill. It was one of several lodgings in the West Country of the Cheddar Rattlers, a secretive organisation born in the area of the famous Gorge, and indeed cheese, of the same name. Their task, it was said, was to perform something of the nature of charitable works for men of similar standing. Yet there were others who accused all men of such interests as being in league with the devil and his minions, and that further, the Rattlers were robbing the men of Somerset of their wits and their daughters of their virginities. As in many legends, there was a seed of truth at the core. One Grand Master, now run from the county, did indeed avail himself of the naive proclivities of the daughter of the Mayor of Axbridge in a now famous and scandalous orgy of sexual wantonness that spilled out upon the square near King John's hunting lodge. From this incident the Rattlers strove to buff the tarnish and cast sun upon their name, yet in vain.

With hunger gnawing upon his soul and with a thirst so deep he felt he could have sunk his head into the River Avon and drained it to its mud floor without hesitation, Hiddon hastily repaired to the nearest hostelry, a scurrilous inn teetering under the name The Pizzle. With what coins he still possessed, he bought a tankard of ale and a platter of dark bread and meats and ensconced himself against the damp stained west wall, where shade and shadow hid him from further unwarranted demonstrations of ill will.

There he sat for an hour nursing flesh and drink, avoiding the glare of the landlord, who desired, as ever, that his customers should not buy but one tankard for an entire evening's refreshment. Hiddon's thoughts ran and tumbled about the two tasks he had about him. One from the vile Bishop. One from the Grand Master of the Cheddar Rattlers. One born from his willingness to spread the message of free thought; one from the over-openness of his purse. A man cannot enter the afterlife with such metal, so it must be spent. Yet, as an atheist, he deemed it also worthy to spend his money. Despite the Bishop's suggestions, atheism and fiscal laxity are not common bedfellows unless they share the name Thomas Hiddon. But then pamphleteering is not a free pursuit; to rid the minds of men of their childishness of thought cannot be done for no cost. What little money he had inherited was not long about him. Imperiled by savage impecuniosity, he sought other sources of income to continue his work, not least as a surveyor in the American colonies.

Feeling undesirous of setting about his onerous, not to say impossible, tasks, Hiddon mustered the last of his coins and administered another ale to soothe his racked and tortured spirit. He was, for the foreseeable future, now penniless. He would, as they say, play out the last vestige of decency upon the fiddle of drink.

By purchasing another beverage, Hiddon avoided the splenetic landlord who was about to launch a broadside of explosive and concussive words in the young miscreant's direction. Instead, the soak tempered his malevolence while he tapped the barrel. As he did so he sullied his breeches with a rapid salvo of malcontent wind but scarce seemed to notice, perhaps through familiarity of such activities.

As he stood at one with the counter, Hiddon was unaware of a trio of taut faced fellows who entered The Pizzle as if they were expecting trouble, like certain members of the King's militia entering a den of thieves. Each man cast his eyes upon a third of the inn and thereupon all at last fell upon the stooped figure of their quarry, caressing his last coins within his palm.

The largest of the three, much akin to a Russian bear topped in a tricorn, moved stealthily of foot to within a few paces of Hiddon whereupon he drew a cosh and smote the young man about the skull.

His chin struck the timbers of the bar, his body, like week-old sullied laundry, fell misarranged upon the floor and for the third time that day, Thomas Hiddon was manhandled away from liberty.

There was a sudden shock of water upon his head and for a few brief moments, while he fought fears of drowning, Hiddon scrabbled his hands about his face and called out. When consciousness was fully restored he found himself upon the floors of an inner chamber within the city courthouse. He sat like a half drowned rat on the deck of a ship and set his mind upon deducing the fearful particulars of his latest predicament.

A rotund gentleman of portly demeanour, like a ship's barrel with grease-soaked cheeks, was swiftly devouring the carcass of a roast chicken like a ravenous street cur.

On one side of the chamber was a long bench, raised so that the occupiers were elevated in rank and status from the accused before them. Here sat the three kidnappers, two of whom seemed than less stirred by the situation, while the Russian bear, hat in lap, studied Hiddon as if at any moment he expected the young man to flee for the door.

On the other side of the room stood a baker's dozen of uniformed militia, of a regiment unknown to Hiddon. Perhaps they were either raised in Gloucester or Somerset. Their scarlet tunics were clean and the white trim was also free of besmirching. Brass buttons reflected the sun that spilled through the leaded lights above the high legal altar. Their eyes were fixed upon some point in the mid-distance. They appeared to ignore Hiddon but their muskets were affixed with bayonets as if forearmed against any incitement to rebellion on his part.

The fat greasy one looked up quickly at Hiddon, as if to confirm that the right man had been brought afore him, then returned to his feasting.

With his mouth full, he mumbled, "I will ask but one question of you, Thomas Hiddon, late of His Majesty's colonies. Are you, as some say, a spy?"

Hiddon frowned in puzzlement.

"Is it recounted that I engage in the arts of subterfuge and espionage? It is a lie."

"For monies, they say, so that you may render unto your creditors that which you owe. Do you deny this?"

"Sir, I do."

For a few moments his accuser was perforce silent, for his mouth was stuffed with roast fowl. The bird was now sundered as if fallen from cannon shot and lay upon the plate like a corpse.

Mopping at his mouth, Hiddon's third nemesis of the day sat back, lifted a goblet of wine and quaffed noisily from its contents.

"Then, do you claim, my spies abroad are wrong in their assessment? But they are trusted men and have yet to fail me or his Majesty's government."

"I pray you cannot find it in your heart to believe me," Hiddon said and moved to raise himself to stand like a proud man against his accuser, but a member of the militia forced him to remain where he was by use of the butt of his musket.

"I do not for one minute believe anything that issues from your mouth. It is a foetid orifice from which spews forth malice and inconsistencies. I am obliged to render it mute."

"I stand within a court of law and decree my innocence."

"Pshaw! If a decision were laid at my conscience as to what to do with you, I would have you thrust against a wall and sent to the next world by the use of lead shot. But I am instructed, against my better judgement, to keep you alive."

"I am honoured."

"Rest that impudent jester's tongue. I am to offer you a King's Pardon, but you must agree to undertake actions to recompense the country."

Rather than defend his dented honour, Hiddon attempted conciliation, but the judge interrupted:

"Your choice is to attend to this task or go to the gallows for treason."

As clear as fresh gin was the course open to the young Hiddon. Despite his ill ease at being accused of such crimes of which he knew himself innocent, it was better to accept the charges than to swing at the end of a rope.

"I accept."

"No defiance in your heart I see. Which may be good or bad depending on one's point of view. The task is this. The King, knowing of the stirrings across the ocean, requires a better understanding of his subjects. Information has come to his ears that malcontents roam the land, treason-filled miscreants who may act against the crown in a time of revolution. You are to seek out these hidden and secret cabals and cadres who may bear the king malice. You are charged with Somersetshire. You are to have a purse enough to render your task, no more than board and lodgings and three meals a day. No gambling, whoring or drunken debauchery. Such misadventures will break contract and you shall swing."

Hiddon's mind laboured on this offered duty. The answer would be yes for liberty; even a minor yoke is better than shuffling off the mortal coil. If the task were hunting for a horse-ladder, he cared little. Coins and a quest were at least, for now, the promise of livelihood.

"I accept the task placed before me."

"Do not test my patience Hiddon. Your devilish smirkings will have you dewitted upon the cobbles of this city. I hasten to remind you that, should you speak of such matters to anyone, I will cut short your sorry existence myself."

The man sat back in his chair and studied Hiddon with eyes much akin to that of a ferret, cornering its prey in the farmyard.

"I meant no disrespect," Hiddon said. "I will not take liberties with the quest."

"You are as oily as an eel fresh caught and writhing on the grass. Be gone from my sight." A purse was cast in Hiddon's direction and narrowly caught by him. "Six months you have. You will lodge in the City of Wells wherefrom your reports will be handed to a man in my service. When you have found rooms, avail me of the address. Do not cross me, Hiddon. I am a man with little patience for godless traitors."

On his command, two infantrymen manhandled Hiddon to his feet and marched him through the halls to the doors of the assize, then cast him into the street.

To priest, creditor and king, Hiddon now was roundly tied, ensnared by cunning traps and deviousness. He cared little for that three-headed beast. Half a year was his contract and within that time he must fulfill his obligations and rid himself of the duty to these other men. Still he could be free of the boundaries now lain upon him, and able to continue his peregrinations unbound, a free man and a freethinker.

To celebrate his newfound employment, Hiddon repaired forthwith to the Admiral of the Narrow Seas, an inn with creaking joists and swarthy patrons on the edge of the docks. Here he intended to drink to the day when true liberty would be his companion once more. But before he could finish even one tankard, the bear-like man appeared, forcefully dragged him from the establishment and threw him unceremoniously onto a Vintner's cart heading south to Wells.

THE QUESTS ARE UNDERTAKEN

From the first folio of collected letters once in the possession of John Tyfold-Piebald.

My Esteemed Sire,

I have taken suitable lodgings not far from that wondrous building, the cathedral, displaying as it does that skill and craftsmanship of the master masons of long ago. To look up at its towers, it takes all my skill in not falling backwards, so precipitous and fabulous is the stonework. Indeed, on my first visit I was assisted by a man of the cloth who espied my troubles and rushed to aid me. I was told that it was not uncommon for newcomers to tumble hence.

I am stationed at the Bulbous Whim in Tucker Street.

Your obedient servant,

T. Hiddon, Esquire.

(This letter was addressed to the representative of his Majesty's government who had charged Hiddon with the task of seeking out the secret men of the county. The tone is light and friendly, at odds it seems with Hiddon's real feelings towards the man. My father suggests this was part of an attempt to 'disarm' his paymaster. *P. P.*)

There was that key again.

'What do you think?' Linda bit a fingernail.

'It's another novel isn't it? It doesn't read like the first extract. It's a different author I should imagine.' I studied the photocopy. It certainly looked genuine (that's the original book I mean not the photocopy). The typeface was certainly of the period and as far as I could tell the printer's marks and the texture of the paper seemed as old as the hills.

'The key,' Linda said, clearly thinking it was important.

'The sun key. Yeah, it's mentioned again. Still doesn't make it real. Maybe this author read the other novel as well. Or both authors sourced Wendell Partridge's library.'

'But why would anyone send this to me?'

'Your article. You mentioned the novel extract.'

'I know, but why send it to me? Why anonymously?'

Half a good point.

'Somebody thought you might be interested.' I moved slowly across the carpet and sat down.

'Yes but why the anonymity?' she asked.

Okay, Linda had a point. Why would anybody deliver unto her a photocopy of an extract from an unheard of book, which related, by way of a key sporting the image of the sun, to a recently found extract of a different novel?

'You sure this isn't from Gus?' I asked.

'He wouldn't send it anonymously. You know him. He'd make a real song and dance about it. He would bound round to my place all gestures and excitement.' Linda reached for the photocopy. I leant over and handed it to her. I watched her examine the words as if they might somehow contain a threat to her well-being.

One minute I'm living my life without this wretched sun key, they next it's coming at me from all directions and making my friends nervous into the bargain. I must admit it was all a bit odd. Whoever it was who delivered the document knew of this Hiddon character. Was Hiddon a real person, adding to the possibility that the sun key was real?

The sun was a universal image, obviously. Helios. The prime mover. The one genuine object that brought life to this planet. Sol Invictus from which Christianity nicked the halo. Aten. The All–Seeing Eye. Etc., etc., etc.

As far as I could recall the sun was important in every culture on the planet, symbolically I mean. Gets me out the house. Pub garden. Onto the beach. It lifts the spirits. I was meandering.

'The sun... the son.' Linda was performing word association. 'Maybe it relates to that.'

'Right.' I wasn't convinced. Rarely am to be honest. 'The son of what?'

'God.'

Here we go... again.

'The sun signifies the *son of god*?' I slurped noisily on my can of 6X.

'It's not unknown for puns and word play to be used by those who harbour secrets.' Linda let the photocopy rest on her knee. I could tell that her mind was starting to work along the lines of wordplay.

'It's stretching it a bit.'

'If the church is threatening to burn anyone who thinks outside the box then puns become very important. Look at alchemy. The whole thing is wordplay and subtext. The language of the birds, for instance.' Linda straightened her back like a schoolmistress.

I rubbed my chin, mostly in an attempt to remove beer that had spilled there, also because I was unconvinced by Linda's reasoning. I had to admit though that it was a tad interesting, especially the idea of lost books. Lost books were more my thing. The only trouble was that the kind of people who read *Codex* were, shall we say, a bit out there, too eager to buy into fads, new age malarkey and conspiracy theories hastily thrown together on the bog by a hard pushed editor looking for something to fill his or her pages with. The undeniable element to all this was the fact that we had two different and unknown texts relating to a Thomas Hiddon with their hints of a mysterious key.

Men had been hanged for less.

'Do you mind if I stay here tonight?' Linda said, looking at her watch, then turning fearful eyes to me. Before conclusions are heavily jumped to, no... I'm not interested. Linda's attractive all right but her head, or rather her mind, it's just too busy for me. I heard her enough times round chez Gus when she was on these full-blown assaults on reality, where the conspiratorial connections came thick and fast. It was an idea onslaught, a tsunami of terrifying possibilities. Exhausting.

'Sure. Spare room isn't tidy though.' It never was.

'Would you mind if I had a bath?' Linda ran strands of hair through her fingers.

'Of course not. Be my guest.'

In an odd kind of way it was good to have a woman about the house again, in that comforting sense of having someone else moving about the place making all those familiar and everyday sounds. Taps running, footfalls on the landing, doors opening and closing. It felt homely.

I really had to sort myself out on that front.

Publishing Conspiracies

The book had been selling well moving quickly out from the underground market, its natural home, into the mainstream. Mark Arden was none too pleased. Despite the message of the book, he was trying his best to maintain his credibility as a vanguard on the walls of liberty, as his Internet website moniker had it. This contrived air of literary isolationism had won him few friends. But increasingly healthy books sales were slowly eroding a decade-long effort to promote his self-image as a lone non-commercial voice calling to the initiated.

Had he been more paranoid, he would have entertained the notion that the book's success was a plot to reduce his status from freethinking maverick to hack writer trying to earn a buck. Yes, he was something of an egotist, often regaling his besieged friends around a pizza and a crate of beer with well-constructed descriptions of dark machinations operating behind the scenes, but fear was not something he had much of. Arden converted his fear into anger, anger at the men in suits whom he thought were making life a misery. He never muddied the waters of his reasoning by claiming that numerous clandestine secret societies were involved, much to the annoyance of his colleagues, who thought otherwise. To him it was just greedy, power crazed men who caused all the suffering, period. The clubs they belonged to were irrelevant.

He clashed with like-minded people at conventions, workshops and rallies. He despised those who were convinced that twelve-foot high lizards had disguised themselves as presidents, aristocrats and stockbrokers. He equally loathed the far right theorists who thought aliens, with apparent 'socialist' leanings, were trying to turn the world into an atheistic and communist super state, and he held in particular contempt those who saw everywhere the hand of the devil working through the Freemasons or the bogus Illuminati.

His book, suitably entitled '?', had been intended to destroy these theories and promote a more down-to-earth view of what was going on behind the scenes. He had intended more particularly, to explode any theory of a pyramidal hierarchy. The question mark referred ironically to the supposed cadre at the pinnacle of power.

But, as he research more deeply, Arden quietly began to change his tune. He became more convinced that some super elite did exist when two colleagues died under highly suspicious circumstances. The word around the underground network was that they had come close to revealing the existence of a genuine ruling secret society. Arden knew, as everyone did in his community of radical writers, that all brotherhoods have never been genuinely secret. Their existences were known, after all. But his two friends had apparently stumbled upon the genuine article.

Three months ago, picking up the phone in the early hours of the morning, Arden had heard the hushed tones of JJ Marsh asking him if he could come round. Assuming he had fallen out with his girlfriend again, Arden agreed. He would get the couch ready. But JJ's voice was edged with fear and punctuated with choking gasps like the sobbing of a child.

Several hours crawled by but JJ failed to turn up. Later that morning an irritated Arden picked up the phone again, to be told by one of his colleagues that JJ's body had been found hanging from a tree in Central Park.

After the funeral, the talk was of motivation. No one could believe JJ was capable of taking his own life. There must have been another reason. Had he come close to something? For about eighteen months JJ had been wrapped up in his own investigations but had refused to talk to anyone about his work. His friends assumed he was on a glory trip and was about to go solo, but Arden voiced another opinion. Maybe JJ was just protecting someone else. Everyone knew that the offices of their small publishing group, if not bugged, certainly drew the attentions of the authorities. They ran a tight ship and maintained a high standard of book keeping and tax returns by way of protecting themselves should the establishment spotlight turn on them. They may have despised those same authorities but they played safe nonetheless. Even their lawyer was impressed by this disparate collection of renegade writers. Yes, they were a thorn, albeit small, in the side of many organisations and multinationals and had broken the law in the name of protest. But they paid their fines and never resisted arrest. They reserved their venom for the written word. If they were going to be brought down in a fit of moral or political pique by those keen to silence them, then the onus would be on the authorities they despised to concoct a web of lies, more difficult if scrupulous records had been kept, to turn against their accusers.

Everyone had their own thoughts on the reasons for JJ's death. But it was not until the group's mentor Jim Eddowes went missing a month later that the silence was broken. Eddowes, or Big Jim, started the radical publishing group fifteen years before. He was without doubt the driving force and inspiration for everyone who worked there. Big Jim's passion was the JFK Assassination; he knew every twist, turn, character and conspiracy. He had torn down the Warren Commission and he demolished wilder and more fanciful notions as they came to the fore. Big Jim's mantra was that the truth is often in the middle, between the extremes. No, he did not think Lee Harvey Oswald, Hoover's lone nut, was responsible but he was clearly involved, if ignorant of his role. Was there a grand plot by Freemasons, Illuminati, or another group, out to destroy Kennedy's presidency? No. But the shootings were not the work of a lone gunman.

Big Jim knew, because he had been in Dealey Plaza that day. He was only three at the time, but he had one overriding memory. He had seen the man behind the picket fence; the man that everyone said could not have been there. He had seen the shot fired, and that crimson spray lit up in the bright November sunshine. Back and to the left – back and to the left. Big Jim knew.

Then, when he was ten, he watched an airliner turning a slow lazy arc against the vivid blue of an afternoon sky above his house. Suddenly from nowhere a glider banked sharply down to avoid being sucked into the engines and span away as the pilot tried to regain control. The news that night denied that both planes had been anywhere near each other. From that moment on he knew that the world was a darker place than people wanted him to believe.

He never forgot those two events. Between them they shaped his outlook. He learnt that most people did not care and were happy to get through their day unhindered by the wider world. Conspiracy theories were the purview of fools, social and political outcasts or misfits. Although he could dismiss most of them, Big Jim knew that sometimes the misfits were right.

Big Jim had also been working on something he was unwilling to discuss. Pursuing a lead in Boston, he had called Arden to say that he would be delayed for a few days. He was following a trail that had led from Dallas to New England and it would be too great an opportunity to let it go. He said he was close to cracking the Big One, which Arden knew to be Big Jim code for the horrific events in Dallas of November 22nd, 1963. Quite what the man had found that had escaped a thousand researchers beforehand was beyond Arden. With Big Jim's disappearance, his discoveries were now perhaps lost forever.

A week had crawled by since, and the mood of the others in the group had become subdued, edged with a degree of irritation. The ship had lost its rudder. Big Jim had always seen Arden as his natural successor and often treated him as something of a second in command. Not that the group had a pecking order per se, but in temperament both Big Jim and Arden shared a similar mindset. It was an unwritten and indeed unspoken rule that, when Big Jim was away, his understudy ran the show and made most of the editorial decisions.

Arden's attention was fixed on the bookshop's window. New York beyond was blurred and melted by a day of rain. Cars rolled by creating low arcing waves that crashed against the sidewalk like winter breakers on a cold grey shore while people raced by, heads bowed against the elements. It was all normal, which for the moment was just what Arden wanted.

He knew that something was dreadfully amiss. Big Jim would always call, wherever he was, and let the group know what he was up to. A week was a long time. He looked at his watch. Time to go home.

Behind him the table that had been covered with hardback copies of his book was now almost empty. The book was creating a buzz. Radio and TV stations were keen to hook up the writer for an interview. Arden had turned most of them down. The few interviews he did do were chosen on impulse.

The book had its critics, despite its popularity. Some described it as wild and unrealistic and asked why such an obviously fictitious work was being touted as a non-fiction book. In fact, all Arden had done was trace the history of the more famous secret societies and their relationships to each other and discussed the roles they might have played in affairs of the West over the last few centuries.

What irritated certain skeptics in the media was Arden's insistence that there was one overall controlling group. His ideas might seem wild, but he was quite prepared to lay out his cards on the table and enjoy the reaction. There was a part of his character that was mischievous. That was what had drawn him to the field of conspiracy theorists in the first place. As he grew older that aspect of his nature was fading, but still, on rare occasions, he gave his inner jester full rein. He and Big Jim had often discussed the possibility of a single pyramid of power but it had never seemed quite credible. People were greedy and selfish, always looking after number one. How could any one group really control all the others, run the world and, more to the point, remain hidden for generations?

Big Jim argued that, if there were a group of that kind, it would have to number no more than a handful. Decision making would be in the hands of a few to avoid the adverse dynamics of a large group, all with their own personal motivations and self-serving desires.

Certainly, codes of conduct and allegiance, a sense of fellowship and the protection of secrets could all act as a kind of cohesive force to circumvent human failings. But nothing had ever succeeded in quelling human desire.

Arden had really written his book just to make people think, to steer them from mute acceptance to a state of questioning. Real patriots ask questions.

As the book signing trailed off, the bookshop staff disappeared out back to make coffee and small talk. Arden was now in two minds whether to stay or go. He felt trapped, even here, a frequent feeling since Big Jim's disappearance. He realised that if he wanted he could just slip out and no one would care, or indeed notice.

After the heat of the bookshop the steady rain was refreshing. He smiled briefly at the thought that he might be the only New Yorker in the city happy it was raining.

As he approached the old brownstone where he had his apartment, the door opened. About to up his pace to get through the door before it closed, he was brought up short as he saw the figure coming out. The man had a classic, chilling, military bearing. He wore dark trousers, a black wool roll neck sweater and a long raincoat.

Arden pulled his coat closer around his face and hurried on by. He heard the door click shut behind him. Was the man was following him? He would only draw suspicion on himself if he looked round.

Up ahead on the other side of the street was a noodle bar, one he and the group often frequented. Weaving through the traffic, Arden pushed open the glass door, trying to appear nonchalant. He produced a smile for Lee, the cheerful proprietor behind the till. Lee grinned back.

"Hi Mark. How's tricks?"

Arden took a seat at the counter and leaned towards him.

"Lee. Tell me. Uptight military-looking guy. Long raincoat. Is he outside?" Arden kept his eyes fixed on Lee who glanced quickly through the big glass windows.

"Yeah, I see him. Other side of the road. You in trouble?"

"I don't know. He's just come out of my building."

"You are in trouble again."

"What's he doing now?"

"Walking on by."

"Did he look over?"

"No."

Arden was about to turn round.

"Wait. He's stopped."

"Looking over?"

"No. He's using his cell phone." Lee continued polishing the counter fittings. "OK. He's leaving. Gone."

Arden turned and looked back out into the rain-washed street. He slowly went to the door and looked out. He could see the man moving quickly away, eventually lost from view behind a huddled, animated group attempting to hail a taxi.

"You want something to eat?" Lee wiped his hands on a dishcloth.

"Yeah. Ah, damn, I don't have any cash. Give me five minutes to go and get some money." Arden opened the door and stepped out onto the sidewalk. He glanced up the street half expecting to see the man heading back towards him, and crossed over to the corner.

Somebody shouted behind him. Spinning round, he saw a woman pointing up and across the road. Suddenly he saw his own apartment window explode showering glass onto people and traffic below. Flames erupted outwards, roaring and hissing in the rain. Arden stood transfixed with horror. He stood for what seemed a long infinite moment, watching clouds of black smoke and flame pouring out of the window. Nobody could have survived that.

Then he pulled himself together and careered through the traffic and up to the door of the building. He punched in the security code. Opening the door he could feel the heat blasting down the staircase. He looked up and saw flames eating their way through the stairs, the paintwork blistering and cracking, peeling away in sheets of molten colour. Smoke rolled greedily down towards him like an angry beast forcing him to back out into the street again. Arden fell, gasping for fresh air.

He was aware of people gathering around him. Someone helped him up. Voices shouted, chattered excitedly. Another asked a question. He couldn't make out the words.

Arden struggled to break free and get into the brownstone but strong arms restrained him. There were a number of smaller explosions – computer monitors detonating in the heat. He saw charred pieces of paper, some still alight, falling like black leaves in the rain.

Now he wanted to run. He fought to free himself from the crowd, flailing his arms at the people supporting him. A man recoiled and slammed awkwardly into a parked car. Arden pushed the others aside and ran across the street and into a side alley. He staggered, tripped and fell into the piles of rank garbage that had accumulated there. He sat up, as the rain began to fall more heavily, and watched the building burn. Someone, somewhere had decided that enough was enough.

He closed his eyes. Then someone screamed among the crowd of horrified onlookers. Unwillingly, his eyes snapped open again. A figure had appeared at the blasted window, a blackened charred figure in a halo of flames, arms waving helplessly. Someone had been in the building, but who? Unable to look away, but more desperate to escape than ever, Arden began to push himself backward up the alley, his feet slipping on the wet ground and rotting pizza boxes. He saw the figure tumble forward, pivot on the windowsill then fall to the sidewalk below.

Madsen stood on the threshold of his home. Beyond, the cool dark interior had the feel of an imposing Cretan labyrinth. Somewhere inside was the beast. His sense of it as a secure haven – his fortress of solitude, as Gregory had often jokingly called it – was rapidly fading. He took a deep breath and stepped in.

For the next hour he went from room to room, checking for any signs of disturbance, any crooked picture or ornament out of place, any sign of violation.

Finishing in his study, he slumped into a large black leather chair and ran a hand across his forehead. He remembered the battle-weary intensity of the past, the psychological rituals he had devised to combat fear. Once before, he had been on the edge of psychosis but had fought his way back from the brink. He had no desire to stare once more into that abyss.

The phone chirped.

He let the answer machine kick in.

"It's Hiroko. Can we meet up? It's about the drawing."

Madsen hesitated.

"I've found out a few things–"

He snapped the phone off its cradle.

"Hi, it's me. I've just got in. How are you?"

"More importantly, how are you?"

Madsen leant forward.

"Okay, I guess," he said, less than convincingly,

"Which means you're not. Chris told me –"

Hiroko let the statement hang.

"That I thought the bomb was meant for me?" Madsen exhaled. He knew Gregory was convinced he was slipping back.

"Are they sure it was a bomb?" She was masking her doubt well. Her voice was warm and comforting. Had Gregory told her all about his past?

"We can meet here if you want." Madsen was surprised to hear himself make the invitation. His subconscious taking over, perhaps.

"When?" Hiroko whispered.

"Whenever. Tomorrow if you like."

"Or today?"

Madsen did not reply immediately. He felt sure this was a personal Rubicon. He could turn her down, yet he wanted to know what the drawing meant; maybe more importantly, he wanted to know Hiroko. Everything seemed to conspire to pull him away from his self-imposed internal exile. Change was growth. Had he simply forgotten that fact?

"Sure," he said warmly. "Why not?"

‡

Hannah made her way again to the temple doorway and peered cautiously out. The wreckage of the Blackhawk, an abstract work of Gothic sculpture, was still burning in the deep gold of evening. Several hours had passed since the attack. She had remained hidden. Darkness would be the best time to move. If insurgents were nearby, she hoped their patience would have run out and that they would have moved on. But why was no one out looking for her? Surely the Blackhawk would be missed. Her presence in Iraq was known to a few people at least. What were they doing? What about her father?

If no one came soon, then she would have to rescue herself. She would have to find a way back to Baghdad, a distance of around one hundred miles, using her own considerable wits and inner reserves.

She considered the pile of blast debris, now filling one side of the chamber, underneath which she could see a booted foot protruding. The dead Agent might have survival rations and other equipment that could help her. If she was to get home she could not afford to be squeamish. Making her way quietly over she began to lift chunks of crude plaster and brick. So as not to alert anyone to her presence, she moved the material one item at a time forming a pile on the other side of the ruined room. It was a long and tedious job.

Hannah freed the arm then the torso of the fallen Agent. The skin was grey and covered in a thick layer of dust and dirt, the fingers tightly clenched in rictus. Then she came to the head. The face was distorted, crushed by the concussion and the weight of debris. She sat the body up and unhooked the equipment vest. She took several clips of ammunition from the man's belt. Knowing there was no time to re-cover the body with rubble, she found the dog tag and snapped off the small stamped plates.

It was now dark enough for her to leave. She hesitated in the doorway, listening intently for any sound that might indicate she was not alone. She could feel a gentle evening breeze on her face. She thought of her home in New England, the wooded valley beyond. But the air here was dry, stale, dusty, not scented with evening blossom, and there was death around her.

If she headed southeast, she could hope to pick up a US patrol on the Iranian border near Qasr-e Shirin. Or she could head down towards the Diyala River some twenty miles or so south. The river seemed the better option. If she could find a boat, then she could travel all the way to its confluence with the Tigris, south of Iraq's capital. But she might spend weeks in the wilderness before she happened upon a military patrol, time she could ill afford. Her father had a strict timetable. She did not want to fail him or herself.

Working quickly and quietly, she loaded the Agent's gun and made a pack of the rations and the spare ammo. She tied up her hair in her scarf and rubbed dirt into the visible parts of her skin. Then she slipped out into the dark. If anyone were watching, their eyes would be on the twisted wreckage of the Blackhawk. She gave it a wide berth.

As she crept carefully up the low, dry slopes to the south she had a picture in her mind's eye of being observed through night sights. But if she had been seen, she would have already been cut down.

After an hour or so, she hit a road. She saw in the distance headlights of what might be a truck, immobile, about a mile away. Looking around, she could just make out a gully at the side of the road. Quietly, she swung herself down its side and began to walk, crouched over, in the direction of the lights.

Arden selected a key then looked both ways up the corridor. He opened the door to Big Jim's apartment a few inches and paused cautiously. He squatted down and gently ran his fingers up and down between the door and its jamb.

He pushed the door open and stood in the hallway. The place was dark and there was a faint smell of rotting food. At least Arden hoped it was food. He half expected to find Big Jim's body propped up in a chair with maybe a bullet wound in the head, or the signs of strangulation around the neck.

Without turning on the lights, Arden walked up the short hall. To his left was the bathroom. A tap was dripping.

An old toothbrush lay on a glass shelf beneath a mirror. The bathtub had a few inches of water in it.

The next room contained Big Jim's bed. A single mattress on the floor with a duvet and a pillow. Nearby was a stack of newspapers, each with sections cut out from scattered pages. Big Jim was famed for his scrapbooks. They contained all the odd stories or the news items that he deemed worthy of note. Arden was convinced people found what they wanted to find. Not everything was a conspiracy. Big Jim developed what he called the Opposite Theory. Whenever anything happened in the world, like a coup or a terrorist attack, look in the opposite direction for its source. It was just his way of thinking about the world around them. Nothing was ever black or white or as simple as the media made out. Everything was grey.

Arden opened another door; Big Jim's living room. It was little more than a storehouse for files, documents and paraphernalia used in the running of an underground publishing house. The place was stacked floor to ceiling with boxes of papers, posters and promotional material. Arden dimly noticed a few early versions of the cover of his book. The place was a tidy mess. No signs that anyone other than Big Jim had been there.

Arden sat down in the old wooden swivel chair, complete with coffee stains and cigarette burns on the armrests. The desk was a miniature Manhattan with tower blocks of paper, box folders and envelopes. There was a yellow-paged legal style jotter covered in doodles made during phone conversations and half a dozen mugs of old coffee, three of which had cigarette butts floating in them. An answer machine read zero.

Having tried the top two drawers in the desk and finding little of interest, Arden opened the third to be presented with an envelope bearing his name and the words *Contract for MS entitled '?'* Big Jim had been promising the contract for months, always making excuses, yet it had been in this drawer all the time.

For a moment, Arden's respect for Big Jim was replaced by anger. He ripped open the envelope and pulled out a document several pages thick. It was blank, except for the last two pages. One of these had only the typed words, 'Howard Hodgson Books, Providence, RI. Sunsphere'. The other was a detailed hand-drawn map showing a large house, a church and a series of caves. 'One of them is with the birds and the serpent' was written beneath in Big Jim's hand.

‡

Waiting for Hiroko to arrive that afternoon, out on the balcony with its view of the bay, Madsen had begun to wonder whether fraternising with a company intern was a sensible move. But Hiroko's presence had defused his paranoia for the first time in as long as he could remember. He did not feel under threat. The shadows had dissolved. The evening had been perfect, the night still more so.

He heard her naked feet on the planking of the balcony, and then felt her arms around him.

"Is this going to be the awkward time?" Hiroko rested her head against his back.

For a second or two he did not answer. Then turning to face her he placed a hand under her chin and lifted her head so that he could look into her eyes.

"For me or you?" he asked. She was wearing one of his shirts. "That looks good on you."

"It's comfortable." She studied him, a little uncertain.

"Then you wear it as much as you like." As he said the words, the ghosts within withered and evaporated. He felt simple joy in life, like the first sight of day after a long dark journey.

Hiroko looked at his face and smiled. "You've let the sun in," she said, and placed a hand on his heart.

"That sounds like Chris," Madsen smiled back.

"He's concerned for you."

"I guessed as much."

"So am I."

They stood in silence for a while, then Madsen broke the moment.

"So what have you found out?"

Hiroko led him off the balcony and back into the bedroom.

Hiroko left the room then returned with her briefcase. She placed it on the bed and opened it. She took out the photocopy of the ornate drawing to which was now attached several handwritten pages and further photocopies. She handed the bundle to Madsen.

"You've been busy." Madsen sat down on the bed. Hiroko reached for her glasses from the bedside table.

"I may be heading off in something of a wrong direction but-" Hiroko hesitated.

"Problems?" Her reticence puzzled Madsen. He studied her face.

"Not really." She paused. "The page definitely came from a book, but..."

"Either it did or it didn't."

"It did. For argument's sake. Several books refer to an architectural manuscript dating from the time of the Renaissance. A kind of manual for designers, like Palladio's *I Quatro Libri*. Wealthy clients could thumb through the book and decide which porticos they were going to have for their palatial homes or what kinds of towers to build. One reference work I've read mentions the Roman Catholic Church trying to have the book banned because it was said to contain occult geometry."

Madsen frowned.

"Occult just means hidden," Hiroko continued. "It has nothing to do with the devil or Satanism, but the Pope issued a Bull to stop its publication. Many copies were rounded up and burnt."

"So this manuscript is more famous for heresy than architecture?"

"Quite. The cathedrals were built using sacred geometry, but the buildings in this lost book weren't about that kind of occult. The illustrators used pagan symbolism, to which the church naturally objected."

"They were afraid that buildings constructed according to these plans might give people a different message?"

"Indeed."

"What was this treatise called?"

"No one's sure."

"And someone found this page from it?"

"Which means it exists somewhere, or at least part of it does."

"But where?"

Hiroko shrugged.

"I've no idea." She moved to sit next to Madsen on the bed. She pointed to one section of text. "This is from a catalogue of Renaissance manuscripts that went up for auction ten years ago at Sotheby's in New York." She allowed him to study the words for a few moments. "Listen to this." She began to read. "Rare MS, probably Venetian 16th Century. Architectural designs and views of the city of Venice. Publisher unknown. Cover and frontispiece missing. This edition once thought to be in the collection of Sir Francis Dashwood of West Wycombe, England."

"Francis Dashwood?" Madsen took the collection of pages from her. "If he's still alive, maybe we could try finding him. You think the torn page came from this book?"

"It's only a guess but it seems likely."

"The auction house will know who bought it."

"But that will be confidential information. Someone might want to steal it." Hiroko pointed out.

Madsen was silent. Someone had indeed stolen it. And had died.

"If the other drawings are as good as that one then I would love to see it."

"So would I. Maybe it is now the only copy."

Hiroko looked up. Madsen felt her eyes on him.

"How about us?"

He turned to look at her and lifted the pile of papers gently away.

"As you said, I've let the sun in." He took her hands, kissed her fingers then drew her close.

The phone rang.

"No." Hiroko murmured.

They let the machine take the call.

"Mister Madsen. This is Detective Kearns. I'm outside your house. Please come to the front door."

Madsen felt a spike of paranoia that swiftly became anger.

"What the hell do they want?" He disentangled himself reluctantly from Hiroko and walked through the upper gallery to the high window overlooking the driveway. There were two police cars parked in the drive. Kearns was looking up at the building and waved as he spotted Madsen. He pointed to the front door.

"I see you have a number of artworks yourself." Kearns cast his eyes over the Futurist illustrations on the wall of Madsen's living room.

"They're mine. Actually, I drew them." Madsen said stiffly.

Kearns leant in close to one of the drawings inspired by Frank Lloyd Wright.

Hiroko entered, shadowed by another policeman. She moved to stand next to Madsen but the cop placed a hand on her shoulder.

"Hey! What's the matter with you?" Madsen took a step forward. He turned to Kearns. "What is all this?"

"You remember the Sheriff," Kearns said directly to Madsen. "Lee Powers."

"Of course I do. He's a friend."

"He came here, didn't he?"

"Regularly."

"A short while ago. He showed you a drawing."

"The Dogana del Mare." Kearns hesitated for a second.

"Yes," said Madsen, a prickle of foreboding starting in his mind.

"Valuable?" Kearns persisted.

"Possibly. I believe it's part of an incomplete book. A rare one."

"A valuable book?"

"I guess."

"Valuable things make people do rash things."

"Undoubtedly. Your point?"

"Mister Madsen, the Sheriff is dead. The illustration he showed you is missing. Stolen."

Madsen felt the ice returning. The shadows were creeping back. "What – how did it happen?"

"He was hung from a tree in Berwick woods behind his house." Kearns said. "And we know it's not suicide. The perpetrator was just clumsy enough to leave a scrap of evidence. And that evidence was enough to bring us here at three in the morning."

Madsen raced through his memory of the day the Sheriff turned up with the page recovered from the body. What had Lee taken or picked up?

"Listen Detective." There was pain in Madsen's voice. "I am not responsible for Lee's death. If he committed suicide, I have no idea why. If he was murdered, I have no idea why. All I can tell you is I had nothing to do with it."

Kearns nodded, but it was clear he did not believe him.

"What did you do with the copy of the drawing Lee gave you, Mister Madsen? Who did you show it to?"

With great effort, Madsen prevented himself from looking toward Hiroko. He said nothing. There was a strained pause.

"Mister Madsen, I may have to return with a warrant to search this place." Kearns made for the door.

"Go ahead."

"And be advised, don't try to leave the area."

Moments later Madsen and Hiroko were alone.

"That bastard."

"He was a piece of work." Hiroko fell back in the wide couch and stared into space.

"You okay?" Madsen sat down beside her.

"No, I'm not. Is he going to have us followed?"

"Maybe. Why didn't they find your notes and the photocopy?"

"I hid them," Hiroko said.

Madsen stared at her. Then he leant forward and kissed her. They sat quietly for a few minutes.

"Did you know the Sheriff well?" she said, eventually.

Madsen nodded, sadness on his face. "I can't imagine he would have killed himself."

"You think he was murdered?"

"That page. The book. It's all connected somehow. What else could be?"

"What if we're next?" Hiroko sounded anxious.

"Yeah. Whoever wanted that page has it. Maybe, just maybe, that's it. They'll leave us alone."

"You don't believe that."

Madsen shook his head.

"No." Hiroko squared her shoulders. "We need to go to New York."

"If we leave, we'll be followed," she said.

"Let them try."

Hannah swore loudly as the gears ground together. With her foot hard down the truck was only able to travel at its top speed of thirty-five miles an hour. Its other more alarming ability was the way it managed to find every pothole in the road, which, in long stretches, consisted of nothing more than rubble and shell holes.

Acquiring the truck had been easy. The two men in the cab had been arguing over a smalltime arms deal when Hannah pulled open the door and aimed the HK at the man nearest her. He had spat and sworn at her, more as a diversionary tactic to allow the other to reach for a pistol. Hannah had fired once killing the man instantly. She had then dragged the other out of the truck and pushed him into the gully, throughout which, he had continued with his venomous tirade against her.

Climbing into the truck she swung the vehicle round and headed off back down the road complete with several boxes of ammunition, half a dozen RPG launchers and several crates of vintage World War two Russian Stechkin machine guns.

After a mile or so she had stopped to off-load the body of the man who had tried to pull the gun on her and the various weapons in the back of the truck. It was a risk worth taking she thought as less weight meant she might be able to get more distance out of the fuel tank. With its defunct gauge she had no idea how much gas was left in the fifty-year-old machine.

She had driven through most of the night. It had taken a long time to travel a short distance due to her lack of knowledge of the area and the seemingly constant traffic, which she did her best to avoid whenever possible. At one point she had found herself heading towards a large roadblock. She could see the lights of numerous vehicles some distance ahead. The terrain on both sides of the road was not exactly vehicle friendly so she parked up and sat there with lights off for two hours. With the first signs of dawn the roadblock slowly dispersed and much to Hannah's relief headed in the opposite direction.

As the sun had risen to her left she had taken out the key to examine it. All this way for something so simple. So many lives taken. So much bloodshed. So much loss. But her father had told her it would be worth it. That the end would justify the methods. She had no idea what he had meant and at best her father was a cryptic man who gravitated towards secrecy and the talk of backrooms so she had subsequently learnt never to ask questions.

When she was around eight years old Hannah had gone through a brief phase of exploring her New England house in a childhood game of fairy tale and had discovered a dark wooden chest in a walk-in closet off her father's study. Intrigued to find out what was inside she searched through his desk trying the various keys she had found there. One of them eventually fitted the lock.

For a long time she harboured a fantasy that her father was a dashing knight riding through the woods around the house. When she eventually asked him if his various evening excursions fitted her romantic view of him he had at first grown very angry but later this had subsided into good humour. He told her that in a way he was a knight but one on a greater mission than just rescuing imprisoned maidens from great towers in the depths of dark forests. Just what his quest was, he never told her but as she grew up she began to realise that in many respects he was not as benign a figure as she had always seen him.

Listening through the banisters to the numerous conversations her father had had with his colleagues during dinner evenings, she had heard him use words like Communism and Atheism, Socialism and Vietnam. Not until she was older did she really understand what those words meant and why her father was so vehemently opposed to them.

Various people were also spoken of. Kennedy was one her father particularly despised. But there were others, many of whom Hannah had simply forgotten. During a brief spell at home on a summer break from Yale she had found her father repeatedly watching a video of the Zapruder film. Every time the gruesome footage of the President's head

116

exploding came round her father would ball his hand into a fist and mutter, 'We got you, we got you.' Hannah could never understand this. At school she was taught that a lone sniper called Lee Harvey Oswald had fired the three shots that had killed the thirty-fifth President from the sixth floor of the Texas schoolbook depository. But to hear her father talk about it made her feel that what she had been taught, the accepted version, was at odds with reality. Some nights it filled her with genuine fear. Was all history like this? A lie?

For many years she became a Kennedy Assassination scholar, learning every nuance of that fateful day in November 1963 mainly, on reflection, as a subconscious desire to prove her father wrong. But the more she read the more she realised that the accepted truth of that terrible event was a distortion. Even applying Occam's razor to the more outlandish ideas something had taken place that day that involved more than the activities of a lone gunman. For instance, surely Oswald would have assumed that the President's car would have had its protective bubble top on. Dallas was a hostile city. The decision to remove it was only taken that morning. And how numerous witnesses, including a secret service agent in the car in front of the presidential limousine, were aware of shots coming from the Grassy Knoll.

Eventually Hannah hit a state of depression. She now knew that if they could lie about the Kennedy Assassination they could lie about anything. Her comfortable view of the world had gone forever. She saw rival power factions hungry for power and it soon dawned on her that all the chaos in the world was caused by the two 'R's, religion and resources and crushed by both were the innocents. Fanatics were happy to murder their fellow species because they believed in a different mythical, non-existent deity while others were happy to lay waste to a far away country because it had oil.

For a few years she despised her father, convinced in her own way that he had been involved with the incident in

Dallas; that he was one of those bringing so much bloodshed and death to the world, all for the sake of a bank balance.

Hannah dropped out of Yale and joined a hippie commune for a few months but realised that they were just as vacuous as those they supposedly despised. They spoke of the world being full of negative energies and that taking vast quantities of narcotics would ease everyone's pain. She realised they were just hiding away and were basically lazy rich kids who were able to drop out because their fathers were millionaires.

Sick of the hypocrisy she saw everywhere, Hannah travelled the world, a solitary figure looking for an answer. The only one she found was that in everything humans do there is greed and corruption, from the great multinational corporations that exploited an indigenous population, all the way down to the man on the street who picked her pocket as she alighted from a train in Rome. Arriving at her hotel an hour later she was alarmed to discover that she had been picked clean, wallet, passport, watch – all gone, to be sold on the black market in all likelihood for drugs. The more of the world she saw the more she grew to hate people. There was no solace anywhere from greed. Cynicism verging on nihilism became her companion.

The antipathy that she felt towards her own race culminated after a vicious assault and near rape that she experienced in Chicago while returning home to New England. Her evangelical attackers told her they were going to force the love of god into her but years on the road and living on her own strengths meant they had chosen the wrong woman. She left both men half-dead, her conscience barely troubled.

On Hannah's return to the family home the readjustment to the life she had once known never happened. She remained an isolated, emotionally neutral individual. The knowledge that her mother had died six months earlier barely registered, warranting no emotional response in her. Her past life was just that, past – dead and buried, gone and forgotten.

She wanted no more to do with that weak young girl with her romantic and unrealistic sensibilities that she had once been.

Initially, her father had been desperately angry with her but as the weeks rolled on he softened. Yet behind this thaw lay a deep ulterior motive. In his daughter Franklin realised he had an asset and one beyond just mawkish familial love. His daughter's total lack of sentimentality meant she would be useful for the intelligence services. At first she refused, claiming that it was just another form of human corruption, but gradually, during long conversations in their now cold and lifeless New England mansion, Hannah was won over by her father's persuasiveness. Inside three months she was rapidly climbing the career ladder within the CIA to the point where, well before it was considered appropriate, she had been sent into Iraq.

A jolt brought her thoughts back to the present. In front of her Hannah could see sunlight reflecting off the water of the Diyala River. She had already crossed it once on the road to Jalula but with the volume of traffic increasing and the risk of more roadblocks she had cut off the road and headed southwest to make her way to where the river ran directly south. Even if friendly Iraqis stopped her, it would be a hindrance she could do without. She had found what she had been sent to retrieve and any further delays would jeopardise what her father and others were trying to bring about. She could not risk the key falling into the enemy's hands.

She brought the truck to a stop and climbed down. The sun was hot but a cool breeze that played across the water eased the temperature. She made her way down the bank to look for a boat but on both sides of the river and as far as she could see there was nothing. Hannah swore under her breath, chastising herself for being so dangerously optimistic.

❉

Sunsphere

'This'll blow yer bits off.' Gus was nothing but colourful with his language. He breezed into the room and threw down a heavily thumbed novel. 'I found this in a second hand bookshop. Last year. I remembered one section that may, as they say, be bloody pertinent. This was the book I was trying to remember the name of.'

Gus's choice of literature was random at best – or would it be safe to say eclectic? Anyway the book was right up his street. It had a cover that reminded me of novels of its type, should I say, and I meant that as a pun as well. It had been designed so that it was similar to a top selling popular conspiracy book that thumped up the book charts and out sold everything else a few years ago. The cover image was a watercolour of Venice with special attention given to the Grand Canal. *Sunsphere* was embossed upon its cover. The author, Mark Arden, who I'd never heard of, had written a series of speculative books. According to the 'by the same author' list, these included *The Holy Legacy of the Secret Michelangelo Scrolls, The Atlantis Heresy, The Titian Heist Conspiracy*, referred to by many of his critics as *The Tit Job, The Botticelli Operation* and *The Golden Bucket of Pissarro*. *Sunsphere* had sold well. The one in my hand was a third edition. A note from the author, on the inside cover, thanked people for alerting him to the grammatical howlers that had littered the previous editions.

Gus reached for a glass, topped it up with the last of the bottle, took a mighty swig then rumbled over to me and while the book was in my hands he flipped the pages through to a section he had marked by bending the corner of the page down.

'Wasn't there an episode of the Simpsons with a sunsphere?' I said, teasing him.

'Dunno,' Gus replied, a touch dismissively.

'Bart and the boys bugger off to a defunct world fair. Expo eighty two or something.'

'Get a load of this bit. Read, read. You'll see.' Gus then went and dropped onto my least threadbare settee.

Knowing Gus wouldn't let me prevaricate, I braced myself and got stuck in... albeit very... very reluctantly.

I was puzzled. How did this fit in with the other sections I'd read? How was it relevant? Gus could see this written in big bold words right across my face.

'Right now flip to... Hang on. I'll have to look.' Gus stood up and took the thick paperback from my hands and flipped a number of pages backwards and forwards. 'There's this bit where this young woman, she's a daughter of a rich right wing power mad senator, has been dropped into Iraq to hunt out this remote mountain shrine near a place called Kifri... I think. Yeah, here we go. Read that bit.'

Minutes later I looked up from the page.

'Ta dah!' Gus could be bloody annoying.

Here was mention of that wretched gold key again. Just what was going on here? I was starting to feel a little, you know, precarious. What if Gus, and especially Linda, were right? Why were all these references coming to light now from so many disparate quarters?

'Has Linda read this?' I flipped the book over to study its cover. The splurge on the back ended with some dramatic hyperbole: *Could the solution to the mystery blow apart one of the world's major religions?*

A great secret. I'd just about had enough of those. They all turned to out to be nothing of the sort.

'She hasn't told you? No? She's read it all right.' Gus flopped his head back, resting it on the back of the settee and stared at the ceiling. 'So what do you think?'

'Great historical revelation in the pages of an airport novel!'

'So say they who know.'

'The publishers? Anyway, knowledge through revelation turns out to be anything but. Fideism is total nonsense.'

'Cynic.'

'I'll take that as a compliment.' I closed the thick paperback and held it in both hands, my elbows resting on the arms of the chair. 'Gus, man, it's a novel.'

'Yeah but the references to sun keys. Surely you can appreciate that it's a wild coincidence.'

'Maybe this Arden bloke found a Hiddon somewhere and referenced the ideas.'

'From an unpublished section of a book over two hundred years old? Doesn't seem likely does it?'

'Have a quick read of the prologue.' Gus closed his eyes.

I did.

Wow!

'Are you going to tell me you think the sun key opens the golden sphere on top of a building in Venice?' Impatient anger fizzed through me. Gus and Linda should really spend less time together was my next overpowering thought.

'Wherein lies a great secret. As in the book.'

'What's the big secret in the book?'

Gus opened his eyes and looked at me.

'You'll have to finish the book.'

That would save me reading the rest of the hefty tome. 'The ending?'

'It's left as a cliff-hanger.'

'A sequel on the cards methinks.'

'Wouldn't surprise me.' Gus leant over and tried to refill his glass, then placed the bottle down remembering he'd drained it earlier. 'Got any more?'

'In the outhouse.' At the back of my small kitchen was a utility room full of old paint tins, a knackered washing machine/tumble drier combination; piles of newspapers and a modest but rapidly depleting wine rack. A small smeary window looked out over a seldom-visited garden.

Gus rattled and clonked about out there.

When he returned I dropped the novel onto a small stack of books that were bound for the toilet.

'So a trip to Venice then. Corkscrew's under that.' I pointed to one of my notebooks spread-eagled and face down on my desk.

'When we have all the keys.' Gus, retrieved the muted metal Ikea device, sat down and placed the bottle between his feet. He sounded a touch irritated. 'And we must go and have a look at Dashwood's place.'

'Who?'

'Sir Francis Dashwood. He of Hellfire Club fame.' Gus twisted off the foil.

'The Hell Fire Club?'

'You know. Toffs carousing and cavorting with ladies of the night. Everyone accused Dashwood of being a devil worshipper, which was total paranoid Christian moralising. In my book most moralists turn out to be idealistic dreamers or top-level shaggers. The other lot I can't stand are the religious hypocrites who bang on about violence in society then demand children should be taught about a mythic figure who was hammered to a cross, in a book replete with genocide, murder, destruction, infanticide, rape, torture and mental dictatorship.'

In went the corkscrew.

'Who was he?' I asked.

'He did everything, man. Ran the treasury, was an MP, wound up the church...' The cork popped.

My kind of bloke then. Especially when it came to winding up the church. There wasn't enough of that as far as I was concerned.

Gus poured himself a glass then stood up and came over to refill mine. He picked up *Sunsphere* and flipped through a few pages until he found another section.

'Read this bit.'

That name...

There was bloody Da Vinci again.

'Gus. Here's Da Vinci. What did I say?'

'It just relates descriptively to an illustration in Dashwood's church. That's all. He's not in the novel per se.'

A combination of tiredness and wine was starting to rub up my fractious gene. I hadn't slept well the night before. Linda had kept me up – no not that way – with frequent visits to the toilet and trips downstairs for glasses of water. Despite my desire for company it had felt odd to have someone else in the house again. Some deep-rooted territoriality had kicked in no doubt.

'Do they find the third key?'

'That's not the point. My point was to show you that there may in fact be three keys to find.'

'Because a novel says so?'

'I know it sounds a bit mad but trust me.'

'Really?'

'Earlier today I contacted the publisher who put me on to Arden. He's agreed to meet us tomorrow.' Gus rubbed his forehead in long languid strokes. I could tell he was frustrated by my less than subtle willingness to not suspend my disbelief.

'Why?'

'To talk about the Hiddon extract.'

'You told him about that?'

'Well, yes. I had to. Arden nearly wet his knickers when I told him I'd found it in an old piece of furniture. That's all. Not where or anything.'

There was a long silence when the pair of us just sat there more than a little annoyed with the other.

'Three keys.'

'That's right.'

'One in Venice, according to the story. One at this church in West Wycombe and…'

'And what?'

'Where's the third?'

'Can't remember but Arden claims he has a real one.'

Well, strap me vitals. There's a surprise.

'Really?'
'He says it's what inspired him to write the book.'

We'd agreed to meet Arden in The Crusader's Head in Temple Road. Gus was to meet him at the station then grab a taxi with the man into town. Meanwhile, I was to take up position and lay claim to one of the private nooks at the back so that we could all talk freely and openly about secret matters.

Oddly enough, and to my complete surprise, I had found a copy of *Codex* in a stack of newspapers near the door almost as if it had been placed there – well yes it had, but I mean covertly, so that I would find it. Christ! I was hanging out with paranoids and it was beginning to rub off. With curiosity getting the better of my scepticism I decided to see what Linda had written.

So-called serendipity or coincidence or conspiracy turned to sweet tweet when I realised that the edition was three months out of date.

No matter.

I purchased a fine ale and took up a seat in the nook furthest from the door.

The cover of the mag sported a rather sickly painting of a crib – all wickerwork and biblical. It had that vomitous air about it often seen in those little booklets dished out by evangelical Christians. You know the ones, Jesus as Teutonic uber-lord, all blond hair and blue eyes, backlit with puke inducing radiant celestial light.

Apparently the *Crib of Our Lord* had been found somewhere west of somewhere Middle Eastern and was now in the hands of dumbstruck archaeologists or rather, and let's be honest about this, the hands of theistic archaeologists working for a creationist university, run by a strident Baptist Church in some southern state of the US of A, desperate for evidence that their ridiculous myths have some grounding in reality.

A chunk of the thing had been sent for carbon dating but the results had proved inconclusive. No, the carbon dates had probably, in fact proved totally conclusive. It was no doubt a 13th century fake and the bible bashers were doing nothing more than quietly spitting feathers in the background and going through that feisty fevered denial that the Shroudies do with that rag from Turin when scientists continuously and metaphorically bash them over the head with the correct date. 'Tis a fake, deal with it.

There were probably in existence enough true cribs of Christ to fill the maternity wing of a modern hospital. Either way it wouldn't stop *Cribbies* from being the next vitriolic minority to start spouting the authenticity of some biblical legend.

The rest of *Codex* was splashing around in similar territory. Bible Codes, misanthropic apocalyptic prophecies, alien abductions, crop circles, auras, crystal bloody healing, Atlantis and all the other dreary, dull and childish shash that however much was proved categorically to be hogwash still managed to attract dimwitted adherents. The magazine, like much of its kind, was an intellectual non-starter. It claimed it was the defender of rejected knowledge cast aside by the material world. Rejected with good reason, I might remind the editors. Oh weary mind... seek the higher intellectual ground...

I found an advert for a T-Shirt emblazoned with *Hug a Freemason, Your Life May Depend on It!* If he's a consultant at a top hospital maybe. Another one, and I thought about buying it, carried the words, *I've Been Probed by a Man from Mars... The Planet not the Chocolate Factory!*

Sheer lunatic joy.

I was starting to despair that I might have to resume thumbing through it again to pass the time when Gus arrived; dragging in his eager wake someone I initially took to be a Mafioso, all black leather jacket, grey shirt, dark trousers, flowing black hair and sunglasses.

Gus hovered at the bar looking around. He waved, bought two drinks and wandered over. We exchanged pleasantries for ten minutes or so then Arden turned matters swiftly onto the topic in question.

'So tell me more about what you've unearthed.' He had a hushed, covert manner as if suspecting members of Her Majesty's intelligence services were listening in.

I was about to respond when Gus cut me off at the pass.

'I found an extract from a novel that mentions the sun key. It was stuck in a secret compartment in an old piece of furniture. It must be two hundred years old. A character called Thomas Hiddon is offered it as a bribe. Then a photocopy of another unknown book, including this same Hiddon character, comes sliding through the postbox. It also mentions a key.' Gus paused. 'What do you think?'

Arden sat there for a moment musing it over.

Gus wasn't going to ask the obvious question so I did.

'So what's your source?'

Arden stared at me. His eyes were full of accusations. I suspected he thought I was extracting the urinary substances.

'If you're suggesting I plagiarised anything, you're wrong.'

I wasn't but then again maybe I was. Anyway, before I could think further on the matter, Arden hunched himself up and slid across the table a little more as if demanding we do similar. A clandestine secret was about to be imparted.

'I think I may have stumbled upon a great mystery.'

I resisted, honestly I did, from rolling my eyes. Gus on the other hand nearly shot his bolt.

'Wow, really? Are you sure?'

'I was in Boston three years ago on a book signing tour for my previous novel. I was sniffing around an antique dealer's place and bought a book that dated from the 18th century. It was about the War of Independence and Freemasonry. I collect books on Freemasonry. But it was only when I got it home that I discovered that sealed beneath the end paper was a letter.' Arden reached into an inside pocket and pulled out a thick wadge of notes. They appeared, via a furtive glance, to be mostly hand written. He removed one sheet and slid it across the table towards me. I was, after all, and Arden knew this, the one who needed convincing. Gus was already squirming on the hook.

With one finger I rotated the sheet of paper and read.

My dear Francis Dashwood, Esq.,

I am much pleased to read that your various trips to that magnificent country and seat of the Renaissance have proved to be so successful on many levels. Our Brothers in that region are most hospitable even when faced with the nefarious activities of the so-called men of the cloth. I am also glad you were able to retrieve the lamp from the George and Vulture, a suitably agreeable conclusion to that particular difficulty. It is a singular and rare item and would be a loss to us all if it had fallen into the hands of those who wish us ill.

I would be willing to assist in the continual development of the noble Brotherhood by way of small recompense for your work in helping to establish the liberated territories in the New World. You must enlighten me as to whether your refurbishment activities have finally drawn to a close. I am most eager to see the sun globe that is now said to adorn the church of St Lawrence.

Your obedient servant as ever,

Benjamin Franklin.

'Is it genuine?' I was full of obvious questions today.
'I had an expert give it the once over and he agreed.'
'Agreed to what?'
'That it was genuine.'
'What's this lamp he's talking about?'

'Sir Francis Dashwood, famous for the Hell Fire Club, founded his Order of the Knights of St Francis in 1746. At first they met at the George & Vulture, a 16th century pub in Cornhill in the City of London. A pub by the way that appears in Charles Dickens' Pickwick Papers. Dashwood and his fellow Knights met in a room lit by a Rosicrucian lamp that was supposed to shine eternally. This was a large crystal globe encircled by a gold serpent with its tail in its mouth, crowned with a pair of silver wings and suspended on twisted serpent chains.'

'I've heard of the Hell Fire Club. Wasn't it all about devil worshipping?'

Arden looked annoyed.

'No. That's a popular misconception and one propagated by the church. They were in fact classical pagans. Earth mysteries, geomancy, bacchanalian revelry, that's what they were into. Real religion. Dashwood couldn't stand Christianity, seeing it for what it really was, so he preferred his own style of worship.'

'I see.'

'You ought to read Donald McCormack's The Hell Fire Club, The Hellfire Club by P. Mannix and Dashwood: The Man and the Myth by Eric Towers. They'll put you straight.'

'I will.' I felt suitably admonished.

To salvage relations, Gus, acting like the UN, stepped in to placate Arden.

'You said you had a key.'

For a second Arden kept his eyes on me then turned to Gus.

'I do.'

'Can we see it?' Gus was trying a conciliatory tone.

'No. I mean not yet.'

'That's a shame.' I smiled but doused the expression liberally with a fresh mint patronising gleam.

'I don't trust you.' Arden reached for the letter. 'We've only just met. For all I know you might be out to stop me.'

I glanced at Gus who look panicked, albeit briefly. Arden was a paranoid. Not unheard of for a writer but I sensed that his mistrust was in the realm of the-Freemasons-might-be-out-to-get-me scenario.

Arden made shifts to move. He drained his orange juice then stood up.

'Thanks for the drink.' Then he was gone.

There was silence for a few moments.

'Christ sake man, why did you have to piss him off like that?' Gus sat back in his chair and folded his arms.

I couldn't answer him because I didn't know.

Gus swore to himself, finished off his drink.

'You off?'

'I'll see you later.' Gus marched out.

Playing Safe

Arden paused before he entered his apartment building. He hated this paranoia but felt perhaps that discretion was the better part of valour. With Big Jim missing, the offices destroyed and at least one of his colleagues killed, perhaps murdered, the thought that maybe he was next gave him no comfort. He was not someone prone to the ravings of a conspiracy theorist who saw patterns of entanglement everywhere but even he had to admit that the events seemed to be connected. Of course he was not sure that Big Jim was dead. But all the facts were far from in and it was at that point, as he knew too well, that wild theories could take over. It was the woeful habit of conspiracy theorists to apply such reasoning in a leap of logic or indeed faith before any real thought was applied. It irritated him completely. It was probably why Big Jim had taken him under his wing. While other members of the group would theorise wildly about certain events in the news, Arden would demolish any proposal with the application of applied reason. At least once a week he read Carl Sagan's *Baloney Detection Kit*, something he wished desperately that the authorities would allow to be taught in schools. It was a perfect antidote to the nonsense that made up society. He had always sought proof. The evidence. There was nothing more important. People demanded it from the police to solve a crime but were happy to have little of it when it came to flying saucers, ghosts and new age healing. Despite humanity's advances, its collective mind was still in the thirteenth century.

For much of the day Arden had hidden himself away in various anonymous bars. Those he never frequented. Despite his resistance to paranoia something was niggling away in the back of his mind. The mental equivalent of a warning bell. For all he knew familiar places may very well be under scrutiny. So he avoided going to see family or friends.

Now, early in the morning he had returned home. The building was just starting to come to life. In a number of windows he could see his various neighbours starting their respective days.

Making his way up the main staircase, he fixed his eyes not on the steps before him but on the staircase ahead, half expecting to see a shadowy figure; the man he had seen outside the office building before the fire, lurking on the landing. Each successive floor proved to be empty. Despite this, Arden's sense of security did not improve.

Opening the door to his apartment, he stood in the hall, hesitating before crossing the threshold. Looking around its open plan interior he once more cursed himself for being so childish. He stepped through and closed the door behind him but did not turn on the main light. Everything was lit coldly in a pale dawn blue.

He stopped. Before him on the breakfast bar was a pile of mail. Someone had very obviously placed it there, which meant someone had been in his apartment. Had that been Big Jim? He picked it up and sifted through the credit card bills, junk mail and the more personal. One of the envelopes had a printed emblem in the top left corner, '*Window on the World Publishing – Open Immediately*'. It was one of Big Jim's creations and he often used it as a way of distributing sensitive material through the national postal system. The whole gloriously crass exterior of the envelope looked genuine but Arden new it for what it was, a fake. He stuck his thumb under the flap and ripped it open.

What's In A Name?

That evening, unable to settle, I picked up *Sunsphere* and flipped through the masterwork. It wasn't exactly a difficult read nor, for that matter, a badly written book. But going on holiday airport style novels always filled me with a little dread. Now, I'm no literary snob. What makes a good book anyway? One that is read by millions and wouldn't tax a twelve year old with a reasonable plot and some interesting ideas or a critically acclaimed indecipherable book written in the highest of highbrow English and read by eight people?

I ploughed my way through a profoundly silly shoot out in a Masonic lodge scene in which our heroes barely escaped with their lives – except one, a bloke called Buchanan who was an ex-special forces Navy Seal geezer whose top training failed him at the last moment – and read on into a short confrontation between this Hannah character and her bigoted Nazi father who roundly chastises her for blasphemy. Finding myself strangely drawn in, I continued.

After the narrow escape our heroes have been taken to a safe house by this we're-not-quite-sure-who's-side-he's-on-chap named Parks.

There was something odd. A feeling that I had missed something obvious. Then it splashed over me like a glass of cold water.

Mark Arden was a character name.

❋

Closing In

M,

I've made progress but at the same time this has brought me more attention - of the wrong kind. I'm going up to Providence. You should have that info from my other correspondence. There's a war on. I don't mean obvious ones like Iraq etc. I mean a war taking place behind the scenes. Ideologies. We're all being blinded. Lied to. It is about resources but remember the other 'r' we always discussed. There's a long term plan, believe me, to stop us thinking in certain ways. Find the Sunspheres. Then you'll know what I mean. I posted this on my journey but I don't think I will get to the end. I am being followed. Be careful.

In all likelihood then, his friend was dead. Big Jim had failed in his quest and was asking his second in command to complete the task. It was obvious too that his friend had succumbed to the paranoia about global conspiracies that Arden had grown to despise. Then again maybe he had had good reason to.

Arden made his way to his refrigerator and took out a beer. Searching through an untidy drawer he found a bottle opener and flipped off the top. There was no hiss when the bottle opened. Something caught his eye. As the crimped top tumbled onto the breakfast bar he noticed something odd about it. He slammed a hand down on the spinning top, and then slowly, almost reluctantly he pulled his hand away.

Holding it between thumb and finger he held the top up to the early dawn light. There was a small puncture mark

133

near the edge. Puzzling over this he turned his attention to the beer bottle. He held that up, shaking the contents.

Opening the refrigerator again he pulled out the other bottles and examined them closely. Sure enough, each one had a puncture mark in the cap. His paranoia returned in a great wave of fear. He looked over at the mail. Was it a warning or a mistake? He now knew it could not have been Big Jim who had left the mail on the breakfast bar. But why had an intruder been so clumsy? Arrogance, perhaps?

Either way, he knew that he would have to leave. Providence seemed the best bet. At least he could keep on the move and maybe test Big Jim's theory that the man had been followed. Now was as good a time as ever.

Locking his apartment door behind him he set off down the stairs breaking into a run as he neared the bottom. The looking glass world he had so despised was pulling him through the mirror.

Holding Hiroko's hand, Madsen led her down through his garden to a set of steps that wound their way down the few hundred yards to the beach. Dawn was breaking in the east and a thin strip of orange light was growing steadily on the horizon. High clouds were edged with pale gold and a lone vapour trail cut its way like a white tear in the fabric of the sky.

Madsen felt elated. The view made him slow his pace. He felt as if he had to absorb it. To drink it in. But he knew at the same time his senses were inadequate to do so. Hiroko overtook him but kept her grip.

"Keep up." Her voice was a loud whisper.

Madsen felt an overpowering urge to stay. How could he leave all this behind? A limb of the sun appeared and a path of light bridged the sea, calm but for a few breakers. A pathway to eternity for ancient peoples.

Feeling him try to slip from her grasp Hiroko stopped.

134

"Josh! We don't have time. Chris'll be wondering what's happened." She brought her face up close to his. "Come on."

With great reluctance Madsen fell into step behind Hiroko now steering them through the undergrowth to the low cliff into which steps had been carved a century or more before.

They ran along the beach, Hiroko turning her head every few moments to see if they were being followed. If they were there were no signs, obvious or otherwise, yet.

Rounding the next headland an eighty-foot yacht, her sails catching the morning sun, moved with skilled precision into the bay.

"He told me he only wanted a forty footer." Madsen smiled. "He's blown his bonus in one fell swoop."

"He's not going to get to us quick enough." Hiroko was looking back along the beach. She could now see Kearns and several uniformed officers clambering down the steep steps to the beach.

"We swim." Madsen grabbed Hiroko's arm and they plunged into the water.

Gregory slowly turned the wheel and the yacht turned her prow out to sea and towards the glowing orb of the morning sun.

"Did the documents come through?" Madsen rubbed a towel vigorously through his hair.

"Yep, everything." Gregory kept his attention on the manoeuvre. "I've copied them onto a CD Rom. It's in the cabin. You destroyed the originals I take it"

Madsen smiled.

"They were hardly originals but yes, they were burnt."

"There's a change of clothes for you in the cabin. That's what normally happens with escapees from the law." Gregory grinned mischievously. "A quick change of identity."

"It's going to take a lot more than a change of clothes to hide us." Madsen took one last look back towards the empty beach. Kearns and his men had long gone. He then made his way down into the cabin behind Hiroko.

‡

It was nearly dark when Hannah made her way down to the river again. There was a rough path that led from the road down to a short ragged makeshift jetty supported on a series of wooden and metal struts. Around each was a halo of opalescent oil. Shining a flashlight around she saw the bodies of numerous fish on the shoreline, a few caught in the reeds. The ground, up-slope from the river, was littered with ejected shells and there was a scattering of abandoned ammo boxes.

The place had obviously been used, up until recently at least, as a weapons market with the merchandise brought ashore and tested in the vicinity. When she had pulled the truck off the road she had seen the remains of an impromptu camp and the tracks of a good number of vehicles both light and heavy.

Nudging the end of the jetty was a small boat, its outboard kicked up out of the water. She shone the flashlight searching the craft for any signs of what the military now called IEDs, improvised explosive devices. Trust the suits to come up with yet another euphemistic name for a bomb. Hannah lowered herself into the boat and checked the outboard's fuel tank. It was nearly empty.

Working quickly, Hannah siphoned off what was left in the truck engine and transferred the fuel to the outboard motor using a rusted Jerry can. With the tank full she cut the rope and pushed away from one of the jetty supports. She tugged several times on the starter cord but nothing happened. Just as she was starting to think she had found the only dud outboard in Iraq the engine kicked into life. In the morning chill the noise seemed unbearably loud. Hannah

raised the HK in her left hand readying herself for any
unwanted attention. But she was alone.

☩

Arden made his way up the steps from the subway.
Not for the first time today he felt as if he was being watched;
the tightening of his neck that suggested someone was
looking at him. Every time he ventured to look around
though, all he saw were the hundreds of commuters going
about their own business. For some unknown subconscious
reason he had taken a circuitous route from his apartment
building through the streets of New York and its subways
pausing briefly in coffee bars and bookshops on his way to
Grand Central. It was perhaps foolish and pandered to his
paranoia but there was little sense in denying that there was
the possibility that he was in danger. It was, in all likelihood,
his way of gaining some psychological control over the
situation if nothing else. Arden had hoped that the noise and
bustle of Park Avenue would distract him from thoughts of
pursuit.

Up ahead he could see the great bulk of Vanderbilt's
Grand Central Terminal building. Even though it offered the
way out, a gateway to freedom, he suddenly felt very
trapped. An overwhelming sense of panic hit him. He began
to up his pace feeling as if any moment there would be
insurmountable obstacles set before him; that there would be
no escape from the city. New York felt more like a labyrinth,
an impossible maze of dark tunnel streets, dead ends and
blind alleys.

Stepping through the main doors and into the
impressive cathedral-like concourse Arden felt, somewhat
peculiarly, that he had found some form of sanctuary. He
smiled to himself, a railway station acting as cathedral. It was
as if he were some renegade in the Middle Ages hounded
onto hallowed ground. The place was busy with small knots
of people gathered around the ticket booths. To his right a

street preacher, moving slowly through the crowds, was holding aloft the stuffed cloth figure of a hanged man. It was a puzzling motif. Surely he should be holding up a cruciform. Then again he did not exactly fit the perception of what Arden had come to expect of these people. At one point the hatchet faced man stared at him, his eyes somewhat bloodshot, a few days worth of stubble on his chin.

Arden made his way to a ticket booth and joined the queue. The street preacher drew level with him.

"Remember JJ. He didn't find the entrance to the labyrinth."

"What?" Arden's anger was edged with panic.

"If you go searching you must not fail. If you do, you will become the hanged man."

"What do you know about JJ?" Arden half turned his head. He did not want to look directly at the man in case he saw something he did not like.

"He failed. He could not find the entrance. He must pay the penalty."

"To who?" Arden turned to look the preacher in the eye but his attention was caught by a familiar looking figure casting his eyes around the busy concourse. It was the man Arden had seen moving away from the office building before the fire started.

Turning his head quickly in the opposite direction, his mind racing hard, Arden eased himself out of the queue.

"If you fail you will have to –" he did not want to hear the rest of what the preacher had to say. Instead he moved swiftly away towards the main doors fearful that any second he would be overtaken. It was a primal feeling, like a child on its way to bed, racing against the dark and shadows. Maybe it was a more primitive sensation still, like an animal being stalked in jungle depths.

He did not want to move too swiftly. It might give him away. So he moved as quickly as possible without breaking into a run despite the urge to put as much distance between himself and his mysterious pursuer.

Arden glanced once over his shoulder and was alarmed to see the man, wearing a look of serious intent, running after him. In his haste to get away his shoes slipped on the floor as he accelerated, his arms flailing as he grabbed air to steady himself.

He ran towards the entrance but as he turned to look once more he careened into a group of businessmen. Arden spun and crashed to the floor. Before he knew it the stranger was on top of him.

The room in the Bow Street Inn was a welcome respite from the journey. Hiroko had hit the large brass bed and fallen asleep within minutes of being shown the room. Madsen, still not yet tired enough to join her, was looking out of the window towards the Piscataqua River and to the Memorial Bridge to his right. Portsmouth was bathed in golden evening light that somehow made the buildings glow. If nothing else their flight from Kearns and his men was exhilarating. Despite his boyish enthusiasm for the chase, he was concerned about the way events were playing out. He chastised himself for agreeing to help Lee with identifying the page from the book. It had led him down a path he now regretted taking. It had made him a fugitive and that was an idea he was not prepared to accept readily.

Gregory had dropped them off in the harbour then, after an hour restocking supplies, had made his way out to sea on his way down to Marblehead, where he often moored his craft and kept a second home in one of New England's favoured addresses. The arrangement was that Madsen and Hiroko would rejoin him there. A split quarry was harder to hunt and if Kearns picked up the trail he would be faced with a choice between Portsmouth and Marblehead.

He turned away from the view and fixed his attention on Hiroko asleep in the warm evening light. Her face had a calm, serene look. He envied her. Sitting down on the edge of the bed he smiled. Somehow, even though his long fought for life of isolation had collapsed, he felt happier than he had in a long time. Let the sun in. It was as simple as that.

He picked up the room's phone, dialed an outside line, then punched in four-one-one.

"Hi, yeah. I want the number for Sotheby's in New York, Roosevelt Drive. Near the East River."

He took the number down then hung up.

For a few minutes he explained, in broad terms, why he was making the request to the inquiries desk at the auction room. After initial resistance the young man who answered the phone put Madsen through to someone who might be able to help, a Mister Parks.

"Parks here."

"Hi. My name's Josh Madsen I'm calling about a rare Renaissance book."

"That's my department Mister Madsen. How may I help?" Parks's voice was friendly but clipped with an air of officiousness.

"I'm an architect and a certain page, torn from a book of architectural designs, was given to me for identification. I had no idea but a colleague did some research and we think it may have come from a book you sold some time ago. A book that's stated in the documentation to have once been owned by one Francis Dashwood."

Parks was silent for a moment.

"I know the book sir."

"Was it missing some pages?"

"I believe it was."

"The cover was missing wasn't it?"

"Yes Mister Madsen. The cover, frontispiece and several pages within." There was a long pause. "Do you have the missing pages?"

"Only one. Well, just a photocopy. The original has gone missing. It was of the statue and gold sphere atop the Dogana del Mare—"

"In Venice," Parks cut him off. "How unfortunate it's missing again."

Madsen was tempted to mention certain other aspects surrounding the elaborate drawing but thought it might make him sound unbalanced.

"Who owns the book?" he asked.

"Who owns it now? I'm sorry, that's confidential."

"Could I talk to Francis Dashwood? Maybe he knows something about it."

"I assure you Mister Madsen, I know all there is to know about this book. And, I might say, you would have severe difficulty contacting Mister Dashwood."

"Why, does he want to remain anonymous?"

Parks snorted derisively.

"Mister Madsen, Francis Dashwood has been dead for two hundred years."

Madsen shook his head slowly.

"I see. Did he really own the book?"

"He did. He used it when he was restoring certain properties in England during the Eighteenth century. He was the gentleman who instigated the infamous Hell Fire Club. A somewhat misunderstood secret society."

"But where did this book come from? How did you get hold of it?" Madsen wanted more answers.

"That I can tell you. A second hand book dealer in Providence by the name of Howard Hodgson. Is there anything else?"

"No I don't think so. Wait, do you have a number for this Mister Hodgson"

"I do." There was a pause for a few moments then Parks returned and read out a number. Parks allowed Madsen time to copy the number down then continued. "Mister Madsen, I would very much like to see the missing page. Would it be possible to send a copy?"

"Certainly Mister Parks."

"Thank you." The line went dead.

Madsen sat back and ran a finger and thumb across his closed eyes. If things had been a little surreal up until that moment then they had certainly grown more so in the space of a few minutes. He felt as if he had crossed a line from the apparently normal world to one in which clandestine secret societies operated. The Hell Fire Club? He had never heard of them. What was their involvement in all this? Did they still exist? There were too many questions and more forming in his mind by the minute. Beyond the window the world seemed calm. He wanted to return to it, to his old life. To step outside and forget everything that had happened. He looked over at Hiroko. Life was a path one could never turn back on. By giving up the past he had found something new, something good. He had found resurrection within life. He remembered words he had seen written across a canvas entitled *The Gospel of Philip* at an art exhibition in the Institute of Contemporary Arts in Boston some years ago. *Those who say they will die first and then rise are in error. They must receive the resurrection while they live...* For years he had never understood what they meant. Now, for the first time, he did.

✝

They had walked for hours in a great circle; Arden always seeking a way to free himself from the presence of the man who finally, when they had reached Roosevelt Drive along the East River, insisted they stop.

"My name is Buchanan. A friend of yours asked me to find you."

Arden took a step back.

"Really? Why the long march?"

"Security reasons." Buchanan paused. "Jim Eddowes."

"Eddowes, who's he?"

"Mark, believe me. I'm not your enemy."

"How do I know that?"

142

Buchanan sighed as if he were a parent whose patience was running thin with a small child.

"I guess you don't but Eddowes expected you to."

"Jim wouldn't think that of me. He'd expect the opposite. He would insist I maintain my doubts, especially when a stranger who knows a lot about me is following me."

"A cynic. Or would you say it's being realistic? Probably both." It was a rhetorical question, but Arden answered it anyway.

"Damn right."

Buchanan turned slightly, his eyes scanning the people of New York.

"When did you last see Jim?" Arden's question tested the water.

"Shortly before he went missing."

"He's missing?"

"You know he is." Buchanan snapped back. "He's missing because of what he got himself into. Listen, we have to find somewhere less open." Buchanan was watchful. It was beginning to unnerve Arden.

"I was told never to go with strangers." There was a level of condescension in Arden's words that made Buchanan grit his teeth. He took a few paces up to Arden.

His voice, although almost a whisper, was forceful and determined.

"Listen. Jim asked me to contact you. He realised his life was under threat because of what he had discovered. The man had lifted the curtain and seen past the veil. He was not meant to so, he had to pay with his life."

"He's dead then."

"Believe me he's dead. They would make sure of that."

"Who's they – the usual *they* of the paranoid's fantasy?"

"Yeah. *They* actually happen to exist, my friend."

Arden smiled and shook his head. This only aggravated Buchanan more. He grabbed the younger man by the coat, his hand balling the thick material with ease.

"Okay. He left two notes for you. Yes?"

Arden's smile disappeared.

"Shall I go on? Okay. You have to get yourself to Providence. To a bookseller. Am I warm?"

Arden nodded.

"At last we're making headway. The only safe way for you to get to Providence is with me. You get on that train, you're dead. You get a taxi, you're dead. You go by yourself, you're dead. Do you understand?"

"Why? I mean who wants to snuff me out?" There was a still an edge of sarcasm in Arden's voice.

"The same people who killed Jim. The same people who blew up your offices. The same people that are fighting a war. A war behind the scenes."

A puzzled look fell across Arden's face.

"Jim's words, my friend."

"Yes they are. But they came from me." Buchanan let his grip slacken.

"I saw you at our offices. Just before the fire."

"You did. I was looking for you. It was just a case of bad timing. I can assume the incendiary devices were already set." Buchanan stepped in close again. "Arden, this is how these people operate. This is what you're up against. You will have to make a leap of faith and trust me."

Arden stared at Buchanan searching for any give away signs in the man's expression. There were none.

"If I wanted to find the book I would already have gone to Providence, yes? Why would I have bothered tracking you down?"

"Yeah, I guess you're right." Arden capitulated. "What do you want me to do?"

An hour later they were heading out of an anonymous car park the exact location of which Arden had failed to fathom. It was in a part of Lower Manhattan he had never been to before despite the fact that he had convinced himself he knew most of the streets in this part of the city.

"Are you military?" Arden asked noticing the way Buchanan handled the car in tight, precise manoeuvres.

"I left after the first Gulf War."

"And…?"

"You name it, I've been with them. CIA, FBI, Special Ops, Special Forces."

"I should've guessed."

"I'm a cliché," Buchanan smiled.

Arden laughed.

"I've never understood why *they* always use ex-military types for surveillance and all that other unpatriotic-against-the-Bill of Rights crap because you guys stand out a mile."

Buchanan said nothing for a moment but he kept his smile.

"But that's just it," he said. "They don't. I'm just a foot soldier. Those who stick out a mile are supposed to. It's all part of the game. Like Oswald, a good old fashioned decoy."

Arden turned his head slowly and studied Buchanan.

"Say what?"

"A war has many fronts." Buchanan continued.

"There you go again. You even talk in military clichés." Arden continued his dismissive tone.

Buchanan's smile began to dissolve.

"Do you really think *they*, to use one of your clichés, are that stupid?"

Arden did not answer. He mulled over the question as a delaying tactic.

"Believe me they're not." Buchanan raised a finger. "They are far from stupid."

"I know that. I know." Arden turned defensive.

"You know nothing. Really, you don't. For generations we have all been played like the saps we are."

"That's nothing knew. We wrote about that all the time, Jim and me. Tell me something I don't know."

145

"It's all about the mind."

Arden rolled his eyes. "Again…"

"Mind. You think you control yours. Hey, I'm not talking about implants and all that crap. That's just hysteria. But do you know where that idea came from?"

"Go on tell me." Arden's voice had regained its sarcastic edge.

"UFOs."

"You're kidding me. It's all nonsense."

"Every single element of that bogus subject was a creation, a work in progress as well, but one in which every single element was part of a test of psychological warfare techniques. You know about NICAP?"

"That's entry level shadow world. Kindergarten stuff. It was a creation of the CIA. The three middle letters rearranged. A smokescreen to promote flying saucers as a way to hide secret weapons testing, taken from and developed with the help of the Nazis. It was there to fool the American people and the Russians by pretending to be something it wasn't."

"But it was more than that. It was about clouding people's ability to question. To frighten them. Fear is the best weapon there is. But there was another level to it. People were seeing real objects. They always let their imaginations run away with them but there were nuts and bolts structures involved. These would then be reported to the authorities and investigated by scientists who would dismiss them as nonsense. People knew what they saw and would therefore condemn science for its inability to explain. It was also a good way to confuse people – the warfare side of it."

"It's a war on science? Come on man, that's dumb."

"That's just it, it isn't. Remember what you and Jim discussed? It's about the two R's – Resources and Religion. You use one to get the other. Remember the myth around Constantine who said he had a vision in which he saw a burning cross that said *In this sign thou shalt conquer*, well you'd better believe it."

"Constantine only legalised Christianity. It was Theodosius I who made it compulsory."

"Names are irrelevant. They come and go. It's the unifying controlling system and what it does that matters."

Buchanan paused to allow Arden a space to think. Then he continued.

"Look how science is demeaned in the press. There are pages and pages of astrology in the daily newspapers but how much astronomy? None. But it's all part of a long-term strategy. Untold millions are spent every year on pseudo-science and its promotion – books, television, magazines."

"But why?" Arden sighed.

"Religion is a useful tool. That little fact has been known for millennia. The priest elite. That's what the ancient peoples had. Egypt for example. And that's what we have now. Science asks questions and where there are questions then answers have to be given and these people do not want to give answers. Science is condemned by people with a vested interest in deceit."

"You control the people you can do what you want."

"Exactly."

"Fill them with unquestioned ideology and they will follow you anywhere. You can use it to get oil for example."

"But how does that – I mean Jim – what did he find?"

"I said it was a war on many fronts." Buchanan checked the rear view mirror, something Arden picked up on.

"We being followed?"

"It doesn't happen that way. But as you know military training is hard to shake." Buchanan smiled.

"Go on." Arden rubbed his forehead. He was tired.

"It's a systematic breaking down of the culture of questioning. Dumbing down I think the phrase is but that's only a tiny percentage of it. See how intelligent design, again another bogus notion, is being allowed to creep back into colleges and universities. You start to attack the walls of science. You make people stupid."

"You make it sound like we all lie down and take it."

"Most of the time people do. But folks like you kick up a shit storm, small ones, but it's enough. The ultimate power is to rule without question and you only get that by keeping people in the dark. Give them a comforting religion and they're putty in your hands. Of course I'm only scraping the surface."

"What about Jim?"

"Jim found out about the war. He found out the next move. He also found out that *they* have a powerful enemy. A resistance movement if you like."

"A resistance?"

"Yeah. An ancient resistance that has kept track over the last millennia and a half or so. While *they* were getting busy, the resistance like all good resistance movements went underground. It fights the war that way."

"I've never heard of anything like that?"

"Of course not. What do you think the Templars were about? Why were they destroyed?"

"Whatever you've got. That's the point. No one knows so they stick whatever fantasy they want onto them."

"The Cathars, The Gnostics, Freemasons. All attacked by the church. Why? There are a host of other facets of this resistance but the one thing they all have in common? They followed their own path. They were free thinkers. So the Church despised them. They've all been said to worship the devil as well as a whole host of other heresies levelled at them. But it's all propaganda. Psych-war. It went on a thousand years ago in Europe. It's going on here, right now. The history of the last seventeen hundred years has been shaped by this war. Powerful men want us to believe their lies so they can do exactly what they want with our permission. The manufacture of consent."

Turning his attention to the outside world Arden watched the people going about their evening routines. Beyond the window of the car, this bubble of super reality, lay the real world beyond. At least, what he once took to be the real world. Arden felt as if he were astride both, not like a

148

colossus but more as an impotent individual; a child taking its first look at the greater reality outside a front door. Alternatively he might very well be travelling with a psychotic who was as paranoid as the worst conspiracy theorist.

"So why do we have to go to Providence?" Arden asked; his eyes focused on the world beyond the windshield.

"Because we have to find a book before they do."

"What kind of book?"

"One that could destroy the resistance."

☦

Hannah cocked the HK and lay down in the boat. She had turned the engine off a short while ago when she had seen headlights up ahead, near the river's edge, and had allowed the craft simply to drift on the current. She could hear animated chatter and the sounds of vehicle doors being slammed. The language though was not Arabic and it was not one she could place and this puzzled her.

Suddenly there were flashlight beams playing across the water. Then someone turned on a searchlight mounted on a large truck. There was no way of controlling the boat. If they saw it they would see her. Quickly she grabbed the mooring rope with her right hand and dropped over the port side into the water. Despite the relatively warm temperature the shock of the water made her gasp. With additional weight on its left side the boat began to turn slowly but the current checked the drift.

In a great sweeping arc the truck-mounted searchlight fell upon the boat. Hannah heard the cocking of several automatic weapons and more excited talk. There was a moment's silence then someone opened up. Bullets blasted and chopped into the boat. The water erupted viciously around her. She closed her eyes and turned her head away for all the good it would do. Half a dozen bullets splintered the handrail above her head. She choked back a shout, took a

149

breath and sunk beneath the surface, her hand still above water holding onto the rope. She felt a bullet smack into her arm; a hot burning fire leapt through her and she swallowed water. She came up for air fighting the pain.

Just as suddenly the bullets stopped. There was more animated conversation that sounded as if it were on the point of getting ugly. Then an argument broke out.

Hannah hung the HK around her neck and grabbed hold of the rope with her left hand. Swinging herself around in the water she held her wounded arm close to her chest. She chanced a look in the direction of the searchlight. Beside it, mounted on a tripod, was a still smoking heavy calibre machine gun. There were half a dozen silhouettes moving about on the shore, two of them in close proximity. The altercation had developed into a full-blown fight. At least it would be a distraction to allow her to drift well out of range.

The searchlight was turned off plunging her into a pain-filled darkness. Gritting her teeth, she dropped the HK into the boat and made an attempt to haul herself back in. It took her a solid five minutes before she rolled onto the wet floor of the craft. She lay there staring up at the stars, entranced for a moment or two by the infinity above her and the light of a billion suns. The pain was too much. She sat up, closing her eyes for a moment. She lowered her head and breathed deeply as a way to control herself. She worked the button of her shirt loose, wet through with blood as well as water, rolled it back and examined the injury. The bullet had a cut a narrow trench in her flesh near the elbow. She searched through the pockets of the kit vest she had taken from the fallen agent and found several bandages and a phial of morphine. She injected the drug then cleaned and dressed her wound.

A sudden exhaustion hit her and she allowed herself to fall back onto the floor of the boat. All she could think of was sleep but if she slipped into unconsciousness she would become vulnerable. Her throat tightened and fumbling in a pocket she pulled out her inhaler. She administered one sharp intake then lay there feeling the weight on her lungs lift. Slowly, the tiredness overcame her and she felt herself collapse into a dreamless sleep.

‡

Madsen woke with a start. He thought for a moment that someone had been trying the door handle to the room. He sat up quickly half expecting someone to come bursting through then chastised himself for being so foolish. He was, he thought, succumbing to paranoia all too readily of late. But he countered this with another thought. He had every reason to feel that way.

Hiroko stirred next to him. She opened her eyes and looked up, smiling.

"Did you sleep at all? You look tired."

Madsen nodded.

"Enough."

Hiroko stretched then sat up in bed.

"Marblehead then. Have you contacted Gregory?"

"Providence."

"Providence? Why?" Hiroko looked puzzled.

"I spoke to a Mister Parks at Sotheby's. The book came from a second hand book dealer there. He won't tell me who has it at the moment but he thinks the missing page is from that Renaissance book. In fact he wants a copy."

"Are you going to send him one?" Hiroko asked.

"Not sure."

"Why not? Maybe he can help."

"He already has done."

"I mean..."

"I know what you mean. I'm just not happy about it. Call it intuition. I don't want to show my hand yet."

Hiroko narrowed her eyes a little.

"If I didn't know you better I'd say you were paranoid."

151

"Probably. But with very good reason. Come on. We need to hire a car and hit the 95."

An hour later they were heading out of Portsmouth and down Interstate 95 to the outskirts of Boston. Heavy rain was falling and the constant repetitive thrum of the windscreen wipers and the hiss of passing traffic were making Madsen feel stupefied. He found himself checking the rearview mirror over and over again like an automaton.

"Are we being followed?" Hiroko asked with a hint of a smile. She turned in her seat to look out the rear window.

"Absolutely no idea."

"Why do you keep checking?"

"Another symptom of my paranoia."

"Were you moving about in the room a lot last night?" Hiroko asked her head angled slightly to one side.

"After I made the phone call I fell asleep. Why?"

"I thought you were wandering around in the dark searching for something."

Madsen felt the hairs on the back of his neck stand up.

"What time?"

"I dunno, maybe it was a dream."

"Are you sure?"

"Why? Do you think someone was in our room last night?"

If he said yes, Madsen realised it would be an admission to his own sense of distrust, an acceptance that they were indeed travelling in a surreal and intimately threatening world. His suspicions were high though that they had indeed been the unwitting hosts to some unwanted prowler. He would have to face facts. His world had changed. The old consistencies were fading into memory while useful mental anchors were being cut. He just hoped he could keep some control.

"Maybe you did just dream it."

"You don't sound convinced." Hiroko smiled.

"I guess, with everything that's been going on lately, my imagination is getting the better of me."

Madsen kept his eyes on the road.

"It's funny, the more you try to keep things the same the more they resist and change." Hiroko placed a hand on Madsen's thigh and gently squeezed. "Variety is the spice of life I suppose."

"Variety is life." Madsen squeezed Hiroko's hand. "You can't control anything. Might as well learn to accept it."

"Even when someone might be out to—"

A dark grey Jeep Cherokee clipped the rear fender, nudging the car sideways. Madsen span the wheel to compensate and swore loudly. The car skidded but he kept control and steered it back into a straight line.

The Jeep lunged again but Madsen was ready. He jammed on the brakes and tucked in behind their assailant.

"Never know why they don't do that in movies."

"What are they doing?" Hiroko, her eyes wide, had one hand up to her mouth.

Madsen then slowed allowing other cars to pass, putting a good deal of distance between them and the Jeep.

"Guess my imagination was right." Madsen looked for off ramps. "When's the next turning?"

Suddenly the Jeep slowed; the driver executed an expert manoeuvre, which brought it back to a position just ahead.

Looking in the rearview mirror, Madsen slipped across lanes to widen the gap again. The Jeep slowed and slipped back and behind.

"Come on!" Madsen was exasperated. "This is no way to take someone out! It's—"

The Jeep raced forward and nudged their car, pushing it into a skid. Madsen pulled hard on the steering wheel to correct the spin. The car aquaplaned, nudging a station wagon ahead, which spun round in a furious one-eighty right into the path of the Jeep. The two vehicles collided sending the Jeep up on its nose and over the hood of the other. There was an explosive detonation of glass and steel. Three other cars smashed into the wreckage while others, braking hard, narrowly avoided joining them.

Madsen pulled over onto the verge. Getting out he looked back. Other cars had stopped and drivers were making their way back to assist. Much to his surprise most of the passengers were clambering out of the wreckage. One of the men from the Jeep fell out and lay on the ground.

"What if Kearns has put an APB out on us?"

"I know, I know." Madsen took a few steps towards the accident. His attention was focused on the man who had fallen from the Jeep, now in the process of staggering to his feet. He looked around then saw Madsen staring in his direction. He reached into his pocket and pulled out a pistol. He fired once in Madsen's direction. Everyone on the road fell back.

"Shit!" He felt the bullet rip through the air not far from his head. He scrambled back into the driver's seat. "My imagination was right." A second bullet shattered the rear window. He slammed the car into drive then accelerated away up the verge, the wheels fighting for purchase on the wet ground. A volley of shots rang out and punched into the car.

Madsen flinched but kept his foot down.

"Are you okay?" he asked, his attention focused solely on trying not to bounce off the loggerhead of traffic that was rapidly building up.

No answer.

"Hey-" Turning to look he saw Hiroko slumped in her seat. A stream of blood was running from the gaping wound in the front of her head. Madsen slammed on the brakes and the car came to a stop in a heavy impact against a truck.

The enraged driver threw open the door and marched round the front of his truck to find Madsen clutching Hiroko's lifeless form to his chest. He was sobbing.

‡

Buchanan returned to the car with two regular sized coffees. Arden, his head resting on a hand in the open window, was watching the steady stream of traffic, his mind wandering through recent events. They had crossed over the Thames, its waters grey and choppy, and had turned off the 95 down towards Groton where Buchanan had made great play of the submarine base there and that it was also the name of one of the preferred schools that Skull and Bonesmen were initiated from. Arden now knew that the first submarine was launched nearby at Old Saybrook in 1776. Why Buchanan had mentioned this he had no idea. He wondered if somehow if was woven into his grand conspiratorial view of the world. Maybe the craft had been full of Freemasons out to dominate the world. Arden smiled inwardly.

"Here yah go. Extra sugar as well." Buchanan leant in through the window and offered one of the coffees to Arden.

Arden accepted.

Buchanan climbed in and slowly wound up the window on the driver's side.

"What you have to remember is this book isn't full of spells of incantations and that kind of crap." Buchanan took a sip of coffee. "It's the architecture that's in it."

"Architecture?"

"Yeah. All those cathedrals in Europe. They were all built using sacred geometry."

"I thought it was just basic geometry. Science, mathematics. They just thought it was sacred. Or it was kept sacred or secret so the masons would continue to be employed." Arden struggled with the lid of his coffee,

"Sure." Buchanan nodded.

"You're not talking about the streets being laid out shaped like an owl or that kind of crap, are you? Might as well be Homer Simpson's head in the streets of Springfield for all the relevance that has."

"That was the Stone Cutters, they're made up." Buchanan's face cracked into a broad grin.

Arden had to laugh.

"It was all part of the war. The Renaissance. Things changed after that. Clued in people were starting to question the power of the church. Not always openly, because that was dangerous. They hid their alternative thinking." Buchanan took a sip of coffee.

"That's not strictly true."

"But science was still a heresy. Different ways of thinking therefore, a heresy."

Arden exhaled noisily to show his impatience.

"Da Vinci did what he did." He said.

"But he still broke the law. He dissected bodies – totally against the teachings of the church. But it's more than that. People had other ideas they wanted to express. Powerful men could see their control starting to slip away. Bibles were in Latin until they were translated into English. The Church didn't like that one bit."

"Hey it's a corrupt world from top to bottom. There's nothing I can do about it."

"Your friend Jim was trying to change it."

"And that got him dead."

"Someone has to keep trying or we'll all lose." Buchanan took another mouthful of coffee.

"Is this some one man crusade of yours?" Arden asked belligerently.

Buchanan said nothing for a while. He looked out the window at the clearing skies.

"No."

Arden sensed the man wanted to say more.

"And?" He pushed Buchanan for an answer.

"I'm part of that resistance." Buchanan allowed the small but important revelation to sink in.

Smiling, Arden shook his head.

"You're kidding?"

"No I'm not. I'm just one of many scattered about the world who are keeping an eye on things." Buchanan turned in his seat and fixed his attention on the younger man. "We're always on the look out for like-minded souls. Jim thought you were a likely candidate."

"Candidate? For what?"

"There's something about your friend Jim you didn't know." Buchanan's face was serious, stern almost.

Arden shook his head.

"What? He was a CIA agent or something equally clichéd and conspiratorial?"

Buchanan's expression remained fixed.

"He was part of that resistance too."

"Do they put something in the coffee here?"

"I'm serious." Buchanan snapped back, his tone made Arden jump. "Have you ever heard of the Ordines?"

"Only once. A super power elite or some such crap. I don't believe in them though. Sounds like they've been made up by the conspiracy nuts. Like the modern Illuminati."

"No, they exist alright. You and Jim discussed the possibility of their existence on a regular basis." It was obvious Buchanan was not buying Arden's feigned dismissal.

"You're going to tell me you're one of them."

"Not exactly. Let's just say my allegiance is with them. The conspiracy nuts, as you so delicately put it, have it wrong. The Ordines are not the problem. They are the resistance."

"Is that right?"

"Yeah."

"So how do I fit in?"

Buchanan raised an eyebrow and turned his head slightly.

"They want to initiate you. To join the fight."

‡

157

Hannah had no idea how long she had drifted. Her watch had stopped, it was now choked with water and she had lost track of the days. She had awoken to a sun that had just slipped below the horizon, which had only added to her disorientation. Sitting up she tried to find out where she was. On the eastern riverbank a young boy, nothing more than a half silhouette in the twilight, was watching her. He was attending a small herd of emaciated goats that had come down to the water to drink.

Hannah grabbed the HK. The boy did not move. She hoped he read the message loud and clear. He stood exactly where he was but Hannah was not sure if it was out of fear, defiance or uncertainty. Maybe it was pride.

A distant pulsing noise was slowly rising in volume. Hannah looked around but could not locate its source. She raised the HK ready to defend her vulnerable position then flinched as a deafening rhythmic roar smashed across her senses. Powerful spotlights turned twilight into day. Dust boiled around her and the water around the boat churned and chopped. She looked up. Descending out of the light was a man in a harness. Above him several of the Blackhawk weapons erupted into life. Staccato flashes roared as tracer raced to its targets.

Over the noise and wash of the rotors the man shouted at Hannah to slip into a secondary harness. She willingly accepted. As the pair of them rose out of the boat the winch-man issued instructions into his headset. The Blackhawk, still firing its lethal barrage of weaponry, began to turn away.

Hannah looked down. On both sides of the river, originally hidden from her view by the banks on either side, was an enormous camp. She could see men rushing to truck mounted ordnance while others had already begun firing at the helicopter with machine guns. An RPG raced towards the helicopter but missed wildly. The dark was lit up with flashes and flames as men kicked out cooking fires, extinguished lamps and flashlights and opened up with an eclectic mix of different calibre weapons.

Within seconds Hannah was hauled aboard and the Blackhawk was racing away. As the helicopter turned west she caught a glimpse of the boy with the goats. He was still looking up at her, his face a sea of calm in a maelstrom of chaos.

The winch-man unhooked Hannah's harness. He grinned.

"Welcome home, Mam." He said in a low monotone.

Hannah allowed herself a smile. She nodded her appreciation.

"See, you can smile," a voice came out of the darkness. A seated figure lit up instantly by a distant explosion.

It was her father.

‡

Gregory, leaning against the doorframe to his office, watched through the glass walls as a sullen Madsen reported what had happened to two stern looking detectives. The design pool was quiet. Gone was the normal ribald laughter, the boisterous chatter and good-natured camaraderie that made working for the company a respected pleasure.

He did not believe in fate, that everyone had a pre-ordained destiny. It was a childish notion at best and he just hoped that his friend would not slip back into the deep mental well that he had been in for so long. Gregory was also hoping that his best friend could weather the storm and that he would not rush home to hide himself away in a prison of his own making or that he would not succumb to some daft notion that life was telling him something.

Somehow he felt guilty. It was after all he who had engineered the meeting; had in many respects pushed them together. Gregory wanted the Madsen of old back. A man, who laughed with life, not cowered against it. He was angry with his friend for being so reclusive, withdrawn, perhaps even defeatist. Madsen's first wife had gone, long gone. Her brief life should be celebrated then set adrift into memory.

159

But he had never had the courage to emotionally injure his friend so, instead of lecturing him, he had let the man sink into melancholy.

Hiroko's death would only convince Madsen that he should hide away for the rest of his life. Gregory knew that was nothing short of a living death.

The two detectives stood up and made their way to the door of Madsen's office and out into the corridor. They headed for the elevators passing Gregory on the way without even acknowledging him. He saluted them by way of a mock thank you then shook his head.

He looked across at Madsen who sensing he was being stared at turned his head. Gregory stepped across the corridor.

"Hi." He closed Madsen's office door behind him.

Madsen nodded.

Gregory hesitated.

"Chris. Don't worry. I know what you're thinking and I know what you're going to say." Madsen stood up. "Not this time. I can't hide away again. Not now." Chris watched the man's hands tighten into fists. It seemed as if Madsen was barely able to contain his anger. "I want to know who and I want to know why."

The Third Key

Linda was up to her elbows in stir-fry. Splashing some seasoned chilli sauce into the mixture, she wiped her nose with a sleeve.

'Have you read *Sunsphere*?' I was fussing with a bottle of wine at the table. It was often my job to fiddle with the wine at the table. As soon as I arrived for dinner a bottle was invariably thrust into my hands for me to deal with. I have never objected.

'Yeah.' Linda let the concoction sizzle. My stomach was at last feeling the urge to digest some food. 'A while ago.'

'But don't you find it a bit pompous of Arden to name a character after himself? Seems a bit, you know… up one's own thing.'

Linda examined the contents of a cupboard. I thought for a second that she'd not heard my question.

'I was thinking. What if?'

Uh-oh. Something suitably nefarious was brewing.

'What if…' Linda selected a pot of spice then continued. 'It's deliberate?'

'It's obviously deliberate.' I retorted, slicing my finger on the foil.

Linda squinted in anger.

'Yes, I know that. I mean more along the lines of autobiography. To suggest that he is somehow involved in real life. That maybe the novel isn't simply a story but is, in fact, real.' She licked a finger, nodded approvingly and added half the contents of the spice pot into the stir-fry. 'That the whole book is a way of revealing secrets but because he's written it as a novel he can rightly claim that it is in fact just a story.' Linda seemed very pleased with her explanation.

'Seems a bit…' I paused before saying 'far-fetched'.

'Plausible deniability, I think they call it.'

'If you're the President of the United States.'

'Think about it. If you've stumbled upon a secret mystery in which these keys are involved… What was it you said? That Arden says he has one? Well, how do you tell the world about this great secret but have the fall back position to say, should anyone hassle you, that it's just a story.'

'Who would want to, as you put it, hassle him?' The cork was one of those plastic ones. I hate them. Always seem so cheap.

'There's no end of secret societies that might want to keep it safe. The Templars for instance.' Linda checked the plates in the oven to see if they were warming.

'I thought they'd all been burnt at the stake.' I knew they hadn't. 'I was just trying to make a point.'

'Which was?'

'Oh I don't know. But there can't be a secret society behind everything in the world. It makes a mockery of reality for a start.'

The doorbell rang.

'That's Gus. Will you go and let him in.'

Gus stabbed the air with a food-laden fork.

'D'you know I'd missed that. How could I miss that? It's so obvious isn't it? I mean the Hannah Franklin character is revealed to be related to old Benjamin in the book.' Gus shook his head and smiled. 'But Arden... Author as character, eh?'

'I suggested that it was something to do with a concealed reveal.' Linda was rolling a glass of wine between her hands. 'Like the Language of the Birds. Have you spoken to Arden again?'

A concealed reveal is what conspiracy theorists call – well, you can guess. Something the old alchemists were fond of doing.

'I had to.' Gus glanced at me. 'To apologise. I spent twenty minutes soothing his ego. He's agreed to come and meet us again. Tomorrow afternoon. I told you you'd just had a bad morning.'

'Why, thank you.' I raised my glass. 'To writers who appear in their own books.' I then drained it in a oner.

'Oh don't get drunk again.' Linda frowned.

'No I won't. I promise.' Never my strong point to make a promise and keep it. But they knew that... all too well. It was one of my well-practiced idiosyncrasies.

'We have to see that key.' Pointing his fork at me Gus came over all officious. 'And that means you apologising and playing ball.'

'Yes.' Linda added. 'You're too dismissive.'

Or rather suspicious. I had to be in my line of work. People turning up with ancient trinkets and demanding to know if they're genuine when it's highly bloody unlikely. Or when you find yourself sinking deeper into a scam that might result in all parties, some international, ending up staring at four blank walls for ten years. I wasn't going to apologise for being a suspicious git. And hell's teeth, in this day and age, you had to be. A constant stream of lies, fibs, scams and rip-offs coming from every direction. Banks, the government, conspiracy theorists and their pseudo-history, the list was bloody endless. If you're asleep at the wheel they've got yah!

'Gus, you said there was no big reveal at the end of *Sunsphere*.' I felt obliged to enter the fray.

'Yeah, that's right. All the protagonists are brought closer to the secret but... well... you ought to read it.' Gus recharged his fork.

'What's the overall plot though? That might shed some light on our theory.' If you can't beat them with common sense, abandon yours.

'Three keys open the golden sphere that's on top of the Dogana del Mare in Venice. The quest is to find those three keys, their connection with certain characters and why those same characters both historic and present day are attempting to keep them, as well as the secret, safe. Set against that is a nefarious secret society working against the good secret society. The bad secret society suspect they know what the secret is and want to keep it that way whereas the good secret society wants to reveal the great secret. The race is on to find the keys. That's it in a nutshell.'

'Sorry, why does the bad secret society want to keep it safe. The secret, that is?' I wasn't quite clear on this point.

'Because...' Gus sounded exasperated. 'You really should read the book. The secret threatens Christianity. The bad secret society is an ultra-right wing theistic group who suspect that the secret in the sunsphere may blow the lid off nearly two millennia of belief. Not only do they feel threatened, spiritually they believe that if Christianity collapses other religions i.e. Islam may rule supreme. Added to that there's the usual right wing repression of third world societies through religion stuff and how that's good for the world... apparently. Well, rich men's bank balances.'

'Okay. So who are the good secret society then?'

Gus raised a finger while he chewed and swallowed.

'The good secret society, called the Ordines, dates back to the Enlightenment, although some suspect they go back much further. To Roman times in fact, as one scene in the book describes three Romans talking about this new plague of a religion called Christianity taking away their old life. Anyway, it was set up by freethinkers who stumbled upon the secret and decided to keep it safe until the world was ready to be enlightened. You assume that it blows the lid of Christianity but that's just a guess because of the bad secret society's desire to contain the knowledge. It's a kind of liberation through freethought versus oppression of the mind subtext.'

'And this secret, whatever that is, is hidden in full view of the Grand Canal?' I asked.

Yes,' replied Gus.

'Like I said, a concealed reveal.' Linda chipped in for emphasis.

'It has a certain irony.' Perhaps Irony was the wrong word but I knew what I meant. 'Why there though?'

'Who knows man? Does it matter? It's an exciting plot device. A mysterious secret right in front of everyone's eyes. The statue of Fortuna high above the heads of Venetians and tourists alike. And of course because Venice was a Templar Base.' Gus smiled. There was a twinkle in his eye. 'Five hundred years ago it was also the biggest brothel in the world.'

'Like the best magic tricks.' Linda gathered up her cutlery and made for the sideboard. 'All in the open but you still can't see how it's done.'

'Dashwood and Franklin et al are all on the side of the Enlightenment. The good guys.' Gus pushed his plate away, his smile gone. 'The main characters like Madsen are accidentally caught up in this quest or as it's hinted at, maybe it is no accident.'

'From the bit I've read, Arden's with the good guys.' I picked idly at a tooth with a fingernail.

'He is. Or rather the character named Arden is. I've no idea about the real one.' Gus sat back and folded his arms.

Linda produced three bowls of Christmas pudding.

'It's July.' Gus giggled.

'It had to be eaten up.' Linda went on the defensive.

'Fair enough.'

Before there are any accusations of sexism here, we took it in turns to rustle up a meal and serve it. The other two relaxed at the table. It's a tradition that goes back years.

'Can we assume that Arden has aligned himself with the good guys for a reason?' Linda licked a finger.

'The character representing the real man?' Gus nodded. 'Yeah I can go along with that.'

I couldn't. Not yet anyway. Perhaps Arden just had a monstrous ego or was doing his Hitchcock bit.

'Does his character have a key in the book?' Seemed like a fair question for me to ask.

'No. One was in the temple of Mithra in Iraq, another was in the church at West Wycombe, the one with the sunsphere on its steeple, it was in a font, and the third was at the bottom of the Grand Canal – but there are hints that it had been found by a scuba diving surveyor checking the foundations along the Grand Canal. A surveyor who was mysteriously murdered in his home in Padova, the wall safe having been broken into.' Gus sounded far too serious as if he thought the book might in fact somehow reflect reality. 'But the key from the canal had been stolen from a powerful family way back when. I'd have to read the tome again to make sure.'

'Have you read any of his other books? What were they, The Holy Legacy of the Michelangelo Scrolls and The

Atlantis Heresy and...?' I rubbed my eyes. I was, I must admit, a little tired.

'I've read The Atlantis Heresy. It's about how the United States planned World War 2 to help them recover from the Wall Street Crash. You know, Europe's power base destroyed so that America could start its efforts to run the world.' Gus prodded his pudding with a spoon.

'Does Arden appear in that one? Linda asked.

'No.'

'How does Atlantis come into the story?' I dreaded the answer, fearing some lost civilisation, drowned city, sphinx-pyramid, lost Ark of the Covenant combo jive.

'America as Atlantis. That the country was known to the ancients before the Vikings and Christopher Columbus. Its manifest destiny to enlighten the world again.'

'I see.' I replied with as much scepticism as I was willing to muster at that time in the evening. 'What about the other one?'

'Never read it.'

'We should check the web.' Linda had already finished her afters and was draining the last of her wine.

Gus nodded.

We spent an hour or so afterwards skimming the web and hunting down references to Arden's oeuvre. There were several websites dedicated to his work, even one that was taking it all far too seriously. Oddly enough there was another set up to denounce Arden as nothing more than a puppet of the shadowy Illuminati. Gus became quite agitated. Turned out the paranoid loon who had launched the website was an American Reverend. This man was convinced that all secret societies were the work of the devil, atheists and, once again, global Jewry.

More tedious far right theistic guffaroo. The man obviously didn't realise that ninety nine percent of secret societies were, or are, religious.

The Internet - every repressed oversexed bigoted lonely male nut job with a vicious axe to grind. Everything rated triple K.

I did wonder if a few of these people had their tongues firmly in their cheeks. I mean you can never really tell except of course for those whose web pages were full of nothing but hate, anti-freethought and more disgustingly, but not surprisingly, anti-Semitism.

Was there anything the Jews hadn't done according to these idiots? *Beware! Christ killers rule the world! Run children run! They'll drink your blood...* adopt mad vampiric laugh.

The more you read, the more interwoven and desperately muddled these people's thinking became. Freemasons controlled by the Illuminati who also controlled the Bilderberg Group via the European Union, the Phoebus Cartel and the Knights Templar, who were in league with the Knights of Malta and the Mafia. It was all one big Gordian knot of bollocks.

None of it made sense and I found it all very childish and paranoid.

We found a few pictures of Arden talking at some conference in London a few months ago. The weekend long gathering had been called *Con-spire*. On a screen behind him was a large image of the cover of *Sunsphere*. In most of the photos Arden looked composed and relaxed but in one an apoplectic middle-aged man, megaphone in hand, who appeared to be frothing at the mouth, had come onto the stage and was jabbing a finger at the author. The caption read *New World Order Critic Alex Fadge accuses Arden of being an Illuminati stooge*. The final snap in the sequence showed Arden's right fist connecting with Fadge's chin.

Beneath was a morticed section enlightening readers to the ongoing lawsuit Fadge had filed against Arden. Fadge, rather bizarrely, was using the 1st Amendment Free Speech ploy but Arden had countered with the fact that this was England where that kind of thing had no power. Besides,

Arden was exercising the very thing Fadge was claiming to defend i.e. free speech, so what was the problem?

It seemed that all these people had one thing in common. They had based their careers on conspiracy theories and therefore needed to propagate them in order to sell more books to pay the rent and put food on the table. Either that or they were just attention seeking, which seemed the most likely – to me at least.

'Don't you find all this just a touch sad. If not totally bonkers?'

My question fell flat.

The one odd thing, and no I don't want to go down that paranoid road, was that there was no mention anywhere of Arden's use of his own name in *Sunsphere*. You would've thought at least one person with too much time on their hands might have made mention of the oddity. There you go; even the conspiracy theorists missed that one.

Tired of glimpsing a virtual world of weirdness, I pretended to go to the toilet as an excuse to go outside and get some fresh air.

Linda's garden was small, surrounded by a 6-foot high dark red brick wall, splashed here and there with fading whitewash. Great hairy plants were running riot throughout, softening all the hard edges. I didn't turn on the outside light and just let the kitchen one illuminate the small patio. Illuminate... Illuminati... was it really all one grand manipulation of reality?

What is it about us that we seek comfort in myths and legends and avoid reality altogether? Why were stupid conspiracy theories so popular? Why all that bloody daft new age thinking. New age! That's a laugh. Nothing new about it. It's the same old ugly dog wheeled out in a new dress. Bogus humpty from top to bottom. It was all right up there with religion.

Why do we do it to ourselves?

Looking up I could just see one or two stars through the sodium funk. I felt better. Staring at the universe always made me feel earthed. All the petty trivia of the day to day serving of the Man fizzled away to its genuine state... meaninglessness.

I'd only ever knowingly met one Freemason. I didn't know he was one at the time but he was just fine. No horns. No cupboards full of kidnapped children. No Machiavellian manipulation of my head. We shared several cups of tea and a packet of orange Club biscuits at a mutual friend's house. He made us laugh with a few jokes and a good time was had by all.

Isn't it all about the projection of our fears? Really. If we're honest. Fear of not being in with the right crowd. Fear that our lives are out of our control. Fear of the big wide world. Fear we don't add up to much. Fear that no one's listening to us. Fear of being alone.

The fear of facing reality.

Isn't that what irrational thought is all about?

As far as I'm concerned the conspiracy is with them. Anything that stands in the way of rationality and reason.

I was about to polish my soapbox further when Gus appeared.

'There you are.'

'Just fancied some fresh air. My head was well and truly, I think the vernacular has it, done in by all that paranoid crap.'

'Yeah, it does get you.' Which was odd coming from Gus because he has a tendency to lap this sort of thing up.

'Found anything more about the man in question?' I sat myself down in a garden chair.

'I think we have to go to the horse's mouth, don't you?'

'Will he talk to us or rather, you?'

'He should do. Linda's keen to interview him for *Codex*. Thinks she might be able to interest the editor in an article on Arden.'

Linda stuck her head out of the door.

'Coffee?'

'Sound.' I gave a thumbs up.

Gus nodded and sat down at the garden table, a dark green metal affair.

'I'll probably tell him about the key I found.'

'You haven't already?'

'I didn't trust him but he wants to see the extract and I want to see the other key, so hopefully...' Gus's voice trailed away and he nodded his head slowly.

'Fair enough.' My thoughts rolled around. 'Okay, there are three keys mentioned in the various extracts and that *Sunsphere* novel. You have a key and he has a key.'

'That's right.'

I had to try and sum things up in order to get my head around all this.

'So presumably two keys have seen the light of day and a third is still out there somewhere.'

Gus nodded.

'If the extracts are to be believed.' Linda placed a tray of coffee mugs on the table. 'Three keys to open the sphere on the Customs house in Venice.' She sat down.

'This doesn't add credibility to the extracts.' I picked up a mug and took a sip.

'Doesn't it?' Linda's voice raised an octave in that way her voice did when she was sharply defending something that was often a little outré. A touch school mistressy again. 'I think it's obvious that the keys mentioned in the books are real. Gus, you have one and so does Arden. That speaks volumes to me. I don't know how you can be so sceptical.'

With bloody good cause!

'So where do we find the third?' My tone was less than amenable. All these documents washing about so soon. Lost manuscripts and gold keys. All sounded too convenient to me. It reminded me of that Hoffman fellow back in the 1980s who was producing fake document after fake document to rip off the Mormon Church. I had often wondered who were the more desperate party, the Mormons who lapped up all the twaddle or Hoffman who was eager to pay off his crippling debts. Or the Priory of Sion spoof that had surfaced out of the columns of a church in the South of France. Only this time a wider audience would suck up the nonsense to launch a thousand ships full of literary fools. The whole thing had rested on the existence of some mythical grail, an idea that had been made up a thousand years ago by the French poet Chrétien de Troyes in his *Perceval*. It would be like a real world conspiracy being based on the quest for a tricorder from an episode of *Star Trek*. If you repeat things enough, if you tell bigger and bigger lies, the more you'll convince the masses.

I could tell this was weighing on Gus who had grown quieter this last day or so. He knew the score. A theory based on feeble evidence was a career crusher. It was not unknown for authors to invent evidence just to back up what they were peddling as a way to bolster their position and of course their careers. Think Roswell. Think Bermuda Triangle. Think alien abduction. Think Knights Templar. To me it spoke volumes about the human species and its willingness to surrender reasoned thought for irrational nonsense. It was all crap from top to bottom. Pardon my cynicism but we're all drowning in it.

'Maybe Arden has an idea where the third key is.' Linda pressed down on the handle of the cafétiere.

'Or hopes we do.' Gus didn't sound convincing. Why would Arden think that? He was just keen to see the Hiddon documents.

'We must be careful though.' Linda began to pour the coffee.

'Why?' Yes, *why?* is my favourite question. Why a conspiracy? Why do we need a god? Why is the world such a mess? Yes there are difficulties with *why?* questions but for the moment it was a failsafe mechanism. If I let go of the *why?* my sanity would sail off into the wide blue yonder shouting *told you so* as it went and I didn't want that to happen again. No sir.

'I still want to know who it was that pushed the other Hiddon extract though your door.' Lifting the coffee to his lips Gus slurped nosily on the rich brew. 'It's significant.'

'Only if we find out who it is.' Linda replied.

Well obviously. If it were the Pope then it would be more significant than if the perp were a small boy simply having a jape at our expense. Not that I think for one moment it was. As for the Pope well, oh, you know what I mean.

'Think about it for a moment. It would have to have been someone who knew that Gus had found the original Hiddon manuscript in that item of furniture.' Linda sat back. She almost sounded like she was talking to herself. As was often the way. I remember in one of her lectures in a local hall she had drifted off delivering her words almost as if she were lost in a trance. 'Who could that be?'

Gus was thoughtful for a moment and adopted that staring into some inner distance look, his eyes fixed on some unknown focal point.

'As far as I know,' he said after a few moments of silence. 'No one. I was on my own in the room when I found it.'

'Perhaps someone realised it was missing.' Linda placed her coffee down and slid her chair closer to the table.

'Then, I should imagine, Gus would be fighting a hefty lawsuit by now.' My words did not go down well. They never do. As the resident sceptic both Linda and Gus should have treated me like the devil's advocate I was instead of the big fat bloated, self-satisfied fly in the ointment they actually took me for.

Once more there was a protracted silence.

Then Linda beamed.

Here it was...

'They meant for you to find the lost manuscript. That's it. They invited you up to look at that furniture item knowing you would find the Hiddon extract.' Linda was smiling.

As was Gus.

To be honest I couldn't think of any genuine alternative to that idea either. It actually sounded quite convincing.

'Hey. You might be on to something there.' Gus leant forward. He tapped the edge of the table with the side of his right hand. 'That's the only logical explanation.'

I entered into the spirit of the occasion. Don't ask. I just felt like going along with it for a while. I often do this but the intention is to throw in a totally daft idea and see what reaction I get. The idea being that I throw them such a silly one that I snap them out of their misfiring senses.

'Sniff out who the person was who sold the chest of drawers to you.' I swirled the coffee around in my cup.

'I only spoke to her twice. Once on the phone and then in person when I was up there.' I could tell Gus's mind was racing. Perhaps the caffeine was doing his work. Gus always did vast quantities of it when he was on one. When his self-induced tizz died down he always crashed through a monstrous series of withdrawal symptoms.

'What was her name?' Linda stood up and made her way back into the house.

Gus made an effort answer but Linda was already inside before he could finish. She returned a few minutes later with her notebook. She opened it up to one of the last few remaining empty pages and sat down again. On a page opposite she had already scribbled a few notes. I could see the words *three keys, sunsphere – Venice and West Wycombe, Hiddon, a Freemason? 2 extracts of books pertaining to Hiddon, Arden – character and author name – claims to have a key similar to one Gus has. What's going on?*

Indeed. What was going on?

'Alexia Carey-Hunt.' Gus sniffed. 'Cracking bit of totty but a bit, you know – haughty. Jodhpurs, white shirt type of thing, blonde hair all over the show. Someone you might see on the cover of a Jilly Cooper novel.'

Great. My kind of scene. Always had a thing for posh girls.

I could tell Linda was feeling uncomfortable with Gus's overtly male talk of the opposite sex. She coughed to make her irritation known.

Gus raised an eyebrow in my direction.

'Maybe we should talk to her at some point.' Linda scribbled *A Carey-Hunt* into her notebook.

'It would be great to see the house again.' Gus had a knowing smile on his face. 'Enormous place. A real old country estate pile, fresh out of a lavish BBC production of a Jane Austen novel. The grounds seemed to go on forever.'

'Wasn't she up to her neck in debt?' My question was pertinent.

'Yes.' Gus replied. 'About two million.'

'How the four and a half does someone get that much in debt?' I asked even though I had some pretty good thieving bank-based ideas as to how that had happened.

'Dunno. Usual ways I guess. I think her old man got himself into hot water over an arms deal to an African dictatorship that went tits up big style,' Gus said in his half arsed street jive. 'I think she said she was in negotiations with an international hotel chain to sell the house for conversion into a country club.' Gus paused. 'If I remember correctly her old man was murdered. I mean the death was suspicious.'

'Hang on, I remember that in the news. An attempted coup wasn't it? CIA backed or something. It was a mix of Old School Tie and US Intel.' Oil was probably in the equation somewhere... as it always is.

Gus nodded.

'Where's the house?' Linda's pen was poised over paper.

'The West Country.' Gus scratched an eyebrow. 'Near the Mendip Hills. I think she said the family had been in the area for centuries.'

'Sadly for not much longer.' I drained my coffee. 'Right I've got to get going?'

'I've arranged for us to meet Arden in the same pub at around three. So behave.' Gus pointed an accusative finger at me.

'Righto.' I deliberately chose not to sound convincing.

'He means it.' Linda added her tuppeny-ha-penny's worth.

'All right. I will.'

I fidgeted in bed that night and felt horribly uncomfortable. My head was sailing directly for the rocks of anxiety on the shifting tides of sanity. Or something like that. About ten years ago I went through a long phase of researching UFOs and read everything I could on the subject. I ate, slept, thought, peed and excreted UFOs for a whole year. It sent me skirting into the abyss of paranoia. I'd watch the evening news, usually Channel 4's, and listened to the barking idiots who ran the world with their doublethink newspeak and thought my head was going to burst. They were all in on it. I didn't know who, what, where, when, and why. I felt insulted and assaulted, got at by unseen enemies and was wracked with fear that every night some slutty little grey pervert was going to burst through my bedroom door and shove his space knob up my bottom while the suits of the CIA looked on in that shadowy *X-Files* way.

It was squalid and I had fallen for it all.

It reminded me of that.

Fear. That's what they wanted. Fear. If it wasn't aliens it was terrorists. If it wasn't them it was some other dubious bogeyman. And by Jove we had to be scared of them all! What a cowed world we'd allowed them to create for us.

From that fear came anger. Not only at myself for believing the drivel but because of the countless bastards who propagated the myths for the sake of their own grubby often political m.o.'s. I hated them all. The world, it seemed to me, was awash with total bogus crapola. It was like an out of control forest fire or more likely a malevolent virus without an effective antibiotic. The far right nuts, throwing Tea Bag tantrums, who made up conspiracy theories about Barack Obama or the same clowns spreading daft rumours about black helicopters and cattle mutilations – all of it engineered to cow the population. Fear of the United Nations, fear of the black man, fear of the Reds, science, Socialists, football... oh and look out, here comes Satan. Ya'll only take mah gun from mah cold dead hand!

I vowed then, in the words of the best Who song, I wouldn't get fooled again.

Yet here I was... once more... skirting the nonsense bandwagon. Conspiracy theories were like pornography, *oh all right... just one more look... then I really must give it up. But no, wait... where's that video tape... for old time's sake...*

I actually ended up convinced that the authorities didn't give a toss about any of it, religion, UFOs, the JFK assassination and all that, because ultimately it kept the people distracted. I was also convinced that the back room suits were just having a bloody big laugh at the idiocy of the populace for believing in a multitude of moronic things. I'm sure they were just playing us like so many creaky old violins in a *we know something you don't* immature playground-level game of wind up the people. They were guardians of empty boxes that some thought were bursting at the seams with barnstorming secrets.

It was all a big psychological game. Cow the people!

Let them live in fear.

Now you know a little more about why I'm the way I am.

Sceptic? You'd better believe it.

When In Rome
Rome, 391 A.D.

It had been a hot august day in the eternal city, the hottest some had said for a generation. Quintus, uncomfortable with the heat at the best of times had spent much of the afternoon reading in the shade of the pillared courtyard occasionally stepping over to the pool to wash his face and hands. More frequently, he would pour water onto his neck and would allow it to evaporate, alleviating the uncomfortable temperature that had been his companion for most of the day.

Eschewing his servants, he had asked to be left alone until such time as the first of his invited guests arrived just after sunset. He had eaten little and drunk even less. His mind was occupied by troubled thoughts. It was clear that the old ways were disappearing fast. The old gods had been replaced by one from foreign shores and Rome itself had been replaced by a new capital, Constantinopolis, a reconstructed Byzantium in the east. The emperor Constantine had realised that Rome was no longer defensible from the threats growing in the north so had cowardly, in the eyes of many, created a New Rome beyond the reach of the barbarian hordes.

Quintus loved Rome. Despite his rural upbringing, albeit one that was wealthy, in the fields of Britannia, he had moved with his family to the heart, the birthplace of the empire some thirty years before. Now he could see his beloved city disappearing under the mantle of unwanted influences. The empire itself was split into two, west and east and could only mean that eventually, and inevitably, it would collapse. The sun would set on the greatest power base the world had ever known and nothing but chaos would follow.

But something should survive. Must survive. The new religion was slowly absorbing and removing the old ways – especially since the Emperor Theodosius had made it the state religion a decade before – despite the willingness in some quarters to hold onto the old beliefs. Old truths must be protected and an old way of life honoured.

Quintus was aware of someone moving hesitantly towards him. Looking up, he saw one of his slaves leading an older man into the colonnade. He nodded. He knew the man well.

"You're early, Sextus." Quintus smiled. He stood up and took his friend's arm.

"I'm old and impatient. Procrastination is no longer part of my character. I've decided that I have little time left for such a luxury."

"To the point as ever, my friend."

"The sun is nearly set. It is soon enough. Helios bows his head again."

"Even the Greeks knew who to worship." Quintus signaled his slave to fetch refreshments.

"Helios or mighty Apollo. It was better in the days of the many." Sextus approached the pool.

"Sit. Sit, my friend."

Sextus, a tall heavy set man, his white hair cropped almost to the scalp, sat down on the edge of the pool, his expression one of racked uncertainty.

"I really thought his lordship Secundus would be here. The man is a slouch at the best of times." Sextus ran his fingers through the cool water.

"He will, in all likelihood, be on time. You arrive too early and accuse everyone else of being late." Quintus returned to his seat. His attention was drawn to the lengthening shadows in the garden. The sky was a deepening salmon pink, the high clouds edged in fiery orange.

"My way of feeling superior." Sextus laughed.

"That I do not doubt." Quintus smiled.

There was a long moment's silence before Sextus spoke again.

"There are only three of us." He said. "Will that be enough?"

"I don't know. But it is a sensible number. There can never be a hung vote. Something the senate should learn." Quintus clasped his hands together

"We are tired old men. What happens when we are gone?" Sextus asked.

"Before such time, we each find a replacement and the other two will vote for which one they desire to see take up the position. That man is then initiated. He swears an oath. And so on."

Sextus leant forward, his hands clasped beneath his chin.

"What is our modus operandi?" He asked.

"To keep the old knowledge safe. Protect it against all enemies, whatever the cost and for all time."

"A noble cause my friend." Smiling, Sextus sat back.

"I hope so. Sometimes fighting a battle is not a way to protect something. Moving stealthily and secretly is sometimes a superior way to defend that which we hold dear and most precious." Quintus stood up again and moved to the threshold of the garden. A gentle evening breeze was strengthening. "We must keep the sun burning. More importantly we must reveal to the world the truth behind this new religion that our esteemed Emperor believes so strongly in. Then they will see it for what it is."

My Esteemed Colleague and Noble Brother,

You will be pleased to know that all is well here. The property with its refurbishments is a handsome spectacle. The church of St Lawrence has seen much by way of similar improvements. The aforementioned reparations are based on the solar temple at Palmyra. You must indeed revisit as soon as your duties allow. But I fear that much time will pass before that day. I do, of course, extend the invitation to your fellow brother Masons who are as welcome here as the sun.

I am aware that the work of the three gathers apace in the Colonies of the New World and for that you must attend with vigour and fortitude. But rest assured your presence here will always be welcome.

Your friend,

Francis Dashwood.

He Was A Friend of Mine
Washington DC, 22 November 1963

He knew he was too old for tears but nonetheless they came and he allowed them to flow. All the years as a journalist he had never felt so emotionally ragged as he had done over the last two hours. He had seen death and he had seen pain in all its multifaceted forms bound up in humanity's inhumanity to its own kind. He had thought for a long while that nothing would ever move him again; that he was in all respects an emotional void. It was a thick shell, it had to be with the things he had seen, but now that hard won redoubt against feeling had fractured.

With both hands on the railings he looked up to The White House. In recent years it has acquired a different name, which some had used in scorn. *Camelot.* Fitting only now in a world that had dispensed with reality to become one that seemed to be entirely make-believe. Why had the man created such a deep affection in the majority, even more so in the manner of his death? Promise was the simple answer. The promise of a better future, a brighter future, the new frontier, where the world was seen as one and not as the many. What was it he had said? *We all share this small world; we all breathe the same air.* Now it seems the sun had set and a new dark night was rolling in. One full of fear and re-invigorated malice and the sense that all was now in vain.

180

Maybe not in vain. There was always hope. But hope, like faith, is based on desire not reality. He could not allow himself that luxury. There were at best, possibilities.

He turned his head to look at the others who had also gathered here. All of them had downcast faces. Several people were weeping. Even a policeman wiped tears from his face with the back of a hand. He was someone who had also seen much but who could not contain his sense of loss anymore than the next mourner.

It was a surreal time. More so because he knew the reasons why the 35th President had been cast aside. Reasons he could not reveal, for who would believe him? There was a power game. A long fought game played over the centuries to its latest strategic move that had been the most decisive yet. For now, the enemy had gained a great advantage and it would take a long time to retake the ground. It might not happen in his lifetime.

‡

"Why the hell should anyone want to initiate me?" For some miles they had said nothing. Buchanan had allowed the younger man time to reflect on what was being asked of him. Now Arden had broken the silence. "I mean, why not some top level scientist? I'm just, or was, a writer from a small publishing house. What use am I?"

"Some scientists are already with us. Yeah, most dismiss it as nonsense and believe me we've asked a good number. I can respect their attitude. They have no time for such things. But it's not just about intelligence."

"Thanks," came Arden's wry response.

"I don't mean it that way." Buchanan's voice had an edge of steel. "Scientists, writers, anyone who thinks freely. That's who they want. Anyone not awash in indoctrination and who can see things for what they really are. True enlightenment comes when you give up believing the bullshit."

"Right out the mouth of the Dalai Lama." Arden sported a mock frown. "They want me because I'm a writer?"

"Yeah."

"They wanted Jim?"

"They did. But he was wiped out."

"But there must be other writers? Other publishing houses?"

"As I said, there are scientists, free thinkers and numerous writers. But we always try to reach the ones we know might be sympathetic to the cause." Buchanan's tone had grown more conciliatory. "Three Roman senators saw how the empire was going. They wanted to hold onto the old ways. They were the first Ordines and their symbol was the sun. It united them in the light. The sun brings light to the day as truth brings knowledge out of the darkness. It illuminates."

"That's a bit flowery for an ex-military man."

Buchanan ignored him and continued.

"They were resisting the arrival of the new religion but this soon became a resistance against all that was deemed untrue or weak minded." Buchanan was searching the road ahead for any exit signs showing Providence. "They tried wherever possible to think rationally. Sure, they had a limited view; science was nowhere near as well developed. But they knew that nature was not the work of the gods."

"They were ahead of their time."

"They were not the first I guess. Who knows? But they were the first to make it official, if you see what I mean?" Buchanan smiled.

Arden watched the landscape roll by.

"So the people running the Ordines show trawl through society looking for people who think..." Arden paused looking for the right word. "...Differently?"

"Yeah, that's exactly what they do. What they've always done. From the famous to the not so. They even approached Leonardo Da Vinci but the only society he joined was the tongue-in-cheek Company of the Cauldron, set up by his friend Rustici. They wanted to make artworks out of food. All that Priory of Sion talk is just crap. It wouldn't have appealed to him."

Arden laughed.

"Never believed that BS anyway. A practical joke. Nothing more."

Buchanan nodded.

"But, look at that on a larger scale, who's pulling whose strings with that one?" he asked.

"Whatever. But Da Vinci was the first scientist. A man of the Renaissance."

"As you so rightly said in your book, the Priory of Sion was a fabrication." Buchanan paused for a moment then continued. "The Renaissance was the work of the Ordines. They wanted to push humanity in the right direction. One great intellectual effort to set us on the right path."

"Are you sure you were in the military? You sound more like my old history teacher."

"I did end my career in military intelligence." Buchanan bore a wry smile.

"There's that old joke about that being an oxymoron." Arden grinned.

"I've heard them all. This, however, is serious." Up ahead Buchanan saw the Providence exit and began to slow the car.

"So why? I mean what's the point? That's what I could never get with the conspiracy theorists. If the Freemasons wanted to control the world why not initiate us all into Freemasonry? It would be so much easier. You're not telling me this is what the Ordines want?"

"It would never happen. Too many diverse and ingrained views. That's why a one-world government could never work. Do you really think Islam will take kindly to being told what to do by Protestants? And vice versa."

"Man, conspiracy theorists don't think, do they? They also forget that everything looks great on paper but when humans are added to the mix it all goes to hell."

"Don't be too dismissive. Some of them are right. Most though are deluded. I guess you could call the Ordines watchmen; on the walls of mental liberty."

"That's a big ask."

"It's never been easy."

"How do I know you're telling the truth? That you're not some psycho?" Arden turned in his seat a little and faced Buchanan.

"You don't."

"So everything you're telling me is a heap of bullshit?"

"What do you think?" Buchanan's tone was cryptic.

"Extraordinary claims need extraordinary evidence." There was a dismissive tone to Arden's reply.

"That's why we're going to Providence, Mister Arden."

✝

They had spent the entire journey in silence. Hannah had seen the nod her father had given her. It was a familiar indication that he was not going to talk in front of unwarranted attention. Even while her wound was dressed he showed no concern for her. When the Blackhawk touched down he maintained his silence. Hannah had slipped into a subservient role. There was a part of her that despised her father for making her feel that way but then he had rescued her and for that she was deeply thankful. Yes, she could have made it all the way back, she knew that, but again maybe her father had come to her aide because he was less than confident in her abilities and feared losing that which she had been sent to find. He had that knack of keeping her emotionally off balance. It left her, for the most part, questioning herself. One minute angry at his psychological manipulation, the next feeling an overwhelming love for him. It was the simple skill of a dictator.

The winch-man opened the side door and saluted Hannah's father as he stepped down. Hannah followed him into the dark. She smiled at the winch-man, a brief thank you for his efforts in dragging her clear. He nodded back but no smile. It was clear he had the utmost respect for her father and would not display any emotion towards the man's flesh and blood.

Rushent was waiting for them. He offered a crisp salute to Hannah's father. Hannah looked around. They were not in the familiar area of the barracks. They were at the main airport.

"Sir. Please follow me." Rushent had lost all that relaxed effortless ease he had shown to Hannah. Now he was as taut and officious as everyone else who found themselves in the presence of Franklin senior.

Rushent guided them to a Humvee.

Moments later they were being driven at high speed across the tarmac towards the far end of a runway. All of the Humvee's lights both internal and external were out; the driver using night vision goggles to see.

Hannah stared out into the dark. Some distant lights were on in the civilian areas. Occasionally she could see the headlights of a car heading somewhere at high speed but for the most part stygian gloom hung over the airport.

The Humvee came to a stop.

Rushent stepped out and made his way round to Franklin's door and opened it, once more saluting as he did so. This made Hannah smile, as it was so dark as to make the gesture meaningless.

Stepping out of the vehicle Hannah was suddenly aware of a large streamlined structure just ahead in the dark. It was a large transport aircraft, a C130, but painted a matt black. There was a whine and a large ramp at the rear of the craft tipped down towards the ground. An internal red light cast a strange infernal glow around the fuselage.

"Sir." Rushent pointed to the ramp but Franklin was ahead of him.

Hannah followed. She nodded at Rushent who saluted her, but kept his eyes staring at some point beyond in the dark.

Making her way under the belly of the machine, she looked up and saw that its surface was a non-reflective material. It reminded her of the stealth aircraft she had seen when visiting a secret development facility with her father years before.

"Hannah." Her father's voice was commanding.

She followed him up the ramp into the belly of the beast. The interior had been stripped of all unnecessary equipment except for a series of seats along both sides of the interior fuselage.

Hannah's father sat down and began buckling himself in. He took a headset off a hook behind his head and spoke into the mouthpiece. "Pilot, earn your pay."

A few seconds later the engines began to whine and rumble into life, filling the interior with a heavy vibration.

Hannah sat opposite her father. She locked her harness together and after a moment staring at the floor, she looked up at him. He was smiling but Hannah knew it was not for her. His lusty delight was for the treasure he would soon possess.

As the aircraft began to taxi up the runway and gather speed Hannah reached into a pocket. At that moment she knew he was smiling not for her but for that something else – in this case the small key she held tightly in her hand.

Opening her fingers she looked down into her hand. On the periphery of her vision she saw her father lurch forward against his harness, eager to see that which he desired above all else.

Madsen was heading south on the 95 not far from the State border when his cell phone chirped for attention.

"Yeah?"

The voice was instantly familiar.

"Mister Madsen. People have a habit of dying around you." Kearns' voice was full of mock concern, as solicitous as a cat for a mouse.

"How did you get this number?"

"I'm a cop. That's what I do. Why did you-" Kearns paused in a well-rehearsed manner, "run, Mister Madsen?"

"Can't say."

"Can't or won't?"

"If you suspect me of killing Lee then you had better come forward with your evidence." Madsen banged the steering wheel with a palm.

"Oh, I do suspect you of killing the sheriff. There's no one else around who remotely fits the profile."

"It wasn't me."

"Maybe it was your accomplice."

"Who?"

"The intern who works, oh excuse me, who worked at your company."

"Hiroko? No way."

"Had you known her long?"

"Long enough."

"But not long enough to vouch for her."

"She didn't do it. D'you think she could have killed a man like Powers? Kearns, whatever you think neither one of us is responsible."

"You see. There's the problem. I think you are."

There was another pause on the line then Kearns continued.

"Why don't you stop, turn around and come back and we can discuss this situation."

"I can't."

"Why not? You're the prime suspect Mister Madsen. I can't negotiate with you."

"Why didn't you stop me in Boston, when the cops there spoke to me about—" Madsen stopped short. The pang of memory stung his eyes.

"By the time I heard about the incident, you were back on the road."

"Then get the Rhode Island police to arrest me." Madsen turned his pain to defiance.

There was no reply from Kearns.

Madsen's defiance continued. "You won't because you're not convinced I did it. You have no evidence. Nothing." Madsen snapped his cell phone shut and tossed it onto the passenger seat.

Kearns was right. Too many people were dying around him. Or was the man just playing on Madsen's paranoia? Another trick perhaps like his bluff about evidence left at the sheriff's hanging.

Yet, as someone had once said, just because you're paranoid doesn't mean they're not out to get you. There had been the bomb in Boston, Hiroko's shooting and the sheriff's hanging. Madsen could no longer dismiss these as unconnected. Subconsciously perhaps, he had made the connection some time back; he was just not ready to accept what he already believed deep down. Admittedly, he had no idea who the body on the beach was, but that too was undoubtedly part of the equation. It had sparked off the whole sequence of events off. But why would anyone be out to kill him? He didn't know anything, or rather, he could think of nothing that would make him a target. Except of course the page from the book. But what was so important about that drawing that meant that anyone who saw it risked losing their life? A single page from a rare book, once apparently owned by someone called Francis Dashwood who was a member of The Hell Fire Club.

Madsen's cell phone chirped again. He ignored it at first assuming it was Kearns but he glanced at the caller display and saw it was Gregory.

"Chris."

"Hey man, you on a computer?"

"No. I'm just crossing over into Rhode Island. Nowhere near a computer, why?"

"Someone's accessing my files. Thought it was you."
Gregory sounded irritated.

"I'd never do that, you know that. What files?"

"The ones you emailed me. The illustration, the auction house records... everything. They're being wiped."

"Wiped? Turn the system off."

"I can't. It's being blocked somehow."

"Pull the plug! Rip the wires out the back!"

There was a long pause. Madsen could hear Gregory swearing as he tried to physically disconnect the computer from the wall.

"Too late. They've gone."

"Listen Chris. Don't worry. If that's all they were after then it's okay. As long as none of our client files were broached I don't care."

"Doesn't look like it. Who the hell's doin' this?"

"I dunno. But someone's trying to clean up."

"Is that all the copies gone?"

"No. I've one on my office system but I guess that's probably been wiped as well. Anyway, I have the CD back up here with me. Someone must have made the trace from my house."

"Who though, that cop?"

"Kearns? Could be. But why would he wipe it? He needs any evidence he can get. He's still trying to pin the sheriff's murder on me and at the moment he has zilch."

"This is all too weird for me."

"Chris. Look after yourself."

"What d'you mean?"

"Just watch your back."

"You getting paranoid again?"

"Paranoid? Probably, but with good reason."

"Call me..."

The line went dead. Up ahead Madsen saw the Rhode Island State line and within moments had crossed over out of Massachusetts. He reached into his pocket and took out the telephone number Parks had given him.

‡

The rains had cleared revealing a late afternoon sun, the light from which spilled across the buildings of Providence, giving them an ethereal, dreamlike quality. Buchanan and Arden drove through the Federal Hill area of the city and continued on through the main intersection and on to Memorial Boulevard where Buchanan took out his cellphone and made a call.

"It's me. Where do we meet? Uh-huh, okay."

He returned his phone to a pocket.

Arden watched the Waterplace Park slide by.

"So where's this bookshop?" he asked.

"There is no bookshop."

"Howard Hodgson's?"

"Bookseller. Not a bookshop."

Arden felt a pang of fear, thinking for an instant that he had been lied to. But the mistake was his. Buchanan had said a bookseller and had made no mention of a shop or otherwise.

Sensing the younger man's trepidation, Buchanan continued in an effort to put Arden at ease.

"He's a one man show. No overheads other than that which he needs to buy and sell rare books. He keeps a low profile. On the very few occasions I've met him it's always been in different locations."

"Why? What's he scared of?"

"Has to keep a low profile with the books he deals in. Remember there's a war on."

"Right. The war." Arden was struggling to contain his sarcasm.

"That's the way it is whether you believe it or not." Buchanan was beginning to sound defensive but more likely he was just weary of the task. Maybe he had done this a hundred times, recruiting freethinkers packed with disbelief and ridicule and was tired of the reaction.

"I've spent the last five years trying to shoot down this kind of thing. The world is not one big conspiracy." It was Arden's turn to defend his position.

Buchanan gave him a look to suggest he was entitled to his opinion.

"Stick to the middle ground. Not everything is a conspiracy. But, they do exist. It's the direct result of the action of power. Caesar's death was a conspiracy as was JFK's. It's about who wants to run the show. Who rules."

Arden did not answer. He still was not sure if he was in the presence of a psychotic or someone who had a great deal to say about the looking glass world. He feared the former. "Nobody's that clever that greed won't force them to screw up. Doesn't matter how many oaths of allegiance they've made to whatever dumb cause."

Buchanan raised a placating hand.

"Just bear with me for the sake of argument."

"Is this man an initiate?" Arden asked, irritated.

"Yeah."

"Okay so he sells books and the Ordines want me as a sunbeam. What's the connection?"

"You'll see."

Coming off the 95, Madsen took exit 22A and continued on until Memorial Boulevard. He turned left onto College Hill at the 4th set of traffic lights and continued on up the hill. There was Benefit Street with the Athenaeum directly before him. He slowed the car looking for somewhere to pull up. He noticed there was a sign indicating there was a car park behind the Greek temple like structure so he continued on. If he remembered his facts correctly it was William Strickland who had designed the building in the Greek revival style popular in the middle of the 19th century. He had seen the photographs in books and architectural magazines but never for real. So it was one of those rare treats to see a famous building close up.

There was a jolt of turbulence and Hannah started from sleep. She was disorientated at first, unsure if she had been out of it for a minute or an hour.

Turning to her left she peered out through a window. It was still dark outside. Far below she could see a coastline slowly giving way to ocean. Beach breakers were edged in white illuminated by a bright moon. The spotlight of a fishing boat was a solitary star in a dark sea of space. It made her feel desperately lonely, as if she were saying farewell to the Earth on a journey to the heavens. Looking up she saw the navigation lights of another plane, a tanker, flying just ahead of the C130. It was beginning to peel away, its refueling task complete.

She looked over at her father. His right hand was clenched tight around the key; his knuckles were white but his face wore a beatific smile as if he were in ecstasy. His eyes were closed, yet somehow she felt he was studying her as if he were in possession of some mystical sense. It was more likely though to be the result of her own feelings of inferiority in the presence of the man. It made her uncomfortable, as it always did.

Her father opened his eyes and looked down at the key.

"What's it for?" Hannah asked.

He did not look up but answered her anyway.

"A guarantee. Of our enemy's demise."

The interior of the Providence Athenaeum was cool and for the first time in a long while Arden felt the tension in his shoulders dissipate. It was one of the oldest libraries in the country and seemed as if little had changed since its 19th century construction. Not that he was particularly fond of its conservative charm, he was used to the noise of New York but at least he could appreciate its seeming defiance to the world beyond its walls.

"Poe came here." Buchanan said in a reverential tone.

"And H.P. Lovecraft," Arden added.

"Who?" Buchanan had taken his cellphone to turn down the ring volume.

"Look him up." Arden felt, for an instant, that he had gained some ground back. "We meeting this Mister Hodgson here?"

Buchanan nodded.

"When?" Arden looked around expecting to see a lone furtive figure staring at them.

"When he calls me."

"I see." Arden nodded gently.

Madsen found himself naturally drawn to the section on architecture but more specifically those books on the Renaissance.

The sanctuary of the library had restored, despite recent horrors, some semblance of a peace of mind. Yes, it was just a veneer but it would get him through.

Hiroko would have known which books to go for. He closed his eyes for a second and saw her face asleep in the hotel room in Portsmouth, lit with soft evening sunlight. The heartache came but he forced it back to quiet anger, the only emotion that was sustaining him.

He found a modern book depicting views of Venice. Flipping it open randomly he came across an image of the Grand Canal. There was the Customs House with the familiar golden sphere. He shook his head at the mathematics of probability that had opened the book at exactly the right page. What was it about that sphere that was attracting so much attention? And why were people dying because of it?

His cellphone chirped. He placed the book under and arm.

"Yes?"

"Mister Madsen. Stay where you are."

The line went dead.

Madsen quickly returned the book to its place on the shelf. He kept his eyes on the wall of books before him but his eyes were not focused on them.

Looking around he saw a man take his cellphone from his ear.

"Was that him?" Arden asked.

"Yeah. The Renaissance section."

"Say what?"

"He's going to meet us there." Buchanan was already making his way across the library.

Arden exhaled noisily. He hesitated. Either he was slipping further in to some madman's weird fantasy on the grand scale or Buchanan was telling the truth. Only one way to find out, he thought and set off after the man.

Madsen realised that two men were now heading his way. He reached down to the pocket in his jacket and felt for the CD-Rom. He turned and tried to focus on a book but was too distracted to concentrate.

Buchanan's attention was drawn to a man whose gaze was fixed, somewhat rigidly, on the books in front of him. The man's demeanour displayed his nervousness. He was obviously uncomfortable, fidgety, as if were expecting something to happen.

Madsen turned just as Buchanan stepped up to him.

"Mister Hodgson?"

"No. My name is...' Buchanan hesitated. 'I thought you might be Hodgson."

Madsen shook his head.

Arden smiled.

"Seems we're part of someone else's little game."

"Who are you?" Madsen asked.

"My name's Mark Arden. I'm here from New York."

Buchanan looked irritated that Arden had revealed his identity.

"I'm Josh Madsen. Boston."

"And Roger Ramjet here is-" Before Arden could finish the older man cut across him.

"Buchanan."

Madsen held out a hand. Buchanan refused to accept it so Arden shook it instead.

"Ever get the feeling you're on a wild goose hunt?" Arden asked Madsen, but it was a question aimed firmly at the ex-military man. "Seems we've come all this way for nothing."

"I'm looking for a Mister Hodgson, a bookseller." Madsen cast his eyes around.

"So are we. He said the man would be here." Arden jabbed a thumb in Buchanan's direction.

"I called him. He told me to meet him here. In this section." Madsen then looked down at his cellphone in his hand.

"Likewise." Arden's tone was derisive.

"I don't understand it." Buchanan's expression was taut.

"Is it part of this mystery man's perverse agenda?" Arden continued with his scathing tone.

"Everyone has an agenda," Buchanan retorted.

His cellphone in his hand vibrated.

"Yes." Buchanan's attention turned to the books then slowly he looked at Madsen then Arden. "We're here."

Madsen cast his eyes around. There were several people looking disapprovingly in their direction but no one making a call on a cellphone.

"He's meeting us in the rare books room." Buchanan turned, looking for a sign to point him in the right direction.

"This is some stupid game isn't it? Does this Hodgson even exist or is it someone you conjured up in that overworked imagination of yours?" His anger barely contained, Arden squared up to Buchanan.

"He exists," Madsen answered quietly.

"Yeah, and who are you? Do you two know each other? Christ, why did I bother with this bullshit?" Turning on his heels Arden made for the exit.

Buchanan studied Madsen.

"He wants to know as much as you do. He won't leave. If you want to find out you'll have to follow me." Buchanan then set off after his charge.

Madsen sighed heavily.

"I've got no choice, have I?"

From her sleep she heard her father's words.

She awoke.

"It's odd how something you dream about takes on a whole new meaning when you see it in reality." Hannah's father had just made another of his cryptic statements.

The aircraft was taxiing down the runway at Groom Lake and was just starting to make a turn towards a series of large hangars.

"What do you mean?" Hannah asked the question but experience had taught her not to expect an answer, at least nothing definitive.

"This." Her father held up the key. He seemed obsessed by it. There had been no emotional reunion, no thank you, and no sense of pride in anything she had done from him. He was happier to see this small inanimate object than he was his own flesh and blood. Hannah felt crushed but hid her disappointment.

The ramp in the floor cracked open and Hannah felt a blast of warm afternoon desert air on her skin. For a moment she thought they were back in Iraq, but as the engines shut off she started to hear familiar American accents. Within a few seconds members of the ground crew were making their way quickly up the ramp to help remove the restraining harnesses. Hannah was quite happy to release her own straps but a blonde woman in her mid to late twenties, who bore no nametag on her uniform, smiled at her and performed the task without seeming to disapprove.

Hannah looked over at her father. He had placed the key inside an attaché case that he was busy cuffing to his wrist.

"Mam. If you'd like to follow me." The blonde woman's tone was comforting but had a military firmness about it.

"Why?" Hannah was puzzled.

"A medical then a debriefing."

"Really? What do I need a medical for?"

Hannah stood up and followed the woman down the ramp. She looked back once to her father but he was lost in his own thoughts, in a daze or delirium of happiness.

As she cleared the fuselage Hannah looked back at the aircraft, incongruously black against the pale yellows, browns and grey of the surrounding Nevada desert. It had that air of menace and deep malevolence. Another psychological weapon no doubt. The occult symbolism of hostile design.

She saw her father being led away to a waiting car, which promptly sped off across the vast open space of the dry lake, criss-crossed with tyre streaked runways.

"Do I know this place?" The question sounded rhetorical but she wanted an answer. Looking round she could see several large but anonymous buildings, odd concrete structures, and a tower that Hannah assumed must contain water, all shimmering in the heat like a mirage.

"It's classified Mam."

"But I have a high security clearance." To her own ears she did not sound convincing enough, despite the truth in the statement.

"Not high enough," the young woman stated.

"But I've seen it. Flown into it."

"We'd deny that."

Hannah turned and looked over her shoulder but the female officer placed a hand on her arm. The grip was strong.

"Please Mam."

Hannah could only think how stupid the whole classified black project programme had become. Looking around it slowly dawned on her where they had landed. The airfield was infamous. Technically it did not exist, yet here it was for the whole world to see, basking openly in the afternoon desert sun.

All she could do was smile.

He was sitting at a table in the rare books room. A small man in a dark suit and a dark roll-neck sweater. His grey hair was thinning and he studied the three men before him over round tortoiseshell glasses like a schoolmaster, about to administer severe punishment for, as yet, undefined misdemeanours.

"Gentlemen, have a seat. I've taken the liberty of hiring this place for a short time to keep unwanted disturbances away. I have an understanding with the staff here."

Buchanan sat first. Madsen looked at Arden who shrugged his shoulders and moved to one of three chairs that had been deliberately placed at the other end of the table.

Madsen followed suit and sat down. There was something familiar in the man's voice.

"I'm glad that both of you have decided to persist despite your doubts and your recent tribulations. For the two newcomers my name is Parks."

"The Parks I spoke to at Sotheby's?" Madsen was taken aback.

Parks smiled.

"Yes, Mister Madsen. The same."

"So who's this Howard Hodgson?" Arden had still not dropped his belligerent attitude.

"It's just a name I use. To buy books privately. I see a lot of rare material and it would be indelicate if I were to put aside all the choice selections for myself. It would be... unseemly."

"So who bought the Dashwood book?" Madsen asked, his own anger rising a notch.

"I did." Parks was unmoved.

"I guessed as much." Madsen shook his head a little.

"Hey, what the hell is going on here?" Arden slammed a hand down on the table.

"Mister Arden, will you please settle?" Parks held up both hands to calm the young man down. He then stood up and brought over a tray of glasses and a jug of mineral water. "Tradition dictates that I offer you something stronger but in the circumstances you will each need a clear head."

"And what circumstances are those?" Madsen sat back and folded his arms.

As he poured them all a drink he fell silent. After placing a glass in front of each man he returned to his seat and sat down.

"I assume Mister Buchanan has told you something of the Ordines, Mister Arden and you Josh, if I may use that familiar term, seeing as we have already spoken to each other. You know about the book and the missing page."

Parks took a drink then studied each man in turn.

"As you have both come this far, you are both intrigued and determined to find out the truth. You have both lost ones dear to you and you have both feared for your sanity." Parks smiled as he spoke the last word. "You have avoided the hangman's noose and the assassin's bullet. In short you're wondering what the hell this is all about."

Parks leant forward in his chair and clasped his hands together.

"At this juncture you have a choice. You can turn around and leave or you can find out the truth. If you desire the truth you will have to cross a particular threshold. Only then can we speak of certain things." Parks sat back and held his palms out. "That is your choice."

Arden sat forward this time, tapping a fingertip on the table as he did so.

"If I walk away what happens to me?" he asked.

"You die," Parks responded tersely.

"What?" Arden screwed his face up. "I said what?"

"Mister Arden, you die. As simple as that."

"Do you follow me out and tap my head with a 38?"

"Not me. The enemy. You walk into the unknown or back to the world you know and die." Parks pointed towards the door.

"The who?" asked Madsen, frowning.

"You of all people should know Mister Madsen." Parks turned to look at Madsen. "You lost someone special. She was killed by the enemy. They wanted you as well."

"I'm sorry?" Madsen screwed his face up in puzzlement.

Parks cut him off.

"The bomb, Mister Madsen. It was meant for you. Both of you know far too much."

"But with all due respect," Arden pointed at Buchanan. "When he told me that heap of hooey, it was all true? If that's the case he trapped me."

"Perhaps a guarantee that you would not turn back. A jab in the right direction." Parks rested both hands on the table in front of him.

"Goddamn." Arden sat back.

"If Buchanan here had told you nothing, your life would still have been in danger. You have stood up above the parapet. You have made your presence known. Your books have been your downfall and your saviour."

"More double talk." Arden shook his head and huffed noisily.

"Your friend Eddowes made certain of your involvement." Parks said matter-of-factly. "If you want to blame anyone, blame him."

Arden glared at Parks then lowered his head. The man was right.

No one spoke for a moment or two.

"What do you want us to do?" Madsen had lowered his guard. Despite his personal reservations and the wall of uncertainty, he had to admit that he was intrigued.

Parks turned and looked directly at Madsen.

"Allow yourself to be initiated into our ranks."

‡

Hannah sat up in her bunk. The ventilation system was generating a low hum that was just at the right frequency to irritate her while the overhead lighting was bright enough to disturb her sleep. She had checked out okay and had been brought to this gunmetal grey room to rest despite her protestations that she did not need to.

The orange boiler suit was stiff and its collar chaffed her neck, increasing her irritability. Swinging her legs over the side of the bed she felt the tightness in her throat and chest and reached for her inhaler. There were no pockets in the boiler suit. Fighting the rising panic she scoured the room. The place was devoid of anywhere to store personal effects.

Gasping for breath she made her way to the steel door but it was locked. Her panic momentarily gave way to anger and she hit the door with an open palm.

"Hey!" Her voice was weak, faltering.

She hit it again but the door was solid, built for security. With body bent over she stumbled back to the bunk and collapsed onto it. Her whole frame was trembling in a cold sweat. Lowering her head to her knees she fought to

201

relax her airways but they resisted. Her head was pounding as her lungs tried to pull in air.

Why had they locked the door? The question repeated itself in a wave of cyclic thought increasing her panic and agitation. Why had they locked the door? Why?

Suddenly there were hands about her face and a mask was placed over her mouth.

"Breathe slow," someone said. "Breathe slow."

Hannah felt the chemical tang of Ventolin. Her taut muscles began to relax. Her eyes focused and she saw the woman who had helped her off the plane.

"Why was the door locked?" Hannah stuttered out the question.

Half an hour later, a fresh set of clothes was brought to her. Still feeling weak from the asthma attack it took her a while to change. Every five minutes she felt the necessity to check that the door was still locked and every time it was. It made her feel foolish to behave in such an untrusting and somewhat childish way. But then it was understandable. She had still not been given a reason for her confinement.

She was just about to try again when she heard someone unlocking the door. The young woman stepped into the room carrying a tray on which sat a plate with a lid and a blue beaker of water. Everything was made of plastic. Hannah could see that trust was not high on the agenda. No metal, therefore no improvised weapons. The secondary effect was to make her feel like a child and to put her in a subservient position. It was patronising at best but she knew, from her training, that it was common practice in such situations. What she still could not fathom was why her? Why Hannah Franklin, when her father was so powerful?

"Are you hungry?" the young woman asked.

"Not particularly" Hannah snapped. "Where's my father?"

"He's already gone. A few hours ago."

Hannah could barely contain her frustration. He had abandoned her again.

"Without me? Is that why the door is locked?"

"National security." The young woman placed the tray on the bed.

"Don't give me that crap. I have a higher security clearance than you!"

"Not here you don't. There's a different command and security structure here that bears no relation to the outside world. We're a state within a state."

"How has that been allowed to happen?"

"I am not at liberty to discuss anything related to the activities of this base."

"Yet here I am. What's to stop me telling the outside world?"

"Nothing. Other than the fact you are to remain here for the duration."

"The duration of what?" Hannah felt her throat tighten again.

"Your father gave the order. You are to remain here until he sees fit. For your own safety."

"Why, doesn't he trust me?"

"I guess not."

Hannah marched to the door and stepped out into the corridor. The woman made no attempt to stop her; she did not have to. There were half a dozen heavily armed sentries lined up in the hallway outside her room.

"Why?" Hannah shouted at the first man. "Why?" she barked at another. "WHY?"

The woman stepped out of Hannah's room.

"Some secrets are meant for the few and the few only." She held out a hand. "Miss Franklin, I could have you restrained. It's up to you."

✝

"Architecture is the mother art because it is the generator of civilisation." Parks refilled his glass. "It is a communicator, a storehouse of knowledge and wisdom, art on the grand scale. Goethe wrote that architecture is frozen music. I am inclined to agree." He then took a drink. "But it can also be subversive, in the best sense of the word. There is power in stone."

"How does that help anyone?" Arden stood up and took a few paces.

"It depends on who you want to help," Parks said cryptically.

"Does everyone you know speak like this?" Arden's question was aimed at Buchanan.

But Parks answered him.

"When what you know is a matter of life and death, then words must be chosen carefully. It they are cryptic it is with good reason." Parks stood. "Gentlemen, your decision please."

Madsen ran a finger along his forehead. He looked up at Arden who was staring at the surface of the table.

"There is a threshold. Do you cross it or not?" Parks pushed his chair in and looked at each man in turn.

Arden finally looked up. He turned to Buchanan.

"Tell me. Is he for real?"

Buchanan nodded.

"And are you for real?" Arden continued.

"It's your decision Mister Arden, no one else's." Parks looked at his watch.

"What d'you think?" Arden's question was aimed at Madsen.

"Will it make a difference to things if we say yes?" Madsen asked quietly.

Parks stepped in to answer.

"It will make all the difference. But you must make a decision fast Mister Madsen."

"Why?" Arden's attention was back on Parks.

"Do you wish to live or die?"

"That's a stupid question."

"Under the circumstances, Mister Arden, it isn't. I suggest you agree. That way we can all leave now before it is too late."

Parks waited for a few moments then started to make his way out.

"I'm in." Madsen was instantly doubtful of his decision but to convince himself he repeated the phrase, more softly. "I'm in."

"And your decision, Mister Arden?"

Arden nodded.

"I've spent my short career writing about this." He said. "I might as well find out what it's all about from the other side. If there is anything to find out, Parks?"

"Plenty," the older man said. "Now will you follow me?"

They took a service exit out of the building and made their way quickly to the street. Above them, the twilight sky was a deep blue and the first stars were beginning to show. Madsen was reminded of a tomb in Egypt he had visited in his post-graduate days, where countless stars had been painted on the stone ceiling perhaps to remind the Ka of the entombed body of its final destination. This led his thoughts to the ceiling of a Masonic temple he had also visited years before when an old school friend was keen to introduce him to the order. That too was rich with decorative stars, gold leafed and random in their patterns.

"Where are we going?" Arden's question was bounded with suspicion.

Parks led them to a large dark blue 60s Mercedes parked in College Street.

"Get in." Parks unlocked the driver's door but held it open for Buchanan, who obligingly dropped into the driver's seat without question.

Both Madsen and Arden exchanged glances, hesitating for a moment. Parks walked around the car to the rear.

"Gentlemen, please." He opened the rear near side passenger door and climbed in.

Madsen felt disorientated. Suddenly he was aware that everything he had known was slipping away into the past; that it was all nothing more intangible than memories of a dream. The once solid known had been replaced by something he felt was more akin to some peculiar charade, one that was verging on the melodramatic. He was losing touch with reality and his old life was now locked behind an invisible door; one he feared he might never find again. He looked up again. It seemed the night sky was the only constant he could cling to.

The situation had confirmed one thing. Her father, despite his supposed assurances that she was being kept at the base for her own security, had abandoned her. It was nothing new, but in the past Hannah had been willing to forgive him, time and time again. Today though, something had changed. The thin threads of attachment that had bound her to her one remaining family member had snapped. She was now, to all intents and purposes, an orphan. With that in mind the last vestige of loyalty to him was extinguished.

This had been exacerbated by the fact that while showering, an armed male guard had watched her bathe and dress. Dignity had been eroded. All part of the game of breaking her will. She was in essence being treated like a prisoner and she still had no idea why.

Back in her room she had been given a fresh inhaler, the old one had in all likelihood been carefully examined then destroyed and for a short time the door had been locked again.

With no loyalty left for her own she figured that an attempt to extricate herself from this prison would at the very least be some form of retaliation towards her father. It would also restore some of her dented pride.

Someone once said that there is always a way to break free. Every prison has a door in and therefore there is a door out. Every entrance is an exit. The door to her room was now unlocked most of the time, that was okay but how was she going to get beyond the walls of the secret facility itself surrounded by hundreds of square miles of Nevada?

She was contemplating this when the door, without warning, was opened by the nameless woman. Hannah was startled, which swiftly evolved into anger.

"When are you going to let me out?"

"Miss Franklin, please follow me."

Hannah refused to move for a second but then realised that this might be an opportunity to see what she was up against. Feigning capitulation, Hannah stood up and went out through the door.

She was led down a series of monotonous corridors until she was delivered to a spartan room not much bigger than the one she had just left. Seated behind a desk was a man, in his mid thirties, dressed in a dark blue suit. He had sand coloured hair and wore tortoise shell glasses that seemed forty years out of date. His attention was on a file and he was running a pen tip down a paragraph of text. On the table next to him was the dog tag she had taken from the fallen agent.

The young woman left.

The man looked up and smiled. Looking round Hannah could see he occupied the only chair in the room.

"Miss Franklin." The young man's eyebrows rose a little but Hannah was not sure if what he had said was a statement or a question. She tried to read the ID pinned to his breast pocket but there was no name, just a long barcode. "You won't get any information off that I'm afraid. We're all anonymous here."

"No names. No comeback. Any accusations will legally fail."

The young man smiled and nodded his head.

"This dog tag. You took it off one of the agents that accompanied you? What about the others?"

"I couldn't get them." She maintained her belligerence.

"Any witnesses to that fact?"

"I'm sorry?"

"The problem is, there's a downed Blackhawk with its crew dead, plus the two CIA operatives and the only one who got out alive was you."

"Meaning?"

"Meaning, Miss Franklin that the suspicions automatically fall on you." The young man sat back in his chair.

"What suspicions?"

"I can see from your file that you've been very resourceful in your short career. You can look after yourself. Good training in survival situations and combat. The usual techniques of – well, need I say more?"

"Yeah, so? Are you accusing me or threatening me?" Hannah took a step forward.

The young man said nothing. His smile was that of a shark.

"Perceptive. That's not in the file."

"Maybe I could add your balls to the file as well."

"This is taking less time than I thought. I prejudged you."

"I'm happy to disappoint." Hannah moved to the wall and leant up against it, folding her arms as she did so.

"It's my contention that you callously murdered the crew of the helicopter and the operatives that were there to assist you. I have a report here, written by a chief medical examiner in the CIA that you have become severely and dangerously psychotic and should be confined to a secure mental institution for the rest of your life." The young man raised his head slightly as if asking for a reaction from

208

Hannah. Her face was the picture of indifference. "Your watch. It houses a GPS homing beacon. Used no doubt for possible extraction by a foreign power."

"Do you know my father?" she asked.

The young man gave no answer but Hannah had gleaned enough to realise that all this was the work of the man.

Pushing herself away from the wall she walked slowly over to the table, and before the young man could stop her, she picked up the file to examine it.

"There are some powerful names here, all destroying my character."

"I assure you all the signatures are genuine."

"I know. They've all been to dinner at my house. So what's the deal? I was told earlier that I was being kept here indefinitely. If that's the case why bother with this crap? Unless of course my father wanted time to pull all this together." Hannah tossed the file back onto the table.

"The file's been ready for a long time."

"Daddy wants me to be a good little girl and not say anything." Hannah shook her head and walked back towards the wall. She turned and looked at the young man who was examining his fingernails. "Bastard."

She caught his attention.

"The choice is yours. Talk to anyone about what you found and it's adios. Keep quiet, you keep your life. It's really very simple."

"When you were tiny was it your ambition to grow up to be an asshole?"

"I'd accept the choice you've been given." The young man paused for effect. "I suggested an alternative to the mental institution idea."

"Oh yeah. What was that?"

"Suicide. That you'd shot yourself out of guilt." The young man put a finger pistol to his head and pulled the trigger. He paused, then standing up, he collected the file together and made for the door. He knocked once and was let out.

The nameless young woman once more appeared. She stared at Hannah,

"Come with me."

✝

"What I cannot, and never could understand, is the persecution of someone to the point of death at the hands of another who is perpetrating the injustice in the name of a mythical non-existent entity." Parks's face was in shadow. "The Inquisition. The Puritans and their notion that all of nature is satanic so the Native Tribes of this country were the work of the Christian devil. Martyrdom, ethnic cleansing. It's all insane. It's death without foundation. Everything is seen in a Manichean sense. It's light or dark, good and evil, right or wrong. All that does is create a worldwide neurosis. Reality isn't black and white. It's shades of grey and the grey depends on one's perspective."

"You sound like a man with an agenda." Madsen, in the back seat next to Parks, was staring out into evening. He was drawn to the lives going on as normal beyond the lit windows of the houses – evening family meals, a man sat at a table helping a child with homework, a couple dancing around their living room to unheard music. Normal life? Or one of a waking sleep? The bliss of ignorance.

"Everyone has an agenda. Mine is the quiet work of centuries."

"Kennedy." Arden turned in the front passenger seat and looked back over his shoulder. His voice was quiet but authoritative. A subconscious dig perhaps aimed at Parks.

"Kennedy indeed Mister Arden. Well done. Do you think he was a Grover?" Parks asked.

"There's no record of him going to the Boho Grove."

"The what?" Madsen turned his attention away from the outside world.

210

"The Bohemian Grove." Arden was grinning. "A social club for the high flying just outside L.A. in California. Kennedy was a New England man and I should imagine with the Grovers' Puritan bias his presence would've been, well-"

"Anathema, Mister Arden. Because he was Catholic. More divisive behaviour. My way of grovelling to a god is better than yours."

"Why did you ask anyway? Arden turned his attention to Parks, whose face was lit momentarily by a streetlight.

"I'm inquisitive."

"About me or Kennedy?" Arden asked.

Parks just dipped his head slightly and let the subject drop.

There was a long silence once more broken by Arden, whose question verged on the rhetorically comedic.

"Hey just where are we going anyway?"

"Do you know Providence Mister Arden?" Parks asked.

"*As I plunged into those mad lanes that wind in labyrinths obscure and undefined*. H.P. Lovecraft."

Parks nodded; satisfied that Arden did indeed know a thing or two about Providence. "In answer to your question, Mister Arden, we're heading to an important rendezvous."

An hour later Hannah was met in her room by a private who looked awkward and apprehensive. It was a final indignity. She would be escorted out of the base by the lowest rank they could find. She wondered what it was they had on him to keep him quiet. This led her to wonder what exactly they had on everyone who worked here. There was in all probability a room in this base somewhere full of files containing lies, fabrication and potentially damaging and life threatening information. Then again maybe this idea in itself was just part of the arsenal of psychological weaponry. Sow a

211

few seeds and allow fear, the most potent of emotions, to do the rest. Shock the rats into following the desired path.

The private led the way through a series of familiar corridors then out through a set of double doors onto a wide gangway. This was not the way she had come in.

Something caught her eye. Looking down on the left-hand side she was stunned to see three craft below her, each one separated by a dividing wall. Around each one numerous engineers and ground crews were working, busy in their tasks. Hannah slowed and shook her head in small movements. She smiled. So this was what all the fuss was about. This was what people were seeing all over the world.

"Mam. You have to keep walking." The private had half turned and was looking back at her over his right shoulder. She nodded but kept her attention on the view below. "Mam. Please." The soldier was obviously very nervous. "You're not supposed to look."

The gangway ended in another set of double doors and before passing through, Hannah looked back once more determined to keep the memories as crystal clear as possible.

As the pair of them descended a set of stairs it dawned on Hannah to ask the simple question, why had they allowed her to see what she had just seen? One minute she was being told that some secrets are meant for the few, the next, she was party to at least one of those secrets. No, it was too good to be true. Was it an extra safe guard to keep her silence? A real way to load the deck in their favour? A test, to see if she would really keep her mouth shut? Or was it, as she really suspected, a game?

Were those craft genuine? Or were they, as she suspected, part of a methodology of building a new myth. As Hitler had so famously said, the bigger the lie the more people would believe it. If the myth was loaded and constantly added to, would it not become more powerful?

Not that she was particularly interested in the subject yet Hannah had seen how the UFO myth had grown, splintered, fractured into different facets, a host of followers proving that it was they who had the truth; that their personal take on the so called alien visitation was the one true way. How many false prophets, deluded individuals, gurus and proponents of doomsday had there been?

Why was she shown a glimpse of these apparent secrets? Maybe they were hoping that she would leave the place convinced she knew the truth and that the sheer weight of this secret knowledge would tip her into becoming another fellow traveller in the flying saucer world or some conspiracy fanatic. Or more likely, if she revealed anything of her search for the key that too could be dismissed as the ravings of a psychotic. *Hannah Franklin also saw flying saucers at a secret base...*

If so, she was not going to play into their hands. She knew it for what it was – extra insurance that she would keep her mouth shut. Anyway, for all she knew the craft she had just seen were nothing more than film props.

The young soldier led her through another set of double doors and along a corridor that had numerous glass panelled doors leading off either side but all the rooms beyond them were empty except one in which a man, seated in a chair was being shouted at by a high ranking officer. As Hannah walked by she watched in horror as this officer placed a pistol at the man's head and upped the volume and the intensity of his tirade. Some five seconds later Hannah heard three shots. She flinched violently at the first and turned to look back.

Another reinforcement?

Part of the game as well?

Undoubtedly.

"Mam. Please." The private held a door open for her. Sunlight was pouring in and she squinted against the brightness. Despite the heat she felt happy to be outside again.

"Where do I go now?" Hannah looked around at the flat terrain around her. Numerous airstrips ran parallel with the buildings and beyond, shimmering in the haze were high mountains.

"There's a private jet coming to pick you up." The soldier slipped back inside the building and shut the door, locking it behind him.

She only had to wait for a minute or two before a Lear jet, free of markings and registration numbers, trundled around the edge of the hangar and rolled to a stop a dozen yards from her.

Not long after, Hannah was looking out of the cabin window as the jet banked east then north. Far below, the numerous buildings were dissolving slowly into the desert haze. Dreamland seemed an apt moniker for the place but Hannah realised that it was more than that. It was part of the mechanism of control. The bigger the lie, indeed. Still the questions haunted her. Was this place as much a façade, a stage set or an agit-prop device as all the other tools of social manipulation employed over the years to sway public opinion had been? Was it in reality nothing more than a heavily guarded empty box?

A decoy?

Pub Talk

Linda had gone up to London to see the editor of *Codex*. She wanted to pitch the Arden article to the man, no doubt backed up with half whispered promises of further exciting developments. Both Gus and I made her swear that she wouldn't talk about the sun keys. In return she made us put hands on heart and declare that if Arden revealed more about the mystery we would not discuss it until she was home.

The Crusader's Head was busier than last time. When I arrived there was a knot of people in the garden blasting away on their ciggies. For some unknown reason I had chosen to come in the back way by heading down the lane at the side and crossing the beer garden at the rear. At the bar I chastised myself for being so silly. Even though I'm a cynic, sometimes that daft sense of paranoia slips under the perimeter wire. It didn't help that some bloke in the corner caught my eye a few times. He was tucked away behind a broadsheet and was doing his best not to be seen so I did my best to ignore him.

Anyway Arden was already there, waiting in the same nook we had used before.

I went over and placed my pint down and said hello. He looked up and flinched a little. He then recognised who it was but his defences remained up.

'Where's Gus?' Arden sounded uncomfortable, in all likelihood due to the fact that he would have to try and make polite conversation with an acerbic sceptic.

'He's on his way. Can I get you a beer?'

'Orange juice and lemonade please. No ice.'

I obliged even though it was bit galling to buy a drink for someone who could probably buy the pub ten times over.

On my return I sat down opposite him. I attempted a conversation. It was a bit of a struggle at first. I had reached that age where I no longer cared what people thought of me – it's too tiring trying to win friends and influence people all the time, so when I realised that Arden wasn't going to be forthcoming, I sat back, took out my notebook and ran through a list of names of those who might be willing to shark my cat's blood.

Arden was suddenly attentive.

'What are you doing?' he was staring at the list of names. To avoid any unnecessary suspicion I had spread the notebook on the table in a kind of policy of openness. So in a sense, I did still care what people thought of me.

'Contacts.' I couldn't resist a little bit of fun so my answer was couched in a conspiratorial tone. Although I should add that most of the names in this book were awash with what the police euphemistically call *form* so the hushed level of my voice was not entirely without merit.

'Contacts?'

'In the antique world.'

'Antiques?' Arden frowned.

'Yeah. I dabble in antiques.'

'What old chairs and things?'

'Sometimes. I'm more into the rare stuff.'

'Like what?' Arden was nothing but terse.

'Dead Sea Scrolls, the Crib of Christ, shrouds... that sort of thing.' I was, of course, joking but I could almost see Arden's brain sparking and fizzing as he processed the info. He had tensed up. I think he thought I was going to try and hawk his sun key. Or maybe the one Gus had.

Arden was thinking this through when Gus turned up. I slapped a fiver on the table and told him to get himself a beer.

Gus in his usual way was more amenable. Soon he and Arden had even swapped a few stories about fare dodging on the underground and drunken journeys home at three in the morning. Then Gus steered the conversation round to the sun keys.

'Where do you think the third one is?' There was a thin white moustache of foam on his top lip when Gus finally asked the question.

In the depths of seriousness there is often humour.

Arden hunched forward a little. I saw him cast his eyes at my notebook.

'I have no idea as yet. I have several theories but until some evidence comes through...' His voice trailed away.

Gus made an appreciative noise. He nodded his head slightly.

'Theories are fine but they don't add up to much unless you can back them up.' I played the role expected of me.

Arden pinched his lips tight and sat back a little.

'I thought maybe with the Hell Fire Club. I wrote that into *Sunsphere*. But I don't think so anymore.' Arden left his left hand on the table. He tapped his fingertips.

'It could be anywhere.' Gus wiped a sleeve across his mouth.

Arden said nothing for about a minute. He looked at both Gus and me then leant forward again.

'Maybe I'll dig up more info at some point. I'd need to find some more of the manuscript of either the novel or the biography.' Arden saw the exchange of looks between Gus and yours truly. His face was one big question.

Gus stared into his beer. He then looked at me. I nodded.

'A friend of ours had a section of the biography shoved through her letter box.' Gus turned to look at Arden. 'The Tarquin Benbow section.'

'Really?' Arden appeared to be on the point of wetting himself.

'A small part of it anyway. But there's no clue to the whereabouts of any key in it.' Gus scratched the back of his neck.

'Doesn't matter,' Arden continued. 'Any Hiddon find is... a blow to the enemy.'

'The what?' Yes, it was my turn to kick up some aggro.

Arden stared at me.

'Don't you get it?' he hissed. 'Hiddon's book and biography were almost destroyed. Sections of them were rescued by certain individuals to protect them. The enemy have been hunting these down for over two hundred years. They've almost succeeded in wiping out anything to do with the man and the history of the three sun keys.'

Silence.

Arden continued although he reined in his anger.

'For all we know the sections we have are all that's left.' He took a swig of his drink.

217

Unwilling to capitulate to drama I popped off another question.

'You might have an idea where the third key is?'

'Hiddon was in Somerset on a quest.' Arden kept his gaze fixed on the tabletop.

Gus stepped in.

'That's right,' he said. "The Benbow document says it was to hunt out secret societies or cabals influenced by the American Revolution who might kick off against the King.'

'That would explain a few things.' Arden smiled and nodded. 'I'd love to see that section.'

'You will.' I chipped in. It sounded mildly like a threat. One a father might say to his son considering a Christmas present in return for good behaviour.

'Go on'. Gus glared at me.

'While ploughing through books in the British Library I came across a reference in a diatribe against Dashwood and his Hell Fire Club mentioning Hiddon turning up at this country house because the owner, a Lord Carey-Hunt, is drowning in debt. There must be a Masonic connection because I can't work out yet why Hiddon would've been there and Carey-Hunt was in the Lodge. Anyway, Carey-Hunt knows about Hiddon's surveying skills so he employs him to find a lost treasure buried within the grounds of the house. A treasure that Lord C.H. hopes will get him out of financial trouble.' Arden paused, allowing this to sink in.

'Carey-Hunt.' Gus spoke in almost a whisper.

'You know the name?' Arden asked.

'I met Alexia Carey-Hunt.'

'Where?' Arden was even more animated now.

'I went to her house. That's where I found the Hiddon novel extract.'

Arden appeared to be on the point of a heart attack or a nervous breakdown, possibly even both. There was something quite comical about watching a pulp writer nearly soil himself. He was excited and agitated and gave the impression he wanted to leave.

'I must see that extract. You don't know how important it is.' Arden rubbed the top of his thighs with both hands.

'Everything's at Linda's place.' Gus said. 'She won't be back until late this afternoon.'

Arden looked at his watch.

'I don't have to go anywhere,' he said, reaching for his wallet.

Arden made for the bar and bought us another round of drinks. Dispensing with the orange juice and lemonade he bought himself a triple G and T. The man was human after all.

For the next hour we spoke of what we'd all found. Arden told us that he had been obsessed with Hiddon for a long time and that the man was the influence behind the *Sunsphere* novel. We asked a number of questions and he answered them succinctly. No, he didn't think that the third key was at Dashwood's place in West Wycombe because of his section of the Tales of Thomas Hiddon. To him the key was at the country seat of the Carey-Hunts, the most likely location. Yes, Dashwood may have been involved. In fact, Lord Carey-Hunt and Dashwood shared mutual friends. Arden wanted to eliminate the Carey-Hunt location before heading to West Wycombe again.

The hour rolled into two, then three, with Arden buying us home made chicken pie and chips to keep us all going. I must admit I was softening to the man. I knew we'd never be chums, as there was a still a great deal I disagreed with him about but he was, after the grand facade had come down, good company.

I then asked him the question I had wanted to ask above all others.

'Why I used my own name in the book? As a character?' He was thoughtful. 'Because it blurred the lines between my quest in real life and that of the protagonist in

Sunsphere. I was on my personal journey to find out who Hiddon was and the whereabouts of the keys. I wanted to associate my name with his in the most personal way I knew. It was somehow... apt.'

To me at least, his answer was less than convincing. It sounded rehearsed, and I suspect one that had been kept in a mental drawer just in case there was any chance in the future he'd come up against difficult sods like us; or rather, me.

'Linda will be cheesed off.' Gus filled his fork with chips, staving them into compliance.

'Why's that?' Arden mopped his mouth with a thick green paper serviette the cutlery had been wrapped in and dropped it on the plate.

'She was convinced it was a Masonic plot. Or something similar,' Gus replied.

'That's what I had hoped for. No disrespect to your friend,' Arden smiled. 'It adds a certain spice to the tale. You shouldn't explain everything. Some mystery must remain.'

I was going to ask why a mystery should remain. Personally, I can't stand them and they get fairly and squarely on my big round ones. I want to know who the silent caller is at three in the morning; I want to know why the odd bit of money disappears from my bank account; I want to know why my ex-cat used to use the floor as a toilet when the litter tray was five inches away from where it squirted and jobbed its business... the list is endless. A life surrounded by mystery displays compliance and laziness on behalf of our species.

Just to add a certain frisson of synchronicity, Gus's mobile chimed. It was a text message from Linda asking where we were. Gus zipped one back telling her to meet us in The Crusader's Head.

Within half an hour Linda breezed in, somewhat breathless and a little overawed to be meeting Arden. For the first half an hour she and Arden sized each other up. Linda was good at this. She never capitulated to fawning or the softly-softly-catchy-monkey routine. Beneath her bluster though she was like a schoolgirl meeting a pop star.

For that time, both Gus and I sat back and let her do her thing. She covered much of the same ground already traversed but Arden seemed not to mind. They also span out into Knights Templar territory and... and... all the usual hoohah.

It soon became clear that the pair of them were, in fact, hitting on each other. You didn't need to be an expert in body language to see what was afoot. Linda was all wide-eyed expectancy and Arden, a touch Machiavellian. For a second I had a spike of that schoolboy jealousy when someone hits on a female friend. Is it territoriality? Arden even agreed to do an interview for *Codex* leaving Linda dizzy with joy.

While the lovebirds cooed, the two gooseberries made for the bar under the genuine pretext (I know what I mean) of buying the next round.

'What's going on there?' Gus asked. He exhaled noisily.

'I have to admit I was suspicious of their mutual reasons,' I replied.

'But not anymore.'

'Oh, I still am,' I said, looking back to our table.

'That's a touch cynical.'

'Maybe. She wants that interview for *Codex*.'

'She just asked him.'

'True.'

'The glamour of a writer, do you think?' Gus smirked.

A writer, glamorous?

'I always thought writers were at the arse end of the social scale,' I said, rather too dismissively.

'Not the successful ones.'

And there are too few of them folks.

Gus looked over his shoulder.

'And who are we to get in the way?' he mused.

For the next hour we did just that, i.e. not get in the way. Then, just as the evening clientele began to arrive, making The Crusader's Head a boisterous confusion of chat and laughter, Linda invited us to reconvene at her place for coffee.

Arden was transfixed. We had pooled together all that we had and it was sending him into something of a tailspin. For half an hour he said nothing. He just sat there and read. And re-read.

Sitting forward he slapped the *Tales of Thomas Hiddon* extract with the back of his hand.

'This is mind blowing.' Arden stood up and began to pace.

Gus and Linda made noises in agreement. I didn't, of course. At the moment there was no mystery, simply a collection of manuscripts, one a photocopy at that, which added up to precisely... nothing.

'You're gonna have a devil of job convincing him.' Gus jabbed a thumb in my direction.

'We can't change his mind,' added Linda. 'He's an irascible old sceptic.' She was one of those who saw scepticism as a symptom of a closed mind. People like me had all shut their brains off to possibilities, according to our Linda. She could simply not fathom the idea that science, by its nature, is just the opposite, it has to be and that scepticism is just a natural defence against the drivel that assaults and insults us on a daily basis.

Arden kept his attention on the document but with great deliberation placed it on the coffee table. He reached slowly into his pocket and took out a small vellum roll. Loosening the ties, he slowly unrolled it in his hand.

He then held up one of the sun keys.

Linda and Gus leant in closer, their mouths and eyes wide, like children pressed up against a toyshop window.

222

'It's beautiful.' Linda reached out to touch it. Arden recoiled a little then reluctantly let it go into her upheld palm. 'There's the sun.'

Gus smiled. He too reached into a pocket and produced a small crumpled brown paper bag. Unfolding it he took out his key. He held it up. Predictably, the light from one of the candles Linda had lit reflected off its polished surface.

'There you go. Snap.' Gus held it out for Linda to take. She did so and placed both keys together in her hand. 'Don't mix them up.' For a second Gus looked panicked.

'Don't worry.' Arden reached for his key and picked it up. 'Look at the rays of the sun.'

Linda's eyes closed in on the rays beaming off the image of the sun.

'Oh yes. They're in the form of a triangle. On this one the left side is missing and on the one belonging to Gus, the right.' Linda leant forward to show me.

I took both keys and studied them carefully. There was the image of the sun with a thick triangular beam coming off it, slightly embossed.

'I assume that the third key has the bottom edge missing.' For a brief while I was genuinely interested, as if to prove Linda and Gus wrong.

Arden nodded.

I examined the keys carefully, rolling them slowly over in my palm.

'Is it a beam or a pyramid?' I asked.

'As in Masonic symbolism? The pyramid and the all-seeing eye. I'd considered that possibility.' Arden sat back in his seat. 'It appears to be too simple and there's no indication that the beam is made of bricks. For the moment I'm seeing it simply as the rays of the sun.'

'What do you think now?' Linda desperately wanted to gloat.

'You're the expert. How old are they?' Gus, too, was on the attack.

Both keys were immaculate.

'I assume they're gold, though not all the way through. Gold is perhaps too soft for repeated use as a key.' I bounced one in my hand. 'Lin do you have a magnifying glass or a loupe about the place?'

'Wait there.' Linda was up and away to a small bureau by the phone under the stairs. She returned a few moments later with a large magnifying glass.

'Can you turn the overhead light on?' I stood up and moved the glass up and down above the keys.

Linda duly obliged.

'Was one of these really found in Venice, as you said in the book? A surveyor who was mysteriously murdered in his home in Padova, the wall safe empty and all that?' Gus asked Arden.

'Yes. He was a real person. Don't you remember that Mafia trial a few years ago?'

None of us did.

Arden continued.

'Mario D'Ambrosio, a surveyor, was tied up with a mob family in Palermo. As it happens that's inconsequential but his name was famous or should I say infamous for a while. For some years he had combined his love of scuba diving with surveying the foundations of Venice.'

'In the waters beneath the Dogana del Mare.' Gus was sounding a shade too melodramatic for my liking.

'Exactly.' Reaching for the coffee pot, Arden refilled his cup. 'Then the key went missing.'

'How do you know it was the key that went missing?' It was a reasonable question for me to ask.

'What else could it be?' Gus sounded indignant. It was definitely three against one here. But then, I was used to being in the minority. It was a hazard of modern living. Even my ex-cat used to bring a few friends round and gang up on me.

'Because, during my research, I spoke to his wife.' It was an ace. A small one, but an ace nonetheless. 'She told me about the key and how D'Ambrosio would sit in his chair for hours just staring at it. He seemed obsessed.'

'You don't think the mob are involved do you?' Linda sounded nervous.

Arden smiled but shook his head.

'I don't think so. There was no evidence to link the mob to the murder or the burglary anyway. Not that that rules them out completely but it seems unlikely. Partly because it appears that D'Ambrosio's wife was looked after very well in the months that followed her husband's death.'

'Doesn't mean they didn't do it.' It didn't and I had to say it.

'It's irrelevant anyway.' Arden had adopted his dismissive air again. He seemed sure of himself sporting that cocky, arrogant manner I had seen before.

Maybe it was irrelevant but I certainly didn't want to wake up in the morning and find the head of a stallion at the foot of my bed or some Johnny turning up at my door making me offers I couldn't refuse and wanting to know why I thought he was funny... *funny how*?

'Gus found one in that chest of drawers or whatever it was so maybe it was yours that came from the Grand Canal.' Linda was playing cod detective.

Arden nodded.

'It's safe to say that your key Gus was probably in that location for two hundred years or so.' Arden took a slurp of coffee.

'Where's the third though?' Standing up, Gus came and stood by me. His question was aimed at no one in particular.

'I don't think the clues lead to West Wycombe.' Arden ran a finger across his chin.

'In *Sunsphere* they do.' Gus kept his eye on his key.

'Yes, but that was just a book. I had no idea. The same with the key from Iraq.' Arden rolled his head to free taut muscles. 'Remember at that time I only knew of one key. The one I had.'

'But how did you get it?' I asked. 'You haven't explained that properly. You keep sidestepping.'

Arden gave us one of his calculated pauses.

'I bought it from a collector.'

'Stolen property.' I lowered the magnifying glass. 'You bought stolen property.'

'But I didn't know that at the time.' Arden sounded defensive. 'It was only later as my research deepened that I realised that I actually had one of the Hiddon keys. It's only now that I know that my key is the one stolen from D'Ambrosio. You found yours in a piece of two hundred year old furniture. That was confirmation that mine was the one from the Grand Canal.'

Fair enough. He couldn't have known. For all I knew he had bought the thing innocently but as for confirmation, that was a bit slim. It was fifty-fifty with the other missing key. But for the moment I let Arden dream his dream.

'So where's the third?' Linda wanted an answer.

Arden was thoughtful. He looked at Gus.

'Do you think Alexia would mind us calling in?'

In The Lodge

Buchanan pulled the car up outside a tall four-storey red brick building. Eight columns made up a portico in which hung a single metal lamp.

"Is that what I think it is?" Madsen craned his neck and looked up at the 19th century building.

Parks smiled but the shadows continued to keep his face in darkness.

"It is. I have friends here." Parks stepped out into the crisp clear air. "Gentlemen, I ask for haste." Shutting the door he made his way swiftly across the street and up to the door.

Madsen gave Buchanan a quizzical look but found no answers with the man.

Arden sighed.

"This is just nonsense." He opened the door slightly but was reluctant to go further.

"You've come this far." Buchanan was staring into the rear view mirror. "Trust him. Believe me it will be worth it. You'll never look at world history again with such..." Buchanan sought a suitable word. "Gullibility." He smiled for emphasis.

"It's a Masonic Hall." Madsen examined the building through the windshield.

"We have friends here. Allies." Buchanan turned and looked back at Madsen. "Please." It was not so much a request as an order.

Another threshold was approaching and Madsen was not entirely sure he was ready. Yes, he had persisted for the sake of Hiroko and his own determination to find those responsible for her death but he felt as far away from that search as he did from his own childhood. To him he seemed to be in a maze, but walking down a path that led away from the centre.

Parks was now on the other side of the road and standing in the light of the portico. He was looking up and down the street and gave the impression he was expecting to see unwanted attention from some quarter. Madsen and Arden crossed the road together to join him. Behind them Buchanan pulled the car away from the sidewalk and drove off.

"Do you want us to become Freemasons?" Arden asked. "Is this your idea of a recruitment drive?"

"No Mister Arden." Parks's voice revealed his growing weariness of Arden's attitude. "You can walk away now but as I told you before you wouldn't get very far." Parks stepped up to the large black door, took out a key embossed with the familiar image of a set-square and dividers and unlocked it. "Follow me. And be quick."

Madsen was last to step over the threshold and before the door was closed he looked back out into the world of the once familiar. Night had come to Providence and with it the continuing sense of malevolent threat.

"Believe me Mister Madsen, they're out there." Parks made his way across the hallway and to a door set under the stairs.

"What are we doing here? This is all too weird for me." Arden was examining the internal decorations of the hallway. Various panels, the cornice and tracery were all richly decorated with Masonic imagery.

"Please follow me." Parks opened the door to reveal a set of descending stairs. "And would the last one through close this door behind them."

"Looking glass world." Arden smiled at Madsen whose expression was one of slight bemusement. "Let's follow the white rabbit."

Both men then followed Parks down the stairs, through another door and into a curtain lined room. All sound was muffled and the only light came from muted up-lights on one of the walls. To their right were a set of double doors, each one bearing Masonic symbols and the letter G. To their left, a single door bearing the image of a skull and crossbones.

"Gentlemen. I know that this may all seem somewhat bizarre. But do you understand the purpose of an initiation?"

"To reject the old world of the profane and to enter a new world of the enlightened," Arden replied as he cast his eyes around the room.

"Indeed. It might also seem ridiculous to go through with it. Why not, as you might ask, cut straight to the chase?" Parks looked at each man in turn. "It is a threshold, a portal, a transition. Call it what you will. But it also shows commitment on your behalf. That you are willing to be loyal to that which you will become."

"Trust."

"Yes Mister Madsen. I know this all seems strange to you. You are after all purely on a quest to find out who it was that was responsible for your friend's death. I assure you it is the only way to find out. You will not find them through orthodox means. The law of the profane world cannot help you."

Parks moved to the single door and selected a key.

"Mister Madsen and Mister Arden you are both here because both your lives became connected at a certain point." Parks unlocked the door.

"What do you mean?" Arden's attention shifted from Parks to Madsen.

Parks smiled.

"Mister Madsen found an unidentified body on a beach. Mister Arden here knows the name of that unfortunate man." Parks paused to allow the facts to sink in.

"I found a body. The police found the page from the book on it." Madsen cast his mind back.

"Jim." Arden wore a blank expression.

"You knew the man?" Madsen asked.

"I did. He was a friend of mine. Jim Eddowes."

"The police drew a blank on the name." Madsen's brow furrowed.

"Kearns didn't." Parks looked up as he unlocked the door.

"Do you know Kearns?" Madsen was genuinely surprised.

"That was the closest they came to getting the missing page." Parks gave him a knowing smile. "At least a copy of it."

"He's not a cop?" Madsen looked worried.

"Oh, he's a cop Mister Madsen, but let's just say he works for the opposition." Parks pushed the door open. "Where the lost missing page is, I'm not sure yet. Do you still have a copy?"

"Yeah. On a CD." Madsen tapped his jacket pocket.

"Excellent. If they had the original we'd know by now."

"I don't understand."

"You will in time Mister Madsen, you will in time. Gentlemen, once more I must ask you to follow me."

Madsen and Arden followed Parks and found themselves in a small changing room. There were numerous brass hooks set into a wooden rail that ran around the wall. Everything was anonymous, no names or numbers, no marks of indication. Even Masonic symbolism was lacking.

"Will you undress to your shirt sleeves and remove your socks and shoes." Parks was searching for a third key as he bent down to open a dark wood chest set against the wall opposite the door.

Both men obliged.

"As you can see this room has no markings of any kind. It is the room of anonymity. A transition point between the profane and the realm of enlightenment."

Arden was about to comment but Madsen touched his arm and gently shook his head.

"I need to do this," he said softly.

Arden acquiesced. Whatever his dismissive feelings were about the situation he could see that Madsen was serious.

This did not go unnoticed by Parks. He smiled to himself.

"Now I will ask you to put on a blindfold each."

Parks held up two thick black velvet bags. Arden was about to say something but restrained himself. A habit of a lifetime was proving hard to break.

"You will feel disorientated at first." Parks continued. "But follow my directions. I will ask you to remain silent unless asked a direct question."

Madsen felt Parks place a section of rope around his neck. Then Parks bound each of their hands behind their backs.

"Now, gentlemen. Please wait until you are summoned."

‡

The Lear jet touched down at Logan Airport into a damp Boston night. The whine of the undercarriage descending woke Hannah from a deep sleep. Looking out of the cabin window she saw the myriad lights of the city rising up to meet her and for a brief moment she felt a lifting in her heart. It was the nearest she had been to reality for a long time. The normal, the everyday, even the boring had become something she craved. She knew of course, that she would have to grab the moment. It was in many respects, like coming up for air or the fleeting moments of freedom on long walks away from her school as she played truant. Her subconscious in rebellion against the strong social constraints that had been built up around her, born of her father's desire for control.

Yes, she still loved him but his latest betrayal would be the last. His deep puritanical ethic had crushed her will but now, at last, she was beginning to have the courage to stand up to him. She had rebelled, conformed and was now about to rebel again. But she must confront him for her sake, not for his.

The plane came to a stop and the co-pilot appeared from the cockpit, opened the main door and let the steps drop to the runway. He nodded but his face was a blank.

Hannah made her way to the door and felt the rain on her face. She was not really sure what she was supposed to do and for a second a sense of helplessness almost overwhelmed her. A foolish, indeed childish emotion, as she was quite capable of looking after herself but fatigue was dissolving her self-control. If she was honest, her sense of loneliness was also playing its part in the emotional equation.

Parked not twenty feet away was a black limousine. Hannah looked at the co-pilot who nodded. It was meant for

231

her. She made her way down the steps to the runway and up to the rear door. As she approached the window dropped.

Her father looked out.

Hannah stopped short.

"Get in." Franklin opened the door and slid across the back seat.

At first she hesitated. Then his commanding voice called to her again.

She did what she was told.

Closing the door she stared straight ahead refusing to make eye contact with the man.

"I'm sorry I had to leave you there." He reached forward and tapped on the partition.

The car began to move.

Hannah wanted to blurt out the planned speech but sat there mute. Her father reached across and took her hand. With the thumb he unclenched her fist. She did not resist.

"Just understand I had to leave you there."

"They locked the room." Hannah replied through gritted teeth.

"For your safety." Franklin could see that his daughter was far from won over. "Certain elements out there would not hesitate to use you to get to me."

"I'm supposed to believe that?" Hannah looked out through the tinted window of the limousine. The streets were a blur in the rain.

"Yes." His voice was soft, hypnotic.

"Why would anyone do that?"

"Please accept that as the truth."

Hannah had never heard her father so conciliatory. She maintained her guard. He had to be bluffing. She loved him but she hated him too and trust was not something that she would readily succumb to. At this point in time she felt as if she was being played with, teased for reasons she could not yet work out.

Her father continued.

"I will let you into a little secret."

✠

For five minutes both Madsen and Arden stood in silence surrounded by uncertainty. Then Madsen felt the rope go tight around his neck. Someone, presumably Parks, was tugging the other end and leading him forward.

He heard a solid loud rap on the double doors. He heard the doors open then a few moments later was led forward again.

Madsen sensed that he had been brought into a sizeable room. The odd but rare noise seemed to echo around him.

A hand was placed on each of his shoulders.

He heard an unknown voice.

"Blind one, kneel." The hands applied pressure and Madsen took that as his cue to do so. He was aware of a number of people around him. Suddenly the rope went taut around his neck. It was enough to make him panic. He gritted his teeth and tried to control his breathing. He swallowed hard but his tongue felt thick and it was difficult to do so. Saliva pooled in his mouth.

He was made to lean forward.

Something sharp was stuck into the back of his neck, and then he felt two more steel points, one at his heart and the other at his right side. He could not be certain but it felt like the tips of swords, their blades unforgiving and unyielding. The tension had become unbearable and in such a quick space of time. His body was rigid. He knew that if he moved the swords would draw blood, they were pressed that deep against his skin.

The commanding voice continued.

"The life you have lived so far is that of the blind man unaware of the greater reality. Around you the walls of ignorance are high. Their bricks are lies and deceit. In every direction there is danger but now you seek enlightenment and a release from enslavement."

There was a long pause.

"Who approaches?"

Madsen heard Parks's voice. The man was only a few feet away.

"One who seeks to leave the world of the profane. A soul staggering blindly on the path of ignorance. A man beset on all sides by danger."

"Why does he approach?"

"He seeks enlightenment. A resurrection in life. He seeks the sanctuary of the Brotherhood of the sun. He seeks to live his life away from the shadows. It is by light we see; by eyes we naught behold. This man seeks the light of wisdom and understanding."

"Is he worthy?"

"I bring him forth as a worthy brother. I found him on the road lost and without sight."

"And who are you?"

"I am the one who was once as he. I recognise his plight and bring him forth so that he may now see as I do. That he may continue on his journey and see the path he must take."

"Does he accept his duty?"

"He does."

"Does he accept the consequences of his actions?"

"He does with full heart."

"Does he accept death?"

"As we all must do."

"Then he must face death."

‡

He had hooked her again with a promise. Hannah felt her anger starting to well up. Not only anger towards her father but also for allowing herself to fall once more, open eyed, into his trap of words.

For the next twenty minutes or so they said nothing to each other until, and despite her own character, she found herself turning to him. She had at last found a spark of courage to face the one person in the world from whom all she wanted was respect, the one person who would not give it to her.

"You didn't even thank me."

For a split second her father was taken aback but he swiftly regained his detached, self-absorbed demeanour.

"Is that what you want from me?"

Hannah felt herself in a mental retrograde slide. She was becoming that small girl again who thought her father could do no wrong. She resisted.

"Yes." She did not want to be that girl again. "You asked me to do what you wanted because you told me I was the only one you could trust. A blood tie." She turned to face him. "I watched good men die. For what? A key?"

Franklin maintained his dismissive reserve. Once it had been the second nature of a politician's mask, now it was inbuilt as if it were part of his DNA.

He smiled.

"You can't even look me in the eye. Are you afraid I will see the lies?" Hannah felt her heart race, the thrill of new emotional discovery.

Her father leant over and in a quiet, angry and threatening voice reprimanded her. For the first time his eyes met hers. There was dictatorial malice in them.

"Good men die everyday. They are good, that is why they die. An irrelevance in the grand scheme of things. Most people's view of life is obscured by their own pathetic grievances. Who cares? It's the duty of a small number of men to change the world and to do that sacrifices have to be made."

He paused for a second.

"There is a war going on. A war for hearts and minds."

"That's your secret is it?" Hannah's question was incendiary.

"No. It isn't," Franklin snapped his reply in her face.

"So you just said that as part of a game. Power play with your daughter. Pretend there's a reward for risking her life." Hannah could feel her body tremble.

"By finding that key you have helped us gain an important advantage over the enemy."

"Enemy? What do you mean?"

"Everyone who stands against me. That's the enemy."

"Are you paranoid?" Hannah studied her father.

Franklin's eyes bore into those of his daughter. The fury within was plain to see. A muscle in his cheek was in spasm from gritted teeth. His hands balled into fists and for a moment Hannah thought he would strike her. In that moment her courage was reborn.

"I'm deadly serious."

"You would hit me wouldn't you?" She asked almost as a taunt. "Your little girl." She stared him down.

Her father's expression remained fixed. But it was a look that betrayed his internal conflict.

"A war for hearts and minds? You're the one with no heart." Hannah turned her attention to the world beyond the limousine. The rain soaked Boston suburbs were beginning to thin.

Inwardly she smiled. She had fought back and although she could not claim a victory she had stood her ground, finding some inner strength to replace the small defenceless girl that had been at the core of her being.

Her father, regaining his composure sat back.

"There is a secret. And I will tell you. Not as a reward but because you are my daughter." His voice was soft and from a man who had retreated.

Maybe Hannah could claim a victory.

‡

For half an hour, maybe longer, Madsen had just about managed to keep himself together. Despite its theatrics, the ceremony was, if nothing else, demanding on the senses.

236

It encouraged fear, an enfeeblement of the will. It was as if his old self was being taken apart, deconstructed and broken down, to be rebuilt in a new form. At one point he felt as though he would cry, at least weep for the past and for all his misdemeanours, both emotional and physical. A great upwelling of memories both good and bad spilled into his head with all their incumbent rights and wrongs, emotional scars, joys and heartaches. It was as if he was searching for something stable to hold onto while adrift in a vast ocean of uncertainty.

He wanted to stop. He wanted to return to his childhood and begin again. He wanted to make amends. He wanted to…

The question was aimed at him.

"As you have been adrift in darkness do you now wish to see the sun again?"

A hand was placed on his shoulder, a cue for him to answer.

"I do." Madsen's voice was cracked. He was not sure if it was the right thing to say. "I do wish to see the sun again. Yes."

The swords were withdrawn.

"Then you are new risen. A resurrection into a world where truth is illuminated by the sun."

There was long pause then swiftly the blindfold hood was removed. Madsen was left blinking in the intense light of an ornate lamp.

He looked around. Apart from Parks, who was holding the hood, the room was empty. The ceiling was a dark blue sky filled with stars. At its centre, from which the lamp was suspended, there was a large representation of the sun with an all-seeing eye at its centre. The floor was a checkerboard of black and white tiles. Directly in front of Madsen were three large chairs each with a sun symbol across the back that reminded him of the carvings he had seen from ancient Egypt, the sun disc carried by falcon wings.

"I heard others." Madsen stood up.

"You did. But their identity must be kept secret. Now, apologies but I must ask you to leave." Parks was making for the double doors.

"Arden?" Madsen frowned.

Parks nodded then stopped. He looked up at the ceiling. By the look on the man's face Madsen understood that something was amiss.

There was a sound. Incongruous. A gun shot.

"Stay here." Parks made for the double doors and opened them. From above came the sound of splintering woodwork. Racing across the curtain-lined room, Madsen not far behind, Parks opened the single door. Arden was in the process of taking his hood off.

"I take it that has nothing to do with the ceremony." Arden was looking up.

"No, Mister Arden. And we must leave."

There was a burst of gunfire.

"Christ!" Arden threw the hood down and grabbed his jacket and shoes. Parks reached into Madsen's jacket and took out the CD but Madsen snatched it from him.

"When we're out of here you can have this." Madsen grabbed his clothes.

"Maybe you're right." Parks moved to the door at the bottom of the stairs and locked it.

There was another burst of gunfire.

"Who are they shooting at?" Madsen asked looking up at the ceiling.

"More importantly how do we get out?" Arden was pulling on his shoes.

Parks returned.

"Follow me please."

"Parks? What is all this?"

"Mister Arden. It is our enemies. They have defiled the lodge."

"I don't understand."

"Mister Arden. Both you and Mister Madsen are here, with the copy of the page. More importantly the Ordines were here. They performed the initiation. The enemy took their chance to kill two birds with one stone." Parks was halfway across the curtain-lined room.

"Kill being the operative word." Arden followed.

There was more gunfire, rapid, an automatic weapon.

All three paused as they heard the door at the top of the stairs crack off his hinges.

"I'll ask again: how do we get out?" Arden was more insistent.

"Through the other room. I'm sorry Mister Arden your initiation will have to wait."

Parks set off. Footsteps could be heard coming down the stairs.

"Come on." Arden tugged on Madsen's sleeve.

They caught up with Parks who was reaching up to the lamp. He pulled on it and a door, carefully concealed in the decorative work, opened in the rear of the room behind the chairs.

"It is on a spring mechanism and will close by itself." Parks was making for the opening.

There was more automatic weapon fire and the door at the base of the stairs exploded in a shower of splinters.

Parks slipped through into darkness followed by Arden. As Madsen made his way through the door was nearly half closed.

"Is this the way the others left?" Madsen could see that the door was thick and weighted, supported on angled hinges.

"Yes." Parks reached for a flashlight from a recess then made his way along a narrow passageway. "This tunnel dates back at least a hundred and fifty years. Civil War I've been told. Personally I think it's older."

Behind them they heard more gunfire, launched probably out of frustration more than at a specific target.

"I'm inclined to agree. It looks Medieval. European."
Madsen studied the construction.

"You sure?" Arden sounded incredulous.

As Parks walked by a particular spot he tapped the wall.

"There."

Arden slowed to look.

There was the image of a skull and cross bones carved into a large stone.

"That's a Templar image isn't it?" Arden traced a finger around the image.

"Something odd to find in a Civil War construction." Parks added.

"But not in a Masonic building surely?" Madsen asked.

"True," replied Parks. "But I'm sure you'll agree these stones in this tunnel are older than the Temple."

Madsen ran a hand along the wall as he followed Parks and Arden. He had to admit that the stonework did indeed look older than a century and a half. Quite what that meant he was not sure but it hinted at heretical notions about history. But then that, in the light of recent events, would be no surprise to him.

"Where does it go?" Arden asked.

"To the rear of the building where Mister Buchanan will be waiting for us."

The passageway veered to the left and began to rise at a very gradual degree and after about fifty yards ended in a series of steps.

Parks raised a hand indicating Arden and Madsen should wait then made his way slowly up the steps until he came to a door. Opening it slowly he glanced out then called down to the others to follow.

When Madsen stepped out into the darkness he saw that the door was recessed into a large plinth topped by a statue that reminded him of something that the sculptor Jacques Juvenal would have created. Taking a pace or two back a short way he saw the figure was of Benjamin Franklin. It was a duplicate of the famous one in Pennsylvania Avenue but here the man was depicted younger and fresher faced holding a pair of golden spheres.

"Mister Madsen, you can study statues when we're less pushed for time." Parks was casting his eyes around the open area behind the Temple, half of which was set aside for parking.

"There." Arden saw the Mercedes first and moved quickly towards it.

"Wait." Parks called after him but Arden was not going to stop.

When he reached the car, Arden pulled up short. Buchanan was in the driver's seat but he appeared to be asleep. There was something about the man's appearance that drew Arden up short. He then saw what was wrong. Buchanan's throat had been cut in a precise wound; sliced from ear to ear. The blood had spilled down the man's front and had spattered the car's steering wheel, dashboard and windshield.

"Christ." Arden turned away in disgust.

"We don't have time for this." Parks was searching the shadows.

There was a distant boom from inside the Temple. All three men turned to look. After a few moments smoke began to billow out of smashed second floor windows.

"What do we do now?" Arden watched the flames ripping through the air.

"Pull Buchanan's body out and take the car." Madsen was reaching for the driver's door handle.

Parks grabbed Madsen's wrist and shook his head.

"We will need a new car. Anonymous."

"Hey." Arden saw a man appear around the corner of the building. He was looking in their direction. "Someone's seen us."

"This way." Parks set off across the open space and up towards a thick wall of undergrowth that formed the rear boundary of the Temple grounds. Bullets whipped and cracked around them.

Pushing his way through the thick and entangled bushes Madsen felt a sense of intense panic. It was a frightening experience to put aside his paranoia and realise once and for all that he was indeed being pursued; that someone was genuinely out to kill him. It was a primeval and animalistic experience; the pretence of the modern world, with all its defensive charades, was torn apart to reveal a state of raw nature beneath. The paper-thin veneer of civilisation had gone and in its place was indifferent existence writ large. Only humanity was capable of building up myths to protect itself from nature red in tooth and claw. Only humanity was stupid enough to hide itself from the reality and truth of all things.

All morality was stripped away. What was morality anyway? Something preached by those who ignored it. There was none inherent in the universe. It was a construct like the notions of good and bad. Just a matter of perspective. Everything is grey, not black and white.

"Mister Madsen, move!" Parks shouted.

There was a low wall topped with railings. When Madsen reached it Parks and Arden were already scrambling over.

The limousine pulled up the drive of the manor and came to a stop, the automatic electric gates closing slowly behind it. Franklin opened the door and stepped out ignoring Hannah. She sat there for a few moments longer, then followed.

In the hallway she was surprised to see a group of dark suited men all of a similar age to her father. They were confident, even arrogant looking, as if they were in possession of great power. They had obviously been awaiting his return.

Franklin led them directly into the main front room where a fire had already been set. Hannah drifted by and made for the stairs. She overheard the tail end of a sentence that one of the men had directed at her father.

"...we've made the first move against them..."

Before the doors were closed Hannah saw a smile fall across her father's face.

She made her way up to her room and sat on the edge of the bed. While massaging her forehead to soothe away the headache that was beginning to form she tried to make sense of recent events. It was not easy. In the present situation she felt more like a puppet, a device, an instrument of her father's machinations. That she was his own flesh and blood seemed to have little bearing on his attitude to her.

She was aware of someone. Looking up she saw her father standing in the doorway. He was studying her.

"Can I come in?" The sternness in his voice had gone.

Hannah made a gesture to suggest it was up to him.

Her father made his way to a chair and sat down. He said nothing for a moment then leant forward.

"You have to understand that the greater good is what is most important to me right now."

Hannah's attention was aimed at the carpet. She did not want to look at him, at least not yet.

"I had to send you, you know that. You were the only one I could trust," he continued.

Hannah shook her head slowly.

"Believe me with what I know, you are the only one I can trust. If I had sent anyone else they might not have returned with-" He fell silent.

"You sent me all that way. For a key. Why?"

Franklin stood up and made for the door.

"I can't tell you. Suffice to say that what it reveals will tear down western civilisation, those parts that matter I mean. We are defending the world from darkness." Franklin left.

Hannah still had a thousand questions to ask him, her mind racing with the conflicting emotions of anger and love. Why had he abandoned her? Why was it so difficult for him to thank her? Why was he dismissive of her achievements? The man was a stone wall. She despised him for it.

Being impulsive was not one of her characteristics, so it took her aback somewhat to find herself heading downstairs to confront her father. Maybe it was symptomatic of her resolve that she would not be treated that way again. That it was he who would have to show her at least a modicum of respect from now on.

She approached the front room and slowed her pace; her desire to belittle him in front of his colleagues rapidly deflated. Her father still held sway. The large double doors were shut but she could hear the conversation taking place within.

One of the voices was saying something about retrieving an object while another spoke of leaving it exactly where it was. Then her father spoke. He wanted to take it but he reminded them they could not safely open the reliquary, as they were still missing the page from a book.

Another asked how the search was developing and was told by Franklin that for the moment it had stalled but they had a key and therefore still had the upper hand. Rest assured the Ordines would be defeated.

The Ordines. Who were the Ordines? It was a name unfamiliar to her. A company? A family name? Business rivals? She had no idea. The way her father spat the name out they were obviously the object of intense hatred; anathema to the man's world view.

She heard him talk of destroying them once and for all. That the world would be a better place without this destructive godless distraction with its corrupting influence. That he would be the man to do it. Beyond the doors and out of sight of his daughter, Franklin was allowing free reign to his extremist polemic. As she listened she now no longer understood him. Had she ever? Or was she now finally admitting to herself that her fight to win his love was at an end. The gulf between them seemed immense, unbridgeable. But, she suspected and if she was honest with herself, it had always been that way. Only now had she the courage to admit it. It was obvious that she had reached a fork in the road in respect to their relationship.

She turned away from the door to make her way through to the kitchen at the back of the house but before she did, she heard her father mention a name. It was someone that was apparently in possession of a copy of the important missing page. The name was Madsen. And Franklin wanted him dead.

When her father found her half an hour later she was sitting at the kitchen table nursing a glass of milk. She had heard his guests leave but had assumed that he would lock up, then go to bed without even stopping to wish her goodnight. His presence surprised her.

"Looks good. The milk."

"Just needed something to fill a void." Hannah fought the urge to look up.

Franklin made his way to the cupboard and took out a plate and some cookies. He went to the refrigerator and poured himself a glass of milk.

He sat down to Hannah's left, at the head of the table.

"Here, have one." Franklin took a biscuit then slid the plate towards her. She shook her head. "Not as good as your mother's. She could bake a damn fine cookie."

Hannah ignored the offer.

Franklin took a mouthful of milk but his attention was firmly on his daughter.

"Do you want me to say thank you?" His tone was bullying. "To say how proud of you I am? Is that what you want?" He bit down hard into a cookie.

Hannah looked up, still fighting the urge to look at him. She was trying to stand her ground.

"You know, one day it might be great if you just showed me an ounce of respect." Hannah fought the tears that were welling up. "Just once. For Chrissake!"

"Don't blaspheme. Not in my house," Franklin snapped back.

She turned to look at him.

"When have you ever shown me any respect?"

Franklin bit into the cookie again.

"Respect? Respect is for the weak. You have to be strong in this world," he snapped. "To get to a position where it matters the people around you deserve no respect. They are meaningless."

"What is that supposed to mean?"

"Take no prisoners. I've told you all this."

"You taught me to be heartless. But it's not the way it's supposed to be at all." Hannah could feel her throat beginning to constrict. She reached for her inhaler and administered two short stabs from her inhaler.

"Sentiment, that's your problem. Now you have to rely on medication to get you through. It's a weakness."

Hannah felt the habit of subservience returning. She struggled to resist it.

Her father continued.

"I taught you self reliance. I had you trained to deal with the outside world. It's a warzone. You have to know how to fight."

"Only because people like you make it one. Where's all that godly love you adhere to?"

"I told you not to blaspheme!" Franklin's face was thunder.

Hannah stood up and made for the back stairs that led up out of the kitchen.

"One day you might do me the courtesy of giving as much love to me as you do to your god."

❊

246

The Mysteries in Alexia's Front Garden

I'm not the best travelling companion on a motorway. I find them, at best, deadly dull. They have taken the fun out of driving. Yes, you may get to your destination more quickly but at what cost? No exploration. No wrong turns to serendipitous discoveries. No interesting byways or lanes to trundle down and get lost in. Then they're always busy and/or at a standstill.

I hate them.

But here I was bashing down the M4 feeling nauseous. I had opted to sit in the back. Actually both Gus and I thought it would be better. We could nod off while Linda could chatter to Arden and no one would notice us catching flies, comatose on the back seat.

The M25 had been a total disaster. Our early start had simply meant we had found the traffic jams sooner than anyone else, or so it appeared. Arden's big old-fashioned Oxford blue Merc somethingorother, I have no idea about vehicular nomenclature, whistled in that way fast cars do, westwards towards Zummerzet.

We had left it too late to call ACH last night but as Gus was swift to reveal, the invite for his return was an open one. I assumed that she was ever willing and keen to get rid of other family heirlooms in order to keep the bastards from her door so the plan was for Gus to call her when we were within shouting distance of the Carey-Hunt's front gate. The claim would be that he was just passing by and thought that it might be wise just to pop in and say hello with a swift casting of eyes over further items Alexia wanted to cast off like so much driftwood. We, of course, would be associates in the man's trade.

'Why doesn't she just sell the whole lot to this hotel chain?' I stretched my leaden limbs.

'I think this is money for her own use. You know, slip it away offshore beyond the grasping hands of the debt collectors. I don't think she'd see much of the proceeds from the sale of the house and grounds,' Gus replied, his eyes still closed.

Wise woman.

Wise woman indeed.

None of us thankfully were that keen to stop and feast on the filthy bilge slopped up in those wretched service stations so we paused for very late lunch in Bath at a drinking establishment with a beer garden. The city was drowning in glorious sunlight making the honey coloured walls of the buildings glow. After a few pints it sent me on one and for a while, things got a bit big on me. My mood was tainted a bit when I thought I saw the bloke from The Crusader's Head sitting inside at the bar. When I looked for a second time he had gone, thwarting my intention to find out if it was indeed him.

Arden held forth about a Freemason who designed part of the city, one of the Georgian Circles with a main road leading off, in the shape of a key. The diameter of the head of the key apparently, was exactly the same as Stonehenge. One or two of the houses in the circle had been designed to mirror the interiors of Masonic Lodges with chequerboard floors and pairs of columns representing *Jachin* and *Boaz*, Forte and Sagresse, strength and wisdom.

'Everything's connected,' was all Linda could say. Technically, I guess, everything was connected, but not in the way Linda thought. She saw conspiracy, whereas as I saw physics and mathematics in respect to matter (told you everything had suddenly grown big in my noggin).

For a time I suspected Arden was playing with her head. Maybe he saw in her something of a disciple. Someone who was hanging onto every word he said. I knew the man had an ego but just how large I had yet to fathom. *Spectacular* sprang to mind. He spoke, rather eloquently if the truth be known, about Masonic symbolism, Rosicrucianism, one big wind up apparently, and the more subtle levels of secret orders. He had no time for Bohemian Grovers and all the modern rubbish, as he phrased it, as there were no deep

248

levels of symbolic meaning within them. Just men who were too rich and powerful for their own good. He preferred the old orders such as the Illuminati who, he said, had nothing to do with the paranoid theistic drivel slammed onto the Internet by loud-mouthed evangelicals across the Pond.

Arden had a fondness for the Illuminati because they had been forged in the fiery dawn of the Age of Enlightenment so that wealthy gentlemen could discuss matters that were heretical to the Church, that over-arching monster of bigotry. He also said he had a soft spot for Freemasons because many early scientists sought, and were given, sanctuary within the lodges of Europe against the fevered machinations of Papists keen to repress knowledge.

Throughout much of this impromptu lecture Gus and yours truly sat listening but not really listening. The beer had worked its afternoon magic and I wanted to simply kick back and soak up the sun. I was happy just to let Arden's words wash over me. Linda was doing enough listening for the pair of us anyway.

Not long after, we made off in the car and headed cross-country towards the heart of Somerset. We took the Radstock road and then on down to Shepton Mallet, which sounded to me like an early apparatus for splitting the atom. I pictured two tweed-clad gentlemen taking it in turns to whack fresh air. Shortly after that I nodded off and when I awoke I had no idea where I was. This was after all, a part of the country I knew next to nothing about.

For this part of the journey Gus sat in the front guiding Arden as to the right roads to take. I say roads: they were rapidly becoming lanes once removed from their cousins, the dirt track. Linda was dozing to my right, her head resting on the window, perhaps a little put out that she had to sit next to me and not next to her dashing knight conspirator.

In Bath Gus had forgotten to phone Alexia, so we pulled into a small grassy lay by to allow the man to fulfil his duty.

'Hi, Alexia, Gus here. Yes. I'm in the area on a business trip.' There was a long pause. 'That would be great. Yes. I have some colleagues with me. Is that a problem?' Another long pause. 'I think that portmanteau should be next on your list. Of course. Yes. I'm not sure. About half an hour. Okay, bye.' Gus grinned. 'See, easy.'

'How far away are we?' Linda asked running both hands through her hair.

Gus didn't answer. He opened the passenger door and got out.

'I'll show you.'

Gus pointed down into the valley beneath us. There, nestling in a small wood on the edge of a gently sweeping lake, was the house. It was a magnificent pile. All mock classical, thrown up in, I would assume, the same stone most of Bath was built with. The walls seemed to glow in the sun. I half expected to see men in tricorn hats riding piebald steeds across the heavily manicured lawns and fey, giggling ladies sporting parasols gliding across the terraces or, more likely, a noisy film crew shooting yet another version of Pride and Jaundice.

Dotted throughout the landscape were follies, small temple-like structures and gazebos and at one end of the lake there was a grand portico with a waterfall tumbling away beneath it. Soon, no doubt to be dug up and landscaped into, and I use the term in the broadest sense, that most wretched of things, a golf course.

'The fat cats are gonna love this place,' I said and not without a hint of sarcasm.

'More heritage lost to global corporations. Will they leave nothing alone? Linda put a hand to her mouth. She looked genuinely distressed. 'Such a shame. It's so beautiful.' They were about to dig up Eden and Linda was almost beside herself.

I resisted the temptation to spoil the atmos by telling Linda that it was big corporate money that built the gaff in the first place, usually on the back of an enslaved country sucked dry of its resources. But such Bolshevism on a glorious afternoon seemed woefully out of place. I beat that grey boiler suit wearing part of my fabric back into submission.

Arden, hands behind his back, remained tacit, like Clint Eastwood weighing up a lawless town he was about to enter. His eyes were mapping the landscape and you could almost hear that Ennio Morricone whistling and twanged Jew's harp music start up.

Whip crack!

'Come on folks.' Gus clambered back into the car. 'Let's see what we can find.'

Alexia was a cracker. Yes, a sexist male orientated statement. But that's us men for you. Much to my disappointment, the jodhpurs were obviously hanging up in the wardrobe. She was wearing a black roll neck sweater and dark jeans with those Chelsea boot things with the stretchy sides. She must have been five eleven. She reminded me of a graceful horse.

She greeted Gus as if they were old school friends. She gave him a big hug and was all dramatic gestures and dahlings.

Gus did the round of greetings and we were all ushered into a long living room that looked out onto the back lawn. The windows here were framed in great columns and arches.

'This used to be the orangery.' Alexia sounded proud. 'But it was converted ten years ago into a breakfast room.'

I think without too much sweating on the problem, I could have fitted the entire square meterage of my house into this one room.

She made us all sit down then called her retainer Retinger in to serve refreshments. He was a short man, with a grey shadow of hair on his pate, who looked down his nose at us. He came across as being all territorial; hacked off that

251

four miscreants had invaded the sanctity of his realm. He wasn't dressed in trad butler regalia but wore dark trousers and a white shirt with what looked like, to me at least, highly expensive silver cuff-links.

We all shirked tea and went full steam for the G and Ts. Arden, to my surprise, ordered a pink gin thrown out. This had the additional effect of making Alexia whoop with joy. She hadn't heard anyone order such a thing since her days as a deb.

'Gus,' she asked. 'What did you want to look at today?'

'I thought we'd start in the dining room. I think we could get at least two hundred thou' for the contents.' Gus tapped the armrests with open palms. 'At least...'

'You know I'm going to push you for more.' Alexia sat forward and reached for a folder on a small ornate footstool on which, guess what?, a sun had been embroidered. 'Now then, let me check your estimates.'

This deserved a witty and vulgar response but I resisted.

Gus apparently, during his last stay, had gone from room to room performing some rough round the houses guesswork as to how much each room was worth.

'Maybe it was more.' Gus pinched his lips in.

'It was. Nearly half a million.'

I let fly a 'Christ!' I hadn't meant to. It had just leapt out without my-

'Indeed.' Alexia smiled.

- consent...

I felt a touch embarrassed. Nothing I'd ever valued had come anywhere near that amount. What a waste of time cat blood trinkets and their ilk had proved to be. All those sandals of the saints, knickers of the immortals, several heads of John the Baptist, including a small one which was claimed to be the man as a twelve year old, robes of non-existent messiahs or the original ten commandments, which had turned up last year apparently, so it was said, from a plundered vault beneath a Baghdad museum. In the fog of conspiracy, it was claimed, that this was the sole reason for the invasion of Iraq – to lay claim to the artefacts of Christendom.

Fake artefacts at that. They might as well have rescued seaside views of Galilee, souvenir pillars of salt and stones of the walls of Jericho.

I vowed there and then to pack that holy crap in.

I could sense from Arden a certain amount of impatience. Not with me but with the situation. It was clear he didn't do preamble. He liked to get straight to the point. In many respects I would agree but not here. I wanted to wallow in the opulence. How often am I in these kinds of places?

'Ah, no, you're right. The painting. That's the clincher.' Gus clapped his hands together once. 'Whenever you're ready.'

Alexia nodded but didn't move.

'Tell me Mr Arden how long does it take to write one of your books?' Bright cookie, Alexia.

Arden smiled, happy again that he was centre of attention.

'It depends on how much research I have to do. But I've always believed in going for it. Once I start I don't like to hang around.'

'I see.' Alexia raised both her eyebrows.

'Mrs Carey-Hunt...' Arden sat forward in his chair.

'Alexia, please.'

'Alexia. During my research for my last book I came across an extract from a book that mentions this house and an ancestor of yours who hired a young man to survey the grounds.'

Alexia sipped from her drink.

'The legend.' She said the words so that they dripped with disdain.

'You don't believe it?' Arden asked.

'Why should I? But saying that, if there's a treasure somewhere in the grounds of the house it might be rather beneficial.' A thoughtful look fell across Alexia's aristocratic face. 'Very beneficial.'

Here's a thing. A legend that might actually help a present day predicament. If only it could be that easy. Or that obvious. Anyway, how could the discovery of a key help anyone? It obviously wasn't going to stop Arden from trying though.

Arden stood up and made his way to one of the large windows. Hands in pockets he looked out over the lawn that slid away, banked on one side by a converted stable block, to distant hedgerows and what appeared to be a small cottage. I couldn't quite see from where I was sitting but it certainly looked like a pokey residence. Maybe it's where Alexia's retainer hung out. Maybe he liked to strut about on the lawn semi-naked, shooed off by the gardener. Then again maybe not. My imagination did have a way with itself.

'Will you allow me... us... to research the possibility of the reality of this story?' Arden turned, perhaps a little over dramatically, as he asked the question.

'If you're certain of such.' Alexia ran a hand through that thick mane of hair she possessed. It was gorgeous. It was the kind of hair you wanted to just walk over to and get all silly with.

'Alexia, I am. I'm convinced it's genuine.' He had a way, I can tell you. A combination, no doubt, of his Mafioso looks, that rich voice of his and a general sense of casual arrogance that he seemed to throw off around him wherever he went.

Smooth bastard.

He was trying it on with Alexia and Linda was well aware of this. It was obvious she was getting a tad tense if not a smidge jealous. She fidgeted in her chair and made odd huffing noises.

'I have to be honest and say that I only ever thought it to be a silly legend that was attached to the house.' Alexia stood up. She had about her a slightly dismissive air, as if people were just inconveniences who got in the way, whether they were associates or simple new acquaintances, like us. I doubt if she had many genuine friends. Was that too harsh? I don't know. I'd met her kind before and was never really impressed. She wasn't a silly small town golf club wife with delusions of grandeur. Alexia was in a different league. It was that aloof couldn't-give-a-damn-for-the-lower-classes or, in fact, an anyone-who-wasn't-earning-over-x-millions-a-year detachment. You would never see her getting down and dirty, unless it was with a stable boy in the Royal Household.

'There's only one way to find out.' Arden spoke with authority. Hell's teeth, he was only a writer but he sounded like a comic book hero. All he lacked was an enormous and over stated hand crafted jawline.

'Where would you like to begin?' Alexia raised herself to her full graceful height.

'The library would be the best place,' Gus answered.

'Follow me then.' Alexia made for the door and one by one we followed. For now, Gus's albeit false raison d'etre for being here would have to take a back seat.

The library was magnificent. I could have spent the rest of my life here and not get bored. Thousands, nay verily tens of thousands, of books stuffed every conceivable shelf space within the room.

'What exactly are you looking for?' Alexia asked as she moved towards a glass topped display cabinet. 'I've only ever been in here twice before. It was more my late husband's preserve. Books don't interest me, I'm afraid.'

Arden made his way over to the cabinet and cast his eyes over what lay within. Gus, Linda and myself wandered deeper into the room and began to explore the shelves. I must admit I had no idea what Arden and Gus would be looking for.

'Hey!' Arden said, not a minute later, raising a hand and beckoning us over to come and look.

We did.

There was a letter signed Francis Dashwood. Faded, but nevertheless, perfectly readable.

My Esteemed Colleague and Noble Brother,

You will be pleased to know that all is well here. The property with its refurbishments is a handsome spectacle. The church of St Lawrence has seen much by way of similar improvements. The aforementioned reparations are based on the solar temple at Palmyra. You must indeed revisit as soon as your duties allow. But I fear that much time will pass before that day. I do, of course extend the invitation to your fellow brother Masons who are as welcome here as the sun.

I am aware that the work of the three gathers apace in the Colonies of the New World and for that you must attend with vigour and fortitude. But rest assured, your presence here will always be welcome.

Your friend,

Francis Dashwood.

'It's the answer to the letter I have a copy of. Amazing.' Arden shook his head, a big broad smile across his chops.

'Who are the three?' Gus tapped the glass.

'No idea,' Arden said. 'Perhaps they were involved with the American Revolution.'

I had the distinct impression from Arden that he in fact knew exactly who the three were. The haste with which he answered the question was a real giveaway. And besides, why the American Revolution? Why not The Boston Tea Party or a host of other historical events of that time?

In fact I had to ask him.

'Franklin was involved with the Declaration of Independence. Francis Dashwood was involved as well although to what extent is debatable. That's why.'

'Oh,' came my short, somewhat embarrassed reply.

'Do you mind if I leave you to it?' Alexia was making for the door.

'No, please do.' Linda's response was swift and to the point.

'There's plenty of room here, why not stay until you've found what you're looking for.' Her offer was genuine and one to which we all gracefully accepted. I, for one, had never stayed in a country pile before and it filled me with a kind of schoolboy excitement. I intended to wallow with as much aplomb as I could muster, which could be quite a bit if given the right kind of circumstances. This one being a fine example.

'I'd appreciate that very much.' Arden kept his attention firmly on the manuscripts.

'I'll have Retinger prepare rooms for you.'

'We may be here for some time.' Arden looked up and gave Alexia a tooth-laden smile dripping with a disgusting amount of smarm, charm and snake oil.

'So be it. I'd appreciate having Gus around to continue his work. The pressure from certain financial institutions has increased dramatically this week. Why I should be beholden to my husband's fiscal laxities is beyond me but the thieving bastards must have their pounds of flesh.' With that, Alexia slipped through the door and was gone.

'This is a gold mine,' Arden half whispered.

Gus moved his way slowly along the bookshelves. There were no paperbacks here. Oh no. None of that startling eclectic disarray of multicoloured spines and lurid titles. Here, the literature was all bound in pale browns, dark reds and delicious wine coloured leather embossed with gold text. I instantly fell in love with it.

'We could be here for years.' Stepping up to one of the shelves Linda ran a finger down the spine of a two hundred year old tome on the history of Boston, Massachusetts.

'What are we looking for?' Yes, me again. I had to ask the obvious questions.

'Anything related to Hiddon of course. Letters, diaries, documents of any kind.' Arden paused. 'Anything that will give us clues to the whereabouts of the third key.'

Of course, how silly of me. How forgetful.

The four of us set off in different direction to hunt down anything that might be related to Hiddon, gold keys and hidden treasure.

We spent an hour wandering, searching the spines of the books for anything of interest, but it wasn't until the sun was setting that Arden made the first discovery. At one point he had turned and while looking around at the higher shelves something had made him pause in his tracks. With eyes fixed upwards on a point above the main door of the library, his attention had been drawn to something interesting. I caught this out of the corner of my eye and turned to follow his gaze.

Into a circular alcove with rays of plaster sunlight radiating out from it, the setting sun was beaming a set of numbers. Arden stepped into the middle of the room and pointed to a circular opening in the opposite wall.

'Look. There's a glass disk set into the wall.'

We all looked. Sure enough there it was. Not exactly well hidden, but nevertheless a touch difficult to spot on a casual glance around the library.

'What do the numbers mean?' Linda was beaming, pardon the pun, then put both hands to her mouth and let out a pert laugh.

'Quick, write them down before the sun disappears.' Arden was hastily rummaging through his pockets. For a writer he seemed to be lacking any kind of note taking facility.

Gus was on the case. He whipped out his mobile and tapped in the numbers as if they were a phone number.

Sure enough, within moments the numbers began to fade as the sun set below a line of trees that edged a river flowing out of the estate.

17-7-6 / 322

'It's the date of the American Independence.' Gus held the phone up for all to see.

'But what's the 322?' Linda sported a puzzled look but beneath it she was genuinely excited. It was as if a treasured dream of hers was slowly coming true.

'Obvious but apt.' Arden was thoughtful. 'I wonder.' The writer then set off again, his eyes scanning the bookshelves.

'Do you have an idea?' Gus watched Arden as the man searched... for something.

'I do actually.' Arden held a finger up.

Turned out his idea wasn't very good. At least that's what I thought initially. He had assumed it was connected to the position of books on shelves, like a grid reference, however, the tattered leather reference work in that location turned out to be one entitled *Hermits of the English Country Gardens: Their Employment and Use Therein*. Arden did however turn to page 322 out of curiosity. The only illustration on that page was an etching of a small four-columned folly before which stood a gentleman in a tricorn sporting a horsewhip with what looked like a miscreant fellow of low moral fibre cowering at his feet. There was a rough-hewn sack of spilled vegetables nearby.

'A dead end.' Gus sounded deflated.

Arden said nothing. I think he thought as well but wasn't going to say anything.

'Maybe it has nothing to do with books.' Looking around Linda touched Arden on the sleeve.

At that moment Alexia returned.

259

'Come along. Dinner is served.' She held open the door in emphasis. 'You can leave your investigations until tomorrow.'

After dinner we repaired to a large room, its walls hung with great tapestries. Hunting scenes mostly and all looked at least five hundred years old. That was guess of course; I had no idea but I'd seen similar ones before in my travels. For half an hour or so Gus and Alexia moved beneath them chatting about value and the best way to sell them, either to private collectors or museums. Throughout, Alexia kept one hand on the small of Gus's back. A rather intimate gesture, I thought. But hey, that was Gus. He had a way with women. A natural way. He seemed to succeed without ever trying. It was perhaps his boyish demeanour, which communicated a perpetual need to be mothered.

Linda and Arden were talking in hushed tones about Templars, *Sunsphere*, Venice and holy bloodlines. Bloodlines of mythical characters. It always struck me as odd that people were all tizzed up about something that was so obviously a fake. A conspiratorial mythology built up around someone who never existed. I always found it to be mind-numbing nonsense or at best a vacuous experiment in publicity from which great wellsprings of spurious nonsense washed away common sense. I don't know about you, but I had become totally cheesed off with that great tsunami of books with words such as *key, lost, heresy, scrolls, Templar, secret* blah, blah, blah, yackety-yack-yack-yawn in the their titles. Books that turned the publishing world into the fourth estate of Gotham.

Myths built on myths. It was sickening.

The odd thing was, I appeared to be wrapped up in one such mystery, which made a mockery of my cynicism.

Feeling a bit twitchy, I decided I needed a leg stretcher and some fresh air. I stood up, told everyone what I was doing but, in a spectacular display of indifference, I was deftly ignored.

The night was warm and with a glass of plonk in hand I strolled along the terrace and out onto the lawns. The sky was alive with stars and for the first time in a long while I felt relaxed. I breathed in the thick scented air and my head spun. It was great to be away from that other part of my life. That sorry, struggling, fiscally inept individual wrestling and half beaten by the daily grind. I could perfectly understand why people who lived in the dizzying highs of the financial opiate became detached from every day reality. Living in a place like this I certainly wouldn't want to come down.

I ambled down to a stream. Its gleeful rushing cheered my spirits even more. It reminded me of children giggling. I followed its course from where it emerged under a stone arch down to the river where its waters mingled with the slow, heavy flow of black oily pitch.

What a place. I felt like I was in a Greek myth. Some dreamy arcadia that I used to imagine when reading about Salmacis, Hermaphroditus, Pan and Hera as a ten year old tucked up in bed. Having never been to Greece, I always imagined it to be a variation on the English countryside.

The effect was enhanced by a small Greek temple on the other side of the river, pale and ghostly in the dark – hang on. That was the folly from the illustration in the book. Coincidence? Not the way things had been going of late.

Oh hell, the mystery was deepening. It was like standing on quick sand. The more you resisted the more you slipped further down. The more you flailed to be pulled free the tighter it took hold.

I squinted into the gloom.

It certainly looked like the etching. I could see no way to cross the river and I certainly wasn't going to go crashing about in the grounds looking for a bridge. I wasn't sure of my bearings anyway. No, it would have to wait until daylight.

I stared at the building a little longer then slowly made my way back up the lawn, glancing over my shoulder every once in a while just to make sure I hadn't actually hallucinated the place. I imagined myself as a protagonist in an old book who, having come to a country house, is lost in a phantasmagoria of disparate realities that swirl around him and where he meets mythological characters who tease and taunt him and if he's lucky gets down and grubby in the greenhouse with a nymph. I added that idea to my growing list of unwritten novels.

Looking back for a final time, I thought I caught a glimpse of movement in the darkness on the left hand side of the folly. A shadowy figure, perhaps. I felt the hairs on the back of my neck bristle. Upping my pace I made for the house but chastised myself all the way back for allowing my imagination to, once again, get the better of me.

The following morning found us all in the garden.

'It is, you know.' Gus had asked Alexia if he could take the book on *Hermits of the English Country Gardens: Their Employment and Use Therein* down to the river so that we could judge if I was talking out of my arse or not. Seemed I wasn't, which pleased me no end.

'I think it is.' Linda sounded equally excited.

'I'm convinced.' Arden was and to prove it he was making his way along the riverbank looking for a way to cross. 'Four Corinthian columns. Same angle on the roof apex…'

We spent half and hour trying to find a bridge. Then I remembered the grand portico that I'd seen from the hill and suggested we all made for that.

Not long after we were standing in front of the temple folly. Okay, it had been a great idea for Arden to check the bookshelves. I stood corrected.

Arden walked around its sides then made his way up the few steps at the front and into the main part of the building. It was open plan inside with a low worn marble bench around the wall. Unable to find anything inside by way of obvious clues and feeling a little dejected we sat down and looked out over the grounds and up to the house.

A part of me felt a little nervous, spooked by the apparition I'd seen in the dark so rather oddly, for me at least; I didn't want to go and investigate. The day was overcast and there was a hint of oppression in the air. A veiled presentiment that things were afoot. Okay, a bit overblown but... well, that was the best way to describe the morning. I hadn't slept well and on a trip to the bog I'd caught Alexia leaving Gus's room at around half three in the a of m. She had seen me, smiled, and had then made her way to her own room somewhere at the far end of the house down a corridor that appeared to be half a mile long. She turned once and gave me a deeply suggestive look, her silky pyjamas shimmering exotically and dare I say it, erotically as well. The image of the pert cheeks of her backside clothed in pale grey opalescence has stayed with me ever since and has kept me going through many a lonely night.

We sat in silence for five minutes then Linda stood up. Something had caught her attention. Without saying anything she stood up on the bench and made her way round to a lintel on the inside front of the folly. Just above it there was a round hole. It was not in any geometric or artistic position, if you catch my drift, and seemed deliberately out of place.

'What's that?' She wasn't tall enough to reach it.

None of us were. Abandoning any attempt to form a human pyramid we spent the next hour trying to track down a ladder. There was one in the greenhouse not far from the orangery but it was a tall double wooden stepladder, splattered with paint, that weighed a ton. It took all four of us, with great effort, some time to manoeuvre across the ornamental gardens to the folly. At one point I managed to crush, with a distinct display of alacrity, a rather large vertical cotoneaster.

Back in the folly we pushed Linda up the ladder.

'It's a stone tube.' There was a long pause. 'There's a crosshair at this end and one at the other.'

'Line them up.' Arden had one hand on his chin, his head lowered in thought.

'Line them up? Oh, yes, I see...' Linda took her time then in a triumphant shout called out, 'It's fixed on a spot on the other side of the house. A low outcrop of rock.'

'Thought it might be something like that.' Arden nodded to himself.

Arrogant sod. He had no idea at all. I was about to say something to that effect but Gus caught my eye and subtly shook his head. Against the imp of the perverse, I capitulated.

We took it in turns to confirm Linda's observations and agreed that the crosshairs did indeed point to a rocky wall of rock on the other side of the grounds and somewhat behind the house. I must admit at this point I felt something akin to a growing excitement. It was all a bit *Boy's Own*. Dashing adventures in country estates. I wanted a banded cap and some knee length shorts to put on. Whacko!

We left the ladder where it was and beetled off across the lawns in the direction of the rocky outcrop. Linda and Arden set the pace with Gus and myself traipsing some way behind.

'Can you believe all of this?' Gus held back a few steps to ask me the question. He obviously wanted to be beyond earshot of the other two or so I thought.

'Having second thoughts? I asked.

'No, I mean isn't it exciting. We're on the trail.'

'Of what precisely?'

'That's the point. Who knows?'

'You're convinced the third key is here somewhere?'

'Yeah, I think so. I know it is.' Gus pointed ahead at Arden.

'He wanted it to be in Dashwood's church, didn't he?'

'That was a novel, man. Everything's pointing to the fact that it's here.'

'Okay, not strictly true.' Well it wasn't. There was something going on here without a doubt but a grand mystery leading us to a key?

'Come on. Look at what we're doing now. Following clues around a country estate. Somebody's hiding something.'

'Possibly. But why? Why hide things where they can be found using clues? If you wanted to protect a great secret why not just destroy the wretched thing and forget all about it? It's the obvious course of action.'

'Maybe the time isn't right for the secret to be known.' Gus smiled. 'Maybe the people doing the hiding want to keep it out of the hands of the enemy.'

Gus, it seemed, had now read too much Arden.

We reached the outcrop of rock but, to tell you the truth, it looked artificial. I mean that the whole pile had been brought there and dumped, albeit rather artistically in that fake folly-esque way. Linda, Gus and Arden began sniffing around while I held back to cast a critical eye over the low cliff face that presented itself for inspection.

'Here we go.' It was Gus's turn. He stood before a cunningly concealed entrance draped in thick foliage that gave the opening a rather lewd and suggestive appearance. 'I've found a cave and look, a labyrinth.'

The rest of us moved to join him.

Just outside the entrance there was a carving of a symbolic labyrinth, a pattern I'd seen on the floor of a cathedral in France. Amiens, I think it was...

Linda traced her finger around the pattern.

'The legend is, that if you failed to find the labyrinth you were hung.' Linda's voice was soft. 'And at the centre there's a flower.'

'Some reward,' I quipped.

'What's the difference between a maze and a labyrinth?' Gus scratched his nose.

'A maze is designed to get you lost while a labyrinth is designed to guide you to the middle.' Linda retraced the labyrinth in reverse. 'A labyrinth is more meditative.'

'Let's go and see what's inside.' Arden crossed the threshold and disappeared into the darkness. A moment later I heard a lighter flick open, followed by a flinty rasp. A small flame lit up the writer's face.

It wasn't really a labyrinth at all; more a series of snaking passages that in odd places, seemed to double back on themselves. At one junction I lost the others and found myself on a small terrace overlooking the countryside. I paused for a breather and allowed my thoughts to drift off across the fields. A bit, as they say, of normality was required.

My head was fuzzy. Of late the old thing had been awash with vast quantities of mad information coming at me from all directions. Hiddon, sunspheres, keys, secrets, mysteries, silky pyjamas. I was starting to feel dopey. I could sense my old way of seeing things drifting away like a lifeboat disappearing over the horizon. Conspiracies were a drug; a dangerous opiate that dragged everyone and everything into a maelstrom of a chaotic netherworld of hysteria. Plots on plots were order of the day but like the bogus hierarchies of historical secret societies; Templars begetting Masons, Rosicrucians controlling the Bilderbergs and so on and so forth; it was a mess of bad history, ridiculous story telling and woeful invention. At least that's what I was trying to tell myself. I had to. To keep a grip.

This whirling, dizzying vortex of half concealed alternative histories blended with misinformation, odd contradictions and half-truths, like a grand game of Chinese whispers, was dissolving my grey matter. It was beating my well-hewn cynicism into submission.

I was also starting to feel hungry.

As I leant on a handrail, movement below caught my eye. Linda had popped out of an opening on a lower level and looked almost as confused as I felt.

'You lost?' I asked. 'I know I am.'

'How did you get up there?'

'No idea. A wrong turn somewhere.'

'This is supposed to be a labyrinth not a maze.' Linda put her hands on her hips and looked around. She turned and went back the way she had come.

I took one last look at the green of the countryside, breathed deeply and reluctantly made my way back into the dark.

When, eventually, I found the others they were standing in a chamber lit from above by weak daylight beaming down a narrow shaft that led all the way to the top of the outcrop. They were looking at a pedestal with a flat surface into which a flower had been carved. It was pitted and eroded from rainwater and much of its surface was blotched with various lichens and mosses.

'There's your flower Lin.' Gus rubbed his hand on the embossed image. 'There you are. Did you get lost?'

'I wish. I took a wrong turn somewhere and ended up… somewhere…' I stepped up to the plinth. 'What have we got here?'

'It's the flower at the centre of the labyrinth.' Linda's smile had something of a reverential nature to it.

'Fair Rosamund,' said I.

'What?' Gus frowned.

'Fair Rosamund. Kept at the centre of a labyrinth by Henry the Second. Built in Woodstock I think.' I tried to sounds as convincing as my feeble memory would allow.

'Or the Minotaur.' Gus smirked.

'The Cretan labyrinth, constructed by Daedalus,' Arden added, his attention firmly on the flower image. 'Not to be confused with the Cretan Conduit which had a thousand turns.'

'Like a summer run in a Blackpool nightclub.' My feeble joke fell firmly infertile upon stony ground.

'The biggest was The Egyptian near Lake Moeris. Designed by Petesuchis.' Arden dropped to his haunches.

'That one had three thousand rooms, half of them underground.' He started to run his hands around the column of the pedestal.

'Thank heaven nobody decided to recreate that one here. We would've been lost for weeks.'

'You would've,' Gus sneered.

'Cheers,' I retorted. I wanted to add a scathing pile of verbose denouncements encompassing everything that had happened in the last few days, but resisted. It wasn't easy. One sharp verbal jab in the wrong place and I'd be off like a geyser.

'Anything there?' Linda's attention was focused squarely on Arden whose fingertips were stroking the stonework.

'Appears to be writing,' he replied, dropping his head to one side.

'Those who seek a mystery will find it. Those who seek the truth must lose it.' Arden read it again, silently to himself, his mouth forming the words.

'What does that mean?' Gus's puzzlement had a hint of irritation.

'What's the 'it'?' Linda bent down to read the words, positioning herself a little too close to Arden for his comfort.

'Is it a code?' Gus was looking around the walls of the chamber. 'Is anything else carved into the pedestal?'

'I'm looking,' Arden snapped back. 'Wait. What's this?'

On the opposite side to the writing was an image of a classic maze. You know the kind. The ones you see in the activity pages of kids' comics.

'I wonder if the couplet refers to the maze.' Linda's mind was off. 'The way,' she added. 'You must find the way then lose the way to get to the secret.'

Well of course the couplet could've meant anything. How about *stupidity*? Or *ignorance*? If anyone had cared to ask me, that's the answer I would've given. But nobody did. I think they sensed my continuing ambivalence coated in a shiny veneer of glistening sarcasm.

'I don't think I've seen a maze in the grounds.' Gus folded his arms then placed one hand over his mouth and tapped gently while he engaged his grey matter. Something caught his eye. 'Look.'

We did.

Above the door to another tunnel, one we hadn't yet taken, was that now familiar image of a sun with the triangular beam of light. It was faint but still legible, coated in dark lichen and softened over the years by damp that had rotted the rock.

'That way.' Arden was up and making his way swiftly down the passage before I'd even registered the image. It was hard to make out.

As far as I could tell, the tunnel led in the opposite direction to the house. It snaked its way through the outcrop and to my reckoning it was by far the longest passage in this so-called labyrinth. There was little ambient light and Arden had to resort to using his lighter again. All I wanted was a Hollywood leg bone wrapped in an oily rag. Where was a rotting corpse when you needed one?

'Hey man, you can't say this isn't exciting,' Gus half turned to speak to me.

'Ooo yeah.' My mocking tone was dressed up in a fake excitement. 'All the garden lacks is a pentagram and Charles Gray in a smock!'

'We might find them yet,' came Gus's reply. 'Come on keep up.'

Egad. Gus was serious.

Arden, who had taken on the role of group leader, an alpha writer by the look of things, stepped out of the tunnel onto a wide patch of grass followed closely by Linda. I wasn't far behind Gus, despite his accusations illustrating my passion for dawdling.

Ahead there was an avenue of trees, which led directly to a gateway in a high hedge.

'Is that what I think it is?' Linda asked. She allowed a smile to flash across her face.

Arden nodded, then without further ado, walked briskly towards the opening.

'Maybe we should go for some lunch.' My suggestion, not totally unexpectedly, ran aground on the sands of deafness. 'A sandwich... or two?'

Gus threw me a look of disdain.

'Where's your sense of adventure?' he asked rather condescendingly.

By the time I reached the maze entrance, the others were already out of sight down gravel paths that spread out in all directions. The hedges were thick and neatly cut. No ragged holes to cheat through and it wasn't long before a mild sense of panic whistled through me. I was lost once, as small boy I hasten to add, in a Marks and Spencer's when, for an instant, my mother let go of my hand. I was experiencing an echo of that panic now. Tall beige slacks replaced with high green hedges to hem me in.

'Hello?' I called not too loudly I admit but... well, I didn't want to sound too helpless.

I heard voices coming along one path and made my way swiftly in their direction but when I turned the corner there was no one there. My mild sense of panic soon became irritation. I think hunger had something to do with it, but I was getting totally hacked off with the whole bloody situation.

The Safe House

"Buchanan said something about a book. The reason for coming to Providence." Arden winced as Madsen dressed his wound. "You said you had it."

"You were too slow getting over the railings." Madsen split the bandage and tied a knot.

"Yes, but I'm keeping it safe." Parks poured hot water into three cups of coffee. "I'm sorry but this is instant. I do not have the facilities here to brew fresh coffee."

"Instant? Is there any other kind?" Arden grinned, his smile turning into a grimace of pain. "That's the only coffee I know."

"Philistine. Don't worry, as the cliché has it, you'll live." Madsen stood. "They–" Madsen paused. "Don't know about this place?"

Parks handed him a mug.

"No. It's been a safe house for a while. It's rented under a false name." Parks then held out a mug for Arden who took it and inhaled the aroma.

"Man, that's good."

"Mister Arden, this is not good coffee." Parks sat down at the kitchen table and Madsen joined him. Arden stayed where he was on the small sofa.

"So they want this book?" Madsen cupped both hands around his mug.

"They do. But more importantly they want that page. The one you saw Mister Madsen and the one your friend was carrying Mister Arden. If they had it they would've stopped following us."

"Listen Parks, I'm Mark, he's Josh. Stop being so old school."

Parks ignored him.

"That page is the most important because it contains clues on how to open the Sunsphere."

"The what?" Arden winced again.

"Do you mean the golden orb on the statue on the Customs House in Venice?" Madsen asked.

Parks nodded.

"The sunsphere represents the Ordines. The Ordines have a great secret that a certain individual and his organisation want destroyed." Parks turned his attention to Arden. "Buchanan told you some of this?"

"A little." Arden nodded. "Mostly about who and what the Ordines were or rather are about. He said some other stuff too that didn't make much sense."

"You were never initiated Mister Arden – Mark. But I will for the moment ignore that fact."

"Thank you. I seem to know too much anyway."

"And that is enough to threaten your life."

"That's a shame. I was looking forward to getting my calf skin apron." Arden grinned.

"Initiation is more than that Mister – Mark. It's about waking up to reality. A new perspective on things. You are no longer one of the herd." Parks sat back looking somewhat downhearted. "Unfortunately circumstances have forced my hand."

"Are the Freemasons allies of the Ordines?" Madsen took a sip of hot coffee.

"Some are. Only the high ranked Freemasons 33 degrees and above know of our existence. Remember we are just the… I can't think of the correct term."

"Foot soldiers?" Arden sat up slowly.

"As good as any. There are only three Ordines at any one time and by that I mean those who run things. There are many of us who know of their existence and what they want but only three who make the decisions."

"Why only three?" Madsen looked puzzled, more so when Arden answered him.

"Because there's never a hung vote."

"Indeed, Mark. The decisions are thought out and planned and every angle considered. There are three at the top and the rest below." Parks raised a hand then lowered it in emphasis.

"A sort of holy trinity."

"Yes, Mister Madsen – Josh. But without the paraphernalia of religion. The decisions are all rational and constructed around reason. There's no calling on of a higher power."

"Why not?" Arden moved to the table and sat down.

"Because there isn't one." Parks studied the younger man for a reaction.

"As I've always thought anyway," Arden quipped.

Madsen smiled.

Parks turned to him.

"And you Josh?"

"No. I just looked around and realised it was all nonsense." Madsen stared into his coffee. "Something full of false hope that has taken us down a dead end full of bloodshed and fear."

Parks nodded appreciatively.

"So what's the secret?" Arden studied his bandage.

"No one knows. Something powerful." Parks was staring into space.

"Nice one Parks. A secret that no one knows. It's another empty room again isn't it?" Arden shook his head.

"Yes, there is that possibility. But like every puzzle there is a solution. Besides, a great number of people have died because of it."

"There's a change." Arden's tone was once more dismissive. "Doesn't make it true though."

"Come on Mark." Madsen held up a hand. "I want to hear more about this."

Arden glared across the table at Madsen.

Parks continued.

"There is a story of a Giovanni Bertorelli, in the early 17th century, falling to his death from the roof of the Customs House. I read about this in an unusual book that came into my possession. Alchemy in Venice by Padrone D'Oro, which had rumours of lost secrets in the city."

"Ouch."

Madsen gave Arden a sour look then turned his attention back to Parks.

"Bertorelli was an alchemist and it was said he was trying to get into the sunsphere on top of the building. It was supposed to contain a great secret. He thought that it had something to do with the great work. In alchemy there is Sol or the sun, which is the masculine principal. The book also said that there is a key. A key to disarm the traps. If that's true or not I don't know." Parks was lost in his thoughts for a few moments.

"A key?" Madsen asked, sensing that Parks was being less than forthcoming.

"Yes. Apparently. But the story goes that it has been missing for four hundred years."

"How does this Francis Dashwood you told me about fit into the story?"

"Dashwood." Parks took a sip of coffee. "Everybody despised him for his humanist views. Yes, he was a carouser but he was so much more. They tried to defame him and for the most part they succeeded. But he never worshipped the devil. He hated the church for its hypocrisy. Reciprocally therefore the church hated him. But he just stood up against something he knew to be wrong. He had a good sense of humour. In the Sistine chapel he managed to convince a group of flagellants that he was the devil and set about them with a whip." Parks grinned, which surprised both Arden and Madsen. It was the first time they had seen him do so. "All he did throughout his life was thumb his nose at the power-hungry who controlled the church."

"I'm all in favour of that," Arden laughed.

"Certainly. Anyway, Dashwood was initiated into the Freemasons, as well as setting up a few of his own secret societies one of which was the Hell Fire Club. Did you know, by the way, that Benjamin Franklin was a member?" Parks allowed that to sink in, then continued. "While he was renovating the church of St Lawrence in West Wycombe in England, Dashwood based one improvement on the Customs House in Venice. A duplicate sunsphere. Thus announcing his allegiance to the Ordines, who go under that sign. This one though had three seats built into it."

"Did Dashwood copy everything from the Customs House sphere?"

"Not sure Josh. He owned the book and therefore knew the sphere and its inherent traps. But it's obvious he didn't have the key, which was lost a hundred years or so before. He could not have known what was inside."

"So are the Ordines protecting this secret?" Arden asked.

"Yes and no," Parks replied cryptically.

"That's hedging your bets." Arden winced a little, his hand above the bandage.

"I mean that, yes, for the moment the Ordines are but only by default. The key was lost. When they find the key the secret will be revealed."

"Can I assume that the Ordines are not the only ones who know what the secret is?" Madsen asked.

"But only that there is a secret and a powerful one at that," Parks said. "They are planning another Renaissance, of sorts. They believe, as I do, that it's time for humanity to put aside superstition and stupidity. It's time to leave the cradle. We've lived in fear far too long. A fear created by those who wish to control us. Unfortunately, these same people are determined to keep the secret for themselves."

"Why bother? Science is blowing away all the bullshit anyway." Arden's tone was bullish.

"And are we any better off? Science needs room to breathe." Parks turned his attention to the younger man.

"I think so," Arden retorted.

"I on the other hand do not. Yes, it's there but this is still a demon-haunted world. People are not allowed to think. We are surrounded by a theatre of lies and deception and if that continues we will all be in danger. There are those who wish to maintain this darkness of ignorance."

"It must be a dangerous secret if people want us dead?" Arden looked sceptical.

"And have killed already," Madsen added.

"Indeed. It's about clouding reality for the gain of a minority." Parks stood up and made his way to the window. "I suggest we get some rest." Looking out, the lights of

Providence offered little comfort. He could see the pale grey of the State House with its tall cupola and pinnacle surrounded by the four smaller columned towers lit up against the night. He had always sought comfort in this view; now it seemed to offer nothing but dread.

"What next?" Madsen closed his eyes for a moment feeling a sudden tiredness.

"May I have the CD? I wish to examine the lost page." Parks turned from the window.

Madsen reached into his pocket and took out the CD. He held it between finger and thumb, reluctant to let it go. He thought of Hiroko.

Parks saw his hesitation.

"You can trust me," he said, smiling.

Arden studied both men. He had concluded that Madsen was a man of his word, but Parks... He had not made his mind up about the man yet. The man seemed driven by a personal agenda. He was just not sure if it was one that included both himself and Madsen.

"Mister Madsen. Josh. You can trust me. I am not the enemy." Parks turned and looked directly at him.

Madsen nodded. He placed the CD on the table. Then, after a long pause, slid it across towards Parks.

"If we don't have the key, what good is looking at the missing page?" Arden drained his coffee.

"I'm not sure. On a purely selfish level I have never seen it. But maybe there's something I can learn from it." Parks reached down and picked up the CD.

For a split second Madsen thought it would be the last he would ever see of it. Now, though, he was too exhausted to care. In many ways he wanted out. He wanted to go back to the way things were. Yet he knew that until this was all over, returning home would be an impossibility. At the very least he owed it to Hiroko and according to Parks, there were greater stakes.

"That's mine." Arden made his way back to the sofa and collapsed into it, screwing his face up as an excruciating pain reminded him of his wound.

"There's a spare room through there." Parks pointed down the short hall to a room at the back of the house.

Madsen stood up, his body leaden with tiredness.

"Thank you. For everything."

"Think nothing of it."

In his dream, Madsen was clambering up onto the roof of the Customs House. Before him he could see the sunsphere and the statue of Fortune. Behind it the night sky was shot with a million suns. Making his way up to the plinth he gripped the edge and pulled himself up. The sphere was cool to the touch. He ran his hands around its surface searching for something. The next moment he was falling – falling – an endless drop… and as he hit the water he lurched from sleep.

The house was quiet. Empty it seemed. The first signs of dawn were visible through the curtains but this only added to his sense of isolation. He felt terribly alone. It seemed as if the world had become a desolate place devoid of love, laughter and humanity.

He sat up on the edge of the bed. His attention was drawn to the window and the houses beyond. They were all bleak, lifeless, full of shadows and washed in the dark blues of morning.

He took out his cellphone to check the time. The battery was dead. He sighed.

Opening the door to the room he could hear the gentle hum of a computer. To his right he could see that a sidelight was on in an adjacent room. Looking through the crack in the door he could see Parks studying the image of the page.

Madsen knocked gently.

"You found anything?" he asked.

Parks said nothing for a moment then sat back.

"I have. Well, a few things actually. Come in." Parks pointed to another seat nearby. Madsen moved the chair closer to the computer and sat down.

"The idea that the sphere is protected is true. There's a release mechanism. That triangle shape there."

"Triangle. Three sides. Three Ordines."

"My thoughts exactly." Parks pointed at the screen. "Extrapolating that idea. It is safe to assume that there are two more of the same."

"Seems logical. If the three are supposed to open the sphere then it would have to be simultaneously." Madsen ran a hand around his chin.

"Unless of course it's just two. Two to make sure that every decision is never a hung vote. But I agree with you. It's a bit like the failsafe keys on nuclear missiles – you need both to turn at exactly the same time before a launch can take place."

"Let's hope the sunsphere is not a nuclear bomb," Madsen said dryly.

"What is inside may be far more powerful." There was no humour in Parks's tone.

"You think so?"

"I do Mister Madsen. Something far more potent."

"Like what?"

"The truth."

"The truth?"

"The most powerful thing there is. It's hard to believe that this statue may contain a secret that could threaten so much."

"Exciting uh?" Madsen's tone was deadpan.

"Oh yes. Very." Parks nodded.

Madsen studied the image.

"So what next?" He asked.

"Good question Mister Madsen. Do you have a passport?"

"Not on me. I can have it sent though. I'll need to make a phone call but my cell's dead. Why?"

"Just as well. There's a pay phone down the road. Use that, it will be safer. But please be careful what you say. I cannot stress that enough. Use a false name."

"Where are we going?"

"England."

In A Maze Or A Labyrinth?

What was it I once heard? In a maze stick to one wall and keep going. Easier said than done. I tried, then discovered that the hedge I was following was a large fat 'L' shape and within a matter of moments I was back where I'd started.

I spent the next half an hour or so beetling this way and that and getting precisely nowhere. I was just about to launch into a vitriolic tirade against the whole caper when I turned a corner and found the dynamic trio standing in an open area in front of a small mausoleum.

'How long have you been here?' I snapped.

'Twenty minutes.' Gus grinned. 'Get lost?'

'Of course I bloody did... and what's that?'

'We're about to find out.' There was an aggressive tone to Arden's response. I hadn't actually expected one from him but there it was in all its rumbustuous glory.

It was a stone edifice some fifteen feet high made of the same stone as the house. There was a column at each corner and a single door on what I took to be the west side. I couldn't be sure of directions anymore. Around the cornicing there were embossed images, one or two with a distinctly Masonic flavour to them. There was a three runged ladder, a gavel, chisel and maul, the familiar compass and dividers and a globe. But there was also the, by now familiar, sun icon. This one though was in gold – a metal inlay.

Arden put his hand on the door and pushed. He stuck his lower lip out a little and made a *hmmm* sound. Stepping back he examined the stonework either side of the door.

'What are those?' Again, there I was with an obvious question. There were plates, roughly six inches a side set into the walls.

Arden tapped one. It sprung open to reveal a keyhole. Above it, again, was the familiar gold sun but this one matched the one on Gus's key in that it was missing the right hand edge of the ray.

Gus slapped his pockets. He then reached into one and lifted out his key as Arden opened the other plate. Sure enough it matched his key.

Both fellows inserted their respective keys. Like a missile silo launch control, it was impossible for one person to reach both locks and turn the keys simultaneously. Arden looked at Gus who nodded. Both men counted down from three then turned.

There was a satisfying clink-clonk and the door swung open a few inches. Linda did the honours and pushed it wider. The inside was empty. Just blank stone walls but in the middle of the floor was a descending staircase. I expected Arden to let Linda have the honours and go first but instead he pushed forward and crossed the threshold ahead of her. Ungracious bastard.

Down we all went into the bowels of the Earth. Well, okay, about twenty feet. Now this was an impressive tunnel. It was lined with red brick and every now and then there were iron torch holders in embrasures. All they lacked was a stick of wood dipped in tar or pitch or whatever it was they lit the things with.

It was just a shame we weren't running from a gun battle in a Masonic lodge. I was tempted to say this out loud, but once more resisted shooting my mouth off for fear of alienating my colleagues even more and upsetting Arden further for having the cheek to take the mickey out of his best selling novel. I think, if the truth be known, I was beyond redemption. To them I was a cynical non-believer blind to the obvious mystery that was unfolding.

But, and it's a big but, I had to admit what we'd found so far was at least intriguing, if nothing else. Trouble is, you can dress some things up to make them look more than they are. It's a staple of modern living and frankly that's how conspiracy theories work – or rather don't. A mystery wraps an enigma wraps a paradox, which encircles... absolutely nothing... fresh air... a void. So much of the world around us is presentation. Show. Artifice. Tinsel and glamour around so much... zip.

I should have gone home there and then. I felt a knot in my insides – anxiety or tension – fight or flight. But I didn't. And do you know why? Because the perverse side of my nature wanted to see spectacular amounts of egg on faces. I wanted to inwardly gloat that my cynicism was justified. I wanted to see people looking sheepish. I wanted to get a kick out of people making right round and royal idiots of themselves. What was that expression? *Schadenfreude*. Oh yes... but writ large.

Only they wouldn't admit they were wrong, would they? Go on admit it. You know they wouldn't. It would be like that Captain Mainwaring mantra, *I was just waiting to see who would spot that...*

On and on we walked. I was suffering under the distinct impression that we were not heading in a straight line. I wasn't sure of course but there was a sense we were heading in a great arc. This, as it happened, proved to be correct, as on reaching a door at the top of a flight of steps, after a good long walk in darkness, we stepped out into the library. Four pairs of eyes blinked with the light and a high degree of surprise.

'What was all that about?' I asked, resisting the temptations to finger point and utter a very childish playground taunt.

'There's obviously a reason.' Linda's reply was aimed not just at me but the other two as well. Doubtless it was also

aimed at herself in a rhetorical way as a comforting answer...
of sorts. She held both hands over her mouth and shook her
head gently, unable to fathom this rather jolly turn up for the
books.

Arden cast his eyes around then walked briskly to the
shelving opposite.

'Did we miss something?' Gus moved out onto the
library floor. He held his hands out and looked up as if to
admonish the gods of high jinks and capering.

I can't say wasn't surprised. Even hard-nosed old me
was smirking at the hilarity of the situation.

Gus's mobile chimed. He answered. It was Alexia
wondering where we were. Gus, in a peculiar move, turned
away to talk to her.

'Why bring us all the way back here?' Linda was still
shaking her head. 'I wonder if there was something back in
the tunnel we missed. Like a hidden room or other turnings?'

'Someone's having a laugh,' I chipped in.

Suddenly, in front of Arden, a section of bookshelf
swung open. He stepped back and held his arms wide.

'How did that happen?' Linda asked.

'I should imagine...' Arden made his way over to the
door to the tunnel and examined the release mechanism.
'That bookshelf wouldn't open unless this door was engaged.
We had to go through the maze and the tunnel to open that
secret room.'

'Alexia said come and eat – wow, what's that?' Gus
snapped his phone shut.

We all made our way to the opening of the newly
revealed room. I say room; it was more like a large cupboard
akin to a walk-in wardrobe. There was a single shelf on
which were stacked a number of books and a series of
manuscripts. Above them was, yeah verily indeed, the
sunsphere logo and above that were the words *Vide, Aude* and
Tace. Latin for *see, listen* and *be silent*.

'Those words are usually found in a Masonic lodge.' Arden tugged at his Adam's apple. 'Look at the floor.' It was a chequerboard pattern.

'If you stand on the wrong tile poison arrows shoot out of the walls.' I had waited for years to use an Indiana Jones reference. It seemed like the ideal opportunity to do so now. I kid you not, all three of them turned to look at me. 'It's a joke.'

Even though I was being flippant, my default state, Arden was cautious when he stepped through the door. He looked up. There was a ridiculously ornate lamp above his head, which had mysteriously come on when the door was first opened.

'Careful.' Gus meant it.

Arden paused. Looking around again his eyes fell on a slot in the inner doorframe. He turned and looked on the other side. He took out his key and tried it in the slot. It didn't fit the one on the right so he tried the other. Click. It fitted perfectly.

'Gus. Your key.' Arden held out a hand. Gus handed it over.

Click.

There was the sound of a mechanism, all whirrs and soft clicks.

'Whatever it was, it's disarmed.' Linda's face carried a worried expression.

Arden placed a foot on the floor.

Rather boringly… nothing happened.

Some time later, we adjourned to the dining room where Alexia, or rather Alexia's sidekick Retinger, had delivered unto us a slap up meal of great sumptuousness. We discussed the day's events leaving Alexia amazed. Although, I had to admit, I detected a little bit of fakery around her demeanour. I couldn't believe that all the time she'd been here she had not taken a stroll around the grounds.

283

Well apparently not. Due to the lavish lifestyle she had once enjoyed. Parties mostly. All round Europe, from Monaco to Paris via Milan and just coincidentally, Venice. Inspired by the Masques there, she and her husband had attended; they swung a few in Somerset to try and recapture the spirit of the times. I should imagine it was far from the romance of Venezia but hey, who am I to scoff?

She told us that her husband had never mentioned Hiddon or grand secrets but she was mightily pleased that the house had some mystique associated with it now. Surely that would increase its value on the open market. Gus was quick to reply in the affirmative. What did he know though? He was no vulturous estate agent.

Arden made a great play of the documents we found in the secret cupboard. Well he would, wouldn't he? Alexia with a whoop of delight demanded that she be shown everything. Retinger, on the other hand, seemed guarded and reluctant to join in. I caught his eye a few times but I didn't detect anything. If he was the sneaking shadow, which sounded like an old radio drama character from the fifties, he was giving nothing away. Anyway he was too short. Over the years I'd had all kinds of rubbish thrown at me, other people's insecurities mostly – I was a crap magnet – but I wasn't about to go doing the same to him.

As the afternoon had cracked on apace into evening, we all agreed to show Alexia our *discoveries* the following day.

To save time we divided the finds and made off to our respective rooms. I didn't want to start looking at anything as old Mister Sandman was starting his nonsense, but I lay there knowing there would be little chance of nodding off until I'd at least glanced at my share of the booty. I reached for the notebook.

I had been given one of the standout items in the collection. It was a thin leather-bound tome, with marbled end papers, that had once belonged to one Gregory Fishlock Squires who, according to some attached notes, added much later, stated that he was an amateur archaeologist and antiquarian working in the early part of the twentieth century. The man had become fascinated by Hiddon after visiting the house in March of 1937 and had spent much of the remainder of his short life dedicated to finding out as much as possible about the fellow and, of course, the secret. Squires, according to the notes, was killed on D-Day, so never completed his investigations. Oddly enough, the notes also say he was shot in the back as he made his way up the beach from a landing craft.

The Garden of Earthly Delights

was inscribed in flowing pen strokes on the first page. The name of that manuscript Gus had found. Well I never...

Over the page Squires had written:

The Garden of Earthy Delights was written sometime within the last hundred years but, as yet, I am unable to ascertain an exact date or the true identity of the author. I have hidden the book due to the undeniable fact that certain individuals, through clandestine activities, have made it clear that they seek this work for nefarious purposes. Only last Tuesday I had returned home to discover that my study had suffered at the hands of miscreant felons who had set about my sanctuary no doubt to uncover the whereabouts of that rare item.

I have thus undertaken a précis of the novel so that should the manuscript itself be lost, there is at least a written record of the story that is a shocking tale of the excesses of largesse, moral imbalance and the machinations of secret societies in a time of Revolution. But one that also offers a startling revelation...

Whoopee! That was the kind of thing I liked to get stuck into.

Thomas Hiddon, unable to make a living as a surveyor, has returned to England from the Colony of America now in the initial stages of Revolution. Unable to convince anyone of his ability in his homeland, he is thought of as an American spy, changes profession and becomes an official debt collector offering his services to the Aristocrats who have been wronged through gambling debts.

He secures his first job and pursues a debt-ridden rake through Europe and succeeds in cornering the man much to the delight of the gentleman who hired him. Hiddon is bribed with a golden key that may unlock a great secret. He is also richly rewarded but subsequently spends beyond his means and he too finds himself in a precarious situation financially. Yet he manages to cover it well. Successive employment, although regular, is poorly paid. The Aristocrats who hire him are reluctant to part with large sums of cash and are more interested in having honour satisfied. He is pursued though by shadowy figures who may be after the key. (*Note: The key itself seems like a side story – and plays little part in the Garden of Earthly Delights per se – its inclusion in the story seems oddly out of place – but I may be very wrong*)

Hiddon is now caught in an unsettled and somewhat peripatetic lifestyle. But his luck may be about to change. As a reward for services rendered he is initiated into a quasi-Masonic order called the Ordines and there he meets an Earl who knows someone who is looking for a man such as Hiddon – tenacious yet skilled in the arts of surveying. Hiddon is puzzled but agrees to the job.

He is introduced to a Masonic agent who informs Hiddon that his services are required by Lord Llewelyn Carey-Hunt, who lives in a rambling generations-old seat in the west of England. Before Hiddon is allowed to travel he is asked to sign a contract, witnessed by other members of the Ordines, that Hiddon will not reveal anything he is told on forfeit of death. With nothing to lose, Hiddon agrees and signs the contract.

Hiddon is then driven to the country estate. It is enormous, stretching almost, it seems, from horizon to horizon, a vast parkland of ornate ponds, deep bowers, a hedge maze and lost, overgrown ruins. At its heart is an enormous lake. If he is to survey this landscape it will take him many months the result of which will mean an increase in earnings.

Hiddon pauses at the door of the mansion house, an impressive pile, yet there are hints of decline – the curtains look somewhat jaded and the doors stick. Damp runs amok in places, the fountains have stopped working and parts of the garden need cutting back.

He is met by one of Carey-Hunt's servants and is led through to meet his Lordship. At dinner that evening the two men sit alone and Hiddon discovers a little more about his host. Llewelyn Carey-Hunt has fallen on hard times and is desperate for some cash to keep up his opulent lifestyle and to keep his three daughters in the manner in which they have grown to expect. He still holds lavish parties, but he is at the point where he will be ostracised from society. At one social function he was talking quietly to a friend of his, who was something of a lush himself, about his perilous situation. His friend told him he knew of a man who chases debts, mostly of a gambling nature and found missing money for aristocrats around the courts and palaces of Europe. He is also a skilled man in the arts of surveying and will certainly be able to help. This man is Hiddon.

Hiddon then asks him why he needs a surveyor. Carey-Hunt replies, saying he needs someone who will stick to their job, be tenacious in the execution of their duties, prove skilled in following clues and also in the land arts. Carey-Hunt says he cannot pay, but is told that the debt chaser will work for a percentage of the retrieved money. Hiddon is somewhat confused but intrigued nonetheless.

Lord Carey-Hunt then reveals he inherited this house when he was ten years old and was told, when he turned twenty-one, that the magnificent garden contained a secret. Hidden around the grounds and in the house itself are clues to the whereabouts of a great treasure. To find it one had to gather all the clues and decipher the code. But his Lordship has been unable to decipher anything. For years he ignored the garden. In short, he was too wealthy, but some bad investments and a lavish lifestyle have put paid to his fortune. Now his interest has grown to the point of obsession and he needs the treasure to save face and to keep himself in society's upper echelons.

The young man agrees to help for a percentage of the discovery. Carey-Hunt is pleased and another contract is drawn up. Both men shake hands. The agreement is made.

Hiddon then sets about making himself comfortable in his master's house and makes the additional stunning discovery that the man has three beautiful daughters. The eldest, Emily, entranced by Hiddon, makes a move first and tries to seduce the young man. But he has his eyes on the middle daughter, Sarah, a stunning raven-haired beauty. None of this is lost on his Lordship who starts to manipulate the situation. If he can substitute one of his daughters as a reward he can then claim all of the treasure. While the young man begins to gather the clues he is seduced by the daughters – something Lord Carey-Hunt allows to happen – and he begins to lose sense of reality. The grounds have a haunting quality to them – or is it just the delusions of love?

Carey-Hunt, having kept a careful eye on Hiddon, then blackmails the young man saying that the fellow has seduced his daughters and soiled their honour. For that he is angry (it's all a put on) and says that if he hands over his percentage of the treasure he will say nothing and allow the young man to leave with his reputation intact.

Hiddon has fallen in love with Sarah despite the attempts of the other sisters to seduce him. And soon he cares more about her than the treasure. The clues come slower now and he spends all night thinking about her, creeping to her room at one point to woo her.

Carey-Hunt begins to worry that things are going too slowly. He has a large social event in two month's time – an elaborate Masque that includes a mock sea battle on the lake using small-scale galleons decked in gold and bright banners and needs the additional money to make the party extra special. It may be his last for some time. Important guests have been invited including Joseph Haydn, Benjamin Franklin and the King. He appears to be no nearer to the treasure and he is starting to panic.

The Lord then decides to keep Sarah away from the young man, locking her away in her room for 'safe keeping' – but he's also using her as a bribe to get the young man to get on with his job. He can have her full attentions when the treasure is found.

The young man continues with his quest, seeing only glimpses of the daughter through windows or from afar. If they do see each other it is always at a distance. Hiddon is also aware of others. There are strangers lurking in the trees and half glimpsed shadows that appear to be watching him. He also comes across a hermit who lives in a fake grotto created by Lord Carey-Hunt. The Hermit is being paid to live there but he is suffering a crisis of conscience and considers himself to be a fake and a worthless individual, as there are genuine hermits out there. He has taken on the life of a real ascetic but is also rattling through a variety of self-revelatory disciplines ranging from flagellation to starvation in an attempt to purge his soul, eating only vegetables in the process.

Hiddon goes to his weekly meetings with Carey-Hunt to tell him what he has found and begins to draw up everything he has discovered so far. Writings in grottoes, stone pillars, statues pointing in certain directions, odd markings in the landscape, *camera obscura* views from the top of the house– a whole host of clues in fact. A pattern is beginning to form and his Lordship is delighted – "his eyes gleamed with the colour of gold but it was not a warm light – it was cold, stark and metallic, full of the potential for great harm."

Hiddon is getting closer to solving the riddle, but he is also desperate to see Sarah, who is likewise desperate to see him. One night she slips from her room and meets the young man by the lake and they enjoy their first kiss – love is indeed in the air. The place has a magical quality about it and they make love in a boathouse and realise great truths about themselves and the nature of intimacy. Hiddon is no longer interested in a percentage of the treasure – all he wants is Sarah.

A short time before the day of the Masque the gardens are converted into a rich pageant of fantastic animals, banners and marquees. This does not help Hiddon, who has to continue his work interrupted by the 'peasants' from a small faux village on the estate who are there assisting the limited staff – suffering through financial cutbacks.

The day of the Masque arrives. Famous and infamous guests have appeared for the revels and despite a few accidents and mishaps the event seems to be going well. The Mystery figures from the woods are seen to mingle with the crowds but they go unmolested as they too wear disguises. While the party is in full swing Lord Carey-Hunt is alerted by one of his faithful servants that Sarah is missing from her room so the incensed man sets off to look for her and Hiddon. When he finds them he threatens to shoot the young man if he doesn't reveal the whereabouts of the treasure. Hiddon agrees and takes him up to a hidden pump room on a hill while fireworks boom and crackle in the sky. Here Hiddon turns off the flow of water that leads through a series of low gentle waterfalls to the lake. Hiddon then takes him to another hidden lock gate room and there he opens the sluices allowing the water to drain from the lake, through an underground culvert and away to a distant river. This takes some time.

As evening falls the next day, the water has gone leaving the ornate boats run aground but revealing a hidden entrance to an underground vault accessed by steps and tunnels deep beneath the earth – at one point joining natural caves.

Hiddon leads them into the vault – a tomb in which several stone coffins are on display. There are several adults and a number of smaller coffins. Carey-Hunt, eager for treasure smashes the lid off one of the coffins and finds the ancient bones of a young child. He's furious. Where's the treasure he was promised? Hiddon tells him this is it. Bones in a tomb.

Hiddon shows him one coffin lid, on which is carved '*Ecce Homo, Ecce Signum*'. Carey-Hunt is puzzled. Hiddon then reminds him of Pilate's words, '*Ecce Homo*' – '*Behold the man...*'

The Shadowy figures then appear – numerous men dressed not unlike highwaymen – black scarves across their mouths, pistols in their hands. They lead Carey-Hunt away and thank Hiddon for finding what they wanted. They knew the treasure was somewhere in England and had been searching for generations, eliminating each lead that came along. Hiddon realises he's been played and the British authorities were right to suspect him – they did think he was a spy – although he himself did not know it. Certain parties need this treasure to take to America, the real New Jerusalem, as some would have it. Like any powerful city, such as Venice, needed the bones of saints to attract the pious to swell the coffers of the church, the soon to be liberated America will need these remains. The masked men remove the coffins from the vault.

Carey-Hunt is taken away along with Sarah. Hiddon is left in the tomb unable to do anything but is his real quest about to begin? Searching for a way out, Hiddon discovers something missed by his captors...

Umm, sounded familiar. I mean a toff on his uppers resorting to treasure hunting in order to sort out his financial problems. Had Alexia's recently shuffled off hubby been thinking along the same lines as those taken by Lord Carey-Hunt?

What was more puzzling was that the rest of the notebook was missing, the pages having been torn out rather crudely as if done in a hurry. Here and there on the page stubs were indications that drawings had been made. I could just make out letters and the odd arrow or two pointing to what looked like walls or columns or whatever. Maybe those miscreant felons that Squires was in fear of had finally got what they wanted.

Stone coffins? Ecce homo?

A tomb of Christ? Under an English lake? Don't tell me that was what we were all looking for? The physical embodiment of the Holy Grail?

Holy Grail, huh?

A story that has spurred a multitude of people both real and fictional, ancient and modern, and who should have known better, into daft adventures and crusades to hunt down a make believe relic. It doesn't get more daft than that.

A body, a cup, a stone... a bloodline. Why not a fishing rod or a pile of week-old Templar laundry? Why not a tin of biscuits... sorry, unleavened bread, a lush carpet from Persia, a toilet bowl or a pair of stout waterproof sandals?

Why anything at all?

It was all just so pointless.

This really did start to hack me off. I could feel a cloud of indifference settle over me. No, more like one consisting of anger, anger that I had wasted any of my time on this fruitless quest.

I put the notebook down and went to the window. Slipping the catch, I opened it and breathed in great lungfuls of heady night air. Although still warm, the air had that edge to it to remind me that autumn was not far off, no doubt to be followed by a bleak and miserable winter. Seasonal disorder? You bet. I had it in bucket loads.

Then movement caught my eye.

That shadowy figure again, this time running across the lawn away from the terrace beneath my bedroom window. Whoever it was they skidaddled away in sharpish time. My first port of call in suspect town was Retinger but this figure was much taller than Alexia's retainer.

Just who the hell was it?

I waited a little longer to see if the figure would reappear but it didn't. I found myself checking the lock on the window and on the bedroom door. Feeling a bit spooked I sat on the edge of my bed and rested my chin in my hands unsure what to do. After a few minutes I decided to clamber back into bed.

I'd smuggled Gus's copy of *Sunsphere* with me when we'd left to come to the West Country, so I sat back to indulge in another section of that. But, as I read, I began to feel even more paranoid. Was it trying to tell me something?

I was being drawn into the intrigue and try as I might I just couldn't walk away. Maybe a part of me did want to see if it was all true. It was the *what if* that was so appealing. There was a part of me, a little voice that chastised my hard baked cynicism. Elements of doubt were creeping in. I mean, who could deny the maze, the tunnels and the keys? This Hiddon chappie. Alexia's husband apparently murdered. Squires shot leaving a landing craft. Were they really all connected like the clues we had followed around the garden?

I decided that I would chew the cud with Gus. I made my way down the hall to his room but heard voices coming from within. I also recognised Alexia's childlike giggling. My suspicions about them had proved pretty spot on. I crept back to my room and locked the door. Why? I have no idea but, maybe it had something to do with strange shadowy figures lurking in the privet hedges.

I was last down to breakfast. Which surprised me because I hadn't slept much and decided that eight o'clock was a good enough time to head downstairs. The dining room was full of idle chatter. Even Arden appeared to be running on fresh batteries. Alexia though was nowhere to be seen.

'Here he is,' Gus chirped. 'Find anything out?'

'Actually,' I paused for dramatic effect, 'I think I have.'

All eyes were on me.

'Okay,' I continued. 'Maybe.'

'Either you have or you haven't,' Arden sniped.

All right mate, less of the lip.

'The notebook contains the story of the *Garden of Earthly Delights*. A synopsis.'

'The Hiddon novel!' Gus was all smiles.

'The rest of the notebook has been torn out.' I helped myself to an enormous plate of bacon and sat down. 'But the upshot is that Hiddon drained the lake and found a tomb beneath it.'

'A tomb?' Linda's fork hovered above her plate.

'Yeah. The synopsis says... Oh, you can read it yourselves. But after following all the clues engineered into the landscape, Hiddon turns off the waterfall and drains the lake.'

'Did we miss a clue or two?' Gus asked.

'The novel makes no mention of what we've seen,' I said. 'It seems to be more of a romance between Hiddon and one of the daughters of the house owner. The clues throughout are different, as far as I can tell.'

'But the house is definitely the same?' Linda beamed.

I nodded.

Arden stood up and made his way to the double door.

'Where are you going Mark?' Linda asked.

'To drain the lake.'

I took my plate with me. Following the others across the lawn, I forked bacon into my mouth. It wasn't easy but I had to. To me, hunger trumps all other desires, except of course the urge for a damn good...

'The stopcock was in a pump room. The portico maybe,' I said, my mouth stuffed with bacon. 'There might not be anything there. It was just a novel. You know, a story.'

'We have to find out.' Linda had adopted her serious schoolmistress tone again.

Bringing up the rear I was the last to stand beneath the sheltering roof of the portico. A light drizzle had started to fall and I was glad to get my bacon under cover.

'Did the synopsis actually say the portico?' Arden asked, arms akimbo, scanning the stonework.

'No,' came my honest reply. 'Just a pump room.'

Arden scowled. He then set off again, more slowly this time to look around.

'You could be more helpful,' Linda roundly chastised me.

'That's all I know,' I protested.

'Well... ' she continued.

'I can't tell you anymore than that.'

'You could just be more... involved.' She fired off a Parthian shot and walked away.

Okay, I'll make it up then in future. Just to satisfy her.

We spent the next hour sniffing high and low, looking for anything that might turn the waterfall off. For some time now I had been aware of Retinger hovering in the near distance. I would catch him looking in our direction while he attended to whatever it was he was doing within the grounds of the house. I was convinced now that he was not the night-time visitor. And when he came strolling over I could immediately tell his whole bearing was different to that of the person I had seen first by the temple folly and then from my window, assuming of course they were one and the same.

'What are you lookin' for this time?' His manner was brusque.

'How do we turn the waterfall off?' I had taken a five-minute breather on the lawn. I think I was almost hoping he would come over so I could suss him out.

He acted, by way of a response, by heading down to the first of the main arches that spanned the water. We'd actually missed a raised step some three feet above the splash. For something to do I followed him. In a recess in the arch was a wheel, which Retinger was now turning when I stuck my head round the corner.

'Mrs Carey-Hunt is keen to see what you find. That's why I'm doing this.' His voice started out loud above the roaring crash of water then softened as the water flow began to ease. I was aware of the others gathering round. 'Anything else?'

'How long will it take the lake to drain?' Gus asked.

'Drain the lake? I'll have to open the sluices to the river for that.'

'Would you?' Linda was all sweetness and light.

'Now?' Retinger asked.

We all made noises in the affirmative.

'It'll take a day or two to properly drain.' Retinger was already walking away. "Maybe longer."

While Retinger toddled off, the four of us made our way back to the house. Alexia was waiting for us, or let's be more specific, Gus. She wanted him to do some more evaluation around the property and he dutifully agreed and that was the last we saw of him that day. Lunch was left for us in the orangery so the three of us made ourselves comfortable. I, of course, felt like a gooseberry or rather did when Linda made me feel like one. It was clear she wanted time alone with Arden.

With nothing better to do, I slinked off to my room and read some more of Arden's novel. The characters were leaving America and heading for England. They were off to West Wycombe to look for another of the keys.

Relative Values

In need of fresh air and to put some distance between herself and her father, at least for a while, Hannah had gone for a walk around the grounds of the house. She revisited familiar locations from her childhood, seeking solace perhaps in the memories of lost and certainly more innocent days.

Her favourite was the boathouse.

The sky was clear and when the twilight hours came she studied the passing of the stars as she had done as a little girl. She watched mists roll down from the gentle slopes that bordered the lake and then the coming of a new sun. She could always breathe here. Her asthma was a symptom of the world beyond. In this place there was no tension in her lungs. No constriction in her throat. It was her sanctuary.

But age had brought experience and her mind could no longer look upon this place with innocence. She had said good-bye to her childhood here with the son of one her father's friends, a young man she had been desperately in love with and who had reciprocated those feelings. He had been killed, shot in the back, leading an advance on a Republican Guard stronghold in Kuwait. She still missed him deeply, but there were times when she wished she could un-know people, including him, that everything she knew about them could be wiped from her memory, especially those who had caused her pain. She felt the same now about numerous incidents in her life, particularly those that had involved her father. There were events, places and people she would rather forget but these were the crosses that she had to bear. She studied the dressing on her arm. It would heal but there were deeper wounds that hurt more than injured flesh.

Returning to the house she heard her father talking on the phone in the kitchen. There was that name again. Madsen.

Walking slowly along the hallway, and turning left into a small corridor that led to the garage and the stable block, she slowed her pace and listened intently to what he was saying.

"It was an intercept. His passport. He called that business partner of his in Boston. No, let it through. I want to find out where he's going. I don't know. Maybe they have discovered something. If they have then we'll find out. No. I have a better idea. I'll send someone. We'll exploit this Madsen's baser instincts. No, I have the perfect choice. She's right here."

Hannah's anger flared for a second but instantly she realised that she could turn the tables on her father. Quickly she made her way back along the hall and up the stairs to her room.

Five minutes later, lying in bed, she was aware of her father as he paused outside her room. She made no move to acknowledge him and remained still, feigning sleep, her body turned away. He waited for a minute then decided to move off.

Around mid-morning Hannah made her way downstairs and found her father waiting for her in the kitchen. Half-smiling at him she moved to the coffee machine and poured herself a cup.

"Sleep well?" Franklin asked, both hands around a large mug.

"Yeah, thanks."

There was a pause.

"Listen. I want to apologise for my attitude last night. It was unfair and unjust."

Hannah detected the false sympathy in his voice. She knew what he was doing. It was bridge building but for a personal, selfish end. Whenever he wanted his daughter to *run an errand* as he euphemistically called the dirty work he made her do, he would always start with this charade of compassion. An act of transparent contrition.

"I guess." Hannah shrugged.

"It was wrong of me to behave in that way." Franklin studied his daughter for her reaction.

She smiled. He had won her over, again. Or so he thought.

Hannah took his coffee cup and poured him a refill. She then placed it in front of him; a gesture of forgiveness albeit one, in these circumstances, that was purely a charade.

"Thank you."

Hannah said nothing and sat down opposite him. A gesture that was just enough to keep her father guessing. She could see he was working things out, considering a line of approach and trying to figure how much honey to pour on his words.

"You really proved your worth by retrieving that key. And I am very proud of you for doing so. You have to understand that I cannot reveal at this stage just what that means to the status quo. But you have helped keep the order of things and for that I am eternally grateful. I have faith in you."

Hannah played along.

"I was beginning to wonder if you ever really appreciated my abilities," she said with a smile.

"Of course I do. I always have. I have perhaps never made my feelings clear, I will admit, and for that I'm sorry."

She watched as his eyes took on a sympathetic charm surrounded by his well-rehearsed expression of understanding. He was a political man to the core.

"You are forgiven." With more polish she could easily outclass the man.

The smile on his face changed almost imperceptibly to one of self-congratulation. One born of the satisfaction that he had succeeded in his charm offensive.

"I was thinking that maybe you could do with a vacation. Time away to recuperate from recent events."

Hannah tried to look as relaxed as possible despite her foreknowledge of what he was about to ask. She was going to suggest England but thought her father might become too suspicious.

"I would like that," she said softly.

"How about, say…" Franklin paused. "England. Our family has history there."

So did most of New England, she thought. She almost felt sorry for him for coming up with such an ill thought out reason.

"Great. I've never been." She hoped her enthusiasm did not appear overblown.

Franklin stood up.

"Right. I'll make the arrangements." Pausing at the door, he turned. Hannah smiled at him; she knew what was coming. "And maybe you'll run an errand for me while you're there. Nothing much and it won't take long, leaving you time to explore the mother country."

Hannah nodded.

Satisfied, her father left.

When Madsen returned he found Arden cooking breakfast. A large frying pan of bacon was cracking and spitting on the stove.

"The only thing that killed me becoming a vegetarian," Arden said, "was the smell of bacon."

"Two eggs. Easy over," Madsen said, taking off his jacket and sitting at the table.

"Hey, no slacking here. Get the coffee going." Arden waved at the coffee jar with a fork.

"The proper stuff this time!" Madsen stood up and began opening and closing cupboard doors. He found a coffee pot.

Parks appeared with the CD. He placed it on the table in front of Madsen.

"Thank you."

"Did you make a copy?" Madsen asked, suspecting Parks would have done just that.

"Would you have objected if I had?" Parks asked.

"No. How could I? I just thought you might be worried it would fall into the wrong hands."

"I'm careful. Too careful. In fact I have a confession to make." Parks lowered his eyes.

Madsen began to prepare fresh coffee.

"And?" Arden was hoping for something salacious.

"It was me who erased the files on your business computer." Parks sat down. "You understand I had to."

Madsen thought for a moment.

"But how did you know where to look?"

Parks held up a hand.

"I apologise, Mister Madsen. But if you think about it there was only one way I could have found out. Hiroko."

"Hiroko?"

Parks stared out the window.

"Hiroko, Mister Madsen. Believe me there was no malice intended. And may I say, to put your mind at rest, her feelings for you were real."

"You had her spy on me?"

Parks hesitated.

"Mister Madsen, believe me it was not to your detriment. We had to protect the page. That's all."

"She worked for you?"

Parks nodded.

"But I was not using her," he added.

"Is that why they... shot her?" Madsen practically choked on the question.

Parks nodded again, this time almost imperceptibly.

"Mister Madsen, they want you dead as well." Parks paused. "The same way they want Mister Arden dead and of course myself. None of us are safe. Please realise Mister Madsen that she was trying to protect you. Her interest in you... her love for you... was genuine."

Madsen stared at the wall. He fought to keep his emotions in check. When he closed his eyes all he could see was Hiroko's sleeping face in their room at the inn.

"Tell you what Parks. This missing page had better be worth all this shit." Arden kept his back to Parks but waved the fork in the air. "It also cost Buchanan his life…"

"Buchanan knew the risks." Parks lowered his head. "He knew he might have to… sacrifice himself."

There was a heavy silence.

"So where is the missing page? Any revelations about that?" There was anger in Madsen's voice.

"I don't know where the real page is." Parks turned away from the window. "I thought it had fallen into their hands but it's obvious now it hasn't. If so, why would they continue to pursue us? All I know is that your Sheriff friend had it. Then it disappeared."

"How do you know I had anything to do with it?"

"Mister Madsen. We had been watching Mister Eddowes."

"Jim? You were watching Jim?" Arden turned to face Parks who pulled back a chair and sat down.

"Yes, Mister Arden. We had been watching him, following him as well because there was a strong rumour he had acquired the missing page. We had to. Where he acquired it I have no idea. You have to understand that we have eyes and ears everywhere but even so; we had been looking for that drawing for years. We are the watchmen on the walls of liberty, remember. When you reported to the police that his body had been found, Mister Madsen, we feared the absolute worst. I don't mind saying I felt an utter sense of dread."

"Really?" Madsen's tone was tinged with sarcasm.

"Yes Mister Madsen. We knew of your line of business. We also knew that Mister Eddowes was coming to see you before he disappeared."

"To see me?" Madsen frowned.

"Does that surprise you, Mister Madsen?"

"I'm flattered, I guess. But why me?"

"Because we have eyes and ears everywhere." Parks gave him a knowing smile.

Madsen walked slowly across the kitchen.

"Surely you don't mean Chris Gregory?"

Parks nodded.

"He and Mister Eddowes were old friends."

"Excuse me?" It was Arden's turn to look mystified.

"I don't think Mister Eddowes knew that Mister Gregory was part of our organization," Parks continued.

Madsen sat down on the sofa still clutching the coffee pot.

"Chris? With you?" Madsen gave Parks a quizzical look.

Parks was unmoved.

"But why me? Why didn't Chris just take Eddowes to Hiroko? Why involve me?" Madsen continued.

"Because of the journey you have to take."

"Journey?" Madsen bore a look of incredulity.

"All of this involves you. You're the focus. The centre around which everything revolves."

"Come on Parks, stop talking in that idiotic way. Make sense." There was a note of anger in Arden's voice. Doubts were creeping in and he too was starting to feel as if he was caught up in some delusional paranoiac's game. "Are you just yanking our chains here?"

"I'm sorry, I just don't understand what the hell you are talking about." Not for the first time Madsen was feeling that he too was getting the run around.

"Damn right." Arden wanted answers too.

"Mister Madsen, you are involved. Whether you like it or not. But not purely because of the missing page and its illustration but because of who you are."

"Who I am? I thought I was here to find out who killed Hiroko?" Madsen worked a finger across his forehead out of frustration.

"Oh you are. But to know yourself is to know your enemy and to do that you have to understand your birthright. You will then know why they are trying to kill you and why Hiroko died."

"My what?"

"Birthright."

"Are you messing with us Parks?" Arden threw the frying pan down. "Is this all some stupid delusion?"

"Mister Arden, were you not shot at? What's that wound on your arm, a fantasy?" Parks was growing more irritated. "Everything out there is a lie from the grinning images on cereal packets to the stories presented on the news, from financial institutions to the voting system. The bigger the lie the more people believe it. We are all being played with, Mister Arden. Every single day of our lives we are manipulated for the good of a very select group of individuals who want one thing – more power. A few of us have chosen not to believe their lies anymore. That is the whole point Mister Arden and believe me it is no fantasy. We are all feeble puppets of flesh and I have chosen to cut my strings. I am trying to make you cut yours."

"You make it sound like one grand conspiracy."

"But you don't believe in them, do you Mister Arden?"

"Damn right." Arden shook his head. "This is dumb. What are you driving at Parks? What is this, a whacko's wet dream?"

"This is no wet dream! This is about the truth. The reality beyond the nonsense that has been spoon fed to you all your life." Parks gritted his teeth.

Parks's outburst startled Arden. He had taken the man for an emotionally stilted academic.

"Okay, okay." Madsen made placating gestures with both hands. "Please. Getting all worked up will help no one. Especially me." Madsen took a breath. "When you said my birthright, what exactly did you mean?"

Arden gave a derisive snort. "You're a descendent of Jesus." He said, pointing a fork at Madsen.

"Hardly, Mister Arden," Parks snapped. Slowly sinking back into his chair he continued: "You are to become one of the three Ordines who will make a stand against the corrupt and stultifying power sweeping across this country.

You are to bring about and lead a new era of enlightenment. You will bring truth back to the people."

"And how the hell am I supposed to do that?"

"You've already started. As I said, you're already on the journey. The initiation was another step on the path." Parks lowered his voice for emphasis. "If we are not careful the world will enter a new Dark Age."

"Uh? With a cure for cancer, genetics, the space shuttle. How is that the work of a Dark Age?" Arden asked, his tone dismissive.

"Look at the bigger picture Mister Arden. Minds are being clouded, questions muted and ignored, civil liberties eroded – liberties great men fought to secure through war, resistance and rebellion. Reason is denied, superstition runs rampant, and the ignorant hold sway. Thirteenth century minds in the twenty-first. They want us to be cattle, Mister Arden. Real patriots ask questions. A civilised country has the answers."

"How is that my birthright?" Madsen's head was swimming.

"Your heritage. It only seemed right." Parks pointed a forefinger at Madsen.

"This is insane." Madsen was slowly shaking his head.

"On the contrary, this is the only sane thing in an insane world," Parks retorted.

"I'm in Wonderland, I must be. This place is full of mad hatters and white rabbits leading me to places I don't want to go." Madsen stood up.

"Will you, won't you, will you, won't you, will you join the dance?" Arden quipped.

"Dashwood was an ancestor of yours and he was a friend of Benjamin Franklin, one of the founders of this country. They had high hopes for a land of liberty. But they knew, as good men do, that one day, power would corrupt absolutely and that a failsafe would have to be put in place."

"I'm related to Dashwood?"

"You are Mister Madsen. It seemed fitting if not unreasonable that you take your place among the protectors of this country. Of truth. Of liberty in the real sense of the word."

"I'm an architect not a politician."

"And your late father was involved."

"My father was a journalist," Madsen said. "He had nothing to do with anything, except witnessing how quickly the world's going to hell in a handcart."

Parks shook his head quietly.

"Parks, man," Arden began. "If you don't mind me saying so, this just sounds like the delusional fantasy of someone who spends too much time on the Internet."

"I have to agree with Mark," Madsen said.

"Like or loathe it, that's the way it is." Parks was terse.

"I need stronger coffee. I have to wake up."

"Click your ruby slippers together Josh, that should get you home." There was big grin across Arden's face.

"Mister Madsen, most people live their lives unaware of the greater reality. They accept what they are told. They accept everything they read and everything they see. Myths are told as truth, while the truth is distorted into myths that can be dismissed."

"So this Eddowes was bringing me the page from the book because of a distant relation?"

"Yes Josh. But it seems fate has brought you down this path regardless of my machinations." Parks clasped his fingers together. "One could almost use the term destiny."

"No such thing." Madsen huffed.

"You'll have to learn how to use a whip." Arden had returned to the bacon and was now serving it out onto three plates. "Breakfast gentlemen."

"What?" Madsen looked quizzically in Arden's direction but did not get an answer. Then he remembered what Parks had told him about Dashwood "So why do I – we – have to go to England?" He turned back to Parks.

"Firstly, that's where I hid the book the missing page came from. Secondly, I believe that we shall learn more of the secrets that Dashwood kept by studying the drawings of the church of St Lawrence on the top of which he constructed a sunsphere to match that of the Customs House in Venice. It's less complicated in design though, but there maybe something when the two spheres are compared."

"Why did he do that?" Arden asked placing the three plates on the table.

"A good question. I don't know is the simple answer but that's another reason for going to England." Parks ignored his breakfast. "You see, Dashwood engaged in numerous expeditions sending out architects and draughtsmen to survey and draw reconstructions of many classical ruins and buildings. This was collected together in the book, which became a treasure trove of information."

"Come on Parks, eat up. It'll do you good."

"Thank you Mister Arden but I'm not hungry. I have more important things to concern me."

Silence descended on the room except for the sounds of Arden eating his breakfast, something that was obviously proving to be of deep irritation to Parks.

"Where did you have Mister Gregory send your passport?" Parks's gaze was directed at the window.

"What?" Madsen looked up from his thoughts. "Oh, here of course. Using a fake name, like you suggested."

"Then here we wait," Parks said, matter of factly.

"Unless they find us first."

"If they do Mister Arden, then we should be ready." Parks stood up and left the room.

Waiting until he thought Parks was out of earshot Arden looked up from his plate.

"What the hell was all that about?"

"Beats the crap out of me. What do you think?" Madsen was looking to Arden for some sort of grounding in reality.

"Josh. I though it sounded like bull to me. But then..." Arden looked down at the bandage on his arm. "I'm the victim of a pissed off freemason armed with a machinegun."

"Hardly." Madsen pulled out a chair and sat down at the kitchen table and began to pick at his bacon.

"Then I think of Jim, Hiroko, a friend of mine hanging in the trees of Central Park, Buchanan. Being shot at. Hell, maybe Parks is right. I just can't see the bigger picture yet."

"I don't see it either, Mark. I don't understand why people are dying because of a page from a book."

"As long as it's not some insane crap like the Bible code," Arden offered. "Wonder if they've found Darwin, evolution and DNA in it yet? What a kicker that would be." A mischievous grin broke across his face. "Ever noticed how prediction is always about telling what happened in the past?"

"What do you think of Parks?" Madsen stared down at his plate.

"Dunno. He seems a bit tightly wound and I can't help feeling he's just another conspiracy nut who's managed to convince two idiots into believing his *we're all under threat* paranoia."

"Trouble is, I think he's right."

"Who's the bigger idiot, the fool or the fool who follows him?"

"Thank you Obi Wan Kenobi." Madsen stood up and made his way to the cupboards. Searching through them he found a glass and went to the cold tap. Looking out across the road his attention was caught by movement through a window in the house opposite.

✳

The Tomb Under The Lake

It was three days before the water finally drained from the lake. The light drizzle had become full blown rainfall for two of them, forcing us all to stay inside. Alexia was a great host and made us all feel very welcome although I imagined that her relationship with Gus made it easier. Even old Retinger was a touch more sociable. He wasn't exactly *hail fellow well met* but at least his humourless armour had slipped a bit.

My nightly visitor had been conspicuous by his absence. I should imagine the bloody awful weather had something to do with it.

Arden had spent much of his time staring out of the window at the slowly diminishing water of the lake. It was like he half expected mythical Egyptian charioteers to come thundering across and invade his promised land.

It was odd how the missing lake made the grounds look ugly. Instead of water there was a sea of mud, rotted wood and slimy leaf mulch, peppered with the odd dead fish. There was even the ubiquitous shopping trolley. How that had got there was anyone's guess. I don't think there was a supermarket for twenty miles in any direction.

On the third day, when a feeble amount of sunlight was fighting for life through thinning clouds, we all made best speed for the *ex*-lake accompanied by Retinger who pushed a wheelbarrow full of planks of wood and other suitable equipment. I think in a funny kind of way, he was enjoying all of this. It was, after all, a break from the norm. Alexia had disappeared in order to attend a meeting of creditors, then it was off to Bath to talk with the boss of the hotel chain that was looking to buy the property. I'd heard the breakfast cereal crack of gravel as she had driven away that morning in a powerful sports car.

'I've only got two pairs of boots,' Retinger said as he lifted a set of waders and a pair of pale green wellies with straps around the top.

Arden took the wellies.

The three of us dithered, so Retinger took it upon himself to don the waders and follow Arden out to the middle. Gus, Linda and myself waited on the shoreline.

For a while both Arden and Retinger wandered about, seemingly aimless but Arden eventually waved Retinger over and both men stood over a spot almost in the centre of the mud.

'What can you see?' Gus's voice shattered the silence.

Arden held up a hand to suggest we wait.

We did.

Retinger came plodding back and zeroed in on his wheelbarrow. He started laying the planks out to the centre.

'What've you found?' Linda was breathless with excitement. Gus wasn't far behind her with an equally weak-kneed thrill.

'It's a trap door of some kind.' Retinger continued with the task in hand. 'Doesn't belong to the drainage system. So it must be something else.'

So the synopsis of *The Garden of Earthly Delights* was right. Who would've thought it? Not me. It was another blow to my hard-nosed cynical rejection of all things spurious. Don't get me wrong I wasn't about to commit one hundred percent to this. A few facts do not back up a way out and outlandish theory. Those meagre smattering of facts are often all a conspiracy theory has to go on but that doesn't make the grand plot true.

'Can we see?' Linda took a step closer to the mud.

'That's why I'm laying these planks out.' Retinger pointed to one. 'Come on. Give me a hand.'

So we did.

In some places the mud was deeper and one or two of the planks disappeared beneath thick, dark brown ooze. But we could jump across those. Not long after we were all standing around a trap door, with a thick metal pull ring, set

311

into a flat square of raised stone standing proud about a foot from the mud.

Retinger came clonking along the planks with a large and powerful torch in one hand and long crow bar in the other. He flicked it on once to test it and nearly blinded me in the process. It was one of those monsters advertised in gadget magazines that thump on about the fact that the light can blind small children at a distance of two miles.

'You had any idea this was here?' Gus asked Retinger.

'No,' came the familiar, terse as ever response.

Retinger handed Arden the torch and set about the ring on the trapdoor with his crow bar. With one great heave he tweaked the door up on its hinges. The thing lifted on the first attempt. Fetid air crawled out.

Ye gods, it smelt like rotted corpse. I say it did but to be honest I'd never smelt a rotting corpse. I just imagined, rightly as it happened, that this was what rotting corpses honked of. There was a ladder leading down into who knew what. It was all very Lovecraftian.

'Who wants the honours?' I leant over the lip and looked down.

'Why don't you go first?' Gus pointed down into the dark maw. 'You're always bringing up the rear. You can go first this time. Prove to us what a man you are.' Even though there was humour in his voice I could tell Gus meant what he said. His tone had an undercurrent of spite about it.

'Okay.' I took the torch off Retinger and aimed it down the hole. All I could see was a damp stone floor. 'If I'm not back in a week send a search party.'

'Get in.' Gus was eager to find out what was below.

I swung my body round and nervously descended the ladder. The metal was cold to the touch and a little greasy with algae. I paused half way down and shone the torch around. The room below was large and was lined with well-constructed walls. I could see a passage running off.

Stepping off the ladder I made my way to the passage and aimed the beam of the torch along it. There appeared to a void some thirty feet beyond. Another room.

My nose was used to the smell but I also think the good hefty draught from above was easing the odours and softening the blow. As I continued along the passage I heard someone coming down the ladder behind me. I turned and saw the familiar form of Arden drop off the ladder. He saw my torch beam and made his way towards me.

Without saying a word we edged our way along the tunnel. Like the room with the ladder it too was made from heavy blocks that looked as though they could withstand an earthquake, not that they had many of those in Somerset.

The void turned out to be another large room but this time there were a number of raised platforms on which were placed... well... they looked like stone coffins.

Was this a crypt?

The pair of us made our way forwards, our breath forming ephemeral clouds.

Beside each stone coffin were the lids that had been drawn back and dropped onto the floor as if a rather hurried search had once taken place. But a search for what?

'The Garden of Earthly Delights was right.' My voice rumbled around the stone tomb.

'They're all empty.' Arden was standing between two of the sarcophagi, if that's the correct plural of the word?

'Any inscriptions on them?' I asked.

'Not that I can see. Shine the torch here,' Arden asked, his hands resting on the edge of one of the coffins. I did. 'There was once something carved here but it's been defaced... smashed away.'

Looking around in the gloom something on the floor caught my eye. I shone the torch in its direction.

'Hey,' Arden snapped.

My silence spoke volumes.

There lying with its back against the wall, head cocked to one side, was a mummified body dressed in eighteenth century clothes. An ornate pistol, dulled by time was lying in the man's lap. I mean, I assumed it was a man. I wasn't in any hurry to get closer. I think I can safely say I had never seen a dead body, even one that was two hundred years old.

'Is that who I think it is?'

Arden hunkered down and ran a hand around his chin.

'What do you mean?' he asked.

Of course I'd forgotten to let them read the notebook.

'Thomas Hiddon. In the novel he was marooned in here by American sympathisers possibly part of some secret order who were after the treasure, whatever the treasure was.'

Arden turned slowly and looked at me.

'Hiddon?' He sported a big grin, somewhat out of place under the circumstances or rather, under the lake.

'Yeah.' I nodded.

'Really?' He looked back at our fallen friend. 'I never took him to be real person.'

'I mean, it could be him. The tomb under the lake. The pistol there. It all seems to fit the bill.'

'Pistol? Of course, Gus's extract he found in the house.'

'Have a look at the handle. According to the manuscript it should have his name on it.' He should also be missing his heart but I wasn't going to look. I suspected that under the circumstances, his ticker being cut out and taken to America was in reality nothing but a misty-eyed myth or a biographical invention for some propaganda purposes.

Arden slowly reached for the weapon, as if at any moment the corpse would move and shout *boo!*, and lifted it into the torch light. There, engraved in the dull metal was the name *Thomas Hiddon* and beneath that *Gabriel Szhell, Vienna*.

I laughed.

'Must be him.' Arden rolled the gun around in his hand. 'Maybe the novel extract is in fact part biography.'

'Careful. You don't want it going off.' It sounded silly but you never know. I have absolutely no idea if a weapon this old could go bang. How would I explain an accident like that in the hospital, where I'm sure they've heard every excuse under the sun for every conceivable injury yet devised by man? *Eh, yeah. I was shot by a writer I hardly know holding a duelling pistol in a tomb beneath a lake as we examined a two hundred year old dead body that we thought didn't exist... Honest...*

'He shot himself. Look there's a hole in the side of his head.' Pointing a finger Arden spoke softly. I didn't want to look but...

He had as well. Poor bastard. Realising there was no way out he had taken himself off. I imagined for a few moments the man standing at the base of the ladder hearing water flowing above him as the lake refilled. Grim, n'est ce pas?

We both turned when we heard someone descending the ladder.

'Where are you?' It was Linda.

'Down here!' As I called out I shone the torch towards the passage. Moments later she was standing next to us.

'I called out a few times didn't you hear?' She paused. 'Is that who –?'

'It is,' came the chorused reply.

There was a long silence interrupted only by our breathing. Arden began searching the pockets of Hiddon's coat. In an inside pocket he found a mouldy bundle of scrap paper tied together with a thin leather cord. Arden held it over his shoulder and Linda took it. He then continued.

He tapped the waistcoat, then slipped his hand into a pocket. Slowly, he pulled out a velvet bag that was half rotted and falling apart.

As he lifted it up the bottom fell away and out tumbled a gold key.

❅

More Secrets

Hannah sat up in bed. She had heard a noise but was not quite sure what it was that had awakened her. She listened. The house was quiet. With her throat tightening she reached for her inhaler and pressed down hard on the canister. It was nearly empty which set off a spark of panic in her. There was just enough medication to ease the constriction.

Reaching the top of the stairs she paused to listen. The house was silent, still yet thick with presentiment. Looking back at her father's bedroom door she could see it was slightly ajar. The curtains were drawn, as dawn light was evident. He never slept with the curtains open. She knocked gently on the door and looked in. The bed had not been slept in.

As she searched through the rest of the house Hannah came to the conclusion that her father had been gone for some time. There was no indication to suggest that he had just left. On the contrary, it all pointed to him having left a long time before.

In his study she sat down at his desk and looked around. The walls were covered in photographs of her father shaking hands with Presidents and senators. There was even one of him sharing a joke with Kissinger. She thought this odd, as she had often heard her father say he despised the man. In another, her father was sitting on a sand-coloured tank surrounded by troops. Others showed him inspecting assembly lines in factories whose manufactured output was not in evidence. There was a copy of the *New York Times* encased in a heavy wooden frame. *Sen. Franklin Stalls Evolutionary Class* ran the headline. There was a *Washington Post* beside it, *Franklin's Revolution on Evolution*. There was a stack of magazines on a shelf above the desk, the top one being a copy of *Nature*, 28 April 2005. *Is intelligent design coming to your campus?* Below that were a host of other magazines that had similar cover questions including one showing her father – *Sen. Franklin, God and Congress*.

In short this room was a living shrine to her father's ego. A cliché writ large. A self-congratulatory edifice to position and power, power that had been exerted outwards in the cause of self-grandisement. Some of the effort should have been put her way, Hannah thought, or even towards her embattled family but it was obvious they were all secondary issues set firmly against Franklin's personality and ones that were doomed to lose.

The drawers in his desk were locked. Nothing unusual there. After her adventures as a child he had made sure that everything he did not wish her to see was securely hidden. The man loved secrets. Secrecy bought power because there was the suggestion of greater special knowledge. A fallacy of course but it played on the human desire to be separate from the herd.

There were half a dozen printed pages, the top one having been torn from a book, placed in a letter tray, all of them held together by a paperclip. The top sheet was a quote:

> "*...The magnificent gilt ball on the top of the steeple, which is hollowed and made so very convenient in the inside for the celebrations not of devotional, but of convivial rites... the best Globe Tavern I was ever in... I must own up that I was afraid my descent from it would have been as precipitate as his Lordship's was from a high station, which turned his head, too. I admire likewise the silence and secrecy which reigns in that great globe, undisturbed, by his jolly songs very unfit for the profane ears of the world below.*"

Her father had written underneath in neat handwriting, *John Wilkes, the Hell Fire Club*.

The second sheet had been printed from the Internet and was a description of a church. There was a colour photograph morticed into the text. It was not an attractive building but it was certainly out of the ordinary. There were no large ornate stained glass windows in evidence nor were there the usual trappings of a religious building. Hannah could see no image of the cross. The entrance was at the foot of a square tower. Just over half way up there was a simple stepped cornice, which marked the dividing line between what appeared to be older stonework and a more modern arched development. This extended up to another wider cornice. The whole structure was adorned with a golden sphere that was mounted on a sturdy copper green pillar.

She scanned the accompanying text. It was the church of St Lawrence situated in an English village called West Wycombe. In the eighteenth century it had been restored by one Francis Dashwood who was the instigator of a secret society called the Hell Fire Club, an organisation with a scandalous reputation.

Hannah smiled. It seemed out of character for her father to be interested in what was basically a drinking den for aristocrats and one with very obvious pagan overtones. Maybe there was another side of her father's character that he was kept tightly under wraps. A roguish, anarchic element perhaps. It was of course an erroneous idea but she entertained it for a brief while. A personal fantasy.

The other pages were a condensed biography of Dashwood, including a black and white portrait of the young dark haired, Byronesque dilettante whose smile was just as enigmatic as that of Da Vinci's Mona Lisa. It gave Hannah the sense that he was in on some private joke or that any second he might break out in a peel of rich laughter.

She replaced the document carefully in the letter tray trying to remember the exact position in which she had found it. She would not have put it past her father to have marked its exact position to see if it had been tampered with. A test of her loyalty perhaps or maybe a test of her skills in some private game of his.

Trust was not a trait she would ever associate with her father and for a second she felt pity for him. Deep inside he must be a very lonely man in a world he simply saw as either something to exploit or as a realm full of fear.

Suddenly, Hannah was a little girl again exploring the castle. She crossed her father's study and tried the door of the walk-in closet, his inner sanctum. It was locked but she knew where he kept the key. It was a discovery she had made years before. Her tenacity and dedication had been equal to her father's security; traits that would stand her in good stead in later years. It was obviously a talent her father had noticed and one he had set out to exploit.

Hannah reached up and ran her fingers until she found the shallow recess in the architrave. Sliding the small panel aside she found what she was looking for.

The closet had changed over the years. It now had the appearance of a small office and had lost its sense of mystery and the romance of a cluttered space. Gone too were the souvenirs of marriage and the sentimental tokens of companionship. Box files lined one wall and a low table was covered in manila folders and documentation. The wooden box was still there, its surface polished but its edges somewhat worn. Hannah resisted the urge to open it and see for the first time in years the costume of the knight of her childhood fantasies.

Instead, her attention was drawn to the stacks of paperwork on the low table. The file on the top was edged in red stripes and had an adhesive yellow and black security tape. But there was no indication it belonged to any of the known security agencies. Typed across its cover, above a single red line, were the cryptically dubious words *IMPLEMENTATION OF SHIELDED POWER BASE.* Most of the files had similarly obfuscated titles, *CONSTITUTIONAL REPROGRAMMING, B.O.R. SOFTENING, CONGRESSIONAL DECONSTRUCTION, COLLATERAL IMPLICATIONS,* and so on. Breaking the seals and reading them would only have alerted her father so she left them alone. Their titles read like the vague, slightly fascistic terms used in *business speak*. But

319

without question, and whatever their contents, it was clear to Hannah that her father was planning something.

At the bottom of the stack was a different file, thicker than the others but equally sealed with several strips of security tape. It was worn with age and its cover flap had also been secured with a dark ruby red sealing wax. Handwritten on its cover were the words *IMPLICATIONS OF SUNSPHERE.*

What was the sunsphere? She wondered.

As she lifted it up the seal cracked open. Hannah quickly replaced the file and tidied the stack. Looking around all she could see were shelves full of paperwork, documents and files.

She had to finally admit to herself that she was looking for the key. Of course her father would not simply leave it lying around. Nor would he lock it away in the house. In all likelihood he would have it on his person. He would never let it out of his sight now.

With the edge of her t-shirt she rubbed down any surfaces she might have touched and left the inner sanctum, returning the key to its recess in the doorframe.

Despite her precautions, she knew that her father would deduce all too readily that she had been in his study. He had ways of knowing exactly what she had been up to in the house. Sometimes she suspected hidden cameras. He was that kind of man.

Back in her room and at her own desk she began to draw the key from memory. Maybe her father had forgotten her years of training and that the CIA took observational skills very seriously. No, she doubted that. It was more likely that in his arrogance he just did not care; it did not matter whether his daughter knew what the key looked like. What could she do with that knowledge anyway? She had no idea what it related to and he had been particularly careful in not being specific.

The details began to return. One end had the image of the sun, while the shaft was triangular in cross section, perhaps three inches long and ending in a right-angled triangle with a notch cut out of it. It could not be mistaken for anything but a very unusual key that gained the owner access to somewhere unusual. But where exactly? Her father had intimated at great secrets but had been no more specific than that. Was it for a room somewhere? A door? A safe? She could theorise all she liked. It would bring her no closer to an answer.

Her father had asked her to go to England but had made no reference to her taking the key. This Madsen was obviously involved and it seemed likely that this same person was close to making a discovery. Did he know what the key opened? Was that the reason she was going to be asked to follow him, maybe even seduce him for her father? If he knew what this key opened what else did he need? It seemed there was a piece missing from the puzzle and that the man was desperate to find it – at all costs. Maybe this Madsen had that piece. It appeared to be the only logical explanation for her father's malicious interest in this individual.

She studied her crude drawing. Someone had gone to great lengths to hide this key. But why hide it? Why not destroy it? If the secret was so powerful why not destroy it, melt it down and make sure it would never see the light of day again? To have it hidden meant that one day someone would want to use it. Maybe that was the motivation for her father's almost fanatical obsession. He was fearful it would be used again. It was clear to her that Madsen had to be protected.

Hannah spent the rest of the day in the boathouse loft, which had been converted into a sitting room by her mother not long after Hannah's birth. Hiding away here from the world would be easy and for a long time she had convinced herself that she would turn down her father's request and not go to England. But it was not in her; she hesitated to use the word fate, to remain in any one place for a long period of time despite her desire to become more reclusive. However much she tried, something invariably came along, without fail, to unsettle her tranquility.

Around half four she heard her father's voice calling to her from the terrace. For now she would have to play along with his game. It was a deception and one that weighed on her newly rediscovered sensibilities but maybe she could redeem herself for past misdeeds by helping this Madsen character survive her father's machinations. She could at least try.

When he called her for a third time Hannah stepped out on to the deck and waved at him. He motioned to her to join him inside the house. She nodded.

Not long after she found him in his study. For a moment she felt a flash of panic convinced that he knew she had been there.

"I wanted to brief you now about the small errand I want you to run while you are in England." Franklin closed a drawer in his desk and kept his eyes on a document before him. Nothing in his demeanour suggested antipathy towards her but then he was a consummate actor when he wanted to be. "I want this man followed."

He pulled a photograph from the document and slid it across the desk towards his daughter. Hannah had to step across the threshold to pick it up. It was further evidence of his psychology at work.

"Who is he?"

"His name is Josh Madsen, a successful architect from Boston who has had the misfortune to step in my way."

"Not deliberately surely?" Hannah studied the image. It was a blow up of an image of a man looking out of a window in the direction of the camera. In the background she could just make out the blurred image of a second figure. "Where was it taken?"

"Madsen has fallen in with a character by the name of Parks who is on a one man crusade to defeat me. He will fail, of course. This is his idea of a safe house. We've known he's been using the place for some time but we just let him think he has a sanctuary."

She could tell from the photo that the man looked weary, as if he had taken a wrong course and was now far from home. He looked haunted.

"Why this man? What's the problem?" she asked.

"It's a complicated story that I won't go into here."

Hannah knew it was just her father keeping his hand close to his chest. He was not about the reveal his cards now. "Parks is the owner of a book with a missing page. Madsen came into possession of that missing page. I want both. Simple as that. I would have dealt with Parks some time ago but he hid the book."

"Why are they going to England?" Hannah played it dumb.

"I would assume that Parks hid the book there. But I'm sure there's more to it than that. That's what I want you to find out."

"I'm spying?"

"Of course."

"That'll take a long time." Hannah knew it would, she just said it to gauge her father's reaction. It was retaliation or at the very least a dig at his notion that it would be a brief errand.

"It may, it may not. Depends how fast you work." He had no bones about laying the emphasis on her ability but again he had made her feel like the weak element. She despised him even more.

The telephone chimed.

"Yes?" Franklin's tone was terse. "It's arrived? Good. Now finish the clean up. What do you think I want done? Exactly." He hung up. "I've booked tickets for you. I'll have my car drive you down to the airport." He looked at his watch. "You're leaving within the hour. Now, I have calls to make."

Hannah knew what he meant. In some respects he could be plain speaking, other times it was cryptic double talk. She just wished he could be more direct with her. The patronising tone he often used made her sound like nothing more than his secretary. Easily dispensable and not worth a damn.

As she turned away from his study she stopped short when a figure appeared in the hallway. His black hair was tightly cropped and he was dressed in a dark suit. Every inch a military man. She noticed the wire coming from an earpiece. He stood there and nodded to her.

"I'm your escort, Mam."

"I don't think I need one." She knew she did not. It was her father again, making sure she did what she was told. She also suspected that not only was this man her chaperone but her assassin as well, should she defy her father. He was there to do as instructed and, to use her father's term, *clean up*. The man also represented the final nail in the coffin of their relationship. Her father saw her as expendable. "I will have to pack some clothes," Hannah said, and headed for the stairs. She was aware that the man had moved to follow her. She turned and gave him an indignant look.

"I've been instructed to – assist," he said.

It was yet another display of mistrust from her father. Gritting her teeth she shook her head slowly but it was an empty gesture. The man was unmoved. Standing her ground, she only continued up the stairs when he pulled back his jacket a short way to reveal a large calibre automatic pistol in a shoulder holster.

Customs Of The Sea

'Will the police have to know?' Gus asked as he swirled a drink round in a tumbler. The ice cubes rattled with a satisfying clinkety-clink.

'I would've thought so mate.' Sitting at a table, I was attempting to untie the leather cord around the scraps of paper. 'Coroner has to get involved.'

'Even for a body that old?' Gus still sounded incredulous.

'Yeah. Don't you remember that extension to All Saints church last summer? They found those Iron Age burials.' It was no good; I would have to cut the strap. 'First person they called was the local coroner. It's the law.' Iron Age burials that had the evangelistas hissing feathers, unappreciative of pagan bodies lurking beside their kirk. The ignorant bast-

'Won't that blow the cover on what we're doing?' Gus stood up and moved to the window. To say he looked troubled was an understatement.

'I guess somebody would want to know why we drained the lake. Where are the other two?' I asked.

'They're in the library. Arden's looking for more of the Garden of Earthly Delights and Linda's helping. Finding Hiddon's body has stoked his boiler again. But it's also made him a bit, you know, paranoid.'

I too had noticed a change in him but despite this apparent shift in his character Linda was still hanging on Arden's every word. Part of the swag we found in the secret chamber had, oddly enough, proved to be of mixed merit. There was a map of the grounds of the house with notes scribbled all over it probably in Hiddon's own handwriting as it matched the scrawl in the notebook remnants I had read. While the most amazing discovery was a page torn from a book that bore an illustration, in a fine architectural style, of the Sunsphere above the Dogana del Mare with its depiction of the dual statues of Atlas and lady Fortune.

As Arden had written:

The Customs House in Venice or rather the ornamentation on its roof. The Customs House or the Dogana del Mare is on the confluence of Giudecca Canal and the Grand Canal. The building underwent various renovations over the course of the centuries until finally in 1677 a design by Giuseppe Benoni was used to build a square tower made from Istrian stone. On top of its roof was placed a bronze group composed of two atlantes, the plural of Atlas who support a gilded sphere on which balances the allegorical figure of Fortune created by Falconi who was living in Padua...

These recent discoveries had indeed sent our author close to the edge. Arden had grown more paranoid in recent hours and finding Hiddon's body had upped the ante completely. He was now convinced that dark forces were operating in his vicinity, conspiring to send him into mental turmoil. Serendipity, coincidence and outright legerdemain all vied for airtime in Arden's head. But despite his fears he wanted to know more, hence his retreat to the library.

Even so, his agitation did seem a bit forced.

There was nothing for it. I had to resort to scissors. The leather strap gave way. I had done my best to preserve it as much as poss... but there we go... it was done. Omelettes and eggs and all that.

I put the remnants of the strap aside and began to unfold the paper.

The paper was thick, blotched with tea coloured watermarks and threatened to fall apart in my hands. But shear bloody tenacity got me through.

To the finder of this note:

Of late my activities have brought certaine enemies unto me. For that which I have uncovered has led directly to a mighty bounty being placed upon my head. It seems that a great lie has been perpetrated and as I am the one who has thus revealed the secrets that made powerful men yet more powerful and people cowed beneath such errors I am therefore duly set for destruction by whatever means my pursuers deem worthy. Callous men may yet stem the new fountain of knowledge that has spilled forth such sweet waters of understanding across our lands. These same men would if they could, return us all unto darkness. But within each of us a light burns that we must keep aflame against fear and ignorance.

My body lies within a tomb but one created to contain a most wondrous secret, which men have removed to keep us all ensnared. I cannot write therein of such but I have left knowledge of it in a most special place. Seek that city and thus keep the light of the Enlightenment ablaze.

Now my lamp dies, as do I. The illumination within me fades as I move towards that great dark of night where we must all enter. I am already interred and therefore need not the attentions of a priest for I have rejected all such zealous folly for what it is. The great secret has been revealed to me.

I hope that fate stands with the Ordines for all time.

T.H. Esq.

Certain letters appeared to be bolder than the others. With Gus looking over my shoulder we gathered all the emphasised letters together. There were thirty in all.
They were:

l a e g u s a l v a s s e u n b i u l m o e o n r u z i n t

The only one underlined was the letter 'v'.
'Why's that do you think?' Gus moved and sat down his attention fully on the piece of paper I was writing my notes on. 'Is it a code?'
I was tempted to respond with sarcasm but resisted.

'I assume it's a code mate. It certainly looks like one.' I mean why would anyone bother writing a note and have thirty letters that stand out? What else could it be?

'Give me a scrap of paper.' Gus reached out. I tore off a sheet and handed it to him. He took a pen from his pocket and began copying the letters down. 'Why underline the v?'

I didn't know.

Gus pursed his lips and made funny noises. He raised a finger.

'What if?' He paused to think on a little further, 'What if the underlined v is the start?'

Good call.

'Seems reasonable. Then what?' I asked.

Gus shook his head. He sat back.

'Kind of falls apart after that doesn't.' I wasn't being very helpful. 'We have nothing to go on. No terms of reference. Do they spell out words? Are they coded? What do they represent?'

Gus tapped his mouth with the end of his pen.

'V... v... v... v.'

'The trouble is. Without something to kick-start us we can make any old nonsense up with this. Slug... Viola... Arse.'

'I had anus,' Gus grinned.

'My point exactly. Is it in English, French... Latin even?'

We were mulling this over when Arden and Linda returned. Arden was looking suitably ponderous as if under a cloud of despair. But the fact that we had discovered some sort of code in the note from Hiddon's body lifted his spirits and for a short while there was something of the possessed man about the writer.

Everyone set about the task with gusto and for the next few hours the thoughtful silence was interrupted, at sporadic moments, by someone shouting out a word or two, heralded by a *what about?*... and followed by an *oh, never mind*.

Then Linda had a brainwave.

'Sunsphere. Dogana del Mare. That's in Venice.' All eyes were upon her. She began to spell out Venice but only reached v... e... n. 'Oh, never mind. There's no c.'

Arden sat forward.

'Not in the Italian. It's spelt Venezia,' he said excitedly.

We all looked at our lists. We had *Venezia* all right. But that still left us with twenty-three other letters.

'How's everyone's Italian?' Gus smirked.

'Ciao and that's about it,' I replied.

'He mentions the Ordines again.' Linda scratched her head. 'Do you think that might infer something?'

'What do we know about the Ordines?' Gus asked.

'A secret order set up initially to defend the old Roman religions from encroaching Christianity, which was being used to control and manipulate a crumbling empire. Theodosius I made Christianity a compulsory religion and that's when the trouble really began. By the time of the Renaissance, the Ordines, having dispensed with ancient belief, turned to defending science and freethought. In the Enlightenment the Ordines fell into defending reason from the same enemy.' Arden stood up and with hands in pockets paced the room. 'No one's sure how many initiates there are but they are overseen by a group of three. So that no decision is hung.' Arden fell silent for a moment. 'During the Enlightenment many Freemasons protected scientists from the attentions of the Inquisition, who thought all experiments to understand the world were heretical, especially when they started to push God aside. The Ordines, with the assistance of the Freemasons and the Illuminati, defended free thought.'

'They're in Sunsphere, aren't they?' Gus rocked back in his chair.

Arden nodded.

'They're the great protecting force throughout the story. Keeping an eye on the main protagonists.'

'Wish I'd brought my copy.' Rocking forward again, Gus turned his attention back to the letters.

'I've got it in my room.' My confession was met with indifference.

'Go and get it then,' Gus demanded.

I did.

When I returned, Arden chose to read aloud the relevant section. I felt like I was at school again. It was the start of the second part of the book.

The genesis of the Ordines. Pure postulation of course but it didn't matter. Arden was swift to state that what he had written was based on the best available evidence and academic research.

'How does that help us?' Yep, I was doing it again.

This time no one answered. I suspected they were ignoring me, tired of my demolishing questions.

'Was Venice around then?' Gus was tapping the paper. 'Ancient Rome, I mean.'

Arden shook his head.

'It wasn't?' Linda asked quizzically.

'There was a Venetia region. And a place called Altinum. But that was it.' Arden was standing at the window looking out. A light drizzle was falling.

'What's the Latin for sun? As in big fiery orb,' Gus asked. He was writing something.

'Sol,' Arden said. 'Why?'

'Thought so. I can make the Latin for Sol and seeing as this whole thing is about the sun...'

Arden and Linda came over to the table.

'He's right.' Linda turned away, writing sol on her own scrap of paper as she did so. 'What if he's mixed up Italian and Latin. They're related. Venice. Sunsphere. Italy. Rome. Ordines. The whole kit and caboodle.'

'Ten down. Twenty to go. Shall we try German next?' I was roundly ignored.

'So what's sphere in Latin?' Linda turned on her heels.

'Globus,' Arden said. 'Have you found that as well?'

'No but I thought it was the next obvious word.' Gus ran his pen nib up and down the remaining letters. 'G... l... o... Globus. There it is.'

'Venezia. Sol. Globus. He is mixing Italian and Latin.' Arden pulled up a chair and sat down next to Gus. 'What do we have left?'

Gus had crossed out all the used letters, which just left:

a e u s a u n i l m r u n t

'Any ideas?' Gus glanced at Arden who was concentrating solely on what remained.

'What else goes with sunsphere and Venice in all this?' Linda moved to stand by the seated Arden.

'It's not Dogana, Ordine, key.' Arden wrote *clavis* down on his piece of paper. 'Definitely not the word key.'

'*I'm a runt*'s there. Look.' Rather childishly I had written it out. Suitably ignored again. What did I expect? A consonant please Carol... *Lament, muse, Muesli, sauna, ruse...*

'Illuminate. Stone. Freemason?' Gus was randomly firing out words. All the time Arden was shaking his head. 'Hidden. Secret. Lost.'

'I think *hidden* and *secret* are the same, *occultus*.' Arden tapped a fist against his lip.

Occultus? Sounded like a superhero villain.

'Light. Dark. Building.' Linda too had resorted to pulling the textural equivalent of rabbits out of hats.

'Light...' Arden held a hand up. 'Light. What's Latin for light?'

I certainly didn't have a clue and the faces Gus and Linda were wearing suggested they didn't either.

'Lux.' Arden wagged a finger. 'There's no *x*. So... it must be... Lu... lum... lumin... lumin... luminus.' He paused. 'Something like that.'

'If it fits, it'll do.' I went to scratch out *luminus* on my sheet.

'No wait. That's all wrong. Light is *lux*.' Arden sat back somewhat frustrated. 'We need a Latin dictionary.'

So it was back to the library. It was good job Alexia had decided to stay away overnight for her meetings. So far, through our larking, we'd mucked up the library, crushed some flowerbeds, drained a lake, found a corpse and possibly stained various carpets and other soft furnishings to boot.

We'd probably out stayed our welcome as well.

At least we'd found a secret room, a third key and magic note.

Whoopee!

'Here it is.' Arden, having thumbed swiftly through a Latin dictionary he'd discovered, stabbed a finger into a page. '*Lumina*, illuminated!'

The opposite being dim – as in… us.

Which left us with:

e u s a r u n t

'Treasure – oh wait… no.' For a second Gus's face lit up like a lottery winner who then realised his ticket was one number out.

'I should imagine that it's going to be another Latin word,' Linda suggested.

'Venezia. Sol. Globus. Lumina. Venice. Sun. Sphere. Illuminated,' I read out. Wasn't exactly inspiring nor for that matter especially revealing.

Suntrue. Untrue (I liked that one – not that it was proper English as she is writ but it had a certain piquancy) *A Suntrue. Aunts. Ants. Rants. Unrest. Arse* was still there. *True Anus*. Never a true anus.

'Ordines for all time…' Arden was reading Hiddon's note. 'For all time. Eternal.' He reached for the dictionary.

'What do you think it is?' Linda took a step closer to Arden.

'Thought so. Eternal, *Aeturnus.*' He tapped Hiddon's letter.

That was a wild stab in the dark.

Venezia. Sol. Globus. Lumina. Aeturnus. Venice. Sun. Sphere. Illuminated. Eternal.

Bingo!

Er...

So what the code is saying is that in Venice there is a sun sphere shining with eternal light or words to that effect. Nothing we didn't already know. I suppose the added spice was knowing that Hiddon had hidden something within the sunsphere atop the Customs House or rather, this was what he was inferring. A secret that would shock the world and fuel the Enlightenment and free men from superstition.

Arden was especially blown away. It was paralleling his book not quite to the letter but close enough to make him think that maybe he had inadvertently stumbled upon a true mystery. He began pacing the room, hands chopping the air as he tried to get to grips with the idea that his novel *Sunsphere* was based on fact.

I on the other hand thought it too good to be true.

Linda, of course, assumed it was all down to some psychic force. A tapping in to a spiritual realm bursting at the seams to reveal its secrets.

It had just made everyone more determined to go.

Venice it was then.

Let loose the geese...

So that we may follow.

We told Retinger to let Alexia know that we were off. Having practically wrecked the house we were scuttling off without so much as a beg your pardon. Gus left a sealed letter for her in the orangery outlining our discoveries although, to be honest, I suspected there was much more in it than just *what we did on our holidays*, having heard their frolicking.

Still, none of my business.

Retinger asked Gus if he would be back to finish off his work here and was assured that the man would be back as soon as possible. I was sure Gus would indeed be back to *finish his work*.

On the car journey home we went through everything we had discovered trying to make sense of the whole shebang.

'The sunsphere Dashwood built. Is that sealed?' I asked out of ignorance.

'It has seats in it,' was Arden's somewhat terse reply.

'No great secrets relating to historical conspiracies then?'

'No.' Arden paused to concentrate on a turning. 'During my research on the novel I went there for a look. I knew Dashwood had modelled his sunsphere on the Dogana del Mare but I thought my plot device about hidden treasure was just that. I had no idea it would in fact turn out to be real.' There was something about Arden's tone that suggested he was unnerved by the whole business, almost all of it – or rather, so far. At the end of his book, according to Gus, the ultimate secret is kept out of reach of the protagonists. Mind you, it wouldn't surprise me if the same fate eventually awaited us.

'Sometimes things just seem to work out. I don't think there's any cosmic conspiracy.' My statement, though aimed at Arden, was intercepted by Linda.

'You have such a closed mind.' She ran her fingers through her hair to lift it from her eyes. 'That's exactly what happened. Mark here just picked up on the zeitgeist, the prevailing cosmic winds. Maybe it was time for the whole idea to surface. This is the dawn of a new age whose time has come.'

It had taken some time but there it was.

Fluffy, vacuous, New Age cop out. The quick fix way. Apply not an ounce of brainpower, just trot out the

Glastonbury hedge monkey fudge. Vibes man! The positive energies! You're harshing my buzz...

Of all of us my mind was the most open. That's why I wasn't accepting, blindly, everything that was coming at me. Even if of late things had seemed particularly odd. However much I wanted to doubt it there did seem to be a thickening mystery but I wasn't going to surrender without a fight nor accept things on a whim.

Not much else was said on the way home. I detected that everyone, for the moment, had had enough of each other with me being at the top of that list. Perhaps we all needed a good shower and a change of clothing. I know I did. I still couldn't get the smell of old corpse out of my nose.

It took us longer to get home as Arden insisted on going cross-country via Hampshire and not along the old M4. Not sure why he did this. There were hints of things troubling him. I'm jumping to conclusions but these high sprung feats of imagination were ones based on my observations of him. He spent a lot of time looking in the rear view mirror. Even on quiet country roads he seemed over concerned as to what was behind, more so than what was ahead. Sometimes he slowed as if waiting for something and at one junction he overshot wildly. Luckily the road we were joining was empty. I nearly messed myself. Gus, who'd been asleep, came round and in all innocence asked why we had stopped. Linda remained quiet throughout, her hands, white knuckled, gripping the seat.

Eventually the familiar outskirts of Sittingbourne came into view. We had come in via Maidstone and had crossed the M20 at junction 7. There was more sense to this than at first appeared. Traffic news had alerted us to a monstrous accident on the M25. Any mentally fragile person might have assumed it was the forces of darkness rallying to hinder our progress. I must admit I entertained the notion for a few seconds then had to beat them down with a big mental stick.

Nothing was said when they dropped me off. I just muttered a *seeyah* and that was it.

It was good to be home. No, it was great. I threw off my clothes and jumped into the shower and spent half an hour trying to get the damp of tombs and smell of two hundred year old death from my skin. Before I knew it I had been splashing about in the water for twenty minutes. Joy.

Throughout my watery sojourn, my mind wandered hither and thither over the events of the last few days. Despite my paucity of acceptance, I was forced to admit to myself that we had indeed found some odd things. Tunnels and mazes. Secret passages and hidden books. They were real and material. I hadn't dreamt them. We had followed less than cryptic clues to reveal more about Hiddon and what he was up to and to crown the proceedings, we had located the third key.

Secrets and keys. Keys and sunspheres.

Three weeks went by before I heard from Linda. She sounded a little annoyed.

'Hi Lin. Whatcha been up to?' I was examining another artefact that had been sent to me for identification and valuation. It was a mandylion. It didn't look particularly promising but it was a favour for an old contact in the business. Twice a year, on average, we sent each other a little bit of work.

'He's gone.' There was irritation in her voice, a tang of betrayal.

'Who has?'

'Mark. He's gone to Venice. He left yesterday.'

'Oh. Why?' I asked in all the feigned innocence I could muster.

'You know why. He's asked Gus to join him.'

'Just Gus?'

'He has the third key.'

'But not us?' Fine. I didn't like flying anyway and the thought of beetling off to Venice didn't appeal. Whatever enthusiasm I had once possessed for the whole *Sunsphere* mystery had now fizzled away. At least I thought it had.

Odd that I found myself feeling somewhat annoyed.

'He didn't say to not come but I feel like we've been abandoned.' Linda's anger shifted to the sadness of rejection. 'After all we've done together.' I think her barely contained feelings for Arden were getting in the way.

'Do you want me to say something to him?' It seemed like a chivalrous think to say.

'Not sure how it would help,' Linda replied.

'I could tell him what an unconscionable twat he's being.'

'Oh now. Come on. You don't have to go that far.'

I thought I had to go that far.

'Do you have his phone number?' I asked, feeling a touch gallant.

'Listen.' Linda paused. 'Let's go anyway. This is as much our quest as it is Arden's. I mean Mark's.'

Yep. She was right. We'd all done our bit and I think you could even class my dismissive sarcasm as a contribution, of sorts. I was the voice of reason. If one were needed. And yes, one was needed... desperately.

'I'd have to dig out my passport. When's Gus flying out?' I couldn't remember where the damn thing was.

'Day after tomorrow. Shall I try and book two seats on the same flight?'

Hells teeth...

'Okay.'

'I'll let you know how I get on.' Linda hung up.

Why was I capitulating so easily? Why? I think I knew. Because I think, secretly, yes secretly, I wanted to know exactly what was in the sunsphere above the Dogana del Mare... more than anyone.

I cracked open a bottle of wine. Made up a shockingly overpriced value for the mandylion, with my fifteen percent, and called my colleague who had sent it to talk business.

I needed the money.

To go away with.

In the airport I dipped into more of Arden's novel. I'm not sure if I was looking for anything specific, like clues. I mean we were past that by now. We knew where we were going. Venice. The Dogana del Mare to be more precise. Maybe the story was pulling me in more than I realised. Our adventures at the Carey-Hunt's had softened my critical faculties. Linda had bagged two seats on the same plane as Gus who, when he saw us trundle into the airport, allowed a look of surprise to crash across his face.

I had the distinct impression he was not pleased to see us, as if we were unexpected and overweight baggage he would have to lug around with him.

On the bench in the waiting area Linda spent an hour trying to wrestle a conversation out of him while I ignored them both and read.

There was a boarding call. Gus, Linda and I made for the gate in a kind of tense silence. Oddly enough I found myself feeling miffed. Arden had caught a separate flight and I immediately thought this was for the sole purpose of getting there ahead of us and claiming all the shiny glory. Maybe the other two felt this as well. If they did they were keeping shtoom but body language was all and it was speaking volumes. I think Linda suspected that Gus was in on a deal that he and Arden had concocted to share the spoils.

Once settled on the plane I got stuck into some more random dabblings in the pages of *Sunsphere* as I did my best to ignore the trundling preparations for lift-off. Lift-offs and landings were supposed to be the most dangerous times in air travel but at least with landing you were heading in the right direction.

My head was pounding and the words on the pages were lost to me. I scan read and nothing would sink in. I tried to concentrate on a paragraph but it was just a jumble. I went over and over the same page but remembered none of it. Letters and sentences darted and danced, forcing me to shut the book. I closed my eyes and tipped my head back. What the hell was going on? Why was I a part of this nonsense? What was I doing on a plane heading to Italy? Dashwood. Sunspheres. Lost manuscripts. Tunnels... What the hell was this all about?

Three keys...

At least we had all three keys so, technically then, we couldn't fail. Whatever the quest was. Or was that a touch presumptuous of me. Steady boy. I'd nearly lost it there. The boundary between reality and literature had disappeared in my head. I was astride two worlds, one real and one... half real? A dazzling and fantastic textual gorgon ready to freeze the senses.

My head...

Nervous? Yes. I needed to occupy myself somehow. The book had failed. There then followed my usual fidgeting before a plane takes off. I think a few people including Gus had fallen asleep. There had been a delay. No idea what, why or for whom. But the aircraft had strolled up to the runway only to be told to stop.

My palms were sweaty. I wiped them on the armrests... Nervous... nervous... nervous.

In a few hours we would be in Venice and hopefully Arden would be there to meet us. I had no idea why he had gone on ahead. Why he couldn't have just waited for us? It seemed so... I don't know... indifferent.

Everyone around me looked calm, relaxed... bored. Maybe even blasé. Lucky swines.

The engines began to throttle up...

To distract myself I decided to dip into some more of his ubiquitous book. Then promptly wished I hadn't.

※

Taking Flight

The 747 out of JFK was only three-quarters full allowing Madsen, Arden and Parks to sit separated from the other passengers. This pleased Parks particularly. Most of the journey down from Providence had been spent in a state of high tension with a near constant study out of the rear view mirror. Parks had decided not to fly from Logan after suspecting a car behind was following them. He had indicated to make the turn into the airport and saw the car behind do the same. When he changed his mind and turned the indicator off, the car behind followed suit.

At the airport Parks had continued his heightened level of awareness much to the irritation of Arden who was convinced that the man's behaviour would do nothing but attract unwarranted attention. This had continued onto the plane with Parks insisting they sit some distance from the rest of the passengers. He only appeared to relax when the 747 was half an hour or so out over the Atlantic.

Madsen had been lost in his thoughts for a while before he too relaxed into the flight.

He turned to Parks.

"Tell me Parks. Why a golden sphere?"

Parks nodded. He seemed eager to talk, a distraction from his unease.

"You see Mister Madsen the golden sphere on both the Dogana del Mare and the church of St Lawrence represent the sun. The source of all religion. The source of all life on this planet." Parks spoke in a stage whisper. "It was regarded as a deity by primitive man. A bringer of warmth, light and heat therefore it had a high place among the belief systems of our ancestors. The Egyptians had Ra crowned

340

with a solar disk. The Sphinx of course was one personification of their sun god and what are the pyramids if not physical representations of the rays of the sun? How about Aten, a sun deity, made the one true god by the pharaoh Akhenaton. The Phrygians had Attis who was later a sun god under the Romans, a god who suffered, died and rose again. Sound familiar? The Persians worshipped their sun god Ormuzd, the Celts Belanos, the Assyrians had Shamash, the Chaldees had Merodach, the Mexicans Tezcatlipoca, Helios or Apollo for the Greeks and Sol for the Romans. Apollo represented a civilising agency that destroyed with its golden arrows the Python, the serpent of the night. The Scandinavians had Sunna, who according to their mythology was fearful of being eaten by Fenris, a wolf – who represented eclipses. In French Freemasonry the son of a Mason is called a *Louveteau* – a young wolf. This is based on the mysteries of Isis in Egypt in which a candidate was asked to wear a wolf's mask, the symbolism being that a wolf will scatter sheep and cattle like the sun scatters the stars and the night on the coming of day as Macrobius elaborates on in his *Saturnalia*. You will of course remember that in the Greek language *lukos* means either sun or wolf. I digress. It is only natural and in many ways obvious that we worship the sun. Without it there would be no life on this planet."

Parks paused as a passenger made his way up the aisle to the restroom. "The basic myth surrounding the sun is that the sun god rises from the darkness, forsakes his first love, the dawn, and continues on his course gaining strength as he does so. He travels symbolically in a chariot or a boat. Having crossed the zenith his strength begins to fail and on the verge of the Western heavens he encounters the monstrous night that fights and devours him. He must then travel through the underground before being reborn again. You can see the basis for numerous myths, legends, stories and religions in the simple passage of the sun. Beowulf, for example, or at its heart the story of King Arthur. And notice how many religions look to the east for the rising of the sun

341

or *son* if you pardon the pun. Planetary laws of motion defined religion. At the heart of all religions is the observation of natural not spiritual events. However much zealots decry science it is, albeit primitive, at the heart of their beliefs. I find that wonderfully ironic, Mister Madsen. Our ancestors observed the heavens and defined them the best way they could but instead of Kepler they used mythical representation. If the earth orbited the other way or there were two suns the myths and legends would change accordingly. Perhaps people would be slaughtering each other all over the world in the name of the duality. The two gods..."

Pausing for a second time to gather his thoughts, Parks then continued. "For the sphere above the Dogana del Mare it was, for its creator, the idea of the beneficial sun pouring warmth, benevolence and success upon the endeavours of the merchants who sailed beneath it. The sun is also a pagan symbol and Dashwood, with his wicked sense of fun, would have employed his sunsphere as something of a gesture to the staid religious and hypocritical establishment he saw around him. He was perhaps being heretical as well. Some sun deities were said to exist in the sun and were a separate entity to the sun itself, others believed the sun was a god. Dashwood was having fun pretending to be a sun god. I also find it interesting that the Masonic jewels of a past master and a senior deacon are images of the sun."

"Didn't Christianity supplant all that though?"

"On the contrary. Christianity which, let's be clear here didn't really start until three hundred years or more after the supposed events of Christ's ministry, deliberately took up the tenets of so-called paganism. Christianity was nearly dead in the water and it needed to survive. What better way to do that than to merge with an older and stronger belief system. Take the halo for instance. It's painted around the heads of a thousand saints. It represents the sun. Christianity is just a blend of Judaism and Paganism. The Christian holy day – Sunday – the day of the sun." Parks paused again. His attention was focused on a man who had stood up to retrieve something from the overhead locker. Something in his manner alarmed Parks.

"You okay?" Madsen followed Parks's gaze. "Problems?"

"I recognise that man. But I'm not sure how and why."

Madsen watched the man sit down again. Casting his eyes over the other passengers, he saw a young woman with honey coloured hair glance quickly in his direction. She smiled then went back to reading her book.

"Relax. What can anyone do thirty thousand feet over the Atlantic?" Madsen said quietly.

"It is enough that we might be under surveillance. Enough to concern me." Parks sat up and looked over his seat. No one was paying him any attention.

"You said something about a new renaissance. A new beginning." Madsen's question was designed to distract Parks from his paranoia.

"That's right. An attempt was made in 1960 to steer the world in the right direction but when Kennedy – the herald of a new hope – was assassinated, his new frontier lay in shreds. It was also supposed to be the new frontier of the Ordines but they too had once more been defeated. Think about the great things that could have been achieved had Kennedy survived."

"Did they help put him in power?"

"They were working in the background. I guess you were too young to know the sense of optimism that existed when he was President. It was indescribable. Instead, we fell into a pointless cold war of ridiculous wastage and idiotic ideologies. We need our enemies, Mister Madsen. Communism has gone. But you can see for yourself that we have developed another. All for the benefit of a distorted minority who perpetuate myths of fear for their own personal gain. There are dark times ahead. The sun must be brought back from the underworld."

Arden was right; Parks did talk in a cryptic way. Madsen studied the man. His face seemed to have grown more weary and careworn, as if he had only now finally succumbed to the weight of his obligation and dedication to the unseen Ordines.

Madsen stared down at the battleship grey ocean flecked with white. Heading east they were going to meet the sun. He smiled. Somehow it all seemed prophetic or was he, caught up in Parks's worldview, simply reading too much into the world around him? He did not want to become a significance junkie seeing symbolic patterns in everything. It was a delusional mind state where obsessional thinking would add fuel to the fire. Conspiracy theories would not be far behind.

Arden, who had been dozing in the window seat, woke up.

"Sorry, I was looking over you at the ocean."

"S'alright Josh. Don't like air travel much. I try and sleep through most flights." Arden yawned.

"Statistically you're safer up here than you are down there." Madsen's smile bore a hint of mischief.

"Yeah I've heard all of that. You can prove what you like with numbers." Arden sat up and stretched.

"Anyway, you've survived this far." Madsen tapped his arm in mock reassurance.

"Just about. I feel like a fifth wheel."

"Parks needs his foot soldiers and you're with us for your protection, remember. You'd probably be-"

"Say it man. I know." Arden was full of mock disappointment. "And I didn't even get the chance to enjoy an initiation. Although, I think I'm with Groucho on that one. Anyway how am I protected by having you two around?"

"You'll get your chance. And I know a few moves." Madsen put his hands up in mock karate stance.

Both men laughed.

"So why are you still here?" The question was phrased as a joke but Madsen could sense the serious undercurrent.

Arden leant forward a little to see if Parks had his eyes closed.

"I just want to find out who killed Hiroko."

"And the rest?"

"I don't know." As Madsen looked up he saw the man Parks was suspicious about glance in his direction then quickly look away.

It was like a virus of the mind. Parks's paranoia was rubbing off on him, taking root in his consciousness. He hated it. It reminded him of his reclusiveness and his sometimes deep felt loathing of his fellow species. Humanity could at times stir him to joy through the works of the great scientists, artists and designers and to abject despair when he listened to politicians, the greedy and the manipulative. He remembered what his mother had told him before her death, that the world was divided into two types of people – the creative and the destructive. The creatives tried to make the world a better place for all, while the majority, the destructive, just made it worse through reckless selfishness and an habitual disregard for others.

Now, more than ever, he wanted to return home but he could no more turn back on the path than he could return to his childhood.

Hannah put down the book. Her concentration had come and gone for the last twenty minutes but was now failing. Looking over to her right she tried surreptitiously to study the man her father had sent her to follow. He seemed down to earth and more together than the photograph had suggested. It did not appear likely that this man was anything like the threat her father had insisted he was. He gave the impression of being more like a man out of his depth, someone who had been thrust into the unwanted spotlight. There was no evidence of a military or intelligence training. His demeanour gave that away. Ex-forces personnel always looked exactly that. Years of training, experience and dedication meant that they had great difficulty stepping beyond the confines of government jurisdiction without revealing who they had once been.

This Madsen looked like he worked for an outdoor sports company or a business selling speedboats. He was tall and well built but he was also in possession of a timidity or a nervousness when among crowds of people. At one point she had caught his eye but simply smiled to disarm him. It had not been difficult. Then she remembered she was on this errand to protect him from her father.

Hannah sat up in her seat a little and looked forward a few rows to where her chaperone was sitting. He was reading a fishing magazine. Not a subject she would automatically associate with his personality but maybe the man was harbouring a dream for his retirement. Unlikely of course. It was just part of the charade. He adjusted his position slightly and Hannah saw the holster for a brief moment. He had been let on board carrying a weapon. It was the work of her father, it had to be. No one else she knew had the clout or the audacity.

A tall brunette stewardess made her way to the man's seat and leant in. She whispered something in his ear and handed him a note. There was no indication; no subtle reveal of body language that suggested these two knew each other. Standing up he glanced back in Hannah's direction then made his way towards the front of the plane.

Looking over at Madsen and his companions she saw the oldest of his associates watching the movements of her chaperone very carefully. He had about him a nervousness, the awareness of a stalked animal. It had to be Parks.

Her father, during a further briefing before she left for the airport, had once again mentioned Parks. As well as being in possession of the book he was an agitator, a man of revolution, an academic with an agenda and the country would be thankful if he was dealt with. Above all else the man was a traitor who wanted to see his homeland collapse into the ruins of a godless apocalypse. Doubtless her chaperone had been told the same information. But Hannah did not believe a word of it. This was, after all, her father and everything he said was loaded with his own personal prejudices and deep bitterness towards anyone who did not fit his narrow view of how the world should be.

Like all men of his kind the root cause of the world's problems were Liberals, leftists, socialists, academics, Zionists, atheists, evolutionists, and the 60s. Her father's list of *bêtes noires* was endless. He was prejudice writ large. There was nothing more destructive, Hannah thought, than an ignorant man with power.

Her chaperone did not return for another ten minutes and when he did there was no glance in Hannah's direction as he sat down. She could see that the dynamic between them had changed. The man looked deadly serious as if he knew a dark and desperate secret.

Looking across she saw Parks staring across at her. He had been watching the interaction between Hannah and the supposed stranger and had obviously worked out the relationship. Their anonymity had been blown.

Franklin returned the phone to its cradle and sat back in his chair, his eyes on the broken seal of the sunsphere file. He had just signed his daughter's death warrant but he could not risk a strategic compromise. Not with something on this scale. She had defied his instructions and now the future was threatened. He would be taking out Madsen and Parks as well, thus losing ground in his search for the missing book but it was a small price to pay. It had to be done.

While the others slept Parks remained wide awake, his attention firmly fixed on the man on the other side of the plane. There was also something about that young woman that had piqued his suspicion. It was obvious she knew the stranger who was sitting several rows ahead of her and Parks knew what to look for in non-verbal communication but his interest had notched up a gear after the man had returned to his seat. He looked as though he now had a dark shadow hanging over him. That he had just stared into the abyss of his final moment. It sent a spasm of ice-cold fear through Parks.

For the last twenty minutes the man had been checking and rechecking his watch. Far below and craning his neck to look Parks could see the English landscape basking in bright afternoon sunlight. The plane was beginning its descent pattern. Why was the time important? To a suspicious Parks, it suggested that some strict schedule was being adhered to. That something had been planned. It had to be more than just flying nerves. The man looked too determined, too focused on something, too primed. When he suddenly stood up, bag in hand Parks lurched forward in his seat his body tense with anticipation. He watched as the man made his way down the aisle towards one of the restrooms.

Parks's agitation stirred Madsen.

"What's the matter?"

"That one. Something about him I don't like."

"What do you mean?" Madsen moved forward in his seat to study the man Parks was referring to.

"I just don't trust him. The first thing he did when he got on the plane was look in our direction. As if he was making sure we were here."

"He's just going to take a leak before we land, that's all. Keep it together." Parks's continuing paranoia was proving to be a constant irritation to Madsen. It seemed that everyone was a threat. "Which can't be long now."

‡

He shut the door behind him. Lifting the bag up onto the sink unit he unzipped it and took out the dark grey laptop. Flipping it open he waited for the system to boot up. Moving the pointer to an icon of the sun he double clicked and opened up a small window then typed in his password, 'Committee 300'. A red line began to fill up in a thin rectangular box. The device had been given a countdown. Always a pointless element, he thought, particularly in a situation like this. An image of his wife and son flitted instantly across his mind's eye. He loved them deeply but knew his actions would also save them and for that he hoped they would understand.

✝

Madsen closed his eyes. He hated landings. The aircraft always felt as if it were in freefall, that the pilots were not really in control. Every odd noise was a part of the plane coming away. Every judder a mechanical failure. Every puzzled look on the faces of the cabin crew a sign that something had gone wrong.

The seatbelt light chimed.

He mentally repeated a mantra, a prayer to the gods of flight, *just land, just land just land, just-*

There was a low boom that made him jump then a long whine as the undercarriage descended. His hands were clammy and he wiped them down the legs of his jeans.

Opening his eyes for a second he caught Arden grinning at him.

"You seen the colour of your face? It's almost transparent –"

Arden's last word dissolved into chaos.

A colossal concussive blast tore through the side of the aircraft ripping debris around the cabin and out into the bright sunlight. Fragments of fuselage spun and arced,

349

tumbling down the side of the plane and careering towards the ground rising up rapidly to meet them.

The aircraft tipped and veered off course, engines howling as the pilots fought to control the plane and return it to its line of descent.

Screams of panic and dread were drowned in the cacophony of air and engine noise as smoke and flame boiled and ripped through the interior swallowing up passenger and cabin crew alike.

Madsen, aware of the oxygen mask bobbing just in front of his face, felt the intense heat followed by a shattering chill as the air blasted in through the gaping hole in the fuselage. He saw an image of Hiroko, she was smiling and he realised he would never find out who it was that was responsible for taking her from him.

On to Act 3

On that dramatic scene, the second section of *Sunsphere* ended. I turned over a few blank pages and began part three, entitled *Eruditio*. Arden had started this section with another letter from Benjamin Franklin.

Before reading on, I paused to take stock. It had been an extraordinary journey. Not just with the novel, but in reality. I mean, here I was on a plane heading to Venice. Was I mad? Had my wits escaped me? Why was I chasing phantoms? I'd maintained throughout that Gus, Linda and Arden were all reading far too much into all this, yet here was I following eagerly – okay, maybe not eagerly – at their heels. Was I, as I had suspected, slowly succumbing to the mystery? It was perhaps academic. I would stick it out to the end, either to confirm my suspicions or become an acolyte of Arden and the global conspiracy he had unearthed. I was hoping for the former whilst fearing the latter.

Eruditio

My dear Dashwood,

I will indeed take up your invitation but we in the newly liberated lands stand upon a new frontier. This will surely be a tentative but industrious time as we strive to bring about new liberties for man. Like all men of ability we have the method and the means to both create and destroy that which we have fought so long to achieve.

My one true fear is that in time others may come to usurp that which they were given and create a government within a government for the sake of their own petty trivialities based on unreason and superstition. We, the people, must not endure such unpatriotic and uncivil behaviour. The ink is not yet dry and I have doubts, but doubts I will share in the knowledge that you will keep them strictly to yourself.

We must be, as ever, very vigilant towards those who yet seek to defy the will of the people. We must stand upon the walls of liberty built to defend truths from those who would take them from us.

Your Faithful Brother,

Benjamin Franklin.

‡

Washington DC, 22 November 1963

They had lost a great soul. Not a perfect man certainly, but who was? He was someone in power who, in his heart knew exactly what was right, not for himself but for everyone. He knew that humanity was one, and as he had said, we all breathe the same air; we all share this small world. For one thousand and twenty-six days he had not only stirred the negative and positive emotions of every American, he had won the heart of the world. He believed that the times had demanded invention, innovation, imagination and decision. But now he was gone and all was in ruins.

Frank Madsen stepped out of the autumnal daylight into the dark of the hall closing the door behind him. Standing there for a moment he tried to absorb the news. He had seen raw emotion on every face, exposed, defiant and defeated. None of the day's events made any sense. All was surreal; every notion of reality washed away, a muted world, silent, bereft, doom laden. Where once there had been optimism now the gathering clouds of menace were rolling in. Above all else he knew one thing. He must escape. It was dangerous to return home, but there were certain items he must destroy and take others into hiding with him. The sanity of the world depended on it.

He stepped into the front room. He was not a drinker but today of all days he was prepared to relinquish his own self-imposed limitations. He unscrewed a bottle of bourbon and poured himself a full glass.

"I didn't take you to be a drinker."

Looking up he saw a figure standing in the gloom at the back of the room. He was returning a slim volume to a bookshelf.

"A salutation to the dead."

"Nor did I take you for a sentimentalist."

"I'm pleased I still surprise you."

"Where is he?"

"Who?"

The figure stepped out of the shadows. He was reaching into a pocket, a smile across his face.

"Parkland Memorial Hospital," Madsen said.

"You know I don't mean him. He's dead and gone, as you knew he would be. You don't throw a challenge down like that and expect to win, do you?" A gun was produced. Reaching into another pocket a suppressor was brought out and attached to the weapon. "And please for the sake of respect don't play dumb."

"You have no respect for what I stand for."

"Why should I? It's all nonsense. Now please answer my question."

"As if I would."

The man shrugged and fired once.

The bullet struck Madsen's leg just above the knee kicking him to the floor.

"Where is he?"

"I don't know what you mean?" The pain was sickening.

The second bullet struck him just above the other knee.

"Please do not persist in this. I will ask you one more time. Where is he?" He aimed the weapon at Frank Madsen's head. "The third man in your council? The third Ordine?"

"You may have stopped us this time but you won't succeed again."

"We can add naiveté to your list of failings. We will always win. Nobody votes for us. We don't need the charade of a voting system to stay in power. Are you going to tell me where he is?"

Josh Madsen was sitting on the edge of the runway wrapped in a thermal blanket. He was staring up at the jagged gaping hole in the side of the aircraft and trying to fathom out the circumstances of their survival. One whole side of the 747 was blackened and scorched, the untouched skin of the fuselage a dance of crisp bright sunlight, heat shimmer and the reflected lights from the emergency vehicles that had swarmed around the crippled plane.

His mind was a scattergun of stilted memories. A heavy landing, the screams, the deafening roar of engines, the 747 sliding to a jarring tilted stop, emergency slides, panic, burnt flesh. A blur of discordant images, flashing lights, faces and above all the brightness of the sun.

He was aware of a figure standing just to his left. Looking up he saw Parks. He was staring up the plane.

"It was him. A bomb. He was trying to kill us." Parks spoke in a dull flat monotone.

"Where's Mark?" There was no sign of him anywhere. There were numerous people scattered over the grass being attended to by paramedics. In all the frenetic chaos Madsen's attention was drawn to a tight knot of people working feverishly over the body of a man. His skin was blackened, oily and the side of his head was a swathe of raw burnt flesh. A doctor, his hands clasped together, was administering vigorous CPR. He appeared to be losing the battle to save the man's life.

"They'll say it was terrorism. They'll use it to further their cause." Parks lifted his head and looked up into the sky that seemed to be as fragile as glass. "They'll just add it to their list of lies." Parks looked down at Madsen. "That was meant for us."

"Because of the book? The missing page?"

"Yes. An irritation that has to be removed. I cannot lead them to the book. It must remain hidden. But the key..." Parks fell silent as a paramedic came to check both he and Madsen over.

"Many dead?" Madsen found himself asking the medic.

"Three. So far. Which is a bloody miracle." The English accent, with its down to earth tone, threw Madsen for a moment. "You all right?" The Paramedic, a fresh faced young man with cropped blond hair, shone a light into Parks's eyes.

Parks nodded.

"And you?" The medic turned his attention to Madsen.

"Just shaken up," Madsen said quietly.

"Understandable mate."

"We're looking for a friend of ours. He was sat with us." Madsen tried to stand up but a wave of nausea spilled through him. He fell back.

"Whoah, nice and easy mate." The paramedic sat down on his haunches and shone the light into Madsen's eyes again. "Mild concussion, I think. As soon as a doctor's free I'll get them to give you the once over. What was your friend's name?"

"Mark Arden."

"I'll find out." Yet another ambulance was pulling up alongside the stricken plane. The paramedic waved it over in his direction.

"Worry about the seriously injured." It seemed the right thing for Madsen to say.

"We have done. It's your turn now."

Madsen smiled as he felt himself begin to pass out. The voices around him disappeared into darkness.

As he opened his eyes he was staring up into the sun. For a few warm seconds he was ten years old again, lying on the dusty grass outside his childhood home, squinting up at the sky and hanging onto the ground for dear life. At any moment he might drop into its eternal depths and be lost forever to the world. It was a thrilling feeling but one created purely of his imagination. Was it like dying? One day he would find out but not today. No, not the sun but a light above his bed.

Madsen was suddenly aware of the frenetic activity of the ward around him. He lifted his head. He was in a cubicle around which a green curtain had been pulled. He could hear two distinct voices just beyond.

Sitting up, he called out.

Parks appeared through a gap.

"What am I, some pariah?" Madsen leant up on his elbows.

"We had to be checked out. I didn't want anyone to know you were here." Parks's voice was almost a whisper.

Madsen sat up and swung off the bed. His head was pounding but other than he felt okay.

"We can't stay." Parks was edgy.

"Aren't there procedures we have to go through?" Madsen asked massaging his temples with a thumb and index finger.

"If there are, we don't have time. We've got to get moving."

"Where's Mark?"

Parks pulled the curtain back a little way. Arden was standing just beyond, a wry grin across his face.

"Why the hurry?" Madsen was looking for his shoes. "Is that suspicious character from the plane lurking in the corridors out there?"

"Mister Madsen, he caused all this. That bag must have been a bomb."

"Didn't do a very good job, did he?" Arden sounded hacked off. "Surely he would've made the bomb more powerful. You know what I'm sayin'?" Maybe Parks's paranoia had finally eaten through Arden's humorous defences.

"You don't need a large amount of explosives to take out a plane Mister Arden." It was Parks's turn to turn on the aggression as he snapped back his reply. "I don't know how we survived–"

Arden cut across him.

"Because of the pilots, man. They brought that plane in like a– "

"I don't know why we survived," Parks continued. "Maybe he did get the explosive amount wrong but I doubt that. That man looked like he knew exactly what he was doing."

"Come on Parks. Do you spend your whole life looking over your shoulder?"

"Yes I do Mister Arden and with good reason." He stepped up close to the younger man and locked his eyes onto him. "I have been watched for as long as I can remember. Now the situation has changed. Now they want me dead because of what I know and who I am with. I was forced to break cover and now I have the hunter's sights on me. I'm a walking target Mister Arden as are both of you. Mister Madsen more so."

"But why? This is so insane."

Parks's voice dropped to a fierce whisper.

"Because of what we represent Mister Arden."

Arden shook his head and turned away.

"Or maybe you're just paranoid. Ever thought that might be the answer?" Arden's question was almost rhetorical.

Parks turned towards Madsen.

"Mister Madsen. With all you have been through would you suggest I am simply being paranoid?"

"No. I just don't understand why, fully I mean." Madsen, after a second's thought, had to shake his head. He made an apologetic shrug towards Arden.

Parks lowered his head for a moment. He then looked up at Madsen.

"Do you remember your father?"

"What? What do you mean?"

"It is a simple question Mister Madsen."

"Why are you asking me about my father?"

"Do you remember him or not? Frank Madsen?"

Madsen gave Parks a puzzled, questioning look.

"Your father died in nineteen sixty three. Did he not?"

Madsen nodded.

"You were a very young boy, away at school. Did they say how he died?"

"Car accident."

"It was no car accident." Parks shook his head. "The man was shot. Executed is perhaps more apt."

"What? No. It was a hit and run accident just outside our house in Washington. A few hours after Kennedy's assassination." Madsen trailed off.

Parks was shaking his head.

"Three bullets Mister Madsen. A hit. Because your father knew the reasons why Kennedy was shot. He was trying to keep history on course and he had tried to save the President." Parks took a few steps towards Madsen. "Because he had tried to keep the world from going to hell. Because he was defending the great work. Because he was an Ordine. His murderer was trying to wipe them out. They'd already killed one – the President. You father was second. But they never found the third Ordine."

Madsen shook his head almost imperceptibly.

"A direction had been set but that fateful day in Dealey Plaza was like switching the points on a track. It changed the direction of everything that had been set in motion. Your father had tried to switch the points back but had failed. For his noble action he was executed by the enemy."

"My father was involved with Kennedy?"

"Yes, Mister Madsen. Kennedy was an Ordine." Parks paused to allow this revelation to sink in. Both Madsen and Arden looked suitably stunned.

"Both men were Ordines? My father and Kennedy? They made decisions together? That's incredible."

"Isn't it?" Arden sounded unconvinced. "Who was the third?

"I don't know. You have to think of the Ordines as the rudder on a ship. The ship of history for want of a better metaphor."

"Can't steer straight," Arden said quietly.

"Because there's a constant battle to control the rudder. It's all control. Control through fear and deception. Fear of terrorism, fear of the devil, whatever that is, fear of failure, fear of free thought, fear of standing out from the crowd. It goes on. History has been about ways to control the human race. Don't ever forget that. The Ordines want to remove the fear that's all. Take that away and we are all free." Parks seemed to deflate, emotionally spent. "Forgive me, I'm…"

"Don't worry. To say we have been through much lately would be an understatement." Madsen rested a hand on one of Parks's shoulders. "Remember we're new to all this. It's not every day you learn how important your father really was."

"Well, wise up because that's the way it is if you step outside the social corral." Parks leant against the bed. "We really have to get out of here. As soon as they learn the plane survived they'll come looking for us."

"Social corral. Are you talking a Matrix thing here?"

Parks looked annoyed.

"What was that but a rehash of Philip K. Dick anyway. No, this is reality Mister Arden."

"You've read the great man?" Arden asked.

"Read him, met him. In California in the seventies. The Ordines contacted him. Now we really must go."

"Wow." For once Arden seemed genuinely surprised. "Anyway, where are we going? Seems silly to ask. We've come all this way." He grinned.

"Not here," Parks snapped back. He stepped out from the cubicle and looked around. The hospital had been put on alert. With the Tube bombings in London still fresh in the memory there was a distinct sense of tension. Parks could see it on the faces of the members of staff and patients alike. "Mister Arden and I will leave now and you follow in a few minutes. We'll meet up outside. Hopefully this will draw less attention." He then set off down the ward.

"If it wasn't for the wound on my arm I'd still say all of this was just a hill of crap. See you outside." Arden gave Madsen a sharp salute.

For a long time Madsen stood with his own thoughts, a stream of confused images and notions. His father and

Kennedy? Ordines? It seemed fanciful, make believe...
extraordinary... both men striving for real change...

Although Parks was no evangelist it seemed his
words, like a virus, had sunk home and Madsen was not sure
he liked what he was learning. Not that everything was too
convenient, far from it. It seemed as if he had taken a side
step in reality to this odd world that existed behind the
apparent artifice of the everyday. What had Parks said, *a
social corral*. Maybe he was right. He took a breath and
paused to clear his head, trying to quickly develop an excuse
in case anyone asked why he was leaving.

Stepping out from behind the curtain he scanned the
ward then set off in the same direction as Parks and Arden,
following the exit signs. The place was busy but something
caught his eye and he looked over and recognised the face of
the young woman that Parks claimed was working with the
man who had set the bomb. A nurse was cleaning a gash in
her right cheek. Sitting on the other side of the plane she had
escaped serious injury but had not avoided a flying shard of
debris.

Sensing someone was looking at her she looked up.
Madsen continued walking but his eyes had fixed to hers.
She smiled at him. It was a warm and friendly gesture
instantly dissolving Parks's transmitted paranoia, which
Madsen had to admit, was starting to affect him quite badly
and to the detriment of his grasp on reality.

He was leaving. She would have to act first to follow
him. He was too far away to attract his attention properly
and why would he come over anyway. They were strangers.
Then she realised that Madsen's companion, Parks, had
connected her with her chaperone despite her father's
insistence they travel separately. It would have been better if
they had travelled as a couple instead. A less obvious
charade. For the foreseeable future at least, Madsen would

understandably still see her as the enemy. She could not help feeling that this is exactly what her father wanted. Maybe he suspected the possibility of her betrayal and this was his idea of another hurdle for her to negotiate. Any vestige of trust for him had now finally withered. Like falling out of love there was a flatness, an emotional void edged with a certain degree of relief. There was neither guilt nor sadness. She had hung on too long. Her attachment to her father was ballast that needed to be cut away so that she could reach the surface and breathe fresh air. Sometimes it was easier to let go than continue a fight.

Madsen and his companions were in England for a reason. For the book certainly but there was definitely more to it than chasing down an old manuscript. There was that description and photograph from her father's study. That unusual church located in England, in the village of West Wycombe. Perhaps the book was there. It all seemed too good to be a coincidence. She would risk her intuition and assume that was the place they were heading for. The main reason for their journey.

The nurse finished by applying a few butterfly stitches to the wound.

"There we are, all done. Just try not to knock them. Allow the wound to close up properly."

"Okay." Hannah paused. "Do you know where I can buy a map?"

Paddington Station was bustling. News of the plane's near miss had exploded across the media, still red hot from the recent attacks on Canary Wharf and the Bank of England. This year at least the targets had shifted from those of a civilian nature to that of business. People tended to be more resilient, the markets less so. Initially everyone assumed that the bomb had been set off to cripple the airlines but then there were doubts due to the intense levels of security. The accusations began with claim and counter claim straining the special trans-Atlantic friendship on one hand, and further afield in the international arena on the other.

People with their own agendas and right across the political spectrum were setting out to accuse the usual suspects, all of them innocent of the crime. Useful gains could be made from manipulative and damaging rhetoric, hot on the heels of which would be the loss of further civil liberties. Politicians spoke of the nature of the way of life not being immutable as a defiant gesture to the acts of atrocity yet immediately set about changing things claiming, in their usual way, that it was for the good of all.

Faces were nervous on the platforms. Unattended bags were stared at, people moved away. Armed Police were everywhere – as if guns were any use against explosions. A good number of people were leaving the trains and heading up to the taxi ranks where a long irritated queue had formed.

"All part of the great game." Parks sounded deeply cynical and world-weary. There was less paranoia about him and more a sense of resignation as if his deepest suspicions had been finally and overwhelmingly confirmed. Both he and Madsen were waiting by the overhead departures and arrivals display as Arden made his way back from an information window.

"Wrong place. We need to go to Marylebone Station. There's a train that takes us to a place called High Wycombe, the nearest town. It's on the Chiltern line or something-" Arden was cut short.

There was a shout. Everyone turned. A group of police officers, weapons raised, were zeroing in on a man carrying a black and grey backpack. There was fear in his eyes as he obeyed their orders to lie down. From a different direction a plain-clothes detective, handgun pointed at the suspect's head moved steadily and purposefully in his direction. The crowds fell away, backing off swiftly to a safe distance.

"What a world we've made," Parks muttered, his face sour with scorn. "Everything played out like a game."

"A game?" Madsen asked.

"All of history is a game. A strategic game of chess with greed as its motivation." Parks watched as the plain-clothes detective launched a verbal tirade against the man, the gun rammed right up against his temple.

"We should go, before this gets too complicated." Arden motioned towards the exit.

The gates to the platforms were shut and more police officers appeared to begin ushering travellers from the station.

There was a bang... that echoed around the building...

A gunshot...

The man with the backpack lay twitching on the floor... blood pooling in the tiles around his head...

Panic set in. The crowd collapsed into an unruly mob fighting for the exits as the primitive urge to survive broke through the paper-thin layer of civilisation.

"Do you think this was all arranged for us?" Arden looked deeply alarmed as he asked the question of Parks while the three of them were harried towards the main entrance.

"What do you think?" The reply was snapped back.

"If I was you, I'd say yes."

"Then yes."

Outside Paddington, Praed Street and Eastbourne Terrace were quickly heading towards gridlock as police and other emergency vehicles moved swiftly into the scene. Anxious crowds of people were being moved back behind police cordons while the traffic was directed away down side streets.

"Guess we walk." Madsen was looking around for a street sign.

"How far? Maybe we should ask for directions." Arden cast his eyes around the nervous crowd.

"It's this way." Parks pointed up Praed Street, now solid with police cars.

Pushing their way against the tide of people they made their way as anonymous figures in the faceless crowds. Looking up at one point Madsen had to smile at the perversity of probability and the juxtaposition of two extremes. Art in a sea of chaos. In the window of a coffee shop he saw a poster advertising an exhibition at the National Gallery. The theme was American artists in Europe and the image used was that of John Singer Sargent's watercolour, *Fortune on the Dogana*.

"Why are you smiling?" Arden asked seeing the knowing grin across Madsen's face.

He replied with a short shake of the head.

There was a tremor and for a few seconds the ground shook. Numerous large windows burst in the vibration, showering the street with sunlit shards to the stilted cacophony of a thousand car alarms. Thick acrid smoke was boiling up onto the road from the slipway exit at the side of Paddington Station.

Panic hit the people like a monstrous detonation.

Madsen found himself running, caught up in a relentless surge. His mind was unthinking and blank, the primitive urge for self-preservation overriding any modern sensibilities. He was a herd animal again racing to escape the predator.

Parks and Arden were lost in the crowd but rather than stop to look for them he realised that his best bet was to make for Marylebone and hope the others were thinking the same thing.

The crowds spilled into Edgware Road and a number of people were struck by cars as they ran headlong into the traffic. Black cabs braked awkwardly careering into others. Buses jack-knifed. A truck bounced onto the curb colliding with a police car and half a dozen people. In a matter of seconds there was gridlock, chaos, more panic. Ruptured fuel tanks spewed petrol onto tarmac. Thick smoke rolled across the road. Car fumes thickened into choking clouds. Screams and car horns detonated in the thick baking London atmosphere.

With the crowds hesitating and slowing, Madsen wove his way through the traffic jam and across the other side of Edgware Road. He crossed quickly into Chapel Street then made his way to Lisson Grove and eastwards along Marylebone.

A middle aged man, his cheeks red with effort and the afternoon heat and carrying several large cameras was moving swiftly down the pavement in the opposite direction.

Madsen ran up to him.

"Can you tell me where Marylebone Station is?"

"Outta my way. I got a job to do mate!" The man slowed enough to adjust one of the cameras. "Up there. Then next right. But forget it. They're shutting all the lines down." He hurried on.

Madsen, sweating, paused to think. He looked around at the traffic pulling up. Horns were blaring. Cab drivers leant out of windows to shout expletives at other motorists who responded in kind. The city was grinding inexorably to a halt.

Maybe Parks was right. This was all for their sake. To stop them reaching their destination. Then he realised the arrogance and stupidity of the man's statement. All this for three men? Parks would doubtless continue to attest to that sentiment but Madsen could not. It seemed the height of paranoiac delusion. Yet, what else could he expect from the man? The world was one grand lie to him. One mighty fabrication in which the entire human race were witless players in a dumb show for the benefit of a few. Pawns in the chess game that Parks called history.

A decision...

Separated from the others Madsen knew that if he wanted he could turn around, disappear into the crowds and head home. He could walk away, step out of these wonderland theatrics and return to Boston to continue the life he had known. He would never know who killed Hiroko but it would be one more loss he would learn to live with. There was no such thing as peace of mind. Life was never that fair but at least he would be in familiar territory, a retreat if not a sanctuary. He could avoid the affairs of men and walk the beach again watching the simple ebb and flow of the tides. Nature's patterns.

A decision.

Made for him.

Arden came barreling out of the crowds.

"Where's Parks?" he asked searching the faces around him.

"I don't know," Madsen sighed. He felt the molten lead of resentment around his sinking heart. A restless agitation made his body tense. He wanted to run.

Looking up a side street Arden saw Parks waving for them to follow.

"There he is. Come on."

"They'll have shut the stations down." His lack of enthusiasm was given away in Madsen's tone.

Arden misinterpreted it.

"Don't worry, we'll steal a car." It was an attempt by the younger man to rekindle his colleague's humour.

In a few moments they rejoined Parks. The man was as nervous as ever, alternately squeezing his hands together.

Between Madsen's apparent ennui and Parks's frayed nerves, Arden tried to rally their spirits.

"I think it's safe to say they'll have stopped the trains running, at least for a while. Why don't we just lie low until things settle?"

Parks turned on him.

"Mister Arden we cannot afford to wait. Time is running out."

"What the hell do you suggest then? What do we do, eh? What?" Arden's cool demeanour evaporated in the London heat.

"What we have to!"

They left the city on a broad circuitous route taking the A40 and then the M40, heading in a westerly direction towards Beaconsfield. It seemed the wisest and safest route to take under the circumstances, not only to avoid the worsening situation in central London but for the simple fact that they had stolen a car, a silver 4x4, a vehicle that looked as though it had never once been off road, much to the cynical delight of Arden.

Madsen had found himself behind the wheel almost by default, a subconscious desire to be in control perhaps, to stem the feelings of helplessness or just a way to concentrate on something other than plots and conspiracies that made up Parks's worldview. He was fighting a rising sense of animosity towards the man. It was anger sure, but he was not certain as to its source. Was it born of his frustration, or his unwillingness to see things the way Parks did? Or was he genuinely exhausted by the whole affair? Were he and Arden just willing dupes along for the ride? Were they being manipulated in some bizarre scheme? He was certainly angry about becoming a target through his involvement but was there something else? Was Parks genuine? It seemed an obvious question and one he had put off asking himself for far too long.

If what Parks had said and at least hinted at was half-true then why had he not been silenced before? If the situation, this grand power play, was as perilous as the man made it out to be why had those involved not silenced him long before?

The man had thought it the right time to break cover. It was, in truth, the only answer. By dragging Madsen and Arden along Parks had effectively had the searchlight shone on them. They were guilty by association. But then Madsen had to remind himself that it was he who had found Parks, not the other way round. He had turned the stones over looking for answers. He had found this strange and dangerous path on which he was now travelling. Maybe Parks was keeping him alive. It appeared that they were only a step ahead of the enemy because of him.

He was blaming others for his state of mind. Maybe Gregory had been right. He had locked himself away for far too long. He had surrendered to fear too easily, too readily, instead of taking life by the horns and revelling in its preciousness. Others talked of life after death. It was a fallacy. He had to live it now and experience it all before it was too late. It was a subliminal, even subconscious drive that may have kept him alive.

He wondered how his friend was getting on. Was he telling their clients that Camelot's king was indisposed; that he was on some strange quest hounded on all sides by forces rallying against him? He did not want to accept the possibility that Gregory had become another victim of this looking glass adventure. There was a pang of guilt. He should have called to see if the man was okay. That the business was doing just fine without him. He would try and call as soon as an opportunity presented itself.

"Don't miss the turning." Arden looked up from a road map, his finger tracing the blue line that led away from London. "Junction four."

"Got it." Madsen nodded.

"So we're nearly there Parks. What have you got in mind?" Arden asked keeping his eyes on the road map.

Parks cleared his throat.

"I'm only interested in the church of St Lawrence. Forget the caves."

"Caves?"

"Yes Mister Arden, caves. The Hell Fire Club used to meet in a nearby Abbey until it was burnt down. Dashwood excavated caves beneath a nearby hill, a pagan refuge in which he and his colleagues could entertain themselves away from the eyes of those who would try and stop them."

"I know the feeling," Arden huffed.

"Precisely the same forces that rallied against Dashwood are trying to stop us Mister Arden. Because of certain secrets, secrets that are held within the confines of the church."

"Where?" Madsen was taking perverse pleasure in trying to catch the man out.

"Mister Arden knows one of them." Parks's statement took Arden by surprise.

"I do?" Looking up from the road map Arden turned to look over at Parks.

"Yes Mister Arden, you do. At least I hope you do."

"You got me. I don't have a clue what you're talking about."

"Your friend left you an envelope."

"Jim?"

"In case anything happened."

"How do you know about that Parks?" Arden reached up to his coat pocket and touched the envelope inside.

"He told me."

"Really?"

"We had an understanding." Parks turned and looked out of the back window.

Arden was thoughtful.

"Tell me Parks, is this the only reason you allowed me to tag along?"

"What do you think, Mister Arden?" Parks asked.

"If you were to ask me I would say yes."

"Then you are correct."

"Buchanan was looking for me that day in New York. But not for my sake... he wanted the envelope. Parks man, you're an ass."

"It's about trust, that's all, Mister Arden."

"Is it hell!" Arden turned to Madsen. "Can you believe this guy?"

Madsen was studying Parks in the rear view mirror. He was enigmatic in the extreme. If he failed to find those responsible for Hiroko's death he would at least make it his goal to find out as much as possible about Parks.

"There's a whole damn universe to move around in and I end up here caught up in your odd world Parks." Arden shook his head and sighed.

"Oh, it's not fate Mister Arden. It's just statistics and probability," Parks stated in a monotone. He then continued and said thoughtfully looking out of the window, "The size of the universe is more evidence for the non-existence of god. And why create something so enormous for the sake of humanity only? Arrogance. You mistake the randomness of events for purpose and fate. There's no purpose to the universe."

"It was just a comment on my state of affairs Parks. I didn't want a lecture on astrophysics or philosophy."

"I meant please get things into perspective, Mister Arden. This is not about you. You are just a minor player. The envelope you possess is just a small part of a larger puzzle. When that puzzle is complete the picture will liberate us. In many respects you are incidental. We are all incidental."

"Here's junction four." Madsen was pleased to have a distraction. It was not so much a banality to bring the conversation down to earth, that was hardly likely, but it was at least something of the everyday.

Arden turned the road map in his hand.

"The A4010 through a place called Booker, then on up to another road, the A40, then left."

Madsen nodded.

"An envelope?" he asked.

Arden reached into a pocket and took out the envelope Big Jim had left him. He held it up.

Parks was suddenly animated.

"There was a contract in here." Arden was matter of fact.

"Anything else?" Parks leant forward.

"Just a piece of paper with the words, 'one of them is with the birds and the serpent'." Arden studied Parks for any sign of recognition. "Do you know what it means?"

Parks reached for the paper but Arden pulled it close to his chest.

"No, I don't, Mister Arden."

"Now you know that, does it make me redundant to your cause? Is my life forfeit?" Arden was only half joking.

Parks sank back into his chair and stayed silent.

"Hey, don't talk that way." Madsen sounded genuinely upset.

All Arden could do was stare at Madsen.

"Look…" Parks leant forward in the back seat and pointed through the windshield.

There before them, to the west, standing atop the bulk of West Wycombe hill, was the church of St Lawrence. The golden globe was burning against the blue sky, a miniature sun somehow incongruous yet fallen from heaven to perch in the English countryside. It demanded attention, so striking was the sunlit orb. A beacon above the landscape from deep within the psyche of a nation, like Silbury Hill or Avebury, Stonehenge or a thousand monuments and buildings since, each one mightier still.

Madsen involuntarily slowed the car. Although it was not the one from the architectural drawing it was just as magnetic, just as beautiful and equally as enigmatic. It had been for so long an image in his mind's eye. Now here it was, a reality, something solid, visible and no longer a phantom of the imagination. It felt to him like a thoughtform, a tulpa created for his own amusement.

"A golden sphere that represents the sun god born at the winter solstice. A solar symbol. The Light of the World." Parks's voice was sonorous.

"Do you mean Jesus Christ?" Arden asked.

"No," came the clipped reply. "He was a construct. An artifice. An image created for the purposes of power. " Parks shifted in his seat, irritated. "Read Philostratus's book about Apollonius of Tyana, The Origins of Christianity and The Jesus Conspiracy by Acharya Sanning, or Gospel Fictions by Randel Helms." Then added, "At least."

"You're a walking library Parks."

"Thank you, Mister Arden. Reading the right books broadens the mind."

"It's beautiful." Somehow the words were less than adequate and Madsen balked at how dumb he sounded.

"I'm surprised no religious zealot has tried to blow it up."

"But there are many who see it as sacrilegious Mister Arden, as something satanic. Some even claim this part of England to be the source of all evil." Parks paused, then added, "They are, of course, insane."

Arden laughed.

"The Victorians with all their twisted sexuality and perverse morality physically attacked the church here seeing it as nothing but a focus for pagan idolatry."

"You've done your homework, Parks."

"Of course, Mister Arden. This has dominated my research for most of my life. Every part of this estate contains deep secrets from pentagons in the graveyard to sculptures in the caves. I could spend years here and still be none the wiser."

"I still say you should get out more."

"And do what precisely Mister Arden?"

"Steal more cars…"

Hannah was thankful for the cool of the interior. For years she had thought England to be a dreary, rain soaked island beloved of Hollywood cliché. To find the place sweltering in a thick heat wave was more than surprising if not a little exhilarating. Perhaps her feelings had more to do with the location and her father's animosity towards the church of St Lawrence than revelations about a country's weather.

Above her was a painting of the Last Supper in which the powerful eyes of Judas seemed to dominate. They were almost hypnotic but equally accusative. Her father had said the depiction was an abomination owing to the fact that it was a representation of an *agape*, a pagan mystical celebration of love. But Hannah had done her own reading and had discovered that the early Christians had always held a love feast before and after Communion and by that she assumed an orgy of sorts. Eventually, she learnt these festivals had grown far too scandalous and were condemned by the Council of Carthage in 397.

The church, if she could call it that, did not seem to be the place anyone would really, in a sense, worship in. It had more the feel of an Egyptian temple, at least a building from the eastern Mediterranean, than a Christian one, with its Corinthian pillars and walls decorated with friezes of olive branches, fruit, leaves and doves. Elsewhere, the sun, including a huge mandala, and serpent motifs seemed to dominate. It felt like a hybrid or a blending of faiths were being exalted, with a sense that the observer was not yet party to some deeper arcane understanding; one that would only be revealed through initiation into some secret school. Perhaps the Judas figure acted as a warning to anyone who might try to reveal the hidden knowledge.

Hannah took a mouthful of mineral water from a bottle then reached up to unpin her hair. She was only vaguely aware that others had entered the interior seeking perhaps swift solace from the heat. As she casually turned to look she saw that it was Madsen, Parks and the younger man Arden. With mock concentration she began to study a frieze keeping her back to the three men while she thought about the best way to approach them.

Maybe an honest and forthright introduction was the best way, assuming of course, that they would be responsive to her. Parks, she realised, would be the most difficult to convince but if she could work on the other two then maybe he would be won over.

"Josh Madsen."

"Yeah?" Madsen looked up from his study of a lectern. Parks was instantly on guard. He recognised the woman standing before them.

"Hey, you were on the plane."

"I was." Hannah paused. "Mark Arden isn't it?"

"How do you know our names?" Parks's paranoia was tipping into anger.

"Because my father briefed me."

"Your father? I don't understand."

"Oh you will Mister Madsen." Hannah took a few paces towards them. Parks watched her like a hawk. "My father sent me to follow you."

"Why?"

Parks stepped in to answer.

"Because a man called Franklin is her father."

"He is. He wants something you have."

"Why are you telling us? Shouldn't you be-"

"Pretending to be your friend before stealing the second key? I could be. But I don't want it. I'm here to warn you." Hannah tried to sound genuine but the more she spoke the less convincing she thought she sounded.

"Second key?"

"For the sunsphere, Mister Arden. I thought Parks would have told you everything."

"He's said lot of things. Little of it makes sense." Arden turned and looked at Parks.

Parks stepped forward.

"Listen Miss Franklin, tell your father to go to hell!" Parks's outburst shattered the peace of the church's interior.

"I already have done. I don't want the key and I certainly don't want my father to have the key either."

"Why should we trust you?" There was still venomous resentment in Parks's voice.

"I guess you can't. You will have to trust me."

374

"But the man who was with you on the plane had a bomb," Parks said, taking a step forward. His anger had given him some degree of confidence.

"He was sent by my father. Who doesn't trust me." Hannah took a step towards Parks for emphasis. "I didn't want him along. And now I detest my father even more because he wanted me dead as well as you Mister Parks. Do you get that? My father's act of betrayal has become mine. He can go to hell."

"That man could have used a more potent explosive on the plane. Made a good job of it. Why didn't he?"

"Come on Parks, calm down." Madsen put a hand on Parks's shoulder.

"No I won't. Seems too convenient for me."

"More paranoia."

Parks spun and stared at Arden.

"It is not more paranoia. It is common sense. Her father tried to have us all killed!"

Rolling his eyes heavenward Arden gave an exhale of frustration.

"Whatever, man."

Hannah reached into a pocket and took out a folded piece of paper.

"As a small token of trust." She handed it to Madsen who unfolded it. On it was her hand drawn image of they key Hannah had handed over to her father. "He sent me to find this one. I did, eventually, but I am also aware of its importance. I assume it's one of several."

"It's one of three." Parks leant in.

"How do we know it's genuine?" Arden asked.

"Oh it's genuine," Parks replied. "One of three that will open the sunsphere on top of the Dogana del Mare in Venice."

"One of them is here or so you say. Where's the third?" Madsen returned the piece of paper to Hannah.

"It will be in Venice of course." Parks turned his attention to the church interior. "But first we have to find the second. Birds and the serpent wasn't it?"

"That's right." Arden reached into his pocket. He took out the envelope and handed it to Parks.

While Parks and Arden began to look around Hannah's eyes caught Madsen's. He was studying her, looking for any tell-tale signs that would reveal her true purpose.

"You still don't trust me do you, Mister Madsen?"

"Josh, please. And, well, maybe not yet. You're the daughter of Parks's bugbear." Madsen half smiled.

"That's no reason for you to dislike me."

"True. But let's just say that the last week or so has been... weird." He smiled. For the moment at least Hannah seemed genuine. He sensed parity in her manner. Years of experience negotiating deals had taught him to recognise troublemakers. He was no people expert but his sensitivity had stood him in good stead, as it appeared to be doing so now. "Franklin?"

"Yes he is. An ancestor I mean."

Madsen gave an appreciative nod. Then he remembered what Parks had told him about his past.

"Seems we have ancestors who both knew each other."

"How so?" Hannah gave him a sideways look.

"Apparently I'm related to a Francis Dashwood who did all this." Madsen glanced around the church. "According to Parks here, Dashwood was great friends with Benjamin Franklin."

"Seems they're both tied to this place, even now."

"I would hesitate to use the word destiny but yeah, I guess you're right."

Hannah looked up at the painting of the Last Supper.

"Do you know the wedding at Canaa, you know water into wine, was really Jesus's own?" she asked.

"No, I never knew that."

"It would make more sense of Da Vinci's Last Supper."

"To be honest, I'm not religious." Madsen sounded almost apologetic.

"It's all about the mysteries of life." Hannah appeared to have ignored him. "Man and Woman, nothing more sacred than that, in a manner of speaking. The alchemical wedding. Take out all the symbolism and you're left with sex. How we all begin."

"Makes more sense. But all those alchemists. If they could defy physics and transform lead into gold, it would make gold worthless."

"More importantly what does all this have to do with keys and sunspheres?" Hannah drew her attention back to Madsen.

"Ask him. He knows." Madsen pointed at Parks who was paying close attention to what looked like a tall thin table on a tripod of small gold legs that stood behind a red rope cordon. On its top were carvings of small birds and climbing up the pedestal was a green-grey serpent, its attention fixed forever on its prey above. Resting next to it on the flagstone floor was another much smaller table with a legend fixed to it.

"You got something there Parks?" Arden made his way over. "Birds and a serpent together?"

"Yes."

"What is that?"

"A font. Of sorts."

Cutting it Short

I'll cut to the chase. Rummaging around the font they found the other key. I say rummaging. They had to break the thing to retrieve the key and not without kicking up some fuss as they did so. It was of course the finale for that part of the book. I guess they'll tell you that on writing courses and film script seminars. And guess where they were going after that? Venice. Of course. Well I can't say I blame them. It is perhaps the most beautiful city in the world. But anyway they had what they wanted and off they were jolly well going, still pursued, I might add, by nefarious forces controlled by Franklin senior.

Venice, Eh?

"You'll have to trust me. I don't want my father to get hold of whatever secret these keys reveal." Despite Madsen's reservation about Hannah, he was at least willing to give her the benefit of the doubt.

"So what do you suggest we do?" Madsen asked.

It was Parks who answered. "Go to Venice and find a way to open the Sunsphere before they do." He was making for the door. "And quickly."

"But, we have the keys…"

"Mister Madsen for now we do but as long as we have them we are not safe from the enemy. They are at our heels."

Madsen felt Hannah's eyes on him. "What do you think?" he asked.

"We follow him," Arden answered for her. "Let's just hope this isn't going to be a spectacular waste of time. A lot has been sacrificed on the way. A lot of people have died for those keys."

Parks turned at the threshold. "Then let's not dishonour them by failing," he said gravely. "When we reveal the secret, we will have won."

378

Ah, Venice

I awoke with a start. A bit clichéd but nevertheless 'twas the truth but sometimes real life is just rich in clichés, always I might add at the most inappropriate moments. The sound of the undercarriage grinding down jolted me from slumber. I think I was dreaming about being pursued down tunnels that didn't seem to lead anywhere while the three sun keys, melting from the heat of my hands, were nothing more than foil wrapped chocolate that tasted bitter when I licked my fingers. Looking out of the window the city was draped in an afternoon haze. The plane banked and dipped and made its final approach into aeroporto Marco Polo.

After the usual wimbling about in customs, passport control etc, blah, Gus, Linda and I made our way to the luggage retrieval machinery where we picked up our small suitcases. We'd thought ahead this time and packed a change of clothes. When I picked mine up I noticed that it had been opened. The fastening straps were loose and the case lid hadn't been replaced properly.

Now I know they have the right to do this but it was still a little unsettling. There's something inherently invasive about having someone rummaging through your smalls. Did the person have herpes? Had they washed their hands after a damn good dump? How do I know they didn't take it in turns kicking everything around wherever it is they open suitcases. Gus too had suffered at the hands of the backroom rummagers. They'd treated his even more recklessly. Half his clothes were hanging out.

Linda tried calling Arden but there was no reply.

On leaving Blighty, having taken my shoes off, I was more than a shade embarrassed by my socks. My right big toe was sticking out of a hole. I'd forgotten about it when wrestling my least dirty socks from the laundry pile in the corner of my bedroom to don for the journey.

To my eternal joy though, I had noticed that at least half a dozen other men were in a similar situation. All of them trying to remain resolutely defiant. All tackling international terrorism had done was reveal the true state of the British sock.

To avoid any suspicion Gus had attached the sun key to his own set of keys. So that when it went through the spot-the-terrorist-machine it went by unseen. It was just another key.

'Where are we staying?' I asked as we made our way out of the main building looking for a taxi.

'The Hotel-' Linda rummaged in her bag and pulled out her notebook. 'Albergo... is that hotel?... Er... Scherzo.' She also rummaged for and produced her Italian phrase book.

In faltering English and crap phrasebook Italian we found and took the ferry into Venice. As we chugged along a busy canal I kept my eyes open for anything remotely golden and sun shaped but saw nothing.

I'd never been to Venice before. I had read a little about it and had been told it was wallet abusing, in that *a tenner for a cup of tea* type expensive, an amount enough to give every right thinking Brit a heart attack. Still, as we chugged our way towards what I think, rightly, is the most beautiful city on planet Earth I couldn't have cared less. I had only seen the place in lavish TV docs presented by grey haired smoothies or in lavish coffee table books. The reality, I might add, was far better.

The hotel was down a side street. We checked in and discovered that we were all on different floors and in remote parts of the narrow corridored labyrinthine building. It wasn't a large establishment from the front, its walls an ochrous stucco, but once inside it seemed to go on forever. I think that I actually went up four flights of stairs then down two and back up one. At one point I thought I'd found my room then realised I hadn't.

When I eventually found my boudoir it had a small window that overlooked an inner courtyard that appeared to get only a small percentage of feeble sunlight during the day.

To my left the walls were dark and splashed with shadow. I could hear a radio somewhere, a rich Italian voice rattling away about something and music from an open window a floor below me. Well fiddle-de-dee, it was *The Magic Flute*, the old *Zauberflöte*, all Masonic or *Massone*, in the local parlance or *gergo*, I should say. It certainly added a fitting soundtrack to the afternoon, although I had half expected all my movements, bowel or otherwise, to be accompanied by lute music or Vivaldi.

I had no idea which part of the hotel the others were in. I'd lost them what seemed like hours ago. This place had a way of disorientating me, not just in space but also in time. Maybe Venice does this to everyone who finds themselves lost in her beauty. It was a heady blend of tiredness and conspiracy theory. I felt a little like I'd had a few drinks – you know, that lunchtime two or three that softens the edges and makes the world a better place. Realising I hadn't had a drink for yonks, I decided to seek out some refreshment and perhaps on the way bump into Gus or Linda. I made my way back through the maze wishing that I had left breadcrumbs in the tunnels to my room. Where was Ariadne when I needed her? Oddly enough and for reasons beyond my comprehension, I stuffed the well-thumbed and now horribly dog-eared *Sunsphere* into my jacket pocket before leaving.

In the Italian style, the floors were all marbled and tiled and my shuffling about up and down multitudinous steps must have sounded ludicrous to anyone with hand cupped to wall wondering what on earth that English berk was up to.

A chambermaid appeared.

'Posso aiutarla?' she asked.

As a wild stab in the dark by way of a response I nodded, assuming her question had something to do my present predicament.

She pointed down a dimly lit corridor. I smiled my appreciation and headed off.

Somehow and much to my surprise I found myself in the lobby. Linda was there, looking nervous and dare I say it, horribly unsettled.

'You all right?' It was obvious she wasn't.

'Mark was supposed to call. Leave a message at the desk. But he hasn't.' Linda was biting her nails. 'Do you think he'll call?'

Actually no I don't, if I'm going to be honest. It was obvious, all along really, that the man had his own agenda.

'I'm sure he'll turn up. Where's Gus?'

'I think we should go to the Customs House and see if he's there.' She moved to look out of the glass panel in the main door. There was nothing to see but the building opposite. 'Maybe he's waiting for us nearby. There's that famous cocktail place across the water isn't there?'

'Harry's Bar. We'll have a Bellini. Is that Gus or Arden?'

'Arden of course.' There was an edge to Linda's voice. A woman scorned, no doubt. 'Gus has gone to Harry's Bar.'

'Well, let's andiamo as they say hereabouts.' Feeling a little confused and not a shade unalarmed at Linda's mental state, I opened the front door. Personally, I would have preferred to have beetled about the city sniffing out the interesting places but I felt obliged, having come all this way, to fall in behind my colleague.

Bedroom Talk

There was a knock at the door.

"Yes?" Madsen got up off the bed.

"It's me. Okay to come in?" Hannah asked.

"Sure."

She pushed opened the door and entered.

"I needed to talk. Did I disturb you?" Hannah looked around. "Your room's smaller than mine."

"What about?" Madsen stood up. "No. I was just thinking about going downstairs and finding something to eat."

Hannah hesitated. She curled a lock of hair back behind her ear.

"Listen. I know Parks doesn't trust me, but you have to believe me, I have no love left for my father and I have no desire to see him win."

"Parks is distrustful of everyone. Although it's not quite a lifetime's work it must feel like it sometimes. All this I mean." Madsen took his jacket off the back of a seat. "It's not you personally."

"I can't be that confident. He knows who I am. In his eyes I'm a spy sent to sabotage the enemy or report on how well he's doing."

"If it's any consolation, I don't trust Parks either. Both he and your father are after the same thing but for different reasons. They're two faces on the same coin."

"You don't trust Parks? Really?"

"Not for a moment."

Hannah smiled. "I'm not alone. I never thought of it that way. Both men are driven to the exclusion of all else."

"Your father wants to suppress whatever it is he'll find and Parks, well, he wants the world to know." Madsen paused. "I'm not sure I trust any of this to be honest. But here I am."

"So why did you come to Venice?" Hannah sat in the chair. Sunlight from the window behind made her hair glow.

"Curiosity. I guess."

Hannah studied Madsen. "You want to know don't you? That all this adds up to something. That it makes sense."

"You caught me out." Madsen sat down on the edge of the bed. "But I don't know what to believe anymore. I've heard theory after theory and to be honest none of it makes any sense. Don't you?"

"I guess I do. I've tried to walk away but I keep hearing things that make me want to get to the bottom of the mystery."

"I know what you mean."

"Too many people have died. I want to know what they died for."

"You've got that right."

There was another knock at the door. Softer this time.

"Yes?" Madsen stood up again.

It was Arden. "You seen Parks?"

"He's not in his room?" Madsen exchanged a knowing look with Hannah.

"He's gone ahead then," Arden sounded irritated.

"Why am I not surprised?" Madsen looked at his watch. "We've got time to catch him up."

Up ahead, Madsen could just make out someone in the dark. At first he thought it was Parks but the figure was taller, stronger built. He slowed his pace and reached out to grab Hannah's arm as she moved ahead of him. He had been more than a little anxious since crossing the Ponte dell' Accademia over the Grand Canal, where just ahead of them he'd seen two figures moving swiftly from the shadows into a doorway just off the little square on the other side of the bridge.

They had kept to the left as they'd exited the square and carried on into a side street. They had now come to another small canal but before crossing over Madsen had caught sight of another figure hiding in a doorway. Rather than go the direct route Madsen, mentally trying to recall the map of Venice, guided the others down to the street that ran along side the Canale della Giudecca. From here they could follow it right round to the customs house.

As they drew nearer the Dogana del Mare, the impressive baroque church, the Santa Maria della Salute, built in thanks to the Almighty for delivering the city from plague, rose up before them, its great dome washed with the lights of the city giving it an otherworldy, magical appearance. The building was octagonal in shape, as Parks had declared, like the mysterious Templar Castel Del Monte in Andria, Southern Italy, with its eight-sided towers constructed on the corners of its eight-sided walls. Numerology as architecture.

"What?" Hannah sounded irritated.

"Look." Madsen pointed to the wall of the Dogana del Mare.

"Is that another of your father's cronies?" Arden asked Hannah.

"Probably. Although I don't recognise him. But my father has contacts everywhere, not all of them political."

"Mob?" Arden grinned.

"Could be," Hannah replied.

"I thought I was joking."

"John and Robert Kennedy, Calvi... The Pope," Hannah said cryptically. "My father was involved in all their murders."

"How do you know that?" Arden asked.

"My father's one flaw: he likes to keep detailed records. Vanity I guess."

"Just like the Nazis. You make it sound like it's all one conspiracy." Arden sounded a shade incredulous. "That it's all connected."

"It is. My father wants to get hold of whatever is in that sphere."

"Why?" Arden asked the obvious question.

"Vested interest. Maintain the power base. A lot of powerful men will lose out badly if the truth comes out." Hannah paused. Her voice dropped almost to a whisper. "One world will end and another will begin unless my father can stop all this. He wants superstition to win out."

Arden exchanged looks with Madsen who shrugged. Both men expected Hannah to grin but her sober expression remained fixed.

"Come on. Let's keep to the shadows." Madsen set off but Arden grabbed his sleeve.

Madsen turned.

The younger man was pointing up at the globe on top of the Dogana del Mare.

"It's Parks."

They could just make out a figure moving tentatively across the flat roof of the building towards the tower on which the statue of Fortune, supported by the two atlantes, was mounted.

"How did he get up there?" Arden asked.

Madsen didn't reply. His attention was fixed on the sphere atop its thirty-foot tower. Here then was the focus for all the trouble, the anguish and the fear. This is what Hiroko, Arden's friends in New York, as well as many others had died for. A secret contained within the sphere that had been kept hidden for centuries. A secret so damning, so earth shattering that the consequences of its revelation might bring about unending anguish and turmoil but one that existed just above the heads of Venetians and tourists alike, unseen and unknown. A secret in plain view.

"The best place to keep a secret is out in the open." Arden's voice was soft, barely whispered.

"He's going for the sphere. He must have the third key." Hannah's voice was soft but forceful. "The sonofabitch lied to us. He had it all along."

"But where did he get it?" Madsen watched as Parks paused beneath the tower crowned with the golden sphere. He tried desperately to recall anything Parks might have said along this labyrinthine journey about possessing the third key; any clue that might have revealed the truth. But any revelation, however small, was now lost down long tunnels of the past and would remain a mystery, forever out of reach.

❋

The Sunsphere Again

I couldn't work out if it was peach pulp and champagne or peach pulp and prosecco that made up a Bellini, either way, we didn't have time to sample the drink. Just as we arrived at Harry's Bar I watched a suspicious individual study our arrival then get up and go, tucking a newspaper under his arm as he left. It was all a bit weird and reminded me of those black and white war films with spies dressed exactly like spies would be dressed when described only in screenplays and naff espionage novels. Either that or Capone's boys were in town. He didn't look particularly Mafia-esque though. I'd experienced a slight frisson of weirdness as the night before I'd had a dream in which Tony Soprano and one of his crew had initiated me into the Mob by having me lie down in public on an eye freshly popped from someone's skull. I was then awarded with very long strawberry flavoured Cornetto style ice creams. No, I've no idea what that was about either.

Anyway sitting in the corner was Gus and surprise, surprise, Alexia. They were huddled in towards each other like lovers, smirking and giggling like school kids at break time.

'Hi you two,' I said in a very loud voice.

Gus looked embarrassed and sat back in his chair. Alexia gave me one of those fake smiles, like a cheesed off shark caught in the act.

'Have you seen Arden?' Linda asked.

'Yeah.' Gus took a sip of his espresso. 'He's gone to open the sphere...'

On The Tower

Parks took out the three keys. He cupped them in one hand. Two genuine; one a copy. Here, after all the long years of searching, all the blind alleys, dead ends and disappointments, was what he sought. The culmination of toil, study and research. The reward for all the sacrifice, hurt and death that had followed his journey. He was on the point now of fulfilling his deepest desire, born of his inheritance of a family heirloom. The end of the road was in sight. The end point of his quest was not four feet from him.

He realised he was trembling. A rich blend of fear and excitement. He closed his eyes and took a deep breath. His whole life, he realised, had been leading up to this moment.

Selecting one of the keys, he pocketed the other two then clambered up the last few feet using a knee of one of the atlantes to position himself close to the sphere. He looped his left arm around the head of the same statue and scanned the gold surface of the reliquary.

His mind flashed briefly to the tattered manuscript replete with clues, half-truths and hidden meanings, many of which he had failed to decipher. One page flashed into his mind's eye, a fine ink representation of the Sunsphere. He remembered that there was a small triangular mark above the equator and in the western half of the hemisphere. He shifted his attention to that part of the sphere and after a few moments found what he was looking for.

Parks found a keyhole. He inserted the first key he had selected. But nothing happened. Reaching in his pocket he took out a second.

He tried that one.

There was a soft click and the whirring of some inner mechanism.

His heart was pounding.

He closed his eyes to think. Yes, above the other statue.

Dropping down, Parks made his way across the small gently sloping roof and clambered up the second supporting atlantes. He slipped, held on, breathing heavily, seeking a foothold to steady himself. His attention was back on the gilded sphere.

The second keyhole. Where? Somewhere near one of the statue's hands.

He tried the first key out of his pocket.

A click again and the sound of whirring once more.

The third keyhole would be more difficult. It was positioned, as he recalled, at the precise location of Venice if a map of the world was wrapped around the sphere.

Pulling himself up, he used the hand of the second atlantes as a foothold while he slid himself up against the body of the sphere.

He ran his free hand around the surface and there under a thumb was the third keyhole. Parks's heart was racing. Pressure throbbed in his temples. He thought he was going to pass out. He breathed deeply a few times and reached up to place the key into the...

From the rooftops somewhere near the street in which Harry's Bar was located came a single shot.

"What?" Hannah cast her eyes around the buildings. They were now positioned directly below the tower next to the high lamppost at the end of the walkway.

"Was that a gun shot?" Madsen asked looking to his right.

"It came from over there..." Arden stopped short.

As they looked up, Parks's body slipped from the sloping roof of the tower and tipped over the side of the customs house bounced once on the edge of the building and plunged into the Grand Canal.

Up On the Roof

We made our way up to the Canal, to the vaporetto station next to the gardens just round the corner from St Mark's Square. Shielding my eyes I could just make out a figure walking along the flat roof of the Dogana del Mare. I wouldn't have sworn on a stack of bibles that it was Arden but then again, who else would it have been? The four of us stood there and watched his progress.

I noticed a familiar figure lurking near the large lamppost of the Punta Della Dogana. I was sure it was the chap I'd seen leave Harry's Bar as Linda and I breezed in, but, from this distance, it was hard to be sure. He kept looking up towards the tower and the gold sphere.

Arden reached the base of the same tower and walked one way and then the next looking, I would assume, for the best route up. I estimated the height of the tower at around thirty to thirty-five feet, a bit of a climb for anyone.

Lo and behold, Arden seemed to duck down for a second before reappearing and lifting up a long telescoped ladder. How convenient I thought. By now a crowd had gathered to watch Arden's antics both beneath the customs house and around us.

After a few moments of faffing about, Arden then began to climb up at about the same time as someone alerted the police.

By now a noisy throng of people had gathered and all them had their attentions fixed on Arden, now clambering over one of the statues supporting the golden ball. At one point he slipped which provoked a thunderous *Ooooh* to chorus out across the Grand Canal.

Unable to put up with the hoohah anymore I slipped quietly away and sought out a suitable venue to squander some Euros on a large cup of coffee.

I don't know how, although I have some pretty good ideas, the media caught up with Gus, Linda, Alexia and myself while we were at a restaurant. Most of the meal had been spent in silence that was until photographers and news crews spilled into the establishment, much to the consternation of the perplexed owner. How they found us or even knew who to look for, I still have no idea.

We were asked about Arden, his arrest and the purported discovery of a scroll. For some reason I was the one that did all the talking. I told them in no uncertain terms that I found Arden to be deranged idiot who had led us all on a merry dance and that I was thinking of suing to get my expenses back.

Well, he was all over the news that night and all through the papers the following day.

Author's stunt discovers lost scroll in secret hiding place... as one headline had in the *Daily Express* had it. Then Arden's stunt seemed to disappear to the sidelines as the contents of the scroll began to garner far more interest.

Far more interest...

I stayed on for two more days but when I went to look for Linda she had checked out and taken the first available flight home. As for Gus and Alexia, I couldn't find them either.

Revelation

And that's how it was for the next five months. I heard nothing, kept deliberately, I suspected, out of the loop. I went back to selling but I made the conscious effort to broaden my horizons in terms of what I dealt with. For the sake of my sanity, if nothing else. No more holy crap for me. Ebay seemed much more inviting now. Perhaps I could get into flogging memorabilia and other retro-tat to fortysomethings keen to recapture their youth from a decade of choice rich in tastelessness.

Oddly enough, I eventually managed to sell the cat blood relic for a thousand quid to some individual in the Far East. Not long after, I read, in a Sunday Tabloid, about a neo-Christian-religio-cult that had sprung up in Manila. At its heart was the veneration of the blood of Christ. Guess what? Yep. In the photo was the Johnny I had sold the cat's blood to. *Felis domesticus* as messiah. But forgive them. They hadn't a clue what they were doing.

Wonder how many times that had happened in the past? And how many more times before people eventually woke up?

I was whipping up some beans on toast when the phone rang. I did my best to ignore it but found myself walking through to my office.

'Hello?'

'It's me.'

'Linda. Hi. What can I do for you?'

'They've translated the text.' She was breathless, as if on the point of collapse.

'And?' I must admit I was more than little impatient. 'What does it say?'

'Mark's presenting the transcript. He's holding a press conference at his publishers' tomorrow afternoon at three. Professor Wilkes will be there as well.'

'Who's Professor Wilkes?'

'The man who translated the parchment.'

'Well enjoy. You'll have to tell me all about it.'

'You're invited.'

'I thought I was persona non grata.'

'Not anymore.' I could hear Linda's smile down the phone. 'Mark's forgiven you.'

'I see. How's his book going?'

'That's what tomorrow's about. The launch. How about it? Are you coming?'

I didn't want to but the big fat shiny curiosity genes kicked in.

'Okay. I'll see what I can do.' After all I had been with them most of the way. I guess, at least, I'd earned an invite.

I caught the train into London and after a stifling hot tube journey met Linda and Gus outside Verba Publishers.

In the large imposing cathedral like foyer the PR team had erected a small stage backed by large colour facsimiles of the scroll. Around these were copies of the covers of Arden's entire back catalogue lit by small but bright spotlights. Wine was flowing in veritable torrents. Sadly it was all white, Italian oddly enough, Pinot Grigio to be exact, but I took a glass anyway so as not to stand out too much. Not that I was doing that anyway. Not a single person stopped to chat. It tends to be another default state of mine, at parties and other social do's. Little old invisible wallflower me.

Gathered in front of the display were members of the press and a few famous faces from television, most of whom also had books published by Verba. My eyes caught those of an attractive but tough looking young woman with honey coloured hair, sporting an American accent and a small scar on her right cheek deep in discussion with a celebrity historian. They were both discussing the destruction of Iraq's archaeological treasures. As I drifted by in a directionless wander to the edge of the literary melee our eyes met and I smiled my best polite Englishman's smile, which she acknowledged. While I edged myself on to relative safety I couldn't help thinking there was something about her that seemed oddly familiar. She seemed similar to that Hannah character in *Sunsphere*... but no, it was just coincidence. It had to be. Maybe she was a friend of Arden's, and he'd put her into the novel just as he had done with himself... I put her out of my mind as much as the wine allowed. Speaking of which, my glass was empty, so I made for the bar.

Freshly re-provisioned, I scanned the crowd, playing spot the face before my attention was drawn to Arden chatting to a knot of journos as he signed copies of his latest for them. One had a stack and was mechanically feeding them to him each time Arden finished flourishing his autograph across the inner title. Not far from my erstwhile companion, I noticed a recently retired newsreader who, through the pages of a thick tome, was blowing the cover on a Middle East invasion. He appeared to be discussing

393

something with someone I took to be his agent. They both looked really hacked off.

Continuing on my slow meandering tour I found Gus staring up at the altar to Arden the book god. He looked somewhat transfixed like those silly people who gawp at fake shrouds and shrivelled bits of long dead saints, who, in reality had been nothing of the sort. Saintly I mean.

'I expect when it's published he'll sell a million or more copies of it and make an absolute packet.' Gus was admiring the cover of Arden's latest literary offering entitled *Sphere of Destiny* positioned at the centre of the stand. *The Stunning and Explosive sequel to Sunsphere* was emblazoned banner-like across the top. The cover image, all reds, golds and dark hues, was a sunsphere glowing in embossed shiny gold above a shadowed mysterious looking Venice.

'Literary alchemy, mate. Wonder if we'll get a mention,' I mused, my words woven throughout with a heady dose of doubt and sarcasm. 'Is it a novel or docu-lit?'

'Docu-lit.' Linda had suddenly appeared at my side. As she spoke Gus slipped away through the crowd. Alexia had shown up. 'It's based on fact of course.' She added rather defensively.

'Well okay,' I replied.

Detecting the sneer in my voice, albeit one liberally honey coated, Linda shook her head.

'You were there,' she said and walked away.

Arden's agent, a robust chap of maybe sixty, then called for order while the man of the moment climbed up onto the stage. There was a burst of applause kicked off by the head of the publicity department, which went on until Arden raised his hand.

'I'm sorry to say that Professor Wilkes could not be here today to share the stage with me so, if you'll forgive the indulgence, I will continue, alone, in revealing what we have discovered.' All of Arden's seriousness had gone, which was perhaps, nothing more than a fake brooding writer persona for publicity purposes. Here on stage in the limelight, he sported a different personality. Affable, chummy, everyone's mate. Mine host. Unless of course, that was the fake Arden...

He then went on to describe the journey he had taken to get to this point. We, of course were pushed to the sidelines. Oh, we had a mention all right but it was as sidekicks or doubting Thomases. But I was happy to be labelled as such. With consummate skill the actor-writer elaborated a florid and verbose epic tale that led from biblical times right up to the present day but one that had a surprise and shock ending.

Boy, was it a shock ending. I must admit I laughed. I had to. If the truth be known that's probably how it all started anyway. It simply didn't surprise me.

The papers went ballistic as did the church, in all its thousands of variations. Everyone from the Pope to pro-religious scribes in tabloid newspapers, especially the Sunday ones, went into fits of apoplectic narrow-minded rage.

Arden was condemned, threatened, vilified and denounced right across the globe. This would explain Wilkes's absence on the day. Well, I thought so anyway.

But the parchment was real... so they said.

It had been carbon dated. Everything about it was consistent. It matched scrolls from that era in all aspects.

It was genuine... supposedly.

Its pedigree was faultless... apparently.

As the words from a broadsheet newspaper article had it...

Airport thriller writer Mark Arden is now the focus of hate throughout Christendom. Why? Because it seems he has stumbled upon the real genesis of the religion that is followed by nearly a billion people, albeit in nearly 34,000 versions. Across the world the outpourings of malice and venom from people associated with a so-called peace promoting faith are aimed at a new anti-Christ. Indeed some have claimed that Arden is indeed the devil writ large.

In fact he's replaced Richard Dawkins as the number one evangelista hate figure. They claim he is a biblical prophecy come to pass and one that heralds the end of time à la the mad hallucinogenic ravings of Revelations.

Many are calling what he has done a crime, including the Arch Bishop of York who is demanding Arden be convicted for, as yet, an unspecified act of secular perversion, to use his term, while the Archbishop of Canterbury is claiming yet another atheist conspiracy. But all Arden has done is simply reveal a lost scroll and the church is guilty once again of simply shooting yet another messenger.

During nearly a year of investigation and research, the basis of his new book, entitled Sphere of Destiny, published this Christmas, Arden has made a discovery that has rocked the foundations of one of the major world belief systems. Stored in the gold sphere above the Dogana del Mare in Venice was an ancient scroll that when translated exposed the origins of Christianity. He had speculated on this idea in his novel Sunsphere but then fiction and reality began to blend into one fantastic whole.

The lost scroll, with a text written in Hellenistic Greek (the same language as the original Gospels) authenticated by Professor Wilkes, who stands by its provenance, pre-dates the time of those of the Dead Sea. Carbon dating has added weight to the parchments authenticity. Others, especially those from the Christian right, are of course virulently opposed to the findings.

It is believed that as Venice was a base for the Templars, the document may have been brought out of the Holy Land by the order sometime in the 13th century. It has been speculated that this was in fact the secret treasure that the Templars were supposed to have had in their possession, one factor that brought about their destruction by Phillip the Fair. A few centuries later Venice was one of, if not the greatest, printing centres in Europe and would have been a hotspot of literary legerdemain. Wilkes also theorised that Valgrasi, the sixteenth century Venetian publisher of

396

heretical books and Donzelino, the book smuggler, who went missing, may very well have handled the scroll. Due to the strongarm tactics of the Vatican by 1606 the book trade had dried up in the city, the list of banned books not being lifted until 1966. "It is conceivable," said Wilkes, "that the scroll could have been hidden there or smuggled away to protect it." Arden himself has added, "The clampdown in the book trade may have been the Church's way of blocking knowledge of the scroll or a method by which to track it down."

In precise terms the scroll states that a set of back room pranksters, twelve young men and a woman, all children of the elite with too much time on their hands, had decided to have a laugh with the Roman occupiers so they drew on myths from around the Middle East to fuel a prank that eventually backfired on them. Their sources were many and various including Mithraism, which, by the third century A.D., would become equal to if not stronger than Christianity, Judaism, Babylonian belief systems, Pagan sun worship and more importantly Egyptian religion, specifically Amunothph III whose annunciation, conception and birth matches, but predates that of Jesus by eighteen hundred years. Scholars, including eminent theologians, of course, had known about these influences for years but the scroll lays it all out in the form of a confession.

The group put word around that a messiah was working miracles. The intention, it seemed, was to set tongues wagging and allow the rumour mill to crank at full steam perhaps as a focus for a revolutionary uprising against the Roman occupiers. They were, in modern parlance, having a laugh. But as in many similar cases it all grew rapidly beyond their expectation and control. The urban legend, the meme, the myth profited and spread well beyond the borders.

What had started as a joke had now become, after nearly two millennia, something deadly serious…

We never did get to the bottom of the mystery of who slipped the documents through Linda's door and the identity of the unknown shadowy figure I saw at the country house and in the streets of Venice. Although one of them turned out to be Arden's publicity manager. I discovered this while reading an article in a broadsheet Sunday colour supplement containing an interview with the now infamous author well on the way to making several million quid.

I'd heard on the grape vine, i.e. Gus, that Alexia had decided not to sell the family estate but instead had opened up the building to tourists to cash in on the global phenomena that was *Sphere of Destiny*, now rocketing off the shelves along with a re-issued *Sunsphere*, that was selling equally well. The latest edition of which had Arden's fizzog on the back – a smooth, all-knowing photograph of the author against a familiar background of the Orangery at Alexia's pad. The words *explosive bestseller* was splashed across the cover – not very fitting, I thought, for this day and age. I envisioned, in a kinky kind of way, piles of Arden's books being confiscated by over-zealous security people from bewildered passengers queuing at Heathrow, *sorry sir it has the 'explosive' on the cover*.

Anyway, within a few months Alexia was out of debt and living the high life, again. Gus even ran guided tours around the gardens. He at least had been mentioned in the follow up book. I also heard a rumour that they even had Hiddon's body on display sans pistol, which had gone missing but, in addition, and rather interestingly, a national Tabloid, in puffed up self-importance, doubted the authenticity of the corpse and was demanding a DNA test. A test it was willing to fund. How that would help, I had no idea.

Gus had also returned the novel extract to Alexia and it now sat beneath the glass of a large cabinet in the library, conveniently beyond the hands of those who wished to verify its authenticity and along side the photocopied one Linda had received.

That aside…

Had someone been out there guiding us, making sure we uncovered what we did?

Had we been part of some clandestine manoeuvrings of a sinister nature?

Had we been unwitting pawns in a conspiracy?

Or was it just my paranoia?

Who knows? I think Arden wanted to drag other people in, perhaps as witnesses. I did wonder at one point whether he knew someone who I had had dealings with in the past and might have unknowingly upset and had dragged me in to make me look foolish by way of a little bit of revenge. When I had refused to play along maybe Arden had then wanted someone like me to add authenticity or am I just saucing it up? Was I acting in the role of cod expert or was I overplaying my role in all this?

Maybe I'd just gone along for the ride and had been just as caught up and excited by the thrill of the hunt as everyone else but was as yet subconsciously unwilling to accept that idea.

I would've asked the Professor what he thought of it all, had his body not been found floating in the Grand Canal not far from the Dogana del Mare a few days after the release of *Sphere of Destiny*. An odd death that paralleled the mysterious demise of that alchemist at the opening of *Sunsphere* and one that Arden had purposefully left unresolved.

What had Wilkes being doing?

There are still times when I wonder how much of *Sunsphere* was true. Arden had after all named a character after himself. A deliberate move to hint at authenticity? A thinly veiled way to say it had all happened? Or was it just another way to add enticing bait to a well-worn literary hook? And who was the American woman at his book launch, the one I'd thought for a moment to be Hannah? Only Arden knew, of course, and he wasn't saying anything.

399

As for that infamous novel, I never finished it... and it remains on my shelf untroubled by my interest.

An Extract from

The Devil's Cathedral

The Sequel to *Sunsphere*
To Be Published in 2012

The Return of the Templar
Piedmont, January 1308

Even though the rain had long since extinguished the fire, in places embers still hissed releasing narrow plumes of smoke that rose a short way before being dispersed by the winter shower. At the centre of the scorched circle, still crudely marked by the stumps of unburnt kindling and piles of clotting ash, was a barely recognisable human shape blackened and crumpled like the stump of a lightning-struck tree.

For at least a mile outside the town he had seen the plume of oily smoke rising, whipped around wet rooftops and darkened walls by stuttering gusts of wind. He knew then what it meant. It was a Papal beacon; a signal fire to alert a cowed populace that in questioning authority they faced a fiery retribution for their disobedience in this world. No hell awaited those fallen souls. The flames of torment would burn them in the material plain denying them salvation. Stripped of justice and their dignity, their flesh popping and cracking, they would scream to their creator watched by their friends and neighbours, afraid to look away less they join the convicted in the fire.

Now, as he lowered the hood of his cloak and looked around at the lifeless town square, the shuttered windows and the shadowed stonework a strange deep blue in the failing winter light, he realised that the inhabitants here were lost to fear. The talons of Rome, far to the south, were squeezing these people's hearts.

In the ten years he had been away so much had changed. He had left a town rich in life and spirit. Although poor, there was enough food, clean water and cattle to create, in crude mimicry of a Greek legend, some rural arcadia. The fields beyond the gates were fertile, the river ran with fish and the orchards bore fruit. While the nearby monastery, situated on the edge of the large wood through which a tributary of the river ran, harboured the sick and supplied food in times of need.

But as he had spurred his horse up the road to the town of his birth he had been struck by how much the place had become barren and uncared for. It seemed as if pestilence and plague had crawled through the region or that the angel of death had swept overhead dipping its wing tips to touch the earth and drain its life.

Leading his horse to a stable block that had once been owned by a friend of his father, he slid the saddle from the animal then rubbed straw along its back to remove as much moisture as possible. He found an old blanket and threw it over his steed, rubbed the animal's nose then left to look for a familiar face of a friendly smile. Near the door he found a large knife. A butcher's tool. There were dark, stale patches of dried blood on the blade. It was now obvious to him why there were no other horses in the stalls.

Turning left he made his way down the street then left again up narrow gently rising lane between a vintner's and an inn. It was all very familiar to him. Even though some dread presentiment hung in the air he felt somewhat at ease. He was after all home. The jumbled cobbles beneath his feet were as familiar to him as the battle scars on his hands. Some of them still bore familiar nicks and cracks that reminded in so much of his childhood. His eyes sought the one made by a young eager boy trying to lift his father's sword above his head only to have it tip him backwards, the blade cutting a gouge in a stone as the eight year old crashed into the wall.

Running his fingers under his hair he could still feel the dent in his skull.

Stepping up to a familiar door he paused on the threshold. There were times when he believed he would never see home again and once, even as he lay brutally wounded as the city of Acre burned around him, he had a vision of this door, which in his delirium he mistook for the entrance to heaven. In a sense it was true but it was the heaven of youth to which no one, not even he, could ever hope to return to. But he vowed then that he would lay down his sword and return to the place of his birth. The memory of his home and this entrance kept him going through those long troubled times.

He pushed on the door. The hinges whined while wood screeched across the stone floor. It jammed and he had to slip through a gap no more than a foot wide.

There was a meagre fire in the grate but one that was being kept alive by shreds of material and the remnants of an old stool. He knelt down before it and rubbed his hands together. It was a scant welcome. Sensing someone watching him he half turned and saw the shadowy figure of his father standing in the doorway to a side room. The shoulders were stooped and the back more bent with care worn age.

"Guido, is that you?"

Having returned briefly to the stable to gather up an armful of straw, Guido had then stoked the fire until the flames caught bringing more warmth to the room. All the while his father sat quietly on a low chair staring into space.

Guido had not seen his father in 18 years. He told him everything, about the loss of the Holy Land, his travels through Europe with Templar Grand Master Jacques de Molay, the Fall of Ruad, the last Templar possession in the East, life in the Templar preceptory on Cyprus and then, to crown it all, the campaign against the Order of the Temple initiated by the French King, Philip the Fair, and the arrest of his fellow Templars. The mightiest warriors Christendom had ever known were now being hunted down. The move against the Order had prompted Guido's return to Italy, in the hope that he might be able to defend the Templars' reputation, and assist his fellow brothers. But there was no opportunity to give help, any help. Guido had spent the last two months on the road in disguise, his beard shaven off, his Templar tunic long since burnt.

They both stared into the fire that Guido stoked, knowing that the world had gone mad.

"You have a genuine skill with flame," his father coughed. "A real art."

"Many nights spent under a cold moon. That's all." Guido remained on his haunches, hands pressed against the growing heat. "I'm no alchemist."

"Don't use words like that." His father looked agitated. "Not here... or now..."

"Why?"

His father was silent for a long while summoning up the courage to say something that it was obvious to Guido he would rather not. A well-practised dialogue honed on lonely evenings waiting for the moment when they could be spoken. But as that moment actually arrived the words seemed hollow, inadequate and lifeless.

"It was three years ago... nearly. They came for your mother not an hour before dawn." His father rested his hand on the tops of his thighs. "How is it that friends can betray you?" Slowly shaking his head he continued, answering his own rhetorical question. "In desperate times people do desperate things."

Guido, his attention on the fire, closed his eyes. He knew what his father was going to say. The kindling, the ash...

"Say nothing father." Standing up Guido placed a hand on the cold wall above the fire. His head was lowered, his eyes on the hungry flames. "I have witnessed enough betrayal of the innocent to know the consequences."

"Then I will say no more," his father sighed.

"How is it that all this has come about? " There was anger in Guido's voice.

"All born of heresy."

"Heresy?"

"At least the fear of it." His father's voice dropped almost to a whisper. "The autumn after you left the town was suddenly rife with rumour. I'm not sure how it all started. No one ever is of course but nevertheless... it was like a plague... of words. Then some blight afflicted the crop. The fields died. A guest of the Frenchman, Thomas Bérard, had been staying in the town and they took him to be the cause. Some nameless individual, a spy mind, overheard him talking. "

"About what?"

"Heretical knowledge, so they say but the witness was too scared to say what exactly." Guido's father contracted his fists. "The moral coward." Then paused to take a long breath. "Then Alphonso, the new priest, was told."

"What happened to Bellini?"

"Exiled once more."

"Exiled? Why?"

"I honestly don't know. He bought a horse from me, said goodbye and that was the last I saw of him." Guido's father pressed a hand to his face then ran it down his beard. "There's been a shift of power here. You can... feel it in the air. I don't trust Alphonso. On a summer day the man has no shadow." He laughed a little. "You know what I mean."

"And Bérard's visitor?" Guido shook his head. "No, don't tell me. I'm sure I know what happened to him."

"They searched Bérard's house for days looking for something. Turned out all his possessions into the street. Whatever it was they didn't find it so they burnt the place to the ground."

"What's going on here? It's as if the devil is upon us."

"Alphonso agrees with you. He's convinced this area is rife with heretical thought and that the Devil stalks the streets. That our souls are all in mortal danger."

"Tyranny then. Alphonso's I mean."

"He has petitioned Rome. I saw a second messenger ride out five months ago."

"Second?"

"They found the first hanging from a tree by the ford on the Via Levarsi Col Sole two weeks after the man had set out."

"Petitioned Rome? For what reason?"

"Alphonso intends to build a cathedral here. A stamp of authority to rid the land of heresy."

‡

www.ingramcontent.com/pod-product-compliance
Lightning Source LLC
Chambersburg PA
CBHW050922120626
46552CB00001B/2